"*As the Wicked Watch* is a terrific read—a propulsive, compelling mystery, but also a nuanced look at class and racial inequality. With Jordan Manning, Tamron Hall has given us a smart, empathetic heroine to cheer on for years to come."

—Alafair Burke, *New York Times* bestselling author

"Wow—Tamron Hall knows how to tell a story! And this timely and compelling thriller is a treat to read. Unflinching, revealing, and authentic. . . . Authentic and life-changing—and completely entertaining—this is the first of what is sure to be a long-running series from a beloved and talented journalist."

—Hank Phillippi Ryan, *USA Today* bestselling author of *Her Perfect Life*

"Tamron Hall's debut novel *As the Wicked Watch* is a singular thriller that brings the vulnerability and systemic neglect of Black girls as victims of violent crime into vivid relief. . . . The cohesiveness and sheer scope of the narrative Hall has woven together is impressive. . . . Readers interested in the gritty details of crime reporting and investigation will be intrigued. . . . Ultimately, *As the Wicked Watch* is an impressive debut—a moving take on familiar but urgent problems and society's indifference."

—NPR

"Hall's first novel blends true crime with illuminating reflections on media representation and the obstacles faced by a Black woman in journalism."

—Oprah Daily

"*As the Wicked Watch*—the first in a three-book series from Hall—is a thoughtful, captivating novel that highlights that, to some, tragedy is just a news story, but to passionate journalists like Jordan, the real people behind these tragedies are where the true heartbreak lies."

—Shondaland

"The first in a series by Emmy Award–winning journalist Tamron Hall, *As the Wicked Watch* has all the hallmarks of a great thriller, with a fast-moving plot, an unforgettable protagonist, and lots of fascinating insights into TV newsrooms and the biases influencing whose stories get told."

—*Real Simple*

"Emmy Award–winning broadcast journalist Hall's outstanding debut and series launch introduces TV journalist Jordan Manning. . . . Hall brings insight and nuance to such matters as journalism ethics, police treatment of murder cases involving Black women, and competition among journalists and their reliance on those behind the scenes. Readers will want to see a lot more of intelligent, ambitious, and assertive Jordan."

—*Publishers Weekly* (starred review)

"A pulse-pounding story that also provides a fascinating and important look into the difficulties of reporting on and finding justice for Black victims. Emmy Award–winning Hall's extensive background as a TV journalist, including reporting for NBC and anchoring for MSNBC, infuses a great deal of credibility and behind-the-scenes verve to her first crime novel."

—*Booklist* (starred review)

"Hall's decades of field experience lend a lot of credibility to the story and provide a strong footing for an intriguing new crime series."

—*Library Journal*

"Tamron Hall's new novel introduces a detective sure to become an icon. . . . It is a powerful, clear-eyed novel that demands accountability, from its fictional world, yes, but also the real one."

—CrimeReads

"The first in a planned series featuring reporter Jordan Manning, *As the Wicked Watch* is a well-paced and thoughtful crime novel that probes questions of race, representation, and community care."

—*Shelf Awareness*

"*As the Wicked Watch* is a promising start to a series sure to appeal to fans of badass women with mysteries to solve and something to prove."

—*BookPage*

"With over twenty years of journalism experience, years spent reporting on crime and tragedies across the country, and her own personal experiences, Emmy Award–winning talk show host Tamron Hall is in the perfect position to launch this exciting new series."

—*Mystery & Suspense* magazine

"*As the Wicked Watch* gives a real glimpse of what successful Black women journalists must have endured to obtain and maintain their positions."

—Salon

"A multifaceted diamond, *As the Wicked Watch* introduces a series that promises to trouble the mind and touch the heart."

—*Free Lance-Star* (Fredericksburg)

AS THE
WICKED
WATCH

AS THE WICKED WATCH

The First
JORDAN MANNING NOVEL

TAMRON HALL

WITH T. SHAWN TAYLOR

𝒲𝓂
WILLIAM MORROW
An Imprint of HarperCollinsPublishers

HarperCollins books may be purchased for educational, business, or sales promotional use. For information, please email the Special Markets Department at SPsales@harpercollins.com.

A hardcover edition of this book was published in 2021 by William Morrow, an imprint of HarperCollins Publishers.

FIRST WILLIAM MORROW PAPERBACK EDITION PUBLISHED 2022.

Designed by Bonni Leon-Berman

Library of Congress Cataloging-in-Publication Data has been applied for.

ISBN 978-0-06-303704-5

22 23 24 25 26   LSC   10 9 8 7 6 5 4 3 2 1

To the countless children missing or taken
by the darkness of the world.
You are more than a story. You are more than
words on a page. You are loved, you are missed,
and you are not forgotten.

AS THE
WICKED
WATCH

1

"Jordan, we're live in sixty," said Tracy Klein, my favorite field producer, nudging me to get into place.

"Okay, hang on," I said, distracted by a rush of butterflies and the sudden urge to pee, which happened every single time I was about to go on the air. I guess it was my body's way of preparing me for the moment that never got old, but soon panic struck. My earpiece was in, but the anchors' voices sounded like Charlie Brown's parents.

"Hey, you guys. I can't hear. You're not coming through very clearly. The echo is killing me," I said.

I looked up.

Please, not today.

In an instant, the sky darkened over historic Bronzeville on Chicago's South Side, a sign of the dip in temperatures I recalled hearing on this morning's weather forecast. Chicagoans and people all across this state have to deal with one inescapable fact, and that's the cold. Sure, I'd heard people who claimed to love the change of seasons. But to a person from Austin, Texas, that sounded like a case of Stockholm syndrome. Or at least that's what I told my friends from the Midwest when they tried to convince me otherwise.

"Guys, are you trying to blow my ears out?" I shouted at the men a few feet away in the news van. Clearly, whatever they did had fixed the problem. The sound coming out of my earpiece could now be heard in the next county. I stretched as far as my arms could go in this super cute, single-button fitted jacket that looked tailored but wasn't—I'd bought it off the rack—and turned down the literal voices in my head.

"Tracy, when are we getting new equipment? This earpiece was around when . . ."

"Jordan, focus," she interrupted. I could tell Tracy wasn't in the mood for my climbing up on my soapbox today. I glanced down and noticed the heels of my most expensive pair of pumps had slowly disappeared into the soft soil beneath the "L" train track. The low-lying area was prone to flashflooding, and my poor shoes were the latest casualty.

What was I thinking?

"Scott, how's your sound?"

Scott Newell hoisted the camera off the static tripod and steadied it against his right shoulder. He signaled *all good* with a left-handed thumbs-up.

So long as Scott's sound is working, I'll be okay.

Scott is my steady hand and the antidote to my impulsive nature. My voice of reason out in these streets. The irony of us falling into stereotypical gender roles was particularly strange in a business where independent, successful women still kept secrets about gender bias and sexual harassment while reporting on these very matters. But I guess it didn't hurt that he had a smile that had melted a few women and, heck, some men, too, when I'd tried to negotiate a longer interview with an unwilling participant.

For that, Scott is my favorite cameraman, but also because he has steady hands and one of the best points of view behind a lens I've ever seen. And he's reliable—probably one of the most reliable men in my life right now, to tell the truth. In television, allies are everything, and for reporters, the natural first ally when you arrive at a new station is the cameraperson. A unique trust developed quickly with long hours on the road, especially on those occasions when we had to chase down some guy accused of foul play in his wife's disappearance—in my case in heels. You need someone willing to drag you along like those poor women in the campy horror films who'd break a heel and fall just as the killer closed in on them with a chainsaw. Leave no screaming injured woman behind due to her poor choice of footwear. That's Scott.

"Thirty seconds, Jordan." The voice in the earpiece had reverted back to a whisper.

"I don't know what it is, Scott, but my sound is terrible. Can you hear me?"

Scott shrugged his shoulders, not worried that I was seconds from being one of those reporters pressing against their ear, yelling, "Can you repeat the question?"

"Tracy, I still can't hear you guys."

"Hold on, Jordan," Tracy said. "Hold on, we are trying to fix it."

If the sound issues weren't enough to make me want to run into the liquor store a few yards away and drown my nerves, the clouds had assumed the starting position and were waiting for a checkered flag. Hanging low and dense like an alien invader, they made Bronzeville appear more sinister than necessary. "Sketchy," as my mother would say: with vacant lots, boarded-up retail shops and liquor lounges, and potholes the size of a kiddie pool.

The wind gusts this city is famous for sprayed a mix of prickly dirt, gravel, and rock against my bare legs. I could feel a few of the pebbles land inside the arches of my black Stuart Weitzman pumps, a splurge I permitted myself for my twenty-eighth birthday, now likely the dumbest purchase of my life but still one of the cutest. I could hear the words of assistant news editor and my newsroom BFF Ellen Holbrook come back to haunt me.

"I'm just saying, if it were me, I wouldn't wear *my* four-hundred-dollar Stuart's—not today, not where you're going. Oh, that's right, I don't own any," Ellen quipped, exposing a hint of the East Coast accent she picked up during summers spent with her grandparents in Menemsha, Massachusetts, a small fishing village on Martha's Vineyard where everybody sounds like a Kennedy.

The wind whipped the air like a strap, and discarded handbills, plastic bags, and food wrappers were violently sucked into the honeycomb cells of the chain link fence surrounding the abandoned playground. Divided between areas for toddlers and for big kids, it was named in honor of Ida B. Wells-Barnett, a Black investigative journalist and a total badass in her day. I wonder if she would have done a show like *60 Minutes* or *Dateline*.

It's amazing where the mind travels at a crime scene. I'm convinced it's how the brain copes with the sick reality of what humans are capable of.

The playground was wholly unrecognizable from its condition just a few weeks ago when Scott and I were the first to arrive at the scene. The city has since rid the cracked concrete slab and the adjacent grassy field of trash, dandelions, and what we back in Texas call horseweed or marestail, which grows more than six feet tall. When I was a child, I used to visit my cousins on my mother's side in Galveston, Texas. A lot of time was spent running in and around the weeds. It was funny how different they looked erupting from the concrete jungle versus the soft soil beneath a Texas sun, as statuesque as pine trees. The bark was so thick that if you cut it, some inexplicable white liquid would've probably squirted out. My lack of appreciation for it all was lost in my understanding of why curious pre-pubescent boys would be drawn to a place that so effectively cloaked their mischief as they pored over their discoveries.

That it once was a children's play area named after a Black woman who paved the way for people like me to work as investigative journalists only made its fate that much more of a shame.

"Jordan, five! Count it!" the producer yelled.

"Scott, you can hear them. Cue me in," I instructed. "Just yell, 'Go!'"

He nodded.

"Okay, Jordan," Scott said. "The desk is about to hand it offffff!"

He pointed and mouthed *Go*, as if a Hollywood director had burst onto the scene. His over-the-top cue nearly made me laugh. I took a deep breath, fighting the visual of his absurd gesturing, and refocused on why I was here in the first place.

"Diana, I'm at the Ida B. Wells-Barnett playground at 45th and Calumet in Bronzeville. It's been weeks since a crew of prisoners from Cook County Jail on cleanup detail made a gruesome discovery here. Now investigators believe they've established a connection between the body of an African American woman found behind a dumpster at a popular South Side restaurant last week and the victim found here."

Other news media had referred to this latest victim as a prostitute. I didn't have the heart to describe her that way after speaking with her mother. She was somebody's child. Labels give people a reason not to care when aired out on the news. A murder? Oh, she was just a prostitute. A victim? Police said she was on drugs. As the forty-five-second clip of my prerecorded interview with the victim's mother played, I thought about her face, hardened by heartbreak long before her daughter was found dead and partially burned outside a dumpster. Trust me, there was no describing the look. You knew it when you saw it watching from your sofa as the local news camera moved in on a heartbroken helpless parent.

"Powerful clip!" chimed in midday anchor Diana Sorano, her genuine enthusiasm making her more audible than I'd anticipated. The wind whipped my hair across my face, and in the moist air, my face morphed from dewy but tolerable into a sweaty mess likely to spark a viewer complaint that I looked too shiny. The first raindrop splashed across my nose. I tried not to frown, but felt my eyebrows furrow, a bad habit.

"Jordan, with yet another murder of a young African American woman, what are some of the community leaders saying? Are they questioning how police are handling these cases?"

Did she lob that question at me to get me to state the obvious? That people had doubts that the police would use all the resources available to draw a connection between these two homicides, if there was one? Or was she oblivious? Of course people were asking that question. Wouldn't you if you lived here?

"Diana, there is a growing wave of discontent over the number of unsolved murders of Black women on the South and West Sides. Now, with the murder of Tania Mosley, that number stands at eight over the last two years."

"Thank you, Jordan, and again, I look forward to your special report, which airs tonight during the ten o'clock broadcast, with Tania's mom."

I wondered whether Diana fully understood what this latest

murder meant. Would she be looking forward to a special report about White girls being killed? My thoughts went dark, realizing my snap judgment was unfair. She wasn't looking forward to a report on anyone's being killed, no matter their race. It was just that scripted language trap many anchors tended to fall into after years of seeing the same kind of story over and over again. In a few seconds, this story would vanish and the commercial break would act as a palate cleanser until the next funny video everyone was talking about or the comforting kicker about someone or some company doing a good thing. From confronting you with a murder to making you feel motivated in twenty-five minutes or less.

"She looks like a fighter," Diana said. "My heart goes out to her. I hope she has someone to lean on for support."

Yeah, me too. But it won't be me. Not this time.

It started to rain lightly, but I was frozen in place, eyes locked on the camera as I waited to hear *all clear* from Scott.

"Okay, we're out!" Scott shouted. "Let's go, Jordan. Run!"

Scott broke down his tripod and was halfway to the news truck by the time I pried my shoes out of the mud that now encased them, and the sky burst like a thumped piñata.

2

October 11, 2007

Scott and I drove up and down Martin Luther King Jr. Drive searching for the perfect spot to set up for the live broadcast. Numerous posters of Masey James' dimpled face become the morbid bread crumbs leading us to where we want to be. She'd been missing for nearly three weeks, and the posters were a sign of time moving forward with no answers. Some were melted into a blob of ink, her face no longer decipherable or the hotline number half missing, erased by time and weather. The worn posters paled in comparison to the signs of time gone by as we looked around the historic Bronzeville community for a place to park. In the 1930s and '40s, this community was known as the Black Metropolis, an enclave of upper-middle-class artists and entertainers, business owners and numbers runners. It possessed the same sentimental notes as Harlem in New York, Baldwin Hills in L.A., or Detroit's Paradise Valley. They were all landmark communities built on black wealth, but the ups and downs of an economy not built on fairness had taken its toll. Today, under a slow boil appreciation, it was slowly gentrifying into something new but remained a crown jewel of a broader South Side community.

Earlier, Scott and I grabbed breakfast downtown before heading south to police headquarters. We didn't want to be late for my one-on-one interview with Detective Mitch Fawcett. This interview was the talk of the newsroom, and the pressure was on for me to hold his feet to the fire. He had been adamant about not sitting down with me to talk about what he called "the case of a potential runaway." It was a surprise to everyone on the crime beat that he had his comms team reach out with the stipulation that he wanted to talk with me. Was it because I was the most visible Black woman at the station? I viewed his offer with suspicion. I refuse to be his middleman to get out some generic message to tamp down the anger. The ol' "We take this seriously and we are working so hard . . . harder than you could even imagine" spiel. Ellen told me I was overreacting.

"Oh, just go for it. Build the relationship. He knows you don't suffer fools, Jordan."

"Look, I know Mitch Fawcett. Either he has an agenda or his boss is making him do it. Let's hope I don't have to call him out."

In contrast, his boss, police superintendent Donald Bartlett, was a pure softy, with a mild-mannered demeanor and a strong resemblance to Santa Claus. I struggled to take him seriously and often wondered how he got the job. This was a tough town. Under all that fluff must be a guy you didn't want to meet in an alley.

Scott and I arrived at Chicago police headquarters a few minutes early. Walking up to the front desk, I felt dwarfed by the massive flags framing the entrance, leading to a well-worn desk. As I approached, it hit me that I hadn't followed instructions. I was supposed to call Fawcett first to let him know we were parked out front.

Strike one! Great. Now this guy has an opening to scold me before we even get started.

I pulled my phone from my bag and called, realizing that since every camera in the lobby was recording my every move, he probably already knew I was in the building.

"This is Fawcett."

"Hello, Detective Fawcett. It's Jordan Manning. We're here. I mean, we're in the lobby."

"Jordan, I told you to call from the parking lot."

"Sir, I got distracted," I said, trying to sound apologetic, but the snark came out anyway. "We are here. Should I go back out to the lot and call again?"

And here we go, Jordan!

"Just have a seat in the lobby," he said. I sensed he was attempting to maintain control.

I can't seem to get off his shit list. I guess I can expect a few extra parking tickets for the next year.

A uniformed officer who introduced himself as Ramirez met us at the security checkpoint. I felt like the kid picked up last from school after her parents admitted they forgot. Ramirez escorted us past the beat-up front desk to a fortified door leading to a series of cubicles, the detectives' wing. I caught a few glances on the way to an elevator bank in the middle of the building. As we waited, I glanced at the many photos of officers recognized for outstanding performance on one side, those killed in the line of duty on the other.

"Ma'am, go ahead," said Officer Ramirez, regaining my attention from the rabbit hole of reading every plaque and framed article on the wall.

"Where are we going?" I asked.

"Lockup," he said with a smirk, proud of himself for injecting humor in what he must have processed as an awkward situation.

"Good," I replied. "I should feel right at home. I'm sure it's just like my newsroom."

Ramirez remained silent after his cop humor fell a tad flat. Scott never said a word.

We got off on the third floor and were directed into a room with double doors already propped open.

"Ma'am. Sir," Ramirez said, motioning for us to go into a conference room with a long rectangular table and a display of the American flag in one corner and the four-star flag of Chicago in another.

Scott surveyed the room to establish the best camera angle. "Can we dim the fluorescent lights?" Scott asked the officer.

Ramirez was looking up at the lights like he'd never noticed them before when Fawcett entered the room, clutching a note-pad against his chest like it was Kevlar body armor.

"Hi, Jordan, thank you for coming," Fawcett said a little too enthusiastically.

Phony does not suit this guy well. "Sure, Detective. I was surprised to hear from you."

"Sit down." He motioned me to the head of the table.

"Have a seat, Jordan," would have been more appropriate.

The top of his pointy bald head glistened under the lights.

"Actually, Detective, if you could sit there instead, with the four-star flag at your back, and Jordan, you sit here." Scott pointed. "If we face the other way, we'll catch shadow from those blinds over there."

"Sure," Fawcett said.

"Detective, before we begin, I'd like to establish the focus of this interview," I said half matter-of-factly, half "don't try and play me, mister."

"All right then," he said. "Shoot."

"Police have consistently called the disappearance of Masey James a runaway case. Is that changing?"

"We haven't ruled it out," he said. "Teens who run away from home can avoid detection for months."

"But something's changed. What?" I asked.

"Nothing's changed, Jordan," said Fawcett, his fake smile now transformed into a grimace of exasperation. "The young lady doesn't fit the profile."

I smile while thinking, *You idiot. And you're just now figuring that out?*

From what Masey's mother, Pamela Alonzo, had shared with me about her daughter, I was confident she was no teenage runaway. She reminded me too much of myself at fifteen—a girlie girl who took pride in her appearance, someone ambitious and sure of herself.

The interview began and ended in a flash. Fawcett's admission off-camera that Masey didn't fit the profile of a runaway wouldn't come so easy on-camera. *Typical.*

"This is an ongoing investigation, but we're adding personnel and considering some other potential scenarios," Fawcett said.

"Can you elaborate?" I asked.

"I'd rather not, but I want to assure the community and all of Chicago that we will exhaust all resources to find Masey," he said.

So that's it? You called me here for this? Is this guy kidding me? I can't take this back to the newsroom.

"Sir, with all due respect, did you lose valuable time dismissing this as a runaway case?" I asked.

"Not at all. We have a protocol and we followed it. But again, let me stress, this is a priority, and we want to assure Masey's family and all of Chicago we are laser focused on this case and on finding Masey. We are working with the family to trace her every move."

And there you have it—that's the agenda. "We are working on it."

I glared at him with the "That's it?" look I'd mastered after years of interviewing cops, but he didn't take the bait and ejected himself from the chair like a fighter pilot getting the hell out of the hot seat.

He didn't even bother to walk us to the elevator. Where was Ramirez? Were we just supposed to pack up and leave on our own?

Scott looked at me shaking his head, his signature move when he had nothing to say or nothing he thought I wanted to hear. As he packed up his gear, I texted Ellen. **What a bust!**

She sent a quick reply. **What happened?**

But I just texted back **Talk soon**, because frankly reliving any part of what had just taken place was a waste of my time.

As Scott and I exited police headquarters, a familiar face stopped me in my tracks. It was Masey James smiling at me, her image captioned with MISSING in bold black letters tacked to a utility pole.

Perhaps Fawcett should pay more attention to what's in his own backyard. It says MISSING, not HELP FIND A RUNAWAY.

Someone was sending a message, but it wasn't getting through. I felt like grabbing the poster and running back inside and slapping it on Fawcett's desk.

Masey's mother had publicly rejected police assertions that her daughter had run away from home. But there still hadn't been an Amber Alert issued by law enforcement, which was what the alert was meant for. This kid was looking at a future where she could write her own ticket. If it wasn't used in a case involving a teenager any parent would be proud of, then when?

The missing posters were the community's way of issuing an alert for one of its own. Fawcett might have tricked his mind into believing that police were doing their job, just following protocol. But I couldn't ignore what I recognized as a plea for help, for the police to care, for attention from the media, and for answers.

Back in the news van, Scott and I headed toward King Drive, and I rolled down the window and tilted my head out and up toward the sky. The sunlight filtered through the trees that stood guard outside of the stately two- and three-flat brownstones—walk-ups, some people call them—that lined both sides of the boulevard. These houses were unlike any I had seen back in Austin, Texas, and portlier than the brownstones in Harlem. I was impressed with the architecture, though, the kind of regal, ornate design work most builders had abandoned years ago for sameness and simplicity.

The tree limbs, heavy with leaves changing into their fall brilliance, cast a shadow like an archipelago upon the ground below. If I was going to do my broadcast from here, the lighting had to be right.

Scott easily found parking on the street. I jumped out of the van and surveyed the sidewalk for rocks and cracks, anything that could trigger a misstep or snag the heel of my pumps during my walk and talk.

"It's hard to look at these, isn't it," Scott said.

"What?" I asked.

"These posters. I mean, what a nightmare for a parent," Scott said. I couldn't pretend to completely understand what it was like for Scott, the father of a five-year-old son and an eight-year-old daughter he sees every other weekend and twice during the week since his divorce. "I mean, there's been no sign of her in three weeks. What are the chances she's still alive?"

I fought to hold back the answer, forcing the air down required to articulate what I was thinking.

Fawcett's pronouncements spun around in my head. Finally, police no longer viewed Masey as a potential runaway. Five more detectives had been put on the case. His mission was accomplished. His effortless PR stunt playing out, leaving me feeling like a useful idiot. My mic and camera the tools he needed to make people think it was all okay.

Scott asked again, "Do you think she's alive? What are the odds, Jordan?"

"Probably not good," I responded. "Most missing persons cases don't have happy endings. You heard what Fawcett said. This is a different investigation now. And they're probably afraid they're going to catch heat for misclassifying Masey as a runaway for damned near three weeks if she turns up dead."

While I couldn't fully wrap my head around what Scott was thinking as a dad, especially the dad of a young girl, I could fully understand the loss and helplessness Masey's family must be feeling.

Jordan, don't go there. Get out of your own head.

"Scott, look, Masey had just started attending this awesome STEM school. She dotes on her little brother and her cousin's baby girl. She shops in her mother's closet and redoes her nails every other day," I said, bragging on Masey, a girl I'd never met, like I'd heard her mother do, a feeling of kinship that gave my words a tone of protectiveness.

My best friend in Austin, Lisette Holmes, and I had talked about this.

"Masey sounds like a loving, happy child," Lisette said. "Not a girl that would just take off like that. Something's not right."

I ignored my own warning and went deeper into the dark recesses of my mind. While Scott set up, I told him about a case I'd covered while working at a Dallas station that haunts me to this day.

"Two sisters, six and eight years old, who lived in a small town about an hour from the city were reported missing by their mother, Luella Buford. She told police she last saw them playing in the backyard, which backed up to a wooded area.

When I interviewed Luella one-on-one, she told me she'd seen a Black man in a black van circling the area, even driving past her house a couple times the day the girls went missing."

A Black man in a black van. The color of fear. The descriptor of evil. Was it possible? Of course. Did I doubt her story? Yes, from the very start. The mental gamble it took to look at a presumed victim and see them as the villain was a hard place to be as a reporter. The urge to look them in the eye and flat out call them a liar was a disorienting circumstance to fight.

But the fact she went overboard with *black*—Black guy, black car, wearing dark clothing—it was something that even now, when I tell people the story, some get it right away. Others, like Scott, struggled to connect the signs and the red flags. I didn't feel like explaining it to him.

"After about two weeks, their bodies were found in a well on an abandoned property," I said. "They'd been sexually assaulted."

"Let me guess. It wasn't a Black guy," Scott said, his tone indicating he knew where my story was going.

"Exactly!" I said, pointing my finger like a game show host when a contestant guessed the right answer. "But the mother wasn't innocent. Luella had a boyfriend named Jerry Branahan. Jerry was well known around the area. A lot of people felt sorry for him because he'd had his struggles, and he was mentally disabled. He wasn't the girls' father. Luella met Jerry at a laundromat a year after her breakup with her baby daddy. His $568-a-month disability check was a big help to her. She was a piece of work. She manipulated him to the point that he knew to hand over that check before he could close the mailbox."

All these years later, I still remember a mundane detail such as the amount of Jerry Branahan's monthly disability paycheck, but not my own checking account number.

By now, Scott and I, but more important, the news truck had attracted attention, like it was an open invitation for someone to come over and ask, "What's going on?"

"To make a long story short," I said, "it turned out Jerry had the girls at an abandoned house that was one of his former foster homes. Luella thought she could play on the townspeople's and her family's sympathy to extort money. But Jerry, high on glue, ended up raping the girls."

"Wow, that's terrible," Scott said. "I didn't know glue sniffing was still a thing."

"It is in rural Texas," I said. "Oh, oh. We've got company."

The few people who'd gathered moved in closer. I was in no mood for random questions. I was here for answers, but I knew I'd have to help Scott escape the growing crew of folks around him.

"Hi . . . yes . . . we're about to do a live shot. Do you mind . . . excuse me, do you mind moving back over this way?" Scott asked the gatherers.

Getting out of the van, I realized we were parked a few steps from a Masey missing poster tacked to a tree. For the first time, I looked beyond her striking features, noticing her perfect posture. The poise anyone who had ever taken a school picture understood. It was unnatural and regal at the same time. The photographer hired by the school accepted nothing less than pinpoint precision. Chin up, shoulders back. Smile.

Scott had managed to escape the enquiring minds. Without thinking, I said, "She borrowed that top."

"How do you know that?" Scott asked.

"Her mother told me," I said, my eyes still glued to Masey's smile.

What a beautiful child.

"Really? When did she tell you that?" he asked.

"It's cathartic, I think," I said, avoiding Scott's question. "You know, for her to describe mundane details like that to someone about her daughter. Anything to keep from going totally nuts."

"So, you've spent some time with her?" Scott asked, rephrasing the question.

I wasn't sure if Scott was probing because he was concerned or if he was just being nosy.

In either case, his questions began to feel like an interrogation. I'm to blame for my paranoia, for letting a potential victim's relative become a tad too familiar with the lady from the news. How else was I supposed to cover this story if not intimately? With genuine concern?

"Oh, a couple times," I said, and shrugged my shoulders.

It had been four, in fact, most recently two days ago. The first time was the day after Pamela reported Masey missing. She left a voice-mail message on the station's tips hotline the morning after her daughter failed to come home. Everybody at the station knows that if it involves missing children, "send them to Jordan."

My last two years of undergrad at Columbia College in Missouri, I chose a minor in forensic science. Later in graduate school, I wrote my thesis on "Covering Violent Crime: What the Media Misses" to earn my master's. Though I'm not a native of Chicago, my prior experience on the crime beat in Texas, combined with my forensic education, gave me the street cred to design my own beat.

"I know my baby wouldn't stay out overnight. I checked every place she could possibly be, and no one has seen her," Pamela explained in a breathless voice on the tips hotline. "Something's wrong, and the police won't help me."

I realized police were simply following protocol, not to take a missing person's report until the individual had been unaccounted for for a full forty-eight hours. I called Pam, who told me the police suspected Masey had run off.

"That's in most cases, they said," Pam said. "The child has run away and usually comes home or turns up at a relative's house in a few days. Masey wouldn't do that. No way!"

Pamela declared emphatically: "Jordan, if the police think I'm not gonna be out here looking for my child, they're crazy as hell!"

She and I met at a coffee shop not far from the television station by the train tracks on Lake Street. It would become our spot. She shared with me Masey's excitement over Picture Day and told me that her daughter chose a blouse from her closet. "She's always in my stuff," Pam said.

Pamela pulled a wallet size of the image from her billfold. The blouse was a very feminine-looking dark blue and white gingham plaid, with a ruffle down the middle. Masey's thick, shoulder-length hair spilled over the collar, slightly open at the neck, which revealed a heart-shaped pendant embossed with a rose that fit tightly across her neck. Her bang made a wide left turn like a canopy swooping across her perfectly arched eyebrows. Her hands weren't visible in the image, but her nails that day were painted a bright pink, aqua green, and periwinkle blue, alternating fingers, Pam told me.

"She loves to make herself up," said Pam, sitting across from me in the booth during our second meeting at the coffee shop. I hated making her come all the way downtown and felt even worse that she'd ordered and paid for my coffee before I arrived.

"I remembered how you like it," she said. "Heavy on the cream."

"Pam, you mustn't do that," I admonished her, then caught

myself, realizing Pam had no clue about the journalism ethics that disallowed me from accepting anything more than a breath mint or a stick of gum from a source, an ironclad but necessary rule to defend against any accusations of impropriety or compromised objectivity. What Pam and I had been doing could be viewed as somewhat unconventional by some journalists' standards. Unlike print reporters, broadcast journalists rarely spend a significant amount of time with their interview subjects without a camera present, which is why Scott wanted to know why he hadn't been invited, I suspect.

Scott is my guy but I don't tell him everything. Obviously, he was feeling a bit left out. After all, we had been together for hours, and this was the first he was hearing of my growing relationship with Pamela. Unlike the Buford girls, who were White, missing Black children don't typically receive the same amount of ink and airtime that missing White kids do. I'm convinced that one of the reasons Pam had shared so many mundane details with me about Masey is to make me care about her daughter. She didn't want me to lose interest in the story. I must admit, that was brilliant on her part.

I got a text from Tracy. **Jordan, how long before you guys set up the shot?**

As Pam's words played over in my head, I turned away from Masey's ninth-grade picture to focus on Scott and the rush of urgency now snapping me back into the present.

"Jordan, let me grab at least one light," Scott said.

The next text raised the stakes. **Jordan, we need to see the shot as soon as possible.**

"Jordan, get over here"—a rare command coming from Scott. "I need to set this shot."

Where did the morning go? I have no time to write a script. I will just have to wing it.

I texted Tracy. Micing now. I don't have a roll cue. When I pause, that's when you will know to play the sound from Fawcett. I'll wing it, but it will be obvious.

My words would likely send Tracy into a meltdown. An absence of control was not in a producer's DNA. Not the good ones, anyway.

I took a deep breath to try to avoid the habitual scrunching of my eyebrows. I looked around to make sure there weren't any cracks or rocks that could cause me to wipe out while walking and talking through this report.

"Five, four, three, two, action!"

"Diana, I'm at 35th and King Drive in historic Bronzeville. As you can see there are missing posters with Masey James's school picture tacked up on just about every tree. There's a similar scene a couple blocks west of here outside Chicago police headquarters. I spoke a little while ago with lead detective Mitch Fawcett, who shared that police no longer believe Masey is a potential runaway. The girl's been missing three weeks, and investigators are starting to feel the heat from a community that is demanding answers."

Video of my earlier interview with Fawcett played. He didn't share any new information. But, as Ellen had reasoned, "just go and build the relationship." I'm pretty sure, though, that by the time I had left, nothing between me and the pointy-headed detective had changed.

..

The next morning . . .

I took two sips of coffee and was about to make a mad dash out the door to the gym when my cell phone rang. I was going to let it go to voice mail until I saw who it was. My good buddy

Justin Smierciak, a freelance photographer whose best friend was a police scanner. I came in second.

"Hey, sis, I've got something for you," Justin said. He always got right down to the point. I liked that about him.

"Is it juicy? 'Cause I'm headed out the door," I said.

"Oh yeah, babe, you're going to want to hear this before you make any plans today," he said. Justin was not prone to exaggeration. If he said it was big, then it was big.

Justin thinks he is so cool. He wanted to be a cop, but that didn't work out. The thing that struck me when I first met him was his physicality. At five-five, Justin was small and scrappy but stereotypically cocky for a guy of his stature, not willing to back down to anyone. He would get right up in a guy's face twice his size, and he was dogged, too. We were at a crime scene on a story once and I witnessed Justin climb a tree in under a minute to get a shot above the other photographers.

"I just heard that human remains have been found in a vacant field east of the Ryan. One of the officers mentioned the name Ida B. Wells. I checked Google maps and found an Ida B. Wells-Barnett playground on the Chicago Park District website at 45th and Calumet. Looks like the 'L' passes right over it."

"Did they describe the body? Male or female?" I asked.

"Only that they found human remains. You know what that means," he said.

"Yeah, the body must be in bad shape," I said. "Are you headed there?"

"I'm here now! I'm waiting on you," he said.

I hung up and immediately called Ellen.

"Dead body on Park District land? Damn, you just said a mouthful!" Ellen said, clearly now on ten. "Okay, get over there."

"Yep, Scott is my next call," I said.

I should've known Justin was already at the scene. Freelance photographers eat what they kill. But Justin seemed to enjoy the hunt. He was nothing like his brother, Jake, whom I met in college.

The Smierciak boys grew up in Calumet City, an industrialized suburb just south of Chicago. Jake was a buttoned-down wannabe newspaper editor. He would overly enunciate words to try to mask his Chicago accent. I used to tease him that he would do better if he adopted a British accent. It would make him less of a wannabe and more interesting. Justin by contrast was the missing member of the Beastie Boys who never got the call. Aside from journalism and their parents, the two brothers had nothing in common.

Jake got married about three years after graduating from J-school and started a family with a real estate broker. When he heard I'd landed a television gig in Chicago, he reached out and told me to look up his baby brother. Justin and I are as unlikely a pair as can be. But Baby Smierciak has proved to be quite useful to me on the crime beat.

I thought about Masey. Human remains. Badly decomposed body. Three weeks missing. I didn't like the way that this series was adding up. My heart raced. I wanted so badly for it *not* to be Masey, but right now I just wanted to be the first reporter on the scene. Justin wasn't the only photographer who slept curled up next to a police scanner. I'd seen a few others. They were easy to spot, especially in bars packed with journalists. They're the guys having all their drinks bought for them but not actually drinking.

We lucked out, and Scott and I were the first television people to arrive. Barricades were already up, creating a restricted zone. Scott got as close as a conspicuous white van emblazoned with the station logo and a satellite on top could take us. We climbed out of the van. Scott was locked and loaded, ready to aim and shoot.

"Okay, let's go. Keep on walking until somebody tells us to stop," I said.

At the quickstep, Scott and I moved toward the intersection. As we rounded the corner, an ambulance came into view. The next thing I noticed was how unkempt the property was, with towering weeds and trash strewn about. I was so fixated on the heap of green gore, I almost didn't notice the cop rushing toward us, both palms facing outward gesturing for us to go back.

"This is a crime scene, and you are not allowed to cross the barricades at the top of the block!" he screamed. "You are going to have to go back!" he said as he continued to wave his arms in a "go on, get out of here" gesture.

"Officer, sir, I'm Jordan Manning with News Channel 8. I have to get closer. Here is my press pass."

"I said back up!"

One minute the cops need us; the next they are ordering us around like children. Scott and I did an about-face and in defiance moved into a slow retreat. I reached into my jacket pocket and pulled out my cell phone. "I'm calling Joey," I said.

Joseph Samuels was a Chicago police detective I'd grown close to, my "get out of jail free" card or in this case, my "get out of my way" card. We met one day at the courthouse at 26th and California and struck up a conversation outside chambers while awaiting a verdict. It's crazy how the stress of crime can bring people together. The verdict that day was a hung jury. The guy had killed his wife, and it set me off. How could the jury ignore the evidence? Joey invited me out for a drink at one of the grimiest bars I'd ever been to. And it was an awesomely delicious night of tequila shots and beer. It was a much-needed Band-Aid to cover the wound after the foreman announced that a verdict couldn't be reached. I considered Joey a work friend. I enjoyed our talks as much as he seemed to, and I appreciated when he praised me for my investigative instincts.

I was surprised when Joey picked up on the first ring.

"Good morning, Jordan," he said in a tone signaling he was aware this was a favor call, not a dinner invite for later. "How are you this morning?"

"I'm good, Joey. It's nice to hear your voice," I said. "Listen, I'm over at a crime scene at 45th and Calumet. Police have the area barricaded about a block in each direction. But I know something's going on."

"You want to know if I've heard anything?" he asked.

"Yeah, what do you know about human remains found in a vacant lot at 45th and Calumet?" I asked.

"Hell, Jordan, you know more than I do! I just got off a double shift. I guess that's why nobody called and told me about it yet," he said. "Do you think it's that missing kid?"

"I don't know if it's her. I got barked at by one of Chicago's finest for getting too close to the scene. I will say that based on the tension, they think it's her. I'm the only reporter here right now, Joey. I want to break this story. Can you confirm? Or at least find out whether it's a man or a woman?" I asked as politely as I could, adding a lilt in my voice to try and sound less bossy.

"Anything else, your highness?" he asked.

It hadn't worked. Or maybe it had. In either case, he didn't say no.

"You're funny," I said, allowing myself to lean into the familiarity of the exchange, something I'd promised myself I'd get better at.

"Let me get on it," Joey said. "I can't get you up close, but I can find out more about the body."

3

Today was shaping up to be one of those days where every ounce of me would be needed to make it through the newscast. Since Scott and I were the first news crew on the scene, that meant we'd have to wait around the longest of all the media types who would show up eventually for an update from a police spokesman.

My heart breaks knowing how this ends. It's the little girl. I have been doing this long enough to read the room. This is an all-hands-on-deck to secure the area effort. No one from the newsroom was calling. Sources were drying up. No one wants to talk, or they see it as too risky to confirm.

It was unseasonably warm for mid-October, but Chicago weather can be funny that way. Sometimes it snows in April. Freakishly, in the summer of 1995, in a city known for its bitter cold and hawkish wind, nearly eight hundred people died here from the heat.

The jewel of the Midwest offered a taste of life in a variety of flavors. And I'd had a dose of just about all of them in the past three years. Covering violent crime was humbling and terrifying. This beat has forced me to go to the dark end of the street my parents warned me about while I was growing up near a sketchy part of Southeast Austin. It was a wasteland of two-bit liquor lounges and abandoned buildings where addicts went to shoot up and dealers went to recruit. All this took place three blocks west of our growing black middle-class neighborhood of split-level, partial brick single-family homes. Since I left Austin for graduate school in Missouri, the area has been regentrified and is home to seven-figure condominiums, trendy restaurants, and music lounges in a city already full of them.

My mother, Eleanor, a brave and fair-minded woman, was convinced I'd become a lawyer. She would have lost all her bingo money winnings on the bet. But her sage advice has gotten me through way too many gut-wrenching moments in which I questioned whether there were any good people left as I stared at a body being loaded into an ambulance at a crime scene. She's warned me not to linger in the dark places for too long.

"You'll fall into despair if you keep trying to step into the shoes of the people going through this kind of trauma. I raised you to be empathetic, sweetheart, but God doesn't require all this of you. Leave it at the office."

But there was no office for me to store the heavy emotional baggage I lug around to do this job. I never understood why colleges and universities stuck courses in journalism and marketing/advertising in the same schools. The disposition my job requires is more akin to a surgeon's or a psychiatrist's. I must constantly remind myself to turn away from other people's despair and move toward the light that glows in my own life. It's a fragile balance; it's made me hard at times, but just as often, softer than I needed to be.

My cell phone vibrated in my pocket. It was Joey. "Hey, Joe-Joe, what you got?" I asked.

"You still at the scene?" he asked.

"Yeah. I'll be here all day, most likely," I said.

"Well, I don't know much yet. One of my guys did confirm that a body was recovered from a weed-infested lot over there. And I got an email about a news conference at 45th and Calumet today at one-thirty," Joey said.

I immediately called Ellen to let her know that I had confirmed the tip with a source inside the police department.

"Did they say whether it was a man or a woman?" Ellen asked.

"No," I responded. Neither of us stated what we feared and tried to remain positive, as if the mind could simply erase the body lying nearby, or will it not to be the person we already suspected it was.

"Okay, I'm heading into the news meeting now," she said. "Good work, Jordan. Keep an eye on your phone. I'll text you when I get out of the meeting."

Down the block, I noticed a crowd had gathered across the street from the crime scene. Neighbors, I imagined. One woman was crouched down on a stoop. I turned back toward Scott.

"I'm going to walk down there and try to talk to them," I said.

"The cops are gonna stop you," Scott warned.

"They can try," I said.

As I gained on the police barricades, an officer who looked all of fifteen years old spotted me and approached swiftly to head me off like a Bears defensive tackle.

Okay, rookie, settle down.

At that moment, I caught the attention of the woman on the stoop, and I waved to her like we were old friends. I stopped in my tracks and waited for the young officer to approach.

"Ma'am, we're not letting anyone past this point," he said, far more politely than the cop had earlier.

"I can appreciate that," I said with a slight smile. "I'm just trying to get to my friend's house over there. See? She just waved at me. See?" I said, and waved again at the stranger, who waved back.

"Okay, but you have to stay on that side of the street," he said.

"No problem," I said.

I walked toward my unknown but willing accomplice, who'd stepped away from the group gathered near the corner. In her mid to late thirties, the woman wore her hair braided with a detailed precision that must have taken hours, pulled into a ponytail that hung down her back.

I surveyed those around her. It was a quarter after nine.

Most of these folks just climbed out of bed.

I extended my hand and introduced myself and instantly got the feeling this woman was glad to see me.

"Hi, how are you? Thanks for your help back there. I wasn't sure they'd let me by," I said. "I'm Jordan Manning with Channel 8."

"I know who you are," she said shyly. "Tanya. McMillan," she said, breaking her name into two distinct parts the way Mama says *JOR-dan* when she is exasperated with me. "So, what's going on over there?"

I wasn't about to tell her that a dead body had been found across the street from her house, not before I tell the rest of Chicago.

"I'm not sure, but police are calling it a crime scene," I said. "Do you live here? Did you see or hear anything overnight?"

"Yeah, I live here with my mother," she said. "I didn't see anything going on last night. Everybody is saying they found someone dead. This morning, a bunch of orange jumpsuits was over there at about seven-thirty. I guess that's who the city finally sent out here to clean up that lot. They worked a good forty-five minutes, and next thing you know, the place was crawling with cops."

"Orange jumpsuits?" I asked. "Did they say *Cook County Jail* on them?"

"Yeah . . . they did," she said in a tone and with a shrug of her shoulders that let me know she thought I'd asked a naive question. "You know how you see those guys out on the expressway picking up garbage? It was that kind of crew."

"Ms. McMillan, have you told anyone else about this?" I asked.

"No, other than my neighbors and my moms. You're the only person I've talked to today," she said.

Damn! I wish I could've gotten all that on-camera. But there was no way I was getting over here with Scott in tow.

My phone vibrated in my pocket. It was Scott. **WE'VE GOT TO GET READY TO ROLL.** I'd missed an earlier text from Ellen. **WE'RE LEADING WITH BREAKING NEWS.**

I turned to Tanya. "Thank you so much, Tanya," I said, making certain to say her name, another valuable lesson I learned from Mom.

"When someone tells you their name for the first time, look them in the eyes and repeat it back to them. You won't forget the name and they won't forget you tried to make a connection. You never know who you will need."

"We're about to do a live broadcast," I told Tanya. "Would you mind saying on-camera what you just told me?"

Tanya McMillan's smile grew sheepish, and she dropped her head a little. "I don't wanna be on TV. Look at my hair," she said, then suddenly looked down at her outfit. "I need to change clothes first!" she exclaimed.

To me she looked great. But as a woman in television who is often criticized for what I wear, the color of my lipstick, and definitely my hair style, I get it. "Girl, I wish we had time for you to change," I said, code-switching into the Jordan my friends knew.

I know we just met, Tanya, but I need for you to trust me.

"I've got to do a live segment in less than five minutes," I continued. "You look beautiful, and the shot will only be from the chest up. I promise. You look great."

It wasn't a lie. She looked like someone on her way to work in a blue polo uniform shirt with a company logo and khakis. She might not look as nice as she would have liked to, but she did look put together and relatable, from my perspective, unlike the people the women at the beauty salon always complained about. "Why do news reporters go out and interview people who make you cringe or still in their hair rollers?" asked Estelle, the receptionist there.

Believe me, it's not on purpose.

"Okay, come on, girl," I said. "Let's go!"

As we hurried back to Scott, a voice called out from behind, "Tanya! Where are you going?"

"I'll be back, Mama!" she screamed. "I'm about to do an interview on TV!"

The commotion drew attention from the officers at the scene. As we passed the baby-faced cop, he gave me the side-eye. I responded, mouthing the words *thank you* with an apologetic smile.

By the time we reached Scott, I had less than three minutes to script the segment. I brought him and the field producer, who'd arrived as I went fishing for information, up to speed.

"I've got a resident interview. This is Tanya McMillan," I said.

"Hi, Tanya, how are you?" Scott asked.

"Good," she responded.

My heart pounded, not only because I was on deadline but because the plot was thickening. A prison crew had discovered a body. Not the surge of cops Fawcett had described earlier out looking for Masey.

Diana Sorano: "We begin today's broadcast with breaking news on the South Side of Chicago. Channel 8's Jordan Manning is in Bronzeville, where we are told there has been a gruesome discovery. We go to Jordan live now to tell us more."

"Good morning, Diana. I don't know if you can see it from here, but in the distance behind me is an overgrown playground at 45th Street and Calumet Avenue that police are calling a crime scene. Sources inside the department have confirmed that human remains were found here this morning below the 'L' tracks."

I turned to Tanya, who had a horrified look on her face. *Shit!* In my haste, I'd forgotten to confirm the rumor she heard well before I got there.

Please, Tanya. Keep it together.

"With me is Tanya McMillan. She lives across the street from where the body was found. Earlier today, she saw a crew of prisoners from Cook County Jail in the lot. What were they doing, Tanya?"

"Um, they were cleaning up," said Tanya, looking and sounding stunned. "Me and my mom were like, 'Hallelujah! It's about time,'" she said, replaying the moment as if her Oscar depended on it. "We've been trying to get the city to come out and clear that lot for months! They ignored us!"

Tanya's rounded cheeks were now puffed up in anger. Her eyes sloped. It now hit her in real time what I had just revealed live. I felt horrible about my omission, but I was on live television. I had to go on.

"Oh my God, and that little girl is missing!" Tanya had officially made the unconfirmed connection and lost it. "Oh my God!"

Why? Why did she allude to Masey? Damn it!

I angled my body to the left, away from Tanya. Scott picked up on my cue and focused the shot on me.

"Diana, as you can see, this news is very upsetting to folks here. Tanya told me earlier that her mother and some of the neighbors went to City Hall only a week ago to file a complaint about the condition of the abandoned playground."

Diana Sorano: "Jordan, what do we know about the victim?"

"Diana, nothing definitive yet. *Obviously people are worried it could be connected to the Masey James case, but I stress, no one here has confirmed that. We have to keep in mind Masey's family are likely hearing this news and fear the worst.* Police have scheduled a news conference today at one-thirty here at the scene. Hopefully, they'll be able to tell us more then. Back to you, Diana."

I pivoted toward Tanya.

"Tanya," I said.

"Yeah!" She was a different person from the one I'd met less than ten minutes ago.

"I'm sorry I didn't tell you about the discovery before we went on the air," I said. "In my haste and on deadline . . . and I was worried about getting back across the police barricades. I'm sorry. I had a lot going on in my head. Are you okay?"

Tanya paused, as if she had to think about her answer, her head tilted slightly to the left. "No!" she exclaimed. "I'm scared! What else do you know that you're not telling me?" she asked.

"That's all I know, and what you told me was very helpful, by the way," I said, trying to calm her down. "Thank you."

A tear slowly rolled down her right cheek. "It's like we take one step forward and two steps back. We're trying to build a safe community. How are we supposed to do that now?"

I didn't have an answer for her.

"I bet it's that girl," Tanya said, shaking her head in disagreement with her own words. "I bet it's that girl," she repeated.

..

The news conference was pushed back to three-thirty. I hadn't eaten anything since I left the house. By the time noon rolled around, Scott and I were no longer the only media on the scene. Police had erected privacy crime scene barriers around the spot where the body had been found beneath the "L" tracks and gradually allowed the media, which had blocked traffic on the residential street, to move in closer.

Scott had done his best before the privacy screens went up to zoom in to capture a decent shot of the overgrown lot from behind the barricades. But it was Baby Smierciak who got the money shot. Putting his agility to work, he'd managed to scale a fire escape on the building adjacent to the playground and got off a few overhead shots that provided the best view of the property's ragged conditions before investigators noticed him and threatened to arrest him.

GOT A GREAT SHOT! UPLOADING IT, he texted, with an image attached of investigators standing around, their necks craned forward, peering down at a dark-colored tarp.

YOU'RE A GENIUS! I texted back.

I forwarded the image to Tracy to accompany my next broadcast. "Hey, this might be good for a teaser before the four o'clock news," I told her.

By 3:20 P.M., all eyes were on Linda Folson, the public information officer for the Chicago PD. She had just arrived on the scene. She was easy to spot: a tall woman, at least five-eleven, with graying sandy blond hair and a perpetually grim look. In her job, though, it worked in her favor.

At three-thirty on the dot, Folson stood before a podium the department had set up adjacent to the crime scene.

"Good afternoon, members of the press," Folson began somberly. "Thank you for your patience."

Then she got right to the point.

"This morning at 8:13 A.M., we received a call from Cook County Sheriff's Police that a crew of prisoners from the county jail on work detail had discovered human remains under the 'L' tracks at 45th Street and Calumet Avenue."

Folson's words came in rapid succession. "The victim is an African American female, approximately five feet nine inches tall. The remains are now with the Cook County medical examiner. Police will continue to work here at the scene collecting DNA evidence. We have no further information on the victim's identity or cause of death. But police have opened a homicide investigation. We ask anyone with any information to call the crime hotline by dialing 311. Also, we're asking the media to please respect the privacy of the residents here in the immediate area. We'll update you as information becomes available. That's all I have. No questions at this time. Thank you."

Before the word *you* had left her lips, Folson went into full retreat. She scampered away from the podium quickly, ignoring calls of "Linda! LIN-da!" at her back. Not from me, though. I'd turned to stone.

"Jordan, we're going back to the desk," field producer Tracy said through my earpiece. "You're clear."

I was grateful. "The victim is an African American female" had temporarily halted my breathing.

Scott saw it in my face. "It doesn't mean it's her," he said, reading my thoughts.

Why would police reveal the race and gender of the victim to the public before they had made a positive ID?

"It's irresponsible!" I said, incredulous, the words struggling to keep up with my growing outrage. "I mean, isn't it?" looking at Scott.

"What's irresponsible? I don't follow you," he said.

"For police to release that kind of detail about the victim when there's a child missing who fits that description!" I said.

Was Pam watching?

Her words were in my head from that day in the booth at the back of the coffee shop at our third meeting. "Masey's always been tall for her age. She says, 'Mama, I can't wait for these little boys to catch up with me in high school.'"

She also told me about a girl who had a "pick at Masey" at her old school in West Englewood.

"I would've thought she'd be afraid to mess with my baby. Mase has got about three inches on her."

Pam went on to explain how her eldest gets up at five o'clock on school days to make it in time for the eight o'clock bell.

"She literally has to go to the suburbs to get to school in the morning," said Pam as she nervously took a sip of coffee. "It takes her almost two hours to get to school."

Pam laid out the entire route for me: Masey leaves the house around 6:15, walks two blocks to catch the No. 75 bus at Damen Avenue, and rides nine or ten stops to the corner of Chicago Avenue and Kedzie. There she picks up the No. 94 bus to Berwyn, a west suburb that shares a border with Chicago and its better-known suburban neighbor Cicero. From there, she has to wait on the No. 49 Pace bus, sometimes as long as twenty minutes, then ride another forty minutes, deboard at Western and Van Buren, and walk another seven or eight minutes to the Carol Crest Academy on the city's Near West Side.

"The program's worth it," Pam told me. "Getting her out of Hilton High School was, too."

"That's odd that she has to go through Berwyn," I said.

"I know right," Pam agreed. "But believe it or not, that ends up being the shortest, most reliable route."

Masey enrolled in Carol Crest Academy her sophomore year to take part in a gifted program for students who excel in math and science. She had received an invitation from Carol Crest's principal, who promised that she could "count on" her and her staff to make the transition as seamless as possible.

"She wasn't challenged at her old school, but God stepped in," Pam said. "It was like hitting the lottery."

The more I learned about Masey James, the more I saw myself in her. Young, gifted, and Black. Hungry for knowledge and motivated by change. Always in her mother's closet, borrowing her things. A girlie girl with model height and an athletic build. I wasn't surprised she was being bullied by a girl who was probably just jealous of Masey for having all those smarts and beauty to boot. I was bullied from sixth grade all the way through my sophomore year in high school. It wore me out, and ended only after my cousin Stephanie started picking me up from school in my aunt Esther's old Lincoln Town Car we used to call "The Love Boat." Steph must have reached six feet by the time she finished high school, and she was straight up and down like a ruler. Uncle Dooley, who had nicknames for all us kids, called her Skinny Pickle. Stephanie's hair was the color of sand and lighter than her caramel-colored complexion, thanks to her Creole genes and Texas's scorching hot sun. Her age and her height gave her a presence that my nemeses couldn't help but respect. Most people who knew Stephanie respected her. All, that is, except one.

After the press briefing, the news crews started to pack up and scatter. But a half dozen or so squad cars remained parked at various angles at the intersection. My guess was, they were intended to protect potential witnesses from media on the prowl.

"What are you doing later?" Scott said. "Drinks on me tonight at the Goat?"

The Goat was slang for the Billy Goat Tavern & Grill, a local bar made famous in skits on *Saturday Night Live* during the Belushi era and still popular with tourists and local newshounds.

"Can I take a rain check, Scott? I'm really not up for it," I said. "It's been a long day, and right now all I want is food and a pair of flip-flops."

I know Scott. He wanted to be close in case police announced the victim's identity.

"I appreciate the offer, though. I do," I said.

I really did. Scott had comforted me at least twice before when a story was too much for me to handle. But it wasn't the sort of thing I wanted to plan for.

The last time was when we arrived first to the scene of a strong-arm burglary. It was just before Christmas. An African American man who owned a cellular phone franchise on 79th Street had been shot to death. His wife arrived on the scene wearing a mink coat over her nightgown. She'd barely put her Cadillac in park before she leapt out the car and ran toward the white sheet that covered her husband's body. Behind her wails, barely audible, I could hear "Un-Break My Heart" playing on the car stereo. Back inside the news truck, I broke down and Scott held me in his arms. I could still hear her screams.

I was grateful for the silence in my car on the drive home. The days were getting shorter, so the sky had grown dim by the time I pulled my convertible Oldsmobile into the garage beneath my building.

It was rush hour. My fellow tenants poured into the complex

at this time of day. As badly as my feet hurt, I took the back stairs from the garage two flights up to avoid conversation on the elevator. Inside my apartment, the serenity of the familiar thunk-click of the door was interrupted by the rancid smell of the garbage I'd forgotten to take out this morning.

I opened the windows and lit the apple-cinnamon-scented candles planted around the living room. I busied myself cleaning out the refrigerator, throwing out old takeout boxes and liquified vegetables I had bought with the best of intentions. About five minutes later, the perfectly chilled bottle of pinot grigio on the refrigerator door beckoned.

I sealed up the garbage bag, set it by the door, and ransacked the cabinet for my favorite wineglass, the last survivor of a set of four red wine goblets Lisette gave me as a housewarming gift. The death of each glass was more dramatic than the one before it. The first got chipped somehow and almost cut my lip. The bottom of another barely clipped the dining table and broke at the stem. And the third perished in soapy water when Mom unwittingly tossed a hot skillet into the sink. I rarely drank white wine, but when I did, I preferred to sip it from a red wineglass; it felt better in my hand. It was one of my little quirks.

I pulled back the sliding glass door and slinked out onto the porch, collapsing gently onto the padded wicker chaise. Then it hit me. *Pam.* I had been so preoccupied that I hadn't checked my cell phone or turned the ringer back up since I'd left the crime scene. I exhaled deeply and pivoted back inside to retrieve my phone from my coat pocket.

I had four messages: one from Ellen, from earlier today; one from Joey; and two from Pam. I dreaded listening to her voice-mail messages. But I couldn't avoid her text.

POLICE SHOWED UP TO MY JOB AND ASKED ME TO
COME DOWNTOWN FOR AN INTERVIEW.

Fifteen minutes later, another.

JORDAN WHAT ARE THEY SAYING? CALL ME.

The place where peace resides in my soul cried out, "Oh no!"
I was no longer in control of my emotions. The first heave of
my chest caught me by surprise. My muscles weakened and
my phone fell from my right hand to the floor. I felt sick to my
stomach. In a missing person case, hope is all you have. And
now this was lost. Police wouldn't involve Pam if they didn't
have some sense that they had found her daughter.

I reached down to pick up my phone and turned the ringer
volume up to high. Had Pam seen the news? Had she heard the
words *the victim is an African American female, approximately
five feet nine inches tall*? If I call her back, until I know more,
what would I say if she picked up?

I'd done it. I'd become too invested. Because I wanted to
get the story and also because I genuinely sympathized, I'd
allowed myself to become Pam's crutch. I had to learn to set
boundaries. This wasn't a relationship; it was a job, after all. It
was no longer simply a pattern in my dating life. It was becoming a pattern in my work life, too. In the competitive world of
television broadcast journalism, especially in a popular market
like Chicago, somebody's always got their eye on your spot.
And with a vulture like Keith Mulvaney lurking at Channel 8,
I couldn't afford to lose my edge.

Ellen and I nicknamed him Tonya after Tonya Harding,
the disgraced Olympic figure skater who was banned from the

sport in the early nineties after she allegedly orchestrated an attack carried out on her chief competitor, Nancy Kerrigan, by two goons wielding a collapsible baton. If a thwack to the knee-cap was all it took to eliminate me, Keith would've tried it by now. But he was going to have to work a lot harder than that. Still, I told Ellen, half jokingly, "If I come up missing, check his basement."

I gathered myself and my roiling stomach began to settle. The biting hunger I felt hours earlier had subsided, not because of anything I'd eaten but because my mind was onto bigger things. *Jordan*, I heard Mama say, *have you eaten?*

I grabbed a handful of cheese crackers from the cabinet and the bottle of pinot and headed back to the chaise on the deck. It was decorated with Southwest-style pillows and a heavy handwoven wrap I'd bought on an Indian reservation in New Mexico, just outside Albuquerque, during spring break back in college. The night air swirled around me as cooler tempera-tures settled in along with my nagging thoughts.

I have to call Pam back. What would I say? Why hadn't I called before? I was at work. I don't have any more information than I reported. I swear.

Out of the corner of my eye, I caught a glimpse of the time on the clock in the living room. It was 9:05. I hadn't realized so much time had passed, and my phone hadn't rung. Pam hadn't tried to call me in more than four hours. Mom hadn't called, either.

The sky grew cloudy and the air smelled of rain. I grabbed the empty wine bottle and headed back inside. I had a mind to call Mom, but my body went for the couch. I plopped down and covered myself with the soft yellow velour throw Mom gave me for Christmas. Sleep must've come quickly, because when my cell phone finally rang, it was 10:30.

If it's Pam Alonzo, I'll take the call.

It wasn't. It was Joey.

"Jordan, it's Joe."

"Yes" was all I could manage. He had news or else he wouldn't have called this late.

"Look," he said, followed by a heavy, knowing sigh, "I wanted to give you a heads-up as a friend. But this is not to be shared, okay? Do we have an understanding?"

"What is it?" I asked.

"Jordan, do we have an understanding?" he repeated, which was unlike him. "I've gotta know. This is off the record until the news conference tomorrow at eleven o'clock. Okay? This is my job."

"Yes, you have my word," I said. "You can trust me."

He hesitated.

"It's her, isn't it, Joey?" I asked. "Isn't it?"

Joey expelled another heavy sigh. "Yeah, it's her."

My head shook from side to side, like Tanya McMillan's, denying what I'd just heard.

"Jordan, are you there?" Joey asked.

"Yes. Thanks for letting me know," I said.

"Mum's the word," he said. "Good night."

I hung up without saying goodbye, sat straight up on the couch, held my face in my hands, and cried.

4

I awoke to rain coming down in buckets and remembered that I'd left my cushions and treasured handwoven wrap out on the deck overnight. They were soaked, no doubt. But I couldn't worry about that now.

She's gone.

Nothing pierces the heart more violently than the moment you learn of someone's demise for all eternity—especially someone you love. I had come to care about Masey James, a girl I'd never met. And now I never would. She was taken from this world, taken from a mother who adored her and denied a future that looked so bright. When the news breaks, people all over this city will mourn her loss as if they knew her, as I did last night.

Even through my sadness, around 7:45, by the time I drank my first cup of coffee, I'd fully recovered from my reluctance to call Pam. I know that once police identified Masey as the victim under the "L" tracks at the eleven o'clock news conference, every media outlet in town would pounce, looking for family members and neighbors to interview.

A woman answered the phone, but it wasn't Pam.

"Jordan," she said. *Pam must have me listed in her contacts.*

"Hello, yes, this is Jordan Manning."

"This is Cynthia Caruthers, Masey's aunt," she said.

I realized then that I hadn't thought about what I was going to say. Police hadn't yet announced publicly that Masey had been identified as the victim. But surely the family knew. I, on the other hand, wasn't supposed to know yet.

"Hi, Cynthia. Is she available?" I felt horrible for asking. It's never easy to butt into someone's life while they're experiencing the worst pain imaginable. Yet it is something I must do again and again in this job. And, if I'm being honest with myself, it can take a toll.

"She can't talk right now. But I'll let her know that you called," she said.

"Yes, I do understand this is not a good time, Cynthia," I said before I realized my gaffe. Just like that, I gave myself away.

"I know she was trying to get in touch with you yesterday," Cynthia said.

My guilt flared up.

"It was a chaotic scene, and I didn't get a chance to return her call," I said, which was the truth. "Is Pam at her house?" I asked.

"No, she's with me here at mine," said Cynthia, trying to hold back her sobs. "Listen, I can't talk right now," she said abruptly.

"Okay, I just wanted to say . . ." but she was gone. Concerned that I might have sounded insensitive, I texted through my tears: Thank you for taking my call, Cynthia. I'm praying for your family.

I wished there had been more that I could do. I was glad to hear that Pam wasn't at her house, which reporters will surely stake out once police make the announcement.

··

BREAKING NEWS

Weekend morning anchor Ron Mancino: As so many had feared, the body of an African American woman found in an abandoned field yesterday has been identified as missing fifteen-year-old honor student Masey James. Police say the teenager was the victim of foul play. Police superintendent Donald Bartlett made the announcement a little while ago at a news conference. Our Simone Michele reports.

Simone: Ron, a clearly shaken police superintendent Donald Bartlett has confirmed the remains are that of the missing fifteen-year-old. Masey James hadn't been seen since she left a family member's home three weeks ago on her bicycle. She was believed to have been headed home but never arrived.

Clip of Superintendent Bartlett at the news conference: Masey James was one of this city's best and brightest. I know I speak for the entire department when I say we couldn't be sorrier for the way this has turned out. It's heartbreaking.

Out of respect for the family, that's all we can share with you at this time. To the media, I know you have jobs to do, but I'm personally asking you to respect this family's privacy as they struggle with this most devastating outcome.

Simone: Ron, police are being tight-lipped about any leads in the case. Certainly the vacant lot where the body was found will likely present some challenges. There have been reports of extensive flooding and water retention in that area recently. That's not going to make detectives' jobs any easier.

Ron Mancino: Simone, such a sad outcome to this closely watched case. Superintendent Bartlett said our hearts are broken. Indeed, they are. Simone, thank you for your reporting.

I was glad to see Simone break the news. She was on the overnight desk, so I'm not sure how she ended up covering the news conference this morning, but better her than Keith. It is technically my day off, which buys me some time to check in with a valued resource. I left a voice-mail message for Dr. Marvin Chan, a renowned forensic pathologist, a regular guest lecturer at the University of Chicago, and a friend.

I met Dr. Chan while I was working on my graduate thesis on media coverage of violent crime at Columbia College of Missouri. One day a flyer in the student commons advertising a lecture by Dr. Chan on the principles of homicide investigation caught my eye, and I attended. He shared incredible insights. I bought both his books and stuck around afterward for a chance to speak with him one-on-one. I'd researched Dr. Chan ahead of his talk and found numerous articles about him and *by* him in academic and law enforcement journals. He had an impressive portfolio of work and admirers around the world. To quote him directly, versus footnoting a passage from one of his books, would give my paper an edge. Blame it on the extra-credit sensibility I developed attending public schools in Austin, where a gifted Black girl could be overlooked if she didn't do something to rise above ordinary.

I got an A on my thesis and shared a copy with Dr. Chan, with a note thanking him for taking an interest in my project. "You're an inspiration," I wrote.

That was years ago, but Dr. Chan and I have remained in touch. I couldn't believe my luck when, after my first six months on the crime beat in Chicago, Dr. Chan was contracted by the Cook County Board of Commissioners to become a special consultant to the chief medical examiner. The Chicago Police Department had come under fire for the rise in unsolved murders, with a growing number of Black women as victims. The Cook County state's attorney lobbied to have a specialist brought in, and Dr. Chan fit the description as one of the most revered in the country. A frequent expert witness in murder cases, he could be counted on to provide candid, court-worthy testimony in our interviews. Too candid, at times.

I thought about what Simone had said about flooding and water retention in the area.

I had a hunch that the chief medical examiner had already reached out to Dr. Chan for his expert opinion on the time and manner of death. I sent Dr. Chan an email requesting an interview this afternoon. He responded by the time I got out of the shower.

"Sure, come on by today at four o'clock," he wrote. "You know, Jordan, there is only so much I can say on-camera."

"I know, Dr. Chan," I said, remembering how much he enjoyed playing the role of teacher to an eager beaver like me. "I'll follow your guidance."

Scott and I decided not to take the station's van to the medical examiner's office. Too conspicuous. We drove separately and, as Dr. Chan had instructed, met him on the lower level of the morgue, where autopsies are performed and bodies are kept in cold storage.

When we arrived, Dr. Chan greeted me warmly. He'd lost weight and his face looked a little gaunt. "Jordan! It's so nice to see you, my dear. How have you been?" he asked.

"You know me, busy as ever. Wow! Look at you! You trying to fit back in the tux you wore to the prom?" I teased.

"Well, of course, I have to work at maintaining my schoolboy figure," he shot back.

"Well, aside from the usual, I've been following the Masey James disappearance. That's pretty much been my life the last few weeks. You remember Scott Newell?"

"Yes, Scott, nice to see you again," Dr. Chan said.

The two men shook hands, and Dr. Chan quickly got down to business. "Follow me. Let's start in the evidence room," he said.

He escorted us through a cavernous basement hallway with double doors at the far end. Dr. Chan held open the left side door for Scott and me to pass through.

"Jordan, you've been down here before?" Dr. Chan asked.

"Yes," I reminded him. But it didn't make it any less unnerving to walk among the last remnants of people who not long ago were living, breathing human beings who met violent ends.

Insulated shelves held boxes labeled with victims' names in bold letters, followed by a series of numbers that included date of death, birth date, and some other numbers I couldn't discern. Dr. Chan stopped and pulled one of the boxes off the shelf and set it down on a table at the end of the row. He began to speak as he reached inside and pulled out its contents. Each item was wrapped in a sealed plastic bag.

"What you see in these bags is what investigators collected from the body," he explained.

Scott started to lift his camera, but Dr. Chan held up his hand. "You can't film this, though. I can show you to help you understand. But you can't film here," he admonished.

Scott lowered the camera. "Okay, sorry about that," he said.

Dr. Chan then held up what looked like it could've been part of a T-shirt. It was so soiled that it was anybody's guess what color it used to be. "This is the only article of clothing retrieved," Dr. Chan said.

"So, the body was partially nude?" I asked.

"Yes, except for the remnants of this top. Her lower extremities were exposed," Dr. Chan said. "See this crusty seam along the edge," he said, pointing to a discoloration in the ragged, soiled cloth. "It was difficult to discern at first, but under a microscope, it's clear that this is representative of charring. Even in the muddy conditions, the T-shirt fabric, which includes some plastic fibers, preserved this key evidence to help paint a clearer picture of what happened to the victim."

"Did you say charring?" I asked.

"Yes, it appears the killer attempted to destroy evidence by setting the body on fire," he said.

I weakened at the knees. "Oh my God!" I said. "I knew it was going to be bad, but . . ." My voice trailed off.

"There's more. Let's go sit down in my office," Dr. Chan said. He returned the contents to the box and the box to the shelf. "This way."

Inside his tiny office, my first thought was *This is the best the city can do for a world-renowned forensic pathologist?* Dr. Chan must've read my mind.

"I know, it's swanky, isn't it?" he joked. "Trust me, what they're paying me makes up for it. That's off the record," he teased.

The lighting was surprisingly not bad in this bland room with cinder-block walls painted a bright yellow and high-beam LED lighting across the ceiling.

While Scott set up, I quizzed Dr. Chan.

"Apparently the area where the body was found had extensive flooding recently. Masey had been missing for three weeks. So I can only imagine what shape the body was in when you got it," I said.

"Terrible," he said. "The worst possible scenario for evidence collection. But that is something I absolutely do not want to say on-camera. I don't want this bastard to think he's going to get away with this, because there's not enough evidence to connect him to the victim."

"Why do you say that?" I asked.

"The conditions. Burning of the flesh, wrapped in heavy duty plastic, in warm, wet conditions for the better part of two weeks," Dr. Chan said. "Exposed to the elements, insects and night creatures . . . the decomposition was accelerated by three times."

"Okay, I'm ready when you are," Scott interrupted.

Dr. Chan came closer to me and put his hands on my shoulders. "Jordan, I've known you, how long?" he asked.

"Oh gosh, a good seven, eight years," I said.

"You do a hard job, but I know you," he said, "you've got a soft heart. Whoever did this to this child is a monster. He cut her up very badly. I can't say for sure the cutting happened postmortem, but due to the extent, I believe at least some did."

I struggled to hold it together. "How'd she die?" I asked.

Dr. Chan sat on the edge of his desk. "My conclusion is death by strangulation, though there was a lot of bleeding from the cutting wounds. That could have been a contributing factor," he said. "She was eviscerated, Jordan. The fire I can say with certainty occurred postmortem. There was no soot in the windpipe . . ."

"Right, so she was already dead when the fire was set," I said, completing his sentence.

"What do you mean by eviscerated?" I asked. I knew what *eviscerated* meant, but I wanted to know what it meant for Masey.

"There were multiple stab and cut wounds to the torso and the legs. And it appears that more than one type of sharp instrument was used to make those wounds," he said.

My heart sank into my stomach.

"By the time the body was found, it was in an advanced state of decomposition called putrefaction. You're familiar with that term, right?" he asked.

"Yes, I recall reading in your second book about how much it can complicate a criminal investigation," I said.

"This process was accelerated by the plastic surrounding the remains in the warm, wet conditions," Dr. Chan said. "There also were signs of what's known as lividity . . ."

"The purplish discoloration that happens when the blood pools when a body lies in the same position for a while," I interjected like I did as a student during one of our lively exchanges.

"Yes, that's right. It pretty much covered the entire back side, down the back of the legs to just above the ankles," he said.

My left hand involuntarily rose and rested on my chest. I closed my eyes, taking it all in. I asked the inevitable question. "Was she raped?"

"Yes. The ultraviolet screening showed considerable bruising and lacerations in the genital area.

"I'm releasing my official report in the morning, Jordan, so you can't run this until after it has been released," Dr. Chan continued. "But you'll be the first and the only."

"What? Are you not doing any other interviews?" I asked, hopeful.

"No. You're in luck. I'm leaving town tomorrow night."

"Where are you headed?" I asked.

"New Zealand. I'm speaking at a conference. I'll be there two days. Then I'm heading to Switzerland for a little R&R," he said. "I've got guest lecturers scheduled to handle my courses while I'm away."

"Good for you," I said, happy to change the subject long

enough to focus on our interview, a watered-down version of the truth.

"I passed a ladies' room on the way down here," I said. "Can you two excuse me for a minute?"

I walked out the way we'd come in. My heart was beating fast, the anxiety building in my chest.

I had barely enough strength to push open the door and steadied myself against the wall. My body shook and tears streamed down my face. All I could think was *This is going to kill her mother.*

A bright young girl who had a bright future ahead of her. The star of the story her mother loved to tell. Eviscerated. Charred. *My God from Heaven!*

I grabbed the makeup sponge from my purse and blotted my face dry before rejoining Scott and Dr. Chan. My eyes met Scott's as I reentered the room. He looked sympathetic and I had to look away to keep the waterworks in check.

"Are you all right?" Dr. Chan asked.

I wanted to ask him the same thing. Dr. Chan looked more fit than I'd ever seen him, but he didn't seem himself.

"Yes, Dr. Chan, thanks for asking," I said. "This is a rough one. Let's get through this. So just talk, as comfortably as you can, about what your investigation has learned. Okay?"

"Sounds good, Jordan," he said.

"I'm rolling," Scott said.

Dr. Chan shared what he knew in slightly less graphic detail.

Cause of death: Strangulation. Evidence of sexual assault. Attempt to destroy evidence, but nothing about a fire, nothing about evisceration. Those are the kind of details that typically don't become public knowledge until trial.

As we were leaving, Dr. Chan pulled me aside. "Hey, Jordan, I didn't want to come out with this on-camera," he said. "But I've participated in hundreds of investigations. And in more than thirty-five years on the job, I have to say when someone inflicts this type of violence on a human being, it's either personal or the work of a serial killer."

"You've shared this theory with police?" I asked.

"Yes, of course. It's speculative. I wouldn't want to raise the public's concerns without more proof."

"Were you able to collect DNA evidence in connection with the sexual assault?" I asked.

"Honestly, Jordan, the body was in such an advanced state of decomposition, there isn't much DNA evidence to salvage. I'm having some tests run on some tissue that was extracted from beneath the fingernails. But please, don't share that in your broadcast. I don't want to tip this guy off."

"Absolutely," I said.

"I trust you." He smiled.

"Thank you, Dr. Chan. Is it all right if I tape my closing right here before we head out?" I asked.

"Sure, no problem. I myself have to step out for a moment. Just come on out when you're done, and I'll escort you back upstairs," he said.

As he walked out of the room, I turned to Scott. "Okay, Scott, let's get this over with."

"Are you ready? You need a minute?" he asked.

"No, no, I'm good. I know what I want to say. I'm ready."

Outside the courtroom, most people would never hear violence against another person described in the horrific detail Dr. Chan had just shared with me privately. We shield them from it. *We* as in the media, police, and prosecutors. Sometimes I wish the public did know. Then maybe people would understand the true impact of violent crime and the destruction of human life.

"I look okay?" I asked Scott.

"You're gorgeous!"

I stared into the camera, and for a moment I forced myself to forget that Pamela might be watching. People had to know the truth, as much of it as I think they can stand.

5

Following my interview with Dr. Chan, I drove back to the studio, one hand clutching the steering wheel, the other pressed against my cheek, in disbelief over what I'd just learned about the inconceivable horror of Masey James's final moments.

She was eviscerated, Jordan.

I could feel my heart beating, not in my chest, but in my head, like a bass drum relentlessly keeping time. Along the way, I called producer Tracy Klein to see if she was available to edit the footage, which is scheduled to air tomorrow night. Tracy is as good as gold, the most gifted editor at the station and certainly one of the most dedicated. God bless her, she worked an hour and a half over on her Saturday shift to sit with me in the dark, cramped editing booth to chop up the interview precisely as I instructed. I am usually not so hands-on, but Dr. Chan has put a great deal of faith and trust in me, so I make it my business to ensure that nothing I report in any way compromises his position.

It was dark when I pulled out of the underground parking lot, and I mourned the loss of the evening sun when the days grow shorter as a precursor to fall. Back in Austin, I looked forward to the change of seasons and the unbridled majesty of fall's mosaic. In Chicago, fall's beauty is the first sign of the inevitability and brutality of the winter to come.

I felt a similar kind of dread wash over me on the way home. After this day, it is the last place I want to be—drinking alone. No stash of cute throw pillows and scented candles from Pier 1 was going to make me feel better, but I could use a drink, so I called Zena. She's usually up for anything and just the person I needed to pull me out of this funk. Just dialing her number, I could feel the tension leaving my body. I asked her to meet me at a wine bar in my neighborhood. Zena Gardner, or Z, is like a little sister to me, but I admirably refer to her as my "big sister" because at twenty-five, she's already so accomplished. She co-owns a clothing and jewelry boutique with her mother in Oak Park. She also has majority stock in an organic coffee company and owns two rental properties—one in her native Brooklyn and another in Philadelphia she inherited from her grandmother and renovated—and she recently moved into a three-bedroom condo she owns in Bucktown.

I arrived first and headed straight for the more private lounge area in the back, with its low, plush blue velvet couches and candelabras on teakwood side tables. I plopped down and let out a deep breath, then discreetly slipped out of my pumps. The server hadn't noticed me yet, but that was okay. I needed a moment to catch my breath and sink into this velvety comfort.

Z arrived about ten minutes later. The couch had me in its grip by then, and I struggled to find my footing to get up and greet Z with a hug.

"Hey, girl! Don't get up. You're fine," Z said.

But Z had no idea how badly I needed that hug. I fought gravity and stood up, holding out my arms and greeting her warmly. "Thanks for coming out. It's been a rough couple of days, girl."

For some people, my opener would have invited questions, such as "Why?" or "What happened?" But not Zena. It wasn't that she didn't care; her default mode was always to listen and pivot to the positive.

"Wait! When did you cut your hair? I love it!" she said.

Zena hadn't seen me since the big chop a couple weeks ago.

I made a drastic change from a bob that kissed my shoulders to a short do spiked at the top and shaved close to my scalp in the back.

"I liked your style before, but this is *you!*" Z said. "Not everybody can pull it off. It suits your face."

"See, I think so, too. But it's still a big debate in the newsroom."

"What are you in the mood for?" she asked.

"You know I love my big reds. Let's get a bottle," I said.

"Bet!"

Z and I chopped it up until just before midnight, when she was distracted by the chirp of an incoming text message on her phone. She grabbed it off the table so fast it looked like a flash of light beaming across the table. I knew something was up by the sneaky grin that crept across her face.

"I know that look," I said. "I'm about to be kicked to the curb."

Z laughed. "I didn't tell you about this guy I met who works at the CBOT?" That's the Chicago Board of Trade, which meant one of two things: Either he has money or he's pretending to have money.

"Do I need to put him through my approval process?" I asked. "Do you know his birthday? I can have Joey run a background check."

Zena laughed. "It isn't even that serious. Trust me."

I know what you mean.

"We're just meeting for a nightcap . . . at his place."

A nightcap. Is that what they call it now?

"Didn't you say you just met this guy?" I asked, playing the big sister now.

"He's cool. I've been over to his place before. He's not an ax murderer, Lois Lane. Your job makes you paranoid," Z said.

I rolled my eyes. "My job should make *you* paranoid," I said. "Chicago might have a serial killer on the loose targeting Black women."

"Huh?" Z said, head down, eyes wide and peering over her glasses.

"Yeah."

"Oh shit! I haven't heard anything about that."

"It hasn't been confirmed. My source at the medical examiner's office has suspicions, though," I said, and instantly regretted opening that can of worms.

I was saved by another chirp from Zena's phone. And just like that, the sneaky grin was back.

"Go have your nightcap. I've got this," I said, and went for the check.

"Uh-uh!" Z said. She reached inside her purse and dropped two twenty-dollar bills on the table, acting like the big sister once again. I didn't protest. I thought about inviting her over for brunch tomorrow with the rest of my crew, something I'd decided to do at the last minute, then thought better of it. Amanda was going to be there, and Z and she don't click.

"Come on," I said. "I'll walk out with you."

Once outside, before I could say another word, Z held up two fingers and hailed a cab and flashed those same two fingers toward me in a peace sign.

"Good seeing you, Jordan," she said. "You're killing it with that hair, girl. Love you," and she disappeared into the taxi.

I turned in the opposite direction and started to walk home in the dark past midnight, ironically, after admonishing Z to beware of her new man and a potential serial killer on the loose. My spirits were up, so mission accomplished. But I still wasn't ready to be alone.

I could use a nightcap myself.

I pulled out my phone and texted Thomas. **ARE U UP?**

Thomas is a personal trainer I met at the gym. He heckled me one day as I was doing squats. I was on my last set, barbell heavy across my shoulders with twenty-pound weights on either side, when he stepped into my peripheral vision. His chin rested against his right hand as he shook his head disapprovingly. I looked at him.

"What?" I said, slightly irritated, as I carefully returned the barbell to the slats.

"Did you run track in school?" he asked.

Ordinarily I would have said, "And you are?" but I didn't want to invite more interaction. I'd seen this shtick before—trainers trolling the gym trying to reel in new clients.

"No, why do you ask?" I said.

"Because you look like you're running the 440 relay."

"Excuse me?" I laughed.

"For real, you're crouched down like you're in position to grab the baton," he said, demonstrating.

"No way," I said.

"With that posture and stance, you're going to end up needing ibuprofen," he said. "Your left leg is too far back, and you're leaning too far forward. You could mess yourself up doing that. Here, let me show you."

As I watched him demonstrate the proper technique, it dawned on me that I'd seen him at the East Bank Club before. There aren't many Black trainers at this trendy, exclusive gym.

"By the way, my name is Thomas."

Here we go. I didn't want to be rude.

"Hi, I'm Jordan."

He didn't say, "I know who you are."

Interesting.

I sized him up. Thomas wasn't handsome in the traditional sense, but his physique was hard to overlook. He has that V-shaped torso men spend hours lifting weights and surviving on protein shakes and red meat to obtain. Before he went too deep into his sales pitch, if that was what this was, I put on the brakes.

"Look, Thomas, thanks for showing me the proper technique. But if you're looking for new clients, I'm sorry. I don't have extra money right now for a personal trainer. I hope to someday, though."

I expected him to say, "Okay, nice meeting you," but instead he said with a grin, "You know, squats can get boring, but they don't have to be. Let me show you something."

Hello? Did he not hear me?

He removed the twenty-pound weights, grabbed the barbell, and eased up behind me within an appropriate range but close enough that I could feel the heat radiating from his body.

Hold on. Wait a minute.

"Is it okay if I spot you?" he asked.

"Why'd you remove the weights?"

"Because what I'm about to show you requires a little more balance," he explained. "Until you get used to it, don't use the weights. The bar itself weighs twenty-five pounds. I don't want you to injure yourself."

My cynicism started to fade. Thomas stood behind me and lifted his hands palms upward just below the bar.

"This time, as you squat, take a step forward."

I did as he instructed, and he flashed me an approving smile.

Was he flirting?

I didn't have the extra money for a trainer, but I returned the flirt, because I did have extra room for something new in my personal life. And, just like that, we started seeing other, but I wouldn't call it "dating." Thomas was clear he had no desire to meet my friends or accompany me to events.

"But I'd like to see you afterward," he said.

He didn't fool me. Seeing me afterward was his way of keeping tabs on me. He didn't want me coming home with anyone else. I decided I could deal with it for now. Our "relationship" was convenient. Thomas worked early mornings at the club, which fit my schedule perfectly. I got the personal training after all without spending a dime. One of the things I like most about him is that he's a night owl, like me. Most people's heart rate dropped after nine o'clock, the quasi fitness guru told me. Around one A.M., "yours is just getting started. That makes you a unicorn," he said.

Thomas is a unicorn, too, and for that I'm grateful. However, he could have told me about his on-again, off-again girlfriend *before* we had sex. He didn't exactly *tell* me; I asked him after his cell phone was buzzing nonstop at two-thirty in the morning. My reaction surprised him. I used his admission to set boundaries.

"It's not like we're a 'thing,'" I told him with air quotes. "That's your business. We're adults, and I never thought we were exclusive. In fact, I don't want to be. I never wanted to be. I assumed we were on the same page," I said with a wink and a nod.

The truth is, I have neither the time nor the energy to maintain a relationship. I don't want to feel obligated to check in with somebody every day or talk about what's for dinner.

But we can creep.

"That's fine," he said. "But I want the time that we do spend together to be quality time."

That was easy, because quality time to Thomas was effortless fun, like a night stroll across the boulders along Lake Michigan's shoreline. And, of course, there was always the obvious. We started getting together once or twice a week, usually after eleven o'clock at night, because that's what you do when you creep. I'm a little surprised at myself. Not for creeping, but for dating a man five years younger than me. We have great chemistry, and I like that he doesn't try to replicate something he'd seen in a porno flick when he was sixteen. I must admit, his sculpted body makes our lovemaking, which has been *phe*-nomenal, feel surreal, like something out of a dream. I can see why his ex or current girl, or whatever she is, doesn't want to let go.

Thomas texted me right back.

THINKING ABOUT YOU. Want me to come over?
Yeah.

It was that easy. Then it occurred to me that I hadn't been home since this morning. My bed hadn't been made and I'd left all my makeup on the counter in the bathroom getting dressed for work. I quickened my steps. I needed time to straighten up and put something sexy on. Inside the lobby, I got distracted by Bass, the security guard on the graveyard shift.

"Joooor-dan!" he called out to me.

"Baaaass!" I said.

Harold "Bass" Brantley got his nickname for the instrument he plays, mostly with his church choir and occasionally on Chicago's jazz scene when he's lucky enough to get a gig on his day off. Bass and I have been tight ever since he rescued me from the stairwell during a blackout in the middle of a dangerous ice storm. Chicagoans are used to snow, but ice is a different story. Neighborhoods west of downtown were affected overnight, but

I assumed the power would be restored by the time I went to work in the morning. The elevator was still out, so I took the stairs but freaked out in the pitch-black stairwell. I've always been terrified of the dark. Bass, about to end his shift, heard me in distress and came up with a flashlight and walked me down.

We've gotten to know each other through long talks at the security desk. Bass, who's twenty-six, is six-six and slender, with perfect posture. It's damned near a superhero stance. Whenever I see him, I'm reminded to stand up straight and pull my shoulders back.

"How are you doing, pretty lady?"

Shaking my head, I said, "I don't know, honestly. Did you hear about Masey James?"

"Naw, what happened?" he asked. "Don't tell me . . . she's dead?"

"Yeah, they found her body yesterday. Confirmed her ID this morning," I said.

"Ah, man, that's horrible!" said the young father, diverting his eyes toward the floor. Bass has a five-year-old daughter with his girlfriend, Sabrina, whom he's nuts about but not ready to marry, which has been the topic of many of our conversations.

"How's Sabrina?" I asked.

"Don't start," he said.

"Hey, by the way, are you ever going to marry that girl?" Bass released a full-throated laugh that reverberated across the marble walls and floor. It was our inside joke. I've asked him periodically and challenge myself to state it slightly different each time.

"You better get out here!" he said. "Where's your other half?"

"Now see, there you go messing with me again."

"What'd I do?" he asked playfully.

"He's on his way over," I said, which elicited more boisterous laughter.

Bass is a novice health and wellness buff, so he and Thomas have struck a chord. I don't have a problem with that. Bass is discreet. Nothing he has seen or heard me do has made it out into these streets.

Thomas creeped in around 1:15 in the morning and was back out again by 5:30. I've barely had a moment to myself. *Good.* I'd gone from Z to Thomas, and now I was about to entertain another welcome distraction. I got right up and started to make preparation for brunch. I prepped the meat for my famous enchiladas and put the pinto beans in the slow cooker. Given the way I'd been feeling and everything that had been going on, I found solace in the kitchen.

I slipped back in bed and set my alarm for 9:30, which would give me plenty of time to get dressed and meet my girlfriend María Elena at St. Matthew Presbyterian for the eleven o'clock service. I've been going to church nearly every Sunday of late. I hadn't attended church this regularly since Catholic grade school. The commitment to attend church is a different sensation as an adult. It's my reset button.

Sleep came easy, but I was awakened by an incoming call on my cell phone. Part of me hoped it was Pamela Alonzo, but part of me was glad when I saw that it wasn't.

"Hey, Mom."

"Miss Jordan! There you are! I was about to send a search party to look for you."

It was just after seven o'clock. I hadn't been asleep more than forty minutes. Mom was right to admonish me. We hardly ever go more than two days without speaking.

"I know, right? I'm sorry I haven't called." I must have

sounded terribly groggy and fatigued. I sure felt that way. "These past few days have been crazy."

She'd heard that before.

"I figured you were busy," Mom said coolly. The Worrier had been getting better at not thinking the worst, which is her default switch. "I saw on the news they found that little girl who'd been missing. I know that must be bothering you."

"You're right. It is. I didn't know her, but I felt like I did. She could've been Dru or any one of my little cousins or nieces. She was smart. She had a future. It's just such a damn shame," I said.

It was the first time I'd correlated Masey with my cousin Stephanie's oldest and surviving child, Drucilla.

"Have you talked to her mother?" Mom asked.

"No, I haven't spoken to her since they found the body. She called me, though, and left a couple messages while I was at the scene. I didn't check my messages until later, and I felt bad. I'm sure she was wondering what happened to me."

"That's worrying you, too," said the woman who knows me better than I know myself. "Okay, so now that this is over, Jordan, you need to cut that relationship off."

"It's not over, Mom. I am still covering the story. And from what Dr. Chan told me, this investigation could take a while," I said.

Mom's voice brightened at the mention of Dr. Chan, whom she had met once during a visit to Chicago. "How is Dr. Chan?"

"Skinny," I said. "He looks like he's lost about twenty pounds."

"Seriously?" Mom asked. "I hope he's not sick."

"He seemed okay, health-wise. He's on his way to New Zealand as we speak. But I got a chance to interview him on-camera, and he didn't talk to anyone else before he left. That piece is set to air later today."

"Dr. Chan loves him some Jordan," Mom said. "So he did the autopsy?"

"Yes." Then I shifted abruptly. "How'd you hear about it?"

"It led the news yesterday on WGN," she said.

Masey's disappearance didn't lead the local news, but her murder did, which made me think back on the profound question Pastor Andrea Byrd posed to the congregation last Easter Sunday. "Would we have ever known Jesus if he hadn't died on the cross?"

"You know I'd much rather watch your broadcast, but I can't get it all the way down here," Mom said. "Are you still in bed?" she asked.

"Yes, I was out with Zena last night, and I invited the girls over for Tex-Mex brunch today after church."

"Somebody's about to eat good! I sure wish you could fax some of it down here to me," Mom said. "So, what are the police saying?"

My mother the crime buff was not going to let me off the hook that easily. She devours murder mysteries and watches an average of twelve hours of TV crime dramas each week.

"The police aren't saying much of anything so far."

"What's Dr. Chan think?" she asked.

My mother was far from satiated. She wanted the gory details.

"Honestly, Mom, I don't want to get into it right now. It's . . . it's devastating," I said, then went into it, anyway. "She was brutalized. I've never heard of anything like it before. Never."

"Was she raped? Beaten?" Mom asked.

"Yes, it appears so. Beaten, I'm not sure, but she was cut up pretty badly," I said.

"Cut!" Mom exclaimed.

"Lacerations over her entire body, and burned." My words

formed an image in my mind that stunted my breathing. "Just imagine your worst nightmare for your child, then multiply that by two," I said. "That's why I'm having the girls over today. I need a distraction. I can't stop thinking about it."

"There is a special hell for people who harm children," Mom said. "If somebody did that to one of mine, they wouldn't have to worry about prison. I'd kill 'em."

"Mom, you know I hate it when you say things like that," I said.

"I'm not playing," she said.

I know she wasn't. My mother grew up around guns. Her father and brothers hunted, and though she was never formally trained how to shoot, she always kept a gun in the house. In Chicago, there's a lot of talk about Black people illegally owning guns but very little discussion about Blacks who legally keep what they see as protection in their homes. They aren't the face of the NRA or the gun enthusiasts who trot out their weapons in open-carry states. Legal gun ownership has been portrayed in the media as a white male privilege. The face of illegal trafficking of guns across state lines is that of a young Black man, and that has influenced perceptions about those we see as victims and perpetrators.

There is a fifteen-year age difference between my mom and dad, but keeping protection in the home was one thing they could agree on. However, if me or one of my siblings ever fell victim to a killer, U.S. Army 1st Lt. Robert Manning would likely beat my mom to any act of vengeance against someone who would harm his children. My father is one of those quiet men people warn you never to cross. I don't know that I've ever seen that side of him, but I've heard his siblings retell stories at our house during the holidays and backyard barbecues after downing a few Lone Star beers. In a bad situation, he was the one they called on. I refer to him as the Warrior, because he's always encouraged me to fight for what I want, for what I deserve.

"Anyway, Jordan, I was calling to tell you about Drucilla."

My heart pounded. "What?"

"She's fine. I just wanted to let you know that she's not going to be able to make it home for Christmas. She's coming home in mid-January. I'm hoping you'll be able to get some time off and come home then, too. But make sure you check with her to get the dates right."

"Oh, no! She's not going to be home for Christmas?" I was disappointed. For the first time in my career, I had Christmas Eve through the day after New Year's off work, and I'd been looking forward to seeing my little cousin.

"No, she won't be on her job for a year. She couldn't get the time off," Mom said.

"Okay, well, thanks for the heads-up. I will definitely plan on coming home then," I said, but failed to mention it would be difficult, if not impossible, to get time off just two weeks after the holiday break.

January was months away, but the thought of seeing Drucilla made me smile.

"All right, I've got to get ready for church, myself," Mom said. "I know you've probably got a lot to do to prepare for your company, so I'll let you go. Try to enjoy yourself today."

"Okay, love you, Mom. Thanks for tracking me down. Smooches."

"Love you, too."

I pulled the phone away from my ear and as I was about to hang up another call came in. It was Pamela Alonzo.

Remember, you promised yourself you'd answer.

"Hello, Pam?" I asked.

Silence.

"Pamela, is that you?"

"Yes," said a voice I didn't recognize. "It's me."

Her breathing sounded stunted and hollow, as if air wasn't passing through her lungs but through a hole in her heart instead. The emptiness in her voice was palpable.

What do I say? My heart breaks for you. No, don't say that. I'm praying for you. Yeah, well, who cares?

Finally, I managed, "Pam, I'm so, so unbelievably sorry."

"Thank you, Jordan. Were you there? When they found my baby?" she asked. "Were you there that day?"

"Yes," I said, measuring my words. "I got a tip that morning . . . but I didn't know . . . until the news conference yesterday."

A lie.

"I can't . . . tell . . . you how . . . devastated . . . I am," she said, struggling to talk and breathe at the same time.

By now I, too, struggled to breathe. My face became hot and there was a ringing in my ears as I desperately fought back my own tears. I didn't want to cry on the phone with Pam. I didn't feel I had the right to. How could I know what she was feeling? I'm not a mother. I lost my favorite cousin, whom I loved like a sister, but what Pam was experiencing had to be twenty times worse.

No matter how many times I'd seen it before, this level of trauma and pain was gut-wrenching. I wondered how a person managed not to collapse into a vegetative state and wither away.

I took a deep breath and tried to speak, but thankfully Pam spoke first.

"The police don't know nothing! They asking me if I know

who could've done this? Why would I know that?" Pam screamed and sobbed. "Why would I know that?"

I recognized what she described as a standard police question. But how do you tell that to a grieving mother?

"I'm not going to survive this," Pam said. "I already know, this is going to kill me."

Say something, Jordan. But what? How does a person respond to something like that?

Pam continued: "But while I'm still breathing, I'm going to do everything that *I* can do to send the bastard to the funeral home or to death row. And I already know, I can't count on the police!"

Unfortunately, Pam, you're right.

"They told me my child ran away from home, ran away from me and her little brother. Mal-co-o-om," she said as her sobbing escalated. "He's traumatized. How am I supposed to explain this to him?"

Pam's voice reached a fever pitch, and I could no longer suppress my grief. It lunged out of me.

"I'm so sorry," Pam said. "I didn't mean to put all of this on you, Jordan."

"Pam, please, you don't ever apologize to me. Okay?" I said. Silence.

How long can we sit here like this? This is not where I want to be.

"Jordan," said Pam, slightly more composed. "Before this pain takes me from this earth, I will see justice done. Somebody out here knows who did this. I want to issue a public plea for anyone who has information to come forward, and I'm going to set up a reward, even if I have to cash in every dime of my retirement. I want to go on the air, Jordan, as soon as possible. Finding the person who took my angel from me, this is my life now."

And all I could say was "All right. Just tell me when you think you'll be ready."

"I can tell you right now," Pam said. "Tomorrow."

..

If I hadn't already committed to meeting María Elena at church, I would've stayed in bed. My soul said, *Uh-uh. Get up and receive the word of God. You're going to need it.*

I wanted to beat María Elena to church for once, but by the time I finished texting back and forth with Ellen and Scott about interviewing Pamela Alonzo one-on-one tomorrow, I had to scramble to put myself together. When I arrived at St. Matthew's, she was already sitting on a stone bench in the attached side garden, her petite frame folded in half, intently reading a paperback romance novel.

"Oh, so that's what you're going to be thinking about during service," I said.

María Elena looked up with a startled smile, stuffed her book in her oversize bag, and embraced me robustly.

"Good morning!" she said excitedly, squeezing my size 6 frame with her size 0 arms. María Elena is small in stature but gives the biggest hugs.

"Hey, gorgeous!" I almost added, *I thought about crawling back in bed this morning,* but thought better of it. I was here now.

"I forgot that Pastor Byrd isn't here today. We have a guest speaker," María Elena Suárez-Sallen said in her thick Latin accent. She came to the United States from her native Bogotá, Colombia, to study to become an optometrist. She performed the first eye exam I had after I moved to Chicago, and we just clicked. María Elena always looked stunning, her long, light brown hair swept to one side. She wore a maroon jumpsuit with a thick matching belt, a black shrug, and four-inch strappy gold sandals. At five-two, María Elena was almost always in heels and one accessory removed from transitioning from day to evening, no matter the occasion.

I, too, had forgotten that Pastor Byrd wouldn't be preaching today. Now I really did wish I'd stayed in bed. When I worked at the station in Dallas, I grew attached to a small Baptist church pastored by a Black woman. She could really preach. Pastor Andrea Byrd, who is White, approached the word in a similar way that resonated with me, relating Scripture to everyday life. She was just as likely to quote well-known literature as the Bible.

We decided to stay, but I was unable to focus. Pam's request had rendered me impenetrable. All I could think about was the exclusive interview tomorrow. *Wait . . . did she say exclusive? Or did I just assume that? Is she ready for this?* A grieving mother was catnip to a television news station, and I didn't want her to be exploited.

After service, María Elena said, "I want to put on something more comfortable. I'll meet you at your place in a half hour."

Good. That will give me time to dress the enchiladas and whip up a pitcher of margaritas. I turned my cell phone back on. Thomas had left me a voice mail. I was surprised; Sunday wasn't our day.

That's sweet. He called to check on me.

After an emotionally exhausting week, I was looking forward to spending some quality time with my Chi-Town posse. All of them, like me, are Chicago transplants. Dr. Courtney Felix, who was born in Detroit, is an OB/GYN who's married to a doctor of internal medicine, Dr. Nathan Blackwell III. They are the most idyllic couple I've ever met. Both thirty-nine, they have two beautiful sons, Elijah and Nathan IV, ages three and five. I have never seen them argue or throw verbal daggers at each other. Not once. They are the real-life Huxtables. Last year on Halloween, Courtney invited me to their home in suburban Naperville for a pumpkin carving party with the kids. It was a scene straight out of *Good Housekeeping* magazine.

Courtney and I met at the annual Susan G. Komen Race for the Cure in Chicago. I hosted the event that year and also participated in it, though I did more walking than running. It was a rare warm October day in Chicago. Our respective groups had common members and blended along the route. Courtney and I struck up a conversation. Her smile is arresting. I imagine that's one of the features her husband fell for when the two of them met while vacationing with friends in Bali. They were always trying to fix me up with a guy, but neither of them had figured out my type yet.

Amanda Pickering, thirty-five, is a native Kentuckian who works for an investment group at the Chicago Mercantile Exchange. She's single and a prolific dater. I met Amanda in a clothing boutique when I came to Chicago to interview at News Channel 8. The zipper had busted in the dress I'd brought to wear for my interview. Thankfully, I tried it on the day before, and frantically ran out to find a replacement an hour before the boutiques closed downtown.

Amanda overheard me describe my situation to the salesperson and started helping me shop like she worked there. "When you get that job, you call and let me know," she said in her southern drawl.

Amanda and I couldn't be more different. She grew up in a homogeneous community outside Louisville, Kentucky. There were only two Black kids at her high school. In my experience, White people who weren't raised around Black people can be more accepting of our differences than some who have lived around Black people their entire lives. There is, however, a learning curve, and Amanda, though well-meaning, can be a bit naive. Zena finds her off-putting, which is why I didn't invite her today. Amanda thought she was complimenting Zena when she set her apart from Black women living in poverty on the West Side. "You live in Oak Park, for goodness sakes!" All it took was one maladroit statement by Amanda and Zena had had enough of her. I hate that it happened, but I believe in accepting people for who they are. I enjoy both women's company, and I refuse to give one up for the other.

María Elena, thirty-five, is still my eye doctor. We bonded over red wine and complicated relationships. Her ex-husband is a Jewish attorney she met in Chicago. The marriage lasted only two years. She didn't get along with his family and resented their assertion that she married him for a green card. "They were assholes," she told me, "and after a while, so was he."

I needed my girls today. Their camaraderie would be like an emollient for my worn nerves, hardened by cynicism and the stories of death that are constants in my life. I hadn't planned on talking about work today. I must've been crazy to think that these smart, worldly, inquisitive women wouldn't want to talk about the Masey James case.

Amanda kicked it off. "Isn't it horrible about little Masey James?" she said, bringing her right hand to rest on her chest.

"Oh my God! Unimaginable," Courtney chimed in.

"Where'd they find the body?" asked María Elena.

"At 45th and Calumet," I said.

"Was she raped?" Amanda asked.

Oh my God, please! Just shut up! This is the last thing I want to talk about.

Courtney bolted off the couch. Her movement was so sudden that it startled me. Her face had been transformed by a painful memory. Amanda and María Elena didn't know that Courtney had been the victim of date rape in college.

I nodded somberly and said, "Watch the news tonight."

"You talk to Dr. Chan?" Courtney asked, not picking up on my cue to change the subject.

"Of course," I said. "He hooked me up."

"Really? What was the big takeaway from him?" asked Courtney, whose interest, I understood, wasn't purely professional, but that was a big part of it.

I hesitated before I spoke. "He said whoever did this is a monster. I suppose you can say that about anybody who takes a life. But . . ."—I paused somberly—"What happened to Masey is beyond the pale. And it's going to be very difficult to solve this case due to the condition of the remains," I said, powering through the sentence.

"I wonder how long she'd been in that watery field," Courtney, who had obviously watched the news, said. "Even if there was evidence of rape, the conditions could've changed the chemical composition of the evidence, making it useless."

Even with my forensic background, I hadn't thought about that. "It changes the composition of semen?" I said, suddenly becoming interested in a conversation I didn't want to have.

Out of the corner of my eye, I saw María Elena grab the tequila bottle to add a smidgen to her glass.

"Correct," Courtney said.

"There was evidence of assault but no traces of semen," I said. "What's more, she was set on fire, postmortem, to destroy evidence," I said.

María Elena froze. She clearly had lost track of how much tequila she was adding to her glass. "That poor mother," she said.

"Whoa, hold the tequila!" I said.

"Oh shit!" she said. "What the fuck am I doing? I need some juice to put in this."

"No, you need a bigger glass," Courtney quipped.

Everyone laughed, releasing some of the tension of the moment.

"Girl, how do you talk to that mother?" María Elena asked.

"Mostly I listen," I said. "I'm not sure what all she knows about what happened to her daughter. I hope to God that she was spared most, if not all, of those details."

"Like what?" Amanda asked.

I paused for a beat. "*Mmm*," I said, and rested my face in my right hand. The doctor in the house got it right away and walked over and put her arms around me.

"Sorry, sis," she whispered in my ear. She pulled away, flashing me that striking smile of hers, and changed the subject.

"So, how's your love life?"

6

Midway through my morning routine—two cups of coffee with a heavy hand of sugar, enough milk to prompt the question *Do you take coffee with your cream?*, a soft-boiled egg, and half a left-over avocado—I was so engrossed in my daily dose of morning news shows that I was startled when my cell phone rang near my elbow.

I glanced down, scrunching my eyebrows and struggling to focus my vision to make out the number on the screen. It was a 773 area code—a Chicago number. I paused a beat. I have no idea who this is, but I answer it anyway, throwing up a verbal roadblock between me and whoever is on the other end with a stern, inquisitive "Hello?"

"Good morning. Is this Jordan Manning?" said a young woman.

"Yes, it is," I said, instinctively raising the mug to my lips but hesitating to take a sip.

"This is Tanya McMillan."

It was a good thing I didn't take that drink, because the name of the surprise caller on the other end would've left me choking and gasping for air. The Bronzeville resident I had interviewed before Masey James was confirmed to be the victim discovered in the tangled, monstrous weeds of a neglected playground had kept my number after all. And, I hoped, had forgiven me for not informing her before going on the air that the body of a child had been found a few yards from her front door.

"Hello, Tanya," I said, clearing my throat. "How . . . how are you?"

Tanya clearly was not interested in small talk. She got right to the point. "I wanted to let you know about a community vigil going on tonight."

"For Masey James?" I asked.

"Yes. It's being organized by Louise Robinson and the South Side Community Council. It starts at seven o'clock in front of my house. Masey's family, her mother, members of the Black Pastors Coalition, and local elected officials will all be there. It's going to be packed. Folks are furious."

Did she say her mother?

"Pamela Alonzo will be there, you say?" I asked.

"Yes."

Why hadn't Pam told me about the vigil? And when did she hook up with Louise Robinson?

I've never met Robinson, but some of my colleagues have covered her infamous clashes with police and city hall over allegations of police brutality, aggressive surveillance of Black men, use of excessive force, and racial bias in sentencing.

"Ms. Robinson is one of the founding members of the council," Tanya added.

"Okay, I've heard of the council," I said, though I hardly had intimate knowledge about its mission and members. "When was it founded?" I asked. "I've only lived here a few years."

"It's been around, oh, about five years," Tanya said.

"Right," I affirmed. "And you say Pamela Alonzo is going to be at tonight's vigil?" I asked again.

"Ye-es," Tanya said impatiently. I heard her the first time, but I was still troubled by the fact that Pamela herself hadn't told me about it.

"Thank you for letting me know, Tanya," I said. "Are you involved with the council?"

"Yeah, me and my mother are members. We're the group

that was on city hall's behind for months to clean up that disgusting playground."

"Oh yes," I said. "I remember that." However, she hadn't mentioned this group earlier.

"We filed a complaint as individual citizens first, but when that didn't work, the council got involved," she said. "It didn't make any sense that it took the city close to a year to do something about that park, if you can even call it that."

"Do you know how to get in touch with Ms. Robinson?" I asked.

"Uh, yeah. She's my auntie," Tanya said. All that was missing from her dismissive response was "Duh?"

Okay, how was I supposed to know that?

"Oh, okay, I didn't realize," I said, raising my voice an octave to mask my annoyance.

It's incumbent that I choose my next words carefully. In one swipe, my initial perception of Tanya McMillan had vanished like the scraggly lines of an Etch A Sketch. She's not as humble as she initially presented herself, and clearly she's no typical bystander. In fact, I was beginning to get the sense that I am not the only person who has underestimated her. Tanya McMillan is more than just relatable; she's Machiavellian. She knows how to work people, and she is working me to get me to tie Masey's murder to her aunt's agenda, which is something I hadn't anticipated. I have no illusion that I am the only member of the press she's reached out to. I don't know her aunt Louise, but I am familiar with her playbook. She is fomenting discontent in the black community, and a groundswell appears to be developing, starting with the vigil. Tonight residents will assemble to express their pain over the loss of another Black child and their interminable displeasure with the systems—the police, city hall, the parks—that have failed them again and again. They intend to stand in solidarity with a distraught mother who is one of their own.

There is a lot to unpack and not much time to do it. Ellen emailed me late last night that she wants to start running promos of my interview with Pamela Alonzo during the four o'clock broadcast, and I still don't know whether or not it is an "exclusive," but I doubt it. Something felt off. My father always told me, "Trust no one more than your own instincts," and my instincts are telling me to pivot, to stop relying on Pamela to do my job and start thinking about how to distinguish my coverage. If I play my cards right, I might be able to flip the script and induce Tanya to work for me as an ally as opposed to a pawn. An ego stroke and a heavy dose of flattery can sometimes be the best card in the deck.

"Tanya, I am so grateful to you for calling me this morning," I said, maintaining my focus on her, "just as I was grateful for your help the other day. You've been wonderful. Thank you so much."

Then I eased into my questions. "I'd like to interview Ms. Robinson, your aunt, and a few of the other speakers *before* the vigil, if that's possible. Will there a pre-gathering? Are you hosting the speakers at your home? Would it be possible to sit down with a few members of the council and Pamela? At your house? In the living room, maybe?"

"Um, I mean, I don't know," she said. "You have to talk to my aunt and Ms. Alonzo about that."

So, your aunt tells your mother what to do in her own house?

"Well, I'm pretty sure Pam will be okay with it," I responded, dropping her name casually. "I talked to her yesterday. I'm interviewing her today at three o'clock."

I'm not the outsider you think I am. But damn it, why hadn't Pam told me about the vigil?

Apparently, while I was having brunch with the *Sex and the City* crew, Pamela was busy getting representation and amassing a coalition bent toward justice for Masey. It included a community-based organization, a fiery activist, a venerable pastors' coalition, furious residents, and at least one broadcast journalist who was eating out of her hand. It wouldn't surprise me if Pamela had been convinced that she needed to retain a lawyer. For now she has Tanya McMillan acting as her de facto publicist.

I admired Tanya's savviness, working the local media reps without any media training, and keeping it real, with a little attitude cherry on top. But there's no time for such pettiness. A child is dead. A killer is on the loose. Fuck decorum.

Then it struck me: these three women—Tanya, Pam, and Louise—coming together as they have in such a short time is one helluva coincidence. I thought back to the way Tanya had lost it during her live interview. "I bet it's that girl," she said. I sensed her concern, but I never would have made a connection between her and Pamela. How old or new is that connection?

Did Tanya know Masey?

I thought to ask but decided not to, at least for now, focusing on orchestrating tonight's media event.

"It'll probably be fine, but let me confirm with my moms and my aunt first," Tanya said.

"Great," I said, hopping off the couch to grab a pen from the kitchen counter and a napkin to write on. "What's your aunt's number?"

By the time we got off the phone, my coffee had turned cold and I'd lost my appetite, but my heart pumped adrenaline. I took stock of the day. I have an interview at twelve-thirty with police superintendent Donald Bartlett. He feigned reluctance to speak to me on-camera, but I was confident he'd relent. Bartlett, unlike his top lieutenant Fawcett, adores me. He's the exact opposite of the stereotypical police chief. He's so bighearted that at times I wonder how long he is actually going to be able to survive in this job. But I take nothing for granted.

"There really isn't anything more that I can tell you, Jordan," he responded in an email this morning at 6:45.

"Superintendent Bartlett, I understand," I typed. "But there's a community in pain that needs reassurance from you that this investigation will remain a priority until Masey James's killer is found."

DELETE

"Superintendent Bartlett, until a few days ago, this was a missing persons case. Now that it's a homicide investigation, I think the community would like to hear from senior leadership in the police department. Don't you?"

DELETE

"Superintendent Bartlett, understood," I typed. "I would just like to spend some time with you on the record discussing what police know thus far. I think the community will appreciate hearing from you in a more intimate setting than a news conference."

"Spend some time with you" should resonate.

SEND

Now, on top of Bartlett and my interview with Pam at Masey's aunt Cynthia's house at three o'clock, I must try and squeeze in community firebrand Louise Robinson and pull together an impromptu roundtable of community leaders with Pamela in Tanya McMillan's living room by six o'clock. I live for days like this. The stakes were rising by the minute, and I was ready to go in hard, to be more than just a reporter relaying a story. Instead I would be acting as an investigator looking for clues and connecting dots. Days like this are why I chose this profession.

I wasn't surprised that Pamela had agreed to participate in the vigil. Yesterday she was emphatic that finding her daughter's killer had become her life's purpose. Still, I'm annoyed, even a little hurt, actually, that she hadn't mentioned it. Maybe she didn't tell me about the vigil because she didn't have to, now that Tanya McMillan and Louise Robinson are representing her. This frees her up to focus on other important things, like keeping her loving arms at the ready for her six-year-old son, Malcolm, enveloped in grief at the loss of his big sister, and managing her lupus, the chronic illness, exacerbated by stress, that killed her mother at age fifty-nine.

Pamela wasn't the problem. The problem was that I had expectations of a source, and I should've known better. Still, as much as I have beaten myself up about getting too close to Pam, the potential downward shift in our relationship dynamic was just as troubling. After the hours I had spent cultivating that relationship, I couldn't help but wonder, *Is Pam pulling away?*

I texted Scott.

Hey U want 2 grab breakfast? We've got a busy day ahead.

Scott suggested that we meet at our usual spot downtown, but I suggested we meet instead at the District Diner. It's a relic that has survived and thrived for fifty years, proudly owning the slogan *Authentic Taste of Chicago*. I've gone there on occasions when the diner was packed with tourists who had ventured miles from Navy Pier and Magnificent Mile shopping excursions to bask in a true South Side Chicago experience. During the week, it was mostly packed with local elected officials, clergy, business leaders, and community activists, and it does enough business to shut down daily at three o'clock. After church on Sundays, there's almost always a wait, and the line sometimes spills out into the parking lot. I myself have patronized the District Diner after church, barely able to focus on Pastor Byrd's sermon for dreaming of creamy cheese grits and Creole-seasoned salmon croquettes.

The District Diner is a listening space for the media, especially those who cover politics and crime. Stories unfold over the retro Formica tabletops. On- and off-the-record tips waft through the air like the smell of warm pancakes and syrup, and secrets pour out like free refills on coffee. There's no cultural line in the sand, but I've found that my White colleagues think of this place only when they need a scoop. They ooh and aah over "what a great place" it is and rave about the food, promising to return with family and friends, but they never do.

"Not the Black Pentagon," Scott said, repeating the nickname he coined for the mom-and-pop dining hot spot, with its orange sherbet-colored walls, which hasn't had an aesthetic upgrade since it opened in 1957.

"Yep. Sorry," I said.

But I wasn't sorry. I have survived and thrived and survived again in predominately white spaces my entire life. Scott usually doesn't balk on the rare occasions he is "the only" or one of a very few White people in the room. When he's whined in the past, I've been dismissive.

"Scott, I've got four words for you," I told him once. "Welcome to my world."

I'm a Black woman who by and large must leave my neighborhood to socialize with my community. The District Diner is where I go for a healthy dose of culture, even if my media affiliation makes me suspect to some people. Today I was going neither for the food nor for the culture but to see what I could find out about Louise Robinson. And I planned to take advantage of being something my White colleagues are not—a source of pride in the black community. That gives me a little more leeway, especially with Black politicians. And I knew just who to ask.

"I'm getting dressed now," I said. "I'll meet you there."

I pulled out a two-piece dark purple suit with a pencil skirt and a peplum jacket to wear during the day, and rolled up a blouse and black slacks to change into with a pair of flats for tonight's vigil.

Scott and I drove separately. On the way there, I got a call from my bestie in Austin, Lisette. As soon as I saw her name pop up in the caller ID, I remembered that we'd been planning a weekend girls' trip to Saugatuck, Michigan. About three hours from Chicago, it sits along a harbor and attracts boaters and water-skiers in the summer. In the fall, tourists are drawn to the spectacular foliage. I'd been looking forward to it but had all but forgotten about our trip with everything that had been going on.

"He-e-e-y, Lisette!" I said.

"What are you up to? I can tell you're driving," she said. "Can you talk?"

"Yeah, I'm hands free. On my way to your spot—the District."

I had taken Liz to the diner the last time she was in Chicago. It was her idea to forgo brunch at the Four Seasons, as we'd planned, for the District in Hyde Park. Liz is money savvy and curious about investments, and she's always looking for her next act. She wanted to drive through a neighborhood she'd read about undergoing regentrification in the emerging South Loop to check out the real estate. I was disappointed. I'd been looking forward to "Brunch is on me" at the Four Seasons, which is above my pay grade. Liz, a brilliant coder, by age twenty-seven had made a killing off a content management software she developed with a classmate at the University of Texas. She could afford to eat there every day.

"*Mmmm.*" She let out a low guttural growl. "The shrimp and grits! I want to go back there, but I don't know, I might not make it this trip. Guess who's back?"

"Mike," I said matter-of-factly.

"Yes, girl! Well, not yet, but he'll be back from Germany next week-e-e-end. He offered to come down here, but I told him you and I were already thinking about driving up to Michigan. So . . ."

Lisette, a manifestation of our home city's "Keep Austin Weird" culture, fell in love with Saugatuck, an artist enclave with quaint little antique shops and boutiques, and wineries and breweries that appealed to her Bohemian proclivities. So did Mike. Liz met Mike Spencer on our girls' trip to Saugatuck last summer. We rented a cabin by the sand dunes with a view of the harbor. The blue-eyed, sandy blond furniture maker from New York was in Chicago for an artisans' conference with his friend Carlo Santi, visiting from Milan, Italy, and drove up to Saugatuck to hang out with some friends for the weekend. The two men were walking along the dunes when they spotted Liz and me on the patio of our cabin noshing on a charcuterie and cheese board and working on a second bottle of a dry rosé we'd picked up at a local winery. Both men looked like they'd stepped out of a J.Crew catalog. Carlo wore an accent scarf loosely around his shoulders for a hint of euro flare. Amanda was supposed to come with us but had had to cancel at the last minute. Just as well—it kept things even.

"I haven't heard you mention Mike in a while. I didn't know you guys were still talking."

"It's been a little off and on lately since he's been overseas. We've never fallen completely out of touch, though," she said.

"And obviously," I picked up where she left off, "he's been thinking about you, because you're the first person he wants to see when he gets back."

I liked Mike. He reminded me a little of my college crush, Jake, Justin's big brother. But unlike Jake, Mike *has* the blue eyes to go with the blond hair, and a California beach-boy body and the thousand-watt smile. The two men turned and walked toward us as if they had an invitation. Lisette and I didn't know whether to panic and retreat into the cabin or to thank God. Once they introduced themselves and we decided they weren't going to kill us, we chose the latter.

Liz hadn't seen Mike since the two met up in Chicago over the spring.

"He called me last night and said he'd be back in Saugatuck in a couple weeks. That's right around the time we'd talked about running up there. Are you still game?"

It should have been an easy yes, but the timing couldn't have been worse.

"Is Carlo going to be there?" I asked.

Carlo and I didn't stay in touch after he went back to Italy. I got the feeling that Carlo, who was in his late thirties, had a wife back home that he failed to mention.

"No, but Mike said he's got a friend for you," Lisette said.

I'm not sure that's what I want in my life right now.

"When do I need to let you know? Is your friend from Detroit still planning to meet us?"

Does Mike have a "friend" for her, too?

"Yes, and she's bringing a friend of hers from work. It'll be fun. Tell me you're not backing out. Are you?"

"I'd love to go, but there's so much going on here right now with this murder case," I said.

"Which one?"

"The missing fifteen-year-old girl. She was found dead the other day," I said.

"Oh my God! I was praying so hard for her to be okay," Liz said.

"I know. Me too."

The last time I mentioned Masey James to my best friend, it was in the present tense.

"What happened?" she asked, but I didn't have time to go into it. I'd arrived at my destination.

"Hey, Liz, I'm here. I'm going to have to call you later," I said.

"Okay, don't forget. Be careful out there," she said.

"I will."

By ten o'clock, the parking lot at the District Diner was so full it looked like the Dan Ryan with an accident blocking two of the express lanes during rush-hour traffic. Scott was in the news van and made up a parking space. I pulled up behind him. I wasn't worried about getting a ticket.

Scott and I walked in and I scanned the cacophonous diner, with its iconic images of local heroes like former mayor Harold Washington; John H. and Eunice Johnson of *Ebony* and *Jet* magazine; Mavis Staples and the Staple Singers; and boxer Joe Louis, to name a few. The people's pride. Depending on the ethnic group, this type of display could be found in diners across America. In Austin, there'd be Willie Nelson and Stevie Ray Vaughan. In Detroit, Aretha Franklin and politicians like John Conyers Jr.; or Frank Sinatra in Hoboken. Each booth and table bore the name of a historic Black figure. There was even a table named for Ida B. Wells-Barnett, the history-making journalist whose name was now linked to an ill-fated playground.

In the far left corner, I spotted a handsome Black man in his late fifties or early sixties who stood out in a maroon suit tailored to accommodate his broad shoulders. The perfectly coifed waves in his hair looked as if he had commanded them: "Don't move." Cook County commissioner Curtis "C.W." Clark looked up. I caught his attention, and he gestured for me to come over.

To my surprise, he was alone, which was rare. He must have just ended a meeting or was waiting for the next one to start. As we made our way through the cramped room and steaming hot plates, I turned to Scott and muttered, "If he invites us to join him, we're saying yes."

Commissioner Clark stood up and extended his hand, greeting us both warmly. "Good morning, Jordan," he said, his mouth barely visible under a thick mustache. "How long has it been?"

Clark held out his arms and enveloped me in a warm embrace as if I were a relative he hadn't seen for a long while. I'm sure Clark didn't hug every journalist he encountered. Because I am a Black woman in this job, there is an unspoken acknowledgment by people in my community of the struggle that it took for me to get where I am. I'm media but also kin. They want me here. In moments like this, when I feel people's distrust of the media melt away, I feel like a local, though their warmth has limits.

"It's good to see you, too, Commissioner," I said. "This is my colleague Scott Newell."

"Hello, young man. Glad to meet you," Clark said.

"Likewise, sir."

"Please, have a seat," Clark said. "So, Mr. Newell, what is it that you do?"

"I'm a cameraman for Channel 8," Scott said.

"Yes, we're colleagues," I reinforced. "Scott's my favorite cameraman."

"Oh!" Clark exhaled a breath of relief. "Well, as long as he can make me look as good-looking on TV as you do, he's all right with me." He chuckled, and Scott's shoulders dropped a quarter inch.

"I hope we're not intruding," I said. "Are you expecting someone?"

"Not for another thirty minutes. Go on and order yourselves some breakfast. Vera!" He threw up his hand and summoned a nearby waitress. "Bring us some menus."

Until the commissioner mentioned food, it hadn't dawned on me that I was in fact quite hungry. I'd lost my appetite this morning and didn't finish my light breakfast. While I'm here, there's no harm in my ordering my favorite meal—salmon cro-quettes with cheese grits and a warm from-scratch biscuit as big as my hand with strawberry jam. It was enough to eat for two people. Scott and I might have shared a large meal such as this someplace else, but not at the District. We had already elicited a few stares—daggers, actually—when we walked in together. I mustn't appear too chummy with my White col-league at the risk of arousing distrust by my inevitable de-tractors, who are convinced that my education and perceived success have distanced me from my community. Also, people don't know a lot about my personal life. The first time they see me with a man, some will assume he's *my man* or will wonder what I'm hiding.

I knew without even asking that Clark's clock was ticking. Once we ordered, I got right down to business. There was a lot at stake. Even though Louise Robinson and I knew of each other, and her niece Tanya had made me welcome to call her, my instincts told me I needed more gravitas than Tanya to use on Louise. A credible introduction from Commissioner Clark, an astute dealmaker and a heavy hitter like she was herself, would get me a lot further.

"Commissioner, do you have a relationship with Louise Robinson?" I asked.

"Oh, so that's who you're after," he said, chuckling.

"I respect your opinion. I'd like to find out a little more about her before I reach out to talk to her today." I smiled.

The commissioner laughed even harder.

What's so damn funny?

He took a deliberate sip of his coffee. I recognize this old-school power move. I couldn't decipher whether he was thinking about his reply or he was toying with me.

"Yeah, I know Louise," he said. "Why do you ask?"

"She and the South Side Community Council are orchestrating a vigil tonight for Masey James. She's one of the founders, actually," I said.

"Ha!" he scoffed. "She likes to tell people that, but Louise Robinson didn't even live in Chicago when the council was established. She was out in the south suburbs up to God knows what."

I'm not sure what he meant by *God knows what.* I took it with a grain of salt, because from what I've read about Louise Robinson, I know that she is an alpha female who has challenged the establishment, which includes Clark. When a woman does this, it can come at a cost to her reputation and make her unlikable to people who feel threatened by her.

"Really, she's not from Chicago?" I asked.

"She's from here, but she married a guy from out there," he said. "They've been divorced for a while now, but she's only been back in the city for about three, four years."

Our food arrived quickly. By now Clark was so deep into his story, he appeared not to notice. So was I. I forgot to ask for hot sauce, but I was hungry, so I attacked the southern dish that was in stark contrast to my normal sushi and food fusion restaurant world fare, and listened intently as he went on to tell me how Robinson barely escaped indictment while serving as an elected member of a south suburban municipal board.

"The village got so far behind on paying its garbage vendor, they didn't pick up residential trash for three weeks! Can you imagine?"

"I wouldn't want to," Scott chimed in.

"The court had to intervene. It was a mess," he said. "That was before your time, Jordan. She resigned. The terms of the rest of the board members expired, and none of them sought reelection. Not even the mayor," he said.

The steam rising off his scrambled eggs finally drew his attention and he grabbed his fork, leaning over his food and taking a bite. That didn't stop him from talking, though. He went on to explain how Louise moved back in with her mother in Englewood, which consistently ranks as one of the most dangerous neighborhoods in Chicago, with the highest rate of homicides and one of the lowest rates of high school graduations.

"She wasn't there long before she started nagging," he said.

"What do you mean by that?" I asked, trying to hide my disgust at his misogynistic commentary about a woman who clearly cares about her community.

"Oh, just constantly complaining, calling my office and city council members with every grievance imaginable. Before she became such a difficult person, I told her, 'Look, if you want to run for office, then run. Just stop tying up my phone.' In fact, you know the playground where that girl's body was found the other day?"

"Yes, I know it well," I said, moving to the edge of my seat.

"She was the one who blasted the mayor's office and the Park District for letting it fall victim to blight. That was a few years ago, and it's still in horrible shape."

"Yes, I know, I saw it," I said. "Nothing says 'I don't care about the children in this community' like a swing set with no swings. They sent a group of Cook County sheriff's office prisoners to clean it up, and they discovered the body."

"Right. I saw you on the news," Clark said. "It's a shame it had to come to that. A couple years ago, Louise finally kept on until the *Sun-Times* looked into it. They busted the ward leader for siphoning off the money for the upkeep."

"What ward leader?" I asked.

"Lucinda Mitchell," he said.

"What did she do with the money?" I asked.

"Hell, she put it in her pocket," he laughed, and sipped his coffee, which by now was bound to be cold.

"And that was two years ago?" I asked.

"Yeah, at least."

I was still doing the math in my head, thinking about how long the playground had been neglected, when the commissioner continued to speak.

"It was a front-page story," he said.

"How long ago was that?" I asked.

"Let's see, that story came out about a year before Lucinda went to jail, so a little more than three years ago," he said.

It was worse than I thought.

"Three years? That's inconceivable!"

Hell, Louise Robinson should've *been tying up elected officials' phones!*

"You mean to tell me that playground was in bad enough condition to make the front page some three years ago, and it still looked like a dump until just recently?" I asked incredulously.

"Ap-par-ently," the commissioner said. "I remember Louise talked about how it was going to become an incubator of crime.

This was supposed to be a place where children could play. The Park District didn't put any real money into it to start with."

Parks in communities of color typically do not feature the new age soft turf used on playgrounds in more affluent communities like Lincoln Park. Kids on the South Side were lucky to get a slide.

"So the story didn't compel the city to act at all?"

"Oh no, the Park District went in and cleaned up the debris and removed the damaged playground equipment, but they never put anything in its place. They let it sit there and rot."

I would've asked Clark why he didn't step in, but because it is Chicago Park District property, technically it wasn't his jurisdiction.

"Look, I applaud her for at least trying," he said.

Finally, something positive.

"She probably would've gotten more done if she wasn't such a nasty person."

I clenched my teeth to hide my disgust. Clark was again making the point that if you're a woman, no matter where you are on the food chain, there's a man somewhere carping about how difficult you are, even when you're right. I wanted to ask him, "How is it possible that her tactics bother you more than the problem?" But I put food in my mouth, instead, to keep the words from flying out. Good thing it was delicious. I usually don't talk with my mouth full, but to move Clark off his misogynistic rant, I made an exception.

"But . . . she is a current member of the South Side Community Council, right?" I asked.

"She's a member, but she's not a founder, no. That I can assure you," he said. "I don't know why she keeps telling that lie."

For goodness sake, Clark. You've called this woman nasty, nagging, lying . . . all that's missing is the B word.

"With all due respect, Commissioner, aren't you being a little hard on her?" I blurted out, momentarily abandoning the ego stroke, which is sadly a requirement of being a reporter. That's something they don't teach in journalism school, but I learned rather quickly out here in these streets.

He took another deliberate sip of that cold coffee. I fixed my smile and remained affable, because I didn't come here this morning to chastise this grown man. I came to borrow his credibility. Besides, he probably isn't interested in knowing that the way he described a dedicated community advocate was as hurtful for me to hear as a woman as some of the tone-deaf remarks from my newsroom colleagues about race. I have good reasons for trying to get along with them and Clark, too. Listening to his bullshit would be worth it. I would just have to play his game a little longer.

"People don't have to get out here and fight for their community. Whatever happened down in the south 'burbs, I'll give her credit . . . When she wants to, she can be relentless," said Clark.

"You sound like you admire her," I said, with a healthy dose of sarcasm. Clark is a smart man, but I wondered whether he picked up on it.

He hesitated before he spoke, then said abruptly, "Weeelll, to some extent, maybe. I mean, we talk."

That's what I figured. That's why I'm here.

"Would you mind giving her a call to let her know I'll be contacting her within the next thirty minutes?"

"For you, I will make an exception."

Clark wore on my nerves, but it got me to the next step. He pushed his plate to the side and pulled his cell phone from his inside jacket pocket.

"It's loud in here," I said.

"Good," Clark said. "That'll keep the call short and save me from the list of things I'm sure she wants to talk to me about."

Clark had her number in his phone. She must've picked up on the first or second ring.

"Hi, Louise? It's Clark. Can you hear me? It's Clark!" he shouted over the chatter. "Listen, I'm here with Jordan Manning . . . What's that? . . . Okay, wait, wait. I can barely hear you. I'm over at the District. Look, I called you because I'm sitting here with Jordan Manning, the reporter from Channel 8. She's going to call you in a few minutes to talk to you, so pick up her call. Okay? . . . Yes, I know about it . . . Okay, well, let's talk later, okay, dear?"

Dear? After all the shit you just talked about her?

"All right, talk to you later," Clark said and snapped his flip phone closed.

As Clark was finishing up my introduction to Louise Robinson, Vera brought the check.

"I've got this, Commissioner," I said.

"You owe me," he said. "We can start with breakfast." He chuckled.

Scott's eyes widened. I would have to explain to him that there was nothing lascivious about that remark. Clark, I now know, is a misogynist, but he has always been a gentleman. He's a politician, so he's used to people picking up tabs, except Scott reached in and grabbed the check first.

"That's okay. I've got this," he said.

"Always good to see you, Ms. Manning," Clark said. He stood up to walk us out and embraced me once more outside the first set of double doors.

"Likewise, Commissioner, and thank you."

I climbed into the news truck with Scott, cleared my throat, and dialed Ms. Robinson.

"Yes?" she answered inquisitively.

"Hello, is this Ms. Louise Robinson?"

"This is. Is this Jordan Manning?" she asked.

"Yes, ma'am, it is."

"Boy, that was fast!" she said. "I just hung up with C.W. He must like you."

"Why do you say that?" I asked.

"Because he called me on your behalf. I'm sure he gave me a glowing review," she said, dripping with sarcasm. "For C.W. to admit I'm right, you have a better chance of seeing a unicorn walk down Lake Shore Drive."

"Well, he did have some interesting things to say about you," I said.

"And the feeling is mutual," Robinson said. We both giggled knowingly, like two women who were sure we'd been called difficult behind our backs many times before.

This wasn't the way I'd planned to launch our conversation, but it broke the ice, nonetheless. I explained that her niece had told me about the vigil tonight for Masey James and that Clark had filled me in on her history with the playground.

"If it's all right, I'd rather talk in person. I'm not far away. I have someone with me, my cameraman, but I'd like to sit down and chat first. He'll stay in the car." Scott shot me a look.

My goal was to get her on-camera, but I needed to go in by myself first and build trust. So far, so good.

"Forgive the last-minute notice, but I have an interview at the police station at twelve-thirty and another at three o'clock," I said.

"That's fine. Come on."

I jotted down her address and handed it to Scott.

"If I'm not filming her, why am I going again?" he asked.

"Scott, you don't just roll up on a woman like Louise Robinson with fifteen or twenty minutes to spare and put a camera in her face. You just don't.

"But . . . if there's a breakthrough," I said, "I wanna be ready."

At 10:45, the District parking lot was still packed tight, like my skirt, which felt two sizes smaller after that huge breakfast. Just as I was about to give up and drive myself over to Ms. Robinson's, I got lucky and grabbed a spot as a car was pulling out. Then I hopped back in the truck with Scott.

To be honest, I didn't want to drive alone through Englewood any more than Scott did. And perhaps if people saw me sitting up front in the passenger seat, nobody would take a shot at the truck, which happened the last time Scott drove through Englewood by himself.

We were only about ten minutes away from Robinson's house, but I'd promised to give her twenty minutes.

"Let's drive around a little," I told Scott. "She probably needs a little time to get herself together."

We passed three girls who looked to be about eight or nine. They were playing hopscotch on the sidewalk.

"See there?" Scott pointed. "Now, that's cute. I wish I could be filming that."

"Black kids playing hopscotch? What's unusual about that?"

"It's cute," Scott said.

A classic white Chevy Impala drove past us. The music was playing so loudly, I could feel it in my throat.

"Okay, just so you know . . . Black kids have been playing hopscotch for-*ever*. It's not new to the hood," I said.

I don't know whether he heard me, because he was busy lambasting a person who had no idea they were being lambasted.

"Damn, dude, turn your music down!" he said, and then to me. "How long do you want to drive around?" he asked. "Her house is a block away."

"It is?"

"Yeah, we passed it already. I just hope those three guys standing on the corner are gone when I pull back around."

"Why, what were they doing?" I asked.

"Just standing there doing nothing!" he said.

So, standing around doing nothing is code for what?

As we circled back to Louise's block and rounded the corner, sure enough, there were three young Black men in their late teens, early twenties, standing on the corner beneath a blue-and-white CTA sign.

"Dude, it's a bus stop!" I said. "What else are they supposed to do while they wait for the bus but stand around?"

Scott frowned. I could tell that he felt exposed and slightly embarrassed, and he didn't like feeling that way at all. But it was a teaching moment I couldn't pass up.

"You know, how a person sees three Black men looks different depending on who you are and how and where you grew up," I said.

"Yes, I know. Fine. Let's drop it. I didn't see the sign," he said.

"Hear me out," I continued. "Do you think it's possible you were so focused on the three Black men that you didn't notice they were at a bus stop?"

"Everything's not about race, Jordan," he said.

No, he didn't.

"It is for those three young Black men. How people see them through the lens of race impacts how their teachers see them, how police interact with them. Will they see a suspect when he's the victim or just a guy waiting on a bus? Black people have been killed for less."

Scott remained silent, and I backed off. Maybe I was taking out my frustration over Clark's comments on him, and that wasn't fair. But he needed to learn, and if being a little uncomfortable was required for him never to forget, then so be it.

Scott parked in front of a two-story redbrick bungalow with a large shaded porch. I wonder if she uses it much. Misdirected gunfire and stray bullets were very real dangers in this community.

"You call me in ten minutes and let me know what's going on," Scott commanded, clearly irritated. "I don't want to sit out here for thirty minutes," he said emphatically, with a disquieting expression.

I reached over and put my left hand on his right and flashed him a smile. "Okay, I will. I promise."

I was met at the door by a boy who looked to be around eleven or twelve.

"Grandma, you've got company!" he yelled toward the back of the house.

"Show her the way!" Grandma yelled back.

"Follow me."

"What's your name?" I asked.

He looked back but kept moving forward. "Marcus."

He faced forward once more, but then twisted around a second later, pointing his index finger at me. "Aren't you on TV?"

"Yes, I am. I'm Jordan Manning from Channel 8 news," I said, extending my hand.

"You've never been here before," he said with certainty.

"You're right. I haven't."

"Well, it's nice to meet you," he said, shaking my hand lightly, sizing me up. "You're very pretty."

"Why, thank you, Marcus."

I followed the Little Charmer down the hallway onto a screened-in sunporch just off the kitchen. Louise Robinson was sitting in a tan wicker chair with red-and-white-striped cushions, her leg propped up on a pillow on the matching wicker ottoman. She wore a dark blue sleeveless shirt and a gray skirt that hit her at the knee, with one sandal on her left foot. Her right foot was expertly wrapped in an Ace bandage. It was neither formal attire nor typical loungewear, but I could tell she had made an effort to get herself together.

"Hello, Ms. Robinson. It's a pleasure to meet you. I'm sorry to see you're injured," I said. "What happened?" pointing to her lame foot.

"I know you didn't come here to talk about my foot," she said, a little terse.

"Well, no, of course not," I said, managing an uncomfortable smile.

Where'd that come from?

When I opened my mouth again, I relaxed my well-trained vocal cords and dropped my voice down an octave. I sensed from that small exchange that maybe she *was* a little nasty, as Clark had said. Even if that was true, I was determined not to let her take me there. In my experience, people often give back what I give them. In times like this, I imagine myself extending an olive branch. It helps me keep my vibe even.

"Ms. Robinson, I came here today to talk to you about your valiant fight to improve the Ida B. Wells-Barnett playground, which has now become a crime scene?"

"Oh. That," she said. "I have to be careful, you know," she said. "This poor mother has lost her child in the most vicious, desecrating manner. Even if the death didn't happen on the playground, this neglected property was going to be somebody's tomb."

Shit. I should be getting this on-camera. Scott can say he told me so all he wants.

"Thank you so much for letting me come into your home to

speak to you today. I want to applaud you for what you tried to do with the playground."

"Tried?" she said, sounding indignant. "Tried? Honey, I did that thing. The Park District is the one that failed. Not me."

"Well, yes, absolutely," I said.

I felt myself slipping down a rabbit hole that I had somehow managed to dig in less than three minutes. The warmth we had established over the phone was getting chillier by the second.

"It's upsetting to see kids not being given the basics to enjoy in life," I said. "But obviously I didn't come here just to talk about the playground."

"Obviously, you didn't. So what do you want?"

Jeez, can you be a little nicer?

"Ms. Robinson, I'd really like to interview you on-camera. I told Tanya, your niece, that the only way to keep this story in the news was for us to do exactly what you did with the playground. Never let our foot off the gas," I said. "The stakes are higher than a swing set."

I'm aware that I'm pouring it on thick, but if Louise Robinson wants me to beg her to go on-camera, she can forget it. I'm here now, in her house, and I'm determined not to leave without footage. It's one thing to get a grieving parent to talk on-camera; it's another to get a professional mouthpiece, like Robinson. Surely she isn't camera shy. Maybe she's saving it for the vigil.

On the way to her house, I googled the article she was quoted in about the blighted playground.

"Why did it become such a struggle to get the Park District to respond to repeated requests to improve the conditions of the playground in a community full of schoolchildren?" I asked.

"Oh, it wasn't just the Park District; it was Lucinda Mitchell blocking us at first, because she didn't want anybody to find out she was embezzling that money. When they finally did do something over there, we as a community had less than we started with. They took out all the equipment, and do you know they've only cut that grass over there TWICE! You hear me, TWICE in two years! After that, they said forget it."

"Who's they? The Park District?" I asked.

"I blame them all!" she declared. "The mayor's office, too. They're as much to blame for that child's death as the person or people who killed her," she said.

Louise had quickly worked herself into a frenzy, so I decided not to bring up the fact that Masey was murdered someplace else and her body was dumped there.

"Ms. Robinson, Tanya said on the phone this morning that people are furious. What are you hearing? Are people concerned there will be other victims? That a killer's on the loose on the South Side?"

"Our children are dying every day," she said, leaning forward in her chair. "There are always others. Do I think somebody in the community did it? Yes. I do. Do I believe he knew where he was going to stash her body before he killed her? Yes. I believe he did."

She hadn't yet answered the second part of my question.

"Are you afraid there will be others?" I repeated.

"God forbid, but yes. So long as he keeps getting away with it, he'll never stop. His thirst to kill can't be quenched. He's already gone after another young lady," she said.

Wait. What?

"Ms. Robinson, you almost sound like you know who did this," I said, trading in my low octave for a near shriek. "What are you telling me?"

I wish I had an extra hand behind my back to text Scott, "Get in here with the camera! Now!"

Louise Robinson moved up in her chair and, leaning forward, looked me dead in the face. "What I'm telling you is that people don't believe what they see with their own eyes. They ignore the truth."

Why is she being so cryptic?

I listened.

"There is a pathology that runs through our community, Jordan. It places our girls in imminent danger every day of their lives. Before the police fail them, before the prosecutors fail to convict those who would harm them, there is in some cases a failure of the community to protect them."

She was starting to sound like Superintendent Bartlett.

"How so?" I asked.

"Oh, I'm sure you've seen it before. Some people would rather shame our girls and blame them for being victimized. They oversexualize them before they even get their period. Some women are just as guilty as men. It's not uncommon to hear, 'She's acting grown,' or 'She's acting fast,' or 'She shouldn't have been wearing that. She was asking for it. She should've known better.'"

She's right; it was a familiar refrain.

"I agree with you a hundred percent. But, Ms. Robinson, you said he's already gone after another young lady. Who are you talking about?"

She leaned back and held on to the chair's armrests, posturing like a queen on her wicker throne, and with the damnedest look on her face, she said, "Red Moley. And you'd better believe, if there's one, there's two."

7

Scott and I had to hustle to make it to the Chicago Police Department headquarters on time to interview Bartlett. Indeed, he had nothing new to say about the investigation, but what he *did* say and *how* he said it was emotive. Sitting behind his desk, in his dress-white short-sleeved uniform shirt, he looked downright despondent when he said: "Every child's life matters. But as someone working in law enforcement for over twenty-five years, I've continually witnessed the unchecked victimization of Black women and girls, and society's failure to protect them," he said. "Masey James was more than just innocent; she was golden." His lower lip quivered. "She was her mother's pride and joy. Any parent would be proud to have raised such a daughter."

For goodness sake, Bartlett! Are you trying to make me cry?

Bartlett is an empath, which I must say is one of the things I really like about him. He had read the autopsy report. He knew as well as I did the extent of Masey's injuries, and that only a monster would be capable of inflicting such unimaginable horror on a human being. But I do worry about him. His malnourished ego and sympathetic leanings, devoid of the machismo that's heralded in this jewel of the Midwest and certainly within his profession, makes him vulnerable to departmental mutiny. The slightest fissure in his armor, and Fawcett would make a play for his job. I'd bet money on it.

The remorseful expression lingered on Bartlett's flat, round face, but its effect on me withered posthaste. Bartlett's a sweet man, but he's also in charge of this police department. The buck stops with him. Thus I didn't hesitate to pose the question I've heard again and again from people in the community while covering this story and many others.

"Superintendent Bartlett, let me be clear, there's skepticism among Black residents that homicide and missing persons investigations are taken as seriously when the victim is Black, and that that's the reason there have been so many unsolved murders of Black women in Chicago."

Then I bore down. "Superintendent, this surely isn't a surprise to you that people feel that way. So why aren't you doing more to ease their concerns?"

Bartlett's face turned from ashen to crimson. He began to fidget with a pen on his desk, tapping it against a brownish folder. My question must have felt like a betrayal, but it's my job to hold his feet to the fire. And in fact I was doing him a favor by giving him the opportunity to speak directly to Black Chicagoans and calm their fears.

"I've spoken many, many times with black community leaders, ward leaders, and clergymen and women right here in my office about these very concerns. I share their concerns. But it's simply not true that police aren't prioritizing these cases. I have tremendous faith in our investigators, and I assure you, we're giving this case everything we've got, and it'll remain a top priority until we make an arrest," he said.

"Thank you," I said, and nodded to Scott: *That's a wrap.*

I stood up and extended my hand to the superintendent. Even if he was put off by my question, he wasn't the type of man to leave me hanging. "Thanks, Chief," I said, flashing a warm smile.

"Anytime, Jordan," Bartlett said, returning a firm handshake.

Scott and I passed Fawcett's desk on the way out. The lieutenant glanced at us but quickly diverted his eyes. I didn't go out of my way to acknowledge him, either. It's been an emotional day already, and I still have Pamela to deal with. I'm nervous, on edge, fragile. I wondered: *Am I about to get my period? Why am I such a wreck?*

Scott and I have two hours to kill. Pamela told me to meet her at her sister-in-law's house at three o'clock. But we couldn't just show up and start filming, as we had done with Bartlett. I haven't seen Pamela since she found out her missing daughter had been murdered. I needed a moment, unencumbered by professional protocol, to acknowledge her loss, and heck, deal with my own grief. Once more, I would have to ask Scott to remain in the news van, so soon after admitting to myself that this might not have been the correct course of action at Louise Robinson's. Then again, once she inserted her cryptic tale about some fictionalized boogeyman character into our very real-life discussion, I couldn't decide whether Louise Robinson was eccentric or insane.

"Who's Red Moley?" I asked her.

"You never heard of Red Moley?"

"No . . . I . . . I can't say that I have. Is that his nickname? What's his real name?"

"It's a story. I can't believe you've never heard of Red Moley. Did you ever go to camp when you were a kid? Didn't you have sleepovers?"

"Well, yeah, I did," I said.

"Y'all didn't tell scary stories?" she asked.

Her line of questioning began to aggravate the hell out of me. Before I could respond, she asked another: "You ever heard of Bloody Mary?"

No, I've never heard of any of this crap!

"No," I said wryly. Then I remembered. "Wait, you mean the

Bloody Mary of folklore? What was she? A witch, right? She lived in the woods and abducted kids or something like that."

"Yes!" she said with excitement. "She'd put 'em under a spell and they would come right to her."

"Yeah, I've heard it. It scared me to death as a kid. I haven't thought about that in years," I said.

Where was she going with this?

"Red Moley is kinda like Bloody Mary, except it's a he—half man, half monster—who preys on children and takes their hearts, because children have the most loving and trusting hearts."

What's that got to do with Masey James?

I'd pictured several versions of the first conversation I would have with Louise Robinson, and so far this matched none of them.

"When Red Moley gets done with you, there's nothing left of you," she said.

Eviscerated.

I didn't need a mirror to know that I looked perplexed. As much as I wanted to ask what she meant when she said, "If there's one, there's two," I'd heard enough of her hoodoo and pushed on to another topic. Louise caught on, floated back down from Planet Strange, and snapped back to reality.

"Ms. Robinson, in the *Sun-Times* article, you warned of criminal activity at the neglected playground. Were there any occurrences or arrests that took place there that you know of?" I asked as a chime filled the room.

"Excuse me. That's my cell phone," she said, retrieving it from her skirt pocket. "Hello, this is Louise Robinson."

Seconds into the call, I gathered that it was one of the pastors who'd be speaking at tonight's vigil on the phone. She relayed the order of the program to him, and I discreetly jotted down the names she mentioned. Pastor Bowman, Pastor Harper, Bishop Toney. After a few minutes, their conversation drifted onto something entirely different: she brought up funding for a kids' camp at a community center over the Christmas holiday break, which was months away. I checked my watch. It was 11:57. *Shit!* Louise was taking her sweet time on the phone. I held up a finger to get her attention and pointed to my watch.

"Oh, okay, Pastor. I'm sorry. Can I call you back? You're good. We're all set. Okay, see you this evening," she said. "Forgive me, Jordan, we're still adding folks to tonight's program."

"Sure, that's quite all right," I said. "Ms. Robinson, unfortunately I'm going to have to go. I'd already set up an interview at twelve-thirty with the police superintendent. But before I leave, I want to ask you about tonight at your niece's house. Can we film a sit-down with you, Pamela Alonzo, and community leaders before the vigil starts? Just me, though. No other media."

"Yes!" she said, so enthusiastically it startled me. "Yes! We're on the same page! Let's do that. I'll be there no later than five-thirty."

"Great! I'll meet you there."

I don't know that I agree with Louise that we are on the same page, but at least I got part of what I came here for. I checked my phone and Scott had texted me a series of question marks.

"My grandson will see you out. Marcus!"

"Ma'am?" he called.

"Please see Ms. Manning out, son."

"Yes, Grandma."

The jury was still out on Louise, but Marcus I liked instantly. I followed the canny mini-man down the narrow hallway past framed family pictures, some in color, some weathered and faded, along the wall. There was the familiar school portrait of a younger Marcus with his two front teeth missing. He's incredibly astute to be so young. He already has a presence.

Where will he end up in twenty years? Will he possess a fraction of the social acuity he has displayed today even five years from now?

Marcus stopped at the door, turning toward me and extending his right hand. "Goodbye, Miss Jordan. Nice meeting you."

"Why, thank you, Marcus," I said, smiling broadly. "I feel the same way. You have a good day."

The instant I stepped out onto the front porch, I heard the news truck engine turn over and a thundering *VROOM*, the sound an engine makes when the gas pedal is floored while the car is in park. Maybe I was being paranoid, but the sound spoke to me. It sounded like "Fuck this."

Was Scott upset that I didn't ask him to come in?

I opened the door to the van, "Hey. Sorry about that. I just saw your text message. You okay?"

"Yeah," Scott responded a tad too quickly.

"You didn't miss anything here. In fact, she spent half the time on the phone talking to one of the pastors leading the vigil tonight."

I didn't tell him about Louise Robinson's bizarre Red Moley story. Frankly, it made her sound like a crackpot. I'd had higher expectations of her after what Clark had shared. And if I felt that way, I could only imagine what Scott would have thought if he'd heard her. It was like Clark said, people don't have to fight for their community. He had given Robinson credit, and for now, so could I. Who am I to rush to judgment from my West Loop address? I didn't have to live in any of the communities she's fighting for to respect her hustle. Even if part of her motivation is self-serving, all of it couldn't be, and I had an obligation to protect that.

I pivoted. "Here's the good news. We're set to film Louise with Pam and some of the pastors and community members tonight at Tanya's house. Just us. No other media!"

Scott let out a sigh of exhaustion and annoyance. "All right then," and pulled away from the curb.

"Oh, sorry, I wasn't thinking. You have to go in at six, don't you?" I asked, remembering the union rules that restrict Scott's hours. I got the feeling Scott had had enough of me for one day anyway.

He took his time responding. "Well, technically, I'm not working for two hours now, but I'm in the truck," he said. "I don't have the kids tonight, so what else do I have to do?"

"Okay, thanks. I appreciate it."

I truly did. I didn't want to end up with afternoon shift camera guy, George Spivey, a heavy mouth breather with some serious BO.

"I'd like to get to Pam's sister's house fifteen minutes early," I said. "She's a grieving mother. I've got a feeling we're going to need the extra time."

..

I should have felt grateful that the day, with all its intensity, was passing quickly. But the closer I came to interviewing Pamela, the more I was dreading it. These were real people, real lives. The psychological game that reporting such tragedy plays on you—that's the part of the job people don't see. On the outside, I appear to be competitive and driven, but inside I sometimes question whether this is the way I want to cover people and tell stories. The irony of a day like today—one filled with hustling, running and gunning—is that a part of me wants to end the race. I was concerned not just about Pamela's demeanor; I was worried about my own. I had interviewed the parents of young victims many times before, but that didn't make me immune to nervousness or reflections on trauma from my past. On our way to Masey's aunt's house, I could feel a low-key panic attack coming on. Ever since Masey was identified as the victim on the playground, I'd done all I could do to suppress thoughts of my cousins Stephanie's and Jaden's deaths at the hands of her abusive ex-boyfriend. It's been ten years, but there are moments when that feeling of tragic disbelief resurfaces like a light switched on in a dark room.

I've heard people say that when they die, let it be quick, not some lingering, debilitating illness. But sudden death scars those who are left behind to grieve. As human beings, we're keenly aware of our mortality, but it's not something we contemplate every day. So when we lose someone we love in a terrible accident, it forces us to focus on our fragility within that mortal coil. When the victim is young, we mourn the truncation of a life. But when someone you love is murdered, it instills in you a heightened sense of foreboding that never goes away. I wondered, *If I still felt it after all these years, what in God's name was Pamela going through?*

From the time a woman becomes a mother, her marching orders are to protect that child at all costs. It is her biggest responsibility, her most important job. It's what made my cousin Stephanie run back into a burning house to try to rescue her four-year-old son, unable to accept or comprehend a world without Jaden in it, hoping against hope that the rolling flames and the excess heat from the fire that burst out the bedroom windows had somehow spared him. I wasn't there, but I've imagined how that scene must have played out a thousand times.

Does Pam carry that guilt of not having protected her daughter?

This wasn't the first time these feelings have crept up before an important interview. I wondered if Scott sensed my perturbation. He was quiet on the trip over. I was looking over my questions when he finally broke the silence.

"The GPS says we're 0.2 miles away," he said, pointing to the Garmin device plugged into the van's cigarette lighter. "It should be just up here to the right."

Cynthia's neighborhood of modest but sturdy midsize brick homes was tucked between Racine Avenue and the Burlington Northern Railroad tracks located on top of an adjacent hill.

"This is Carpenter Avenue up ahead, so the house should be up here around the cor—" Scott paused, "Oh, nice."

"What?" I said, looking up. A Channel 11 news van was parked outside Cynthia Caruthers's one-story brown-and-tan brick bungalow. Scott and I looked at each other knowingly.

"Well, that answers one question," I said, and retrieved my cell phone from my purse to call Ellen, who picked up on the first ring.

"Newsroom, Holbrook."

"Hey, Ellen. It's Jordan. We just pulled up to the Pam Alonzo interview, and there's another news truck here. Is the promo set to go at four?"

"Yes, it's ready, but I'll let the desk know it's not an exclusive," she said.

"Okay, thanks."

So much for my plan to arrive early.

Scott pulled up behind our competitor. A few minutes later, the news crew were coming out of the house. It was Pamela who had suggested we meet at three o'clock. So clearly, she had scheduled this interview before mine. Or was this her PR agent Tanya's doing?

"Should we wait?" Scott asked. "We *are* early."

"Sure, let's give her a little time to get it together," I said.

I checked my hair and makeup, and before I knew it, five minutes had passed.

"Do you want some time with her before I come in?" Scott asked, signaling that he was fully on board with my plan this time.

"No," I said sternly. "In fact, come on. Let's go."

I stepped carefully along the walkway on the balls of my feet to keep from catching the heel of my shoe in one of the cracks. The main door was flung open, but I tapped on the screen door to announce our arrival. Cynthia Caruthers, the woman I'd spoken with the day of the news conference, answered the door. I am taken aback by how much she favors her niece—tall, leggy, with smooth dark skin and thick jet-black hair with a few early gray strands.

"Good afternoon," I said. "Are you Cynthia?"

"Yes. Come on in. It's nice to meet you, Jordan," she said, and gave me a light handshake.

"It's nice to meet you, too. This is my cameraman, Scott Newell," I said.

"Hello. Nice to meet you, Scott," she said.

Her salutations belied the pain etched in her face. Cynthia closed the front door behind us and led us into a surprisingly lavish dining room, with gold jacquard drapes fitted with regal valances trimmed in tassels and matching tasseled tiebacks against a red wall. The room was excessively dark for this hour of the day. The sheers were black, effectively blocking the sun from breaking through. The room was anchored by an oversize black lacquered dining table far too big for the room. It was ornate and looked expensive, but there was no chance that it was an antique passed down in the family. Clearly, though, the dining room was the most important room in the house. Pam was sitting at the head of the table, which had six full place settings with charger plates, napkins, and matching napkin rings. Two of the settings had been moved to the center of the table to make room for a photo album and a smattering of pictures. Pam had spread them out in front of her, and for the first time I noticed she was wearing a wig I hadn't seen before—a simple bob that hit her mid-cheek with a flat bang.

"Pam," I said gently, sitting down in the chair closest to her and placing my hand sympathetically on her right forearm. "We arrived a little early and I saw the other news crew just leaving. Do you need a minute?"

To my surprise, she said decisively, "No. I'm ready when you are."

"Okay, um . . . this is Scott Newell. And, um, he's going to film us today. He needs a few minutes to set up. Okay?"

Keep it together, girl.

"Yes. That's fine. I have some pictures here that you can shoot," she said, pointing to a manila folder on the table. "Cynthia, can you bring me a bottle of water, please? Would you like one, Jordan? Scott?"

"Uh, no thank you," I said.

"No, but thank you very much," Scott said.

I searched Pamela's face for a sign of the woman I had gotten to know over the last few weeks. She simply wasn't there and might never be again. Yet she appeared remarkably composed. There was no evidence of tears. In fact, there was something stately about her. When Pam and I first met, she was frightened and desperate, pleading for someone to pay attention to the fact that her little girl didn't come home. I didn't have any answers for her, but I'd always had something to say. Now I was unsure of what to say to her. I was discombobulated, thrown off my game. What do you say to someone who's lost everything? Especially when that loss didn't come as a result of a disease or an accident? I knew only what I dare *not* ask, which was "How are you doing?" It's an innocuous conversation starter that's appropriate in most circumstances, but not in this one.

Then it dawned on me: Pamela was wearing the blouse Masey took her ninth-grade school picture in. I decided to start there. "Your blouse . . . it looks like the one Masey wore in her school picture," I said.

"This *is* it. Remember, I told you she stole it out of my closet. Well, she borrowed it. She was always in my closet," she said. Right then, an unnatural expression froze on Pamela's face for a few seconds. It was the first sign of emotion, and it was terrifying. Pam wore the expression of a mother who just learned that her missing daughter was dead—without sound. Then, as quickly as it came, she snapped out of it.

"I was going through some photos and I couldn't believe it, Jordan—out of all these, I only found two pictures of me and Masey together. I guess I was always the one taking the pictures," she said, emitting a laugh that wasn't really a laugh. She reached across the table and picked up a five-by-seven picture frame and rubbed her hand affectionately across the glass before turning it around to show it to me. It was an image of Masey and her with mountains in the background. They were both wearing boonie hats, drawstrings dangling beneath their chins, and had fanny packs around their waists, standing shoulder to shoulder, hands on hips.

"This is us at the Grand Canyon," she said.

"Ahhh, how old was she?" I asked.

"She was eleven on this picture. We had our family reunion in Vegas that year, and a few of us took a tour of the South Rim. Malcolm was too little to go, so he stayed behind at the hotel with my mother. That was the last trip we took together before she died."

To evoke her deceased mother's memory in this terrifying moment without collapsing into tears—I was in awe of her.

"Where is Malcolm?" I asked.

"Oh, he's here with me," she said. "He's in the basement watching TV."

I picked up on her emphasis of *here with me*. When you lose one child, there's no way you're trusting the one you have left with anybody else, not for a while at least.

I pointed to an image on the dining table of a little girl playing on a swing set wearing a Scooby-Doo T-shirt and cutoff denim shorts. There was a man standing directly behind her and a playground full of children and equipment, a sharp contrast to the crime scene.

"Who's this with Masey?"

"That's her father," Pamela said, resting her chin against her left hand. "She was about three, I think, in this picture. This wasn't taken in Chicago, though. We were visiting his side of the family that summer in Memphis. Whew, it was hot! I remember that."

Pamela had previously told me that Masey's father is an electrician who lives in Seattle with his girlfriend. The two were high school sweethearts who continued to date postsecondary. He attended Dawson Technical Institute on the Near South Side and she was enrolled in Chicago State University. Pamela had just started her sophomore year when she became pregnant with Masey. They never married, but she gave Masey her father's last name. She told me everybody in her family expected her to go back and finish college, but she never did.

Stephanie dropped out of college after she became pregnant with Drucilla her freshman year. Like Pamela, we all thought she'd go back, but just as she was planning to reenroll, she got pregnant with Jaden. I remember hearing my aunties, uncles, and older cousins lamenting her decision. "What a shame." "She's too smart to waste her life." Not finishing college didn't make Stephanie any less intelligent, but admittedly, I too, questioned her decision to put her romantic relationships above everything else in her life. Pamela reminds me a little of Stephanie. Both were naturally smart, but the breaks don't always line up for people like them. Pam, even without a degree, worked her way up to general manager within the Omni grocery chain and helped open its Ultra Foods store in Ashburn a few months ago. She had more time to find herself. I wonder what Stephanie might have done if her life hadn't been interrupted.

I wanted to ask Pam whether Masey's father had been an active part of her life but felt it was none of my business and, frankly, had nothing to do with anything that mattered anymore. So, instead, I asked, "What's his name?"

"Anthony, but everybody calls him Tony," she said. "He gets in sometime this afternoon."

"Is he Cynthia's brother?" I asked.

I'd wondered about their connection, because Pam told me that she never married Masey's father. She must have sensed my curiosity.

"Cynthia and I became best friends in high school after I started dating her brother. I've always thought of her as my sister-in-love," she said.

"Ladies," Scott said, "sorry to interrupt, but I just want to let you know I'm good to go here. I just need to get you two mic'd up. Pamela, let's start with you."

Just like that, the nervous energy returned. I fumbled through my purse looking for my notebook with the questions I'd jotted down, then realized I had left it in the news truck. I only wished I'd done a better job of masking my disgust with myself.

"What's wrong?" Pam asked.

"Oh, nothing. I . . . I, uh, left my notebook in the truck. I'll be right back."

A freaking novice, are you?

I was half embarrassed, half annoyed with myself. My plan was to get to Cynthia's and take control of the situation. Now it felt more like the situation was taking control of me. When the woman whose child has been murdered must ask *me* what's wrong, I was clearly not the one in control.

I ran out to the news truck to find my notebook, and the heel of one of the half-size-too-big pumps I'd bought because they were on sale got stuck in a crack and came off.

"Damn it!" I retrieved the shoe, which now had a deep, ruinous crevice down the back of the heel. Nervous energy pulsed through me like an electric shock. I paused and took a deep breath. Pam had kept it together so far. I couldn't let her see me sweat. Once the interview starts is when things can get hard.

Jordan, you cannot fall apart.

I checked my makeup in the rearview mirror and smoothed my skirt and jacket, slipping on the flats I'd brought for this evening before returning to Cynthia Caruthers's elegant dining room.

"Sorry about that," I said as I looped the microphone underneath my jacket and hooked the battery pack onto the back of my skirt.

"Pamela, before we get started, I wanted to ask, what do you hope to accomplish in this interview today?"

She dropped her head and closed her eyes as she thought about her answer. By the time she looked up, her eyes were filled with clarity. "I want people to know who my daughter was. But let me be clear," she said, stabbing the table with her forefinger. "I. Want. Her. Killer."

Pam looked down at the table and covered her mouth with her left hand, then held up her right in a gesture I interpreted as "I need a minute."

Scott took the opportunity to ask Cynthia if there were any cell phones nearby and to turn the ringers off. "And, Cynthia, if you wouldn't mind, the house phone, too?" he asked.

"Those are already off," she said.

Yes, off since the previous interview with Channel 11, which I must now follow, which I hate to do, in such an emotionally charged situation.

The dining room curtains were drawn closed, and the room was dark. Too dark, in fact. I should have asked Cynthia to tie back the panels and let in some natural light. Scott flipped on the light atop his camera.

I started the interview. "When was the last time you saw your daughter?"

"Why are you asking me that? I told you I was at work. I left . . . I left that morning a-a-at six o'clock," she stammered. "You-you-you know that!"

Pamela and I had talked about the last time she'd seen Masey at the coffee shop, but we'd never had the conversation on-camera. I should have prepped her. I should have explained to her that some of the questions I would be asking were about situations the two of us had talked about previously but were unknown to viewers. Expecting Pam, in her current state, to account for that was a rookie mistake. If I hadn't been so lost in memories of my own trauma, I would have remembered that. Now Pam was triggered. Her face twisted and leaning forward, she said with conviction, "Why do our kids always have to be runaways? Huh? Unparented and misguided? Neglected and unloved? The police instantly go there. She was fifteen years old! She was a straight-A student *invited* to attend a prestigious STEM school! How did she accomplish that without a loving family to support her?"

I agreed with everything she said, but this wasn't the reaction I had expected. I thought about asking Scott to stop filming so that I could explain why I asked the question. Instead, I let the camera roll and searched Pamela's eyes, trying to connect with her soul. I realized she was expressing her frustration with police for falling back on stereotypes and their own biases, not with me.

"Pam, I know. I hear you, and I *agree* with you," I said. "But we've never spoken about your recollection from that day on-camera. Okay? I should have prepared you for that question. I'm sorry."

"No, it's okay. I'm just . . . ," Pam said irritably.

"Let's take a break," I suggested.

"No, really. I'm fine. I'm fine," she said.

I'm not.

"You sure?"

"Yeah," she insisted.

I looked back at Scott. "Let's do that take again."

I rephrased the question.

"Pamela," I said, "what were Masey's plans on the day she disappeared?"

Pamela gulped hard before she spoke. "Well, it was a routine Saturday for us. Mase knew I'd be gone to work by the time she got out of bed. So the night before, she asked me if she could ride her bike over to her cousin Yvonne's house after her aunt Cynthia picked up my son for swim lessons that morning. Yvonne's house is pretty much a straight shot, about a mile or so from where I live."

"And did Masey arrive at her cousin's?" I asked.

"Yeah, she texted me to let me know she'd made it, and that her aunt Cynthia had said Malcolm could stay at her house until I got off work. She wanted to spend some time with Yvonne's little girl . . ." She paused.

"Imani," I said.

"Yeah, Imani. She loved that baby. She was supposed to watch Imani while Yvonne ran around and got stuff together for a birthday party she was throwing for her husband that night."

Husband? I thought Manny was her boyfriend.

"But I told Mase to ride back home before dark. She didn't have no business at no grown folk's party. About an hour before my shift was over, Masey called and asked me if she could run to the mall with her cousin and said that Yvonne would drop her off at the house if it started to get dark, and she'd just leave her bike over there."

"Masey told me, 'Mama, the party doesn't start till nine o'clock. I'll be home way before then.'"

In a shattered voice, she continued, "And I told her it was okay."

Pamela hadn't previously shared with me the detail about Masey's going to the mall with Yvonne. I wondered why.

"What mall did she say they were going to?" I asked.

"Evergreen Plaza over on 95th and Western," she said.

I'd been there. Not to shop but to cover the aftermath of a violent altercation between gang members that left two people dead. That was more than a year ago.

"So, she went to the mall with Yvonne. Do you know around what time of day that was?" I asked.

"Not exactly, but it was sometime after she called me, which was about an hour before I got off work, like I said," Pam said.

The new information about the mall threw me. If Pam could pick up Malcolm from Cynthia's after work, couldn't she have grabbed Masey from Yvonne's place after she got back from the mall?

"Did Masey ride home on her bicycle that night? Or did Yvonne give her a ride home because it was getting dark, as you'd requested?"

Pamela clasped her hands together and brought them up to her mouth and breathed a deep, heavy sigh. When she took her hands away, I thought she was going to answer my questions, but she shook her head instead. "I don't . . . I don't . . ." Pam hesitated. "Uh . . ."

"Pam, after you picked up your son from his aunt's house, did you hear from Masey again?"

"No, no, I didn't talk with her any more that night," she said.

"And did you head home after you picked up Malcolm? Is it possible Masey arrived at home before you did, or went back out?" I asked.

Pamela slumped back in the chair and closed her eyes. "I don't know," she said, shaking her head. "I can't . . . I'm sorry. I can't do this right now. I thought I could, but I can't."

Masey's older self, her aunt Cynthia, stepped in. "It's okay, sis. That's enough for one day," she said, then turned toward me and Scott. "She's tired. It's been a lot and the day ain't even over."

I know what you mean.

"Okay, I understand," I said, looking back at Scott with a nod.

When I turned back around, Pam was staring down at the table in a near-catatonic state. I wanted to say something. To grab her by the hand and look her in the eyes and let her know, "I'm not just here for the story; I'm here for you, too." But Pamela was in outer space. When she finally looked up, I placed a hand over my heart and whispered, "Thank you." But her gaze passed right through me. I had hoped to speak to Pam off-camera so that I could ask her how she hooked up with Louise Robinson, but I didn't want to burden her with such details in her fragile condition. Still, there were some housekeeping items I needed to take care of ahead of tonight's vigil and roundtable, so I used Cynthia as her surrogate.

"Cynthia? Can I speak to you for a moment?" I asked.

Cynthia and I stepped into the living room and I told her about the plan to film Pamela with community members to-night before the vigil.

"Okay, I'll let her know," Cynthia said. "But I have to tell you, I don't know how that's gonna go. I wouldn't expect too much from her tonight, either."

"I understand," I said.

I was about to head back into the dining room when it dawned on me to ask, "Cynthia, where does Yvonne live?"

"She's over on 71st and Peoria," she said.

I'm not all that keen on streets on the South Side, but I could've sworn Scott and I passed Peoria today on the way to Louise Robin-son's house.

"Is that over by Louise Robinson's house?" I asked.

"I don't know," she said.

"Is that close to, um, what's that street? Sangamon? I'm bad with streets here. I'm from Texas," I said.

"Yeah, Sangamon is in the next block," Cynthia said.

Interesting.

"Do you know Louise?" I asked.

"Not personally," she said.

Hmm. But something tells me Yvonne does.

I returned to the living room to say goodbye to Pam, who was still sitting at the table staring at the Grand Canyon photo.

I noticed Scott wasn't packing up. He was still filming! I might be glad for the footage of Pamela poring over the image of her and her daughter in the larger scheme of things, but right now it felt wildly inappropriate. I shot Scott a look and reached down and shoved the camera bag in his direction.

Thank God Pam hadn't noticed.

"Pamela? I approached her and leaned down to meet her at eye level. "I'll see you later, okay?"

She nodded and mouthed the word *okay* without a sound.

..

Scott was quiet back in the news truck. I should have been grateful he didn't call me out for getting handled in that interview, especially after my visceral reaction to catching him filming unbeknownst to Pam.

"Look, Scott, I totally get why you were doing that, filming her, but I didn't want to come off as disrespectful. She clearly wasn't doing well."

Scott shot me a look but didn't say a word. The day had been marked by an unusual level of tension between us. But when you spend as much time together as Scott and I do, you're bound to have some off days.

"Can you drop me back at my car?" I asked.

"Sure, but we don't have much time before we have to be at Tanya's," he said.

"I know. I'll meet you there."

I needed time to beat myself up over the interview with Pam and get over it before I had to be back on again for the round-table. I wanted so badly to ask Scott, "Was what I said that horrible?" but I couldn't bring myself to do it.

I never would have imagined that asking, "When was the

last time you saw your daughter?" would have set Pamela off the way that it did. I wasn't questioning her attentiveness as a parent. No way! *Did it sound that way to her?*

Scott dropped me off in the District Diner's now-empty parking lot. It felt good to be by myself and back in the driver's seat. I didn't bother to ask Scott to check in with the producer to schedule a boom mic and an intern for tonight's roundtable. I texted the producer myself.

I had a little over an hour to kill before Tanya's, and I knew exactly how to spend it. Pamela had said that Yvonne's house was pretty much a straight shot from hers at 82nd Street and Damen in the Auburn Gresham neighborhood. I needed to re-trace Masey's journey. If she did, in fact, ride home that night, I wanted to see what she saw just before night fell. Was it a straight shot? Did Masey take a detour or a shortcut that cost her her life?

If Masey did, in fact, ride her bike home, it would be good to know what time she left Yvonne's. I'm guessing that if Pam was still at work when Masey called to ask if she could go to the mall with her cousin, and Pam didn't get off that day until four o'clock, she could've been heading home between four and five-thirty, right around this time of day.

I typed 71st and Peoria into the GPS and jumped on the Dan Ryan southbound. On the way, the more I thought about Pamela's outburst, the more I became convinced that her raw outrage encapsulated how I think a lot of people in her position would feel over the police's mischaracterization of the circumstances surrounding the disappearance of such a dutiful child. Once edited, her anger wouldn't come across as directed toward me.

Traffic was thickening on the Dan Ryan just as I exited at 71st Street, aka honorary Emmett Till Road, and headed west. About a quarter mile or so down I came upon Peoria and, sure enough, a block later, Sangamon, Louise's street, with the blue-and-white bus sign Scott had missed earlier near the corner. Cynthia said she didn't know Louise personally. Now I am convinced that Louise's connection to the family must be through Masey's cousin, Yvonne.

I circled back around to Peoria. I didn't know which house was Yvonne's, but the street looked like so many others to the north and south of this street renamed in honor of a Black child who also was brutally murdered. About 40 percent of the houses on the block, almost all of them made of brick, were either boarded up or severely damaged by fire. I'd seen similar styles of properties on the North Side of the city that went for half a million dollars or more.

So, Masey, what route did you take from Yvonne's house?

I entered Pamela's address into my phone's GPS. Within a few blocks, it directed me to turn left on Racine. I thought there were a lot of churches on 71st Street, but Racine was a whole other level of ecclesiastical landscape. For half a mile, there was at least one church per block, sometimes two located across the street from each other or side by side. Some are large, formidable structures like Shiloh Baptist and St. Sabina, but the majority are one-level storefront churches with magnanimous names such as Prince of Peace, the New Revelation of Holiness Missionary Baptist Church, and Holy Miracle House of Prayer of Apostolic Faith.

Racine is a wide but well-traveled street. Considering the volume of traffic on a Saturday evening, it was quite possible that Masey rode her bike up on the sidewalk. However, that would have been nearly impossible for her to do on 79th Street, where the GPS instructed me to make a left turn. The traffic was perpetual, both from motor vehicles pulling in and out of the White Castle drive-through on the corner or into the Dollar Store parking lot, and from pedestrians flowing in and out of retailers, restaurants, and micro boutiques selling hair extensions, cellular phones, and culturally inspired treasures. There was little room to ride a bicycle safely, not even on the sidewalk. Convinced this couldn't be the route she took, I turned down the first residential street to my left, and circled back around to 71st and Peoria, reset the GPS, and assessed the side streets. Some homes are well kept, others boarded up or uninhabitable. Some lawns are well groomed; others are blighted patches of land dotted with abandoned cars and discarded furniture. Up ahead, there is a sign on a telephone pole that reads SAFE SCHOOL ZONE. Ironically, the school I drove past looked shuttered, and not safe at all. Withered vines clung to the building's facade and to the heavy metal bars that crossed the street-facing windows. The speed bumps on either side of the crosswalk seemed beside the point.

These tattered images of life in West Englewood provided a snapshot of the constant ups and downs of the economic circumstances of residents desperately trying to hold on to what they've worked hard for in communities that lack investment and access to economic opportunity.

There were fewer boarded-up, burnt-out houses the closer I came to the Auburn Gresham community, where Pam lives. I checked the GPS. I'd already traveled 2.3 miles from Yvonne's block. Pamela had described the distance between her house and Yvonne's as a straight shot, a little over a mile. By the time I got to the narrow turnoff for her semi-gated neighborhood at Damen at 82nd Street, I had traveled nearly 3 miles. That's a nothing bike ride for an energetic fifteen-year-old. But if I were a mother, would I allow my daughter to ride alone through the city's consistently most dangerous neighborhood, even during the daytime?

I don't think so.

..

If I had anticipated that things at Tanya's house would be somewhat chaotic, I would've been spot-on. Cars were lined up all the way down the block in front of the house. I parked about a block away just past the "L" tracks where Masey's body was found, still cordoned off with police tape. I looked around to make sure no one could see me and moved the seat as far back as it would go, slid down and shimmied out of my skirt. I thought I was careful until I heard the familiar sound of a slight tear in the fabric as I tried to manage this uncomfortable position, praying no one saw me. That would be creepy. Pulling the pants on was much easier. I was running about fifteen minutes behind, and I didn't see a Channel 8 news truck, though I was grateful there wasn't a truck from a competitor present yet. Louise had so far kept her word.

But where the hell was Scott?

I surveyed the adjacent blocks, a blend of single- and multi-family properties. The number of vacant spaces stood out. There's one directly west of the crime scene, another directly across the street, and another next to Tanya's house. Under cover of night, I can see how someone dumping a body could've gone sight unseen.

At the intersection, city workers hopped out of a municipal pickup truck and set up barricades to block traffic. As I walked toward Tanya's, two squad cars pulled up, cutting off the north- and southbound lanes on Calumet Avenue, while maintaining the throughway on 45th to MLK Drive. It's chilling to think that just a few days ago, while Scott and I were filming my live update on King Drive in front of missing posters with Masey's likeness, the honor student's body lay less than half a mile away.

The community showed evidence of regentrification. Tanya's house appeared to have had some work done on the redbrick facade. It was a nice-looking property landscaped with fresh shrubs and seasonal mums in dark purple. The house next door was mid-makeover. I steadied myself against the banister, going up the steps to the front door to face the unknown. So far I had misjudged everybody I'd dealt with today, except Superintendent Bartlett. My now-fragile ego couldn't afford another misstep.

Tanya greeted me at the door wearing a white T-shirt that had Masey's ninth-grade school picture printed on the front, in color, revealing the tenderness of Masey's young skin and even the shine of her lip gloss. Tanya's hair was pulled up into a tight chignon atop her head. Her movements made the image on her shirt come alive.

"Hey, girl. How are you?" she said, like we were old friends.

"Hi, Tanya. I'm good and you?"

"Good. Come on in. We're ready for you," she said.

Unfortunately, I couldn't say the same. Where in the hell was Scott?

Tanya led me into a bright room with light-colored hardwood floors and an open floor plan. There was a gray sectional with a matching overstuffed chair, a vintage glass-top coffee table that held fruit and vegetable trays and red paper plates with matching plastic cups. I surveyed the room, trying to figure out how to set up the interview, which is what Scott should be doing. I'd just pulled out my cell phone to text him when

Louise strolled up to me without so much as a limp. The Ace bandage was gone; she'd made a miraculous recovery.

"Welcome, Jordan. Nice to see you," she said, more amiable than earlier today. A woman stood slightly behind her. From their resemblance, I surmised she must be Tanya's mother.

"We're just waiting for Pamela and Bishop Toney to get here," she said, turning slightly to her left. "This is my sister, Patricia."

"Hi, Patricia, it's so nice to meet you. Thank you so much for allowing us to come into your home," I said, except there was no *us*, only me.

"You're welcome," Patricia said.

"I'm actually waiting for my camera to arrive. If you'll excuse me for a second, I need to call him to find out how far away he is."

I know Scott was rubbed a tad raw when I left him, but he wouldn't stand me up for an assignment because he was pissed off. That could cost him his job. But why hasn't he called or texted? My call went straight to voice mail. My patience worn down to a nub, I called the desk, and Ellen picked up.

"News, Holbrook."

"Ellen, it's Jordan. I'm at the pre-vigil shoot and I don't know where the hell Scott is. He's not picking up his phone," I said. "He agreed to meet me here. He's never done this. Do you know what's going on?"

"Let me check the log."

Ellen put me on hold but was back in thirty seconds. "The assignment desk pulled Scott off the clock and gave it to George. He isn't there yet?"

"Great," I said sarcastically. "No, he isn't. Pamela Alonzo hasn't arrived yet, either, thankfully. But I'm running out of time here."

"Okay, don't panic. I'll see if the desk can track him down and get his ETA," Ellen said.

"All right."

I wasn't panicked; I was mad. I felt as if Scott was sending me a message but couldn't figure out what he had taken so much to heart that he would ghost on me, without so much as a text.

Tanya's doorbell rang. My head was on swivel, but it wasn't George, it was Pamela, locked arm in arm with a man I didn't recognize. She was followed by Bishop Lamont Toney, pastor of one of the city's largest megachurches; Cynthia; and a cohort of a half-dozen women, all strikingly tall with long thick jet-black hair. They're a formidable group, representing both strength and beauty. Each one could easily be taken for either a supermodel or a WNBA star.

This family has one stunning gene pool.

They bore a resemblance to the man on Pam's arm, and I connected the dots. He must be Masey's father, Anthony James. Masey looked more like her dad, whose side of the family was obviously where her beautiful Kenyan features came from. Just behind the family processional appeared George's round, bearded face.

Finally!

I was grateful the family was occupied greeting the ministers and local politicians so that I could work with George to set up the shoot. He was accompanied by an intern, a young woman who'd recently graduated from Northwestern University and joined the newsroom staff, carrying a bag of equipment.

"Where have you been?" I asked him.

"Sorry, Jordan. The desk didn't tell us about the boom mics until I'd left the station. So I had to go back for them and get somebody to work 'em. Have you met Grace?"

The young woman sat down the clunky equipment bag and stuck her bony right hand out enthusiastically. "Hi, it's so nice to finally meet you, Jordan," she said. "Oh my God, I've watched you, like, since my sophomore year in college."

She was practically bouncing as she spoke.

We don't have time for this.

"You, too, Grace," I said hurriedly, "but time's a-ticking, so we've got to figure out how we're going to set up this room."

I pointed out Tanya to George. "See that lady? Work with her to figure out how we can rearrange this room, because the sectional is too low and the picture window is problematic."

"Okay, will do," George affirmed. "Oh, and we've got one more mic coming in. He's assembling it in the truck," he said.

"Awesome!"

As I surveyed the room, I started to think to myself, *Maybe this wasn't such a good idea.* It was complete chaos. Folks were going in and out of the kitchen, fixing plates of food and standing around eating. The noise level had subsided a bit but pitched upward again once the family arrived. Louise was hugging and saying hello to everybody. An attractive young woman with blond streaks in her short brown hair sidled up to Louise, who turned toward her and gave her a warm hug. It was so loud in the room, I couldn't hear what they were saying. But clearly they were well acquainted.

I'll credit George for making quick work of setting up the shoot. He even had Tanya helping him to move the dining room chairs into two rows.

"Hey, Jordan!" George yelled across the room. "How many people are going to be in the shot?"

I counted in my head but rather than shout back, I held up six fingers.

By now, it was going on six-fifteen. I walked over to Louise, who was talking to Pamela, and tapped her on the shoulder. "Are we ready to get started?" I asked.

"U-u-u-h-h, just a minute," she said, holding up a finger. "Did Tony get something to eat?" she asked no one in particular.

"Does he have time to get some food first?" She turned to me to ask. "He just got in about a couple hours ago."

"How long is that going to take?" I asked.

Masey's father overheard the exchange. "Don't worry about me. You all go ahead," he said. "I'm not in the interview."

Since no one introduced us, I took it upon myself. "Hi, Mr. James. I'm Jordan Manning with Channel 8. You have my deepest condolences."

"Thank you," he said, backing away slightly. "I don't want to be on-camera, though," he said emphatically.

Louise turned and asked, "Why not?" But Pamela cut off the exchange with a stern shake of her head.

"All right," Louise said, shrugging her shoulders.

George and Tanya had arranged a seating area with six chairs, three in front and three in back, and asked everyone to take a seat. Louise made sure to cop a spot next to Pamela and ordered Tanya to remove the third chair in the front row.

"I'll sit in that one," I told George.

Louise quieted the room, and everyone took their seats. The two interns holding boom mics stood on either side of the group, and George was positioned far enough away from me that I wouldn't be distracted by his heavy breathing. What ensued was nothing like what I, nor I am certain Pamela, expected. As savvy as they all believed themselves to be, this group of community activists didn't have the forethought to unify around a common theme. So they leaned on what they knew best. Before I posed my first question, Bishop Toney asked the group to stand up and join hands with the people next to them; then he led a prayer. I shot a look at George, who was already filming, which he confirmed with a thumbs-up.

"Father God, we ask you to bless this family. Bless this mother and father, who have lost a daughter. Bless Masey's little brother, who has lost a loving sister. And bless this community, oh Lord, so that we may go on even as we live in fear and frustration. Lord, we have suffered an unimaginable loss. Tonight we come together as a community to grieve and for a little grace, oh Lord. In Jesus's name we pray. Amen."

Once they reassembled, I started the interview. "Thank you all for taking the time to speak to me. Tonight I suspect we will learn just how deeply the community has been impacted by this stunning tragedy. What are you hearing?"

Each one had their own agenda. Pastor Charles Bowman used this time to try and solidify his reelection to the state senate by promising to fight for more resources in communities of color. Louise stood on her soapbox about the neglected park and blamed city hall and the Park District for the disrepair of the neighborhood, which attracted crime and malfeasance. As they were speaking, Pamela dropped and shook her head. I recognized her movements as a sign that she was about to blow any second.

Thankfully, her church pastor, Reverend Clement Harper, spoke up next. "When my sister in Christ, Pam Alonzo, called and told me her daughter didn't come home one night, and that the police said she had probably run away and they wouldn't do anything about it for two days," he said, holding up two fingers for emphasis, "I knew then that they were wrong. Masey was an excellent student. She loved the Lord. She loved her church and she was excited about her future. If they'd known her like *we* knew her, they would've known she wasn't no runaway. They were wrong not for a day, not for three days, but for three weeks!" His voice rose. "Stop misrepresenting our youth! Stop misrepresenting Black mothers and fathers! Listen to the parents! We know our own children! Look at the facts, CPD! She didn't fit the profile of a runaway, period!"

The next voice, surprisingly, was Pam's. "The police wasted precious time," she said. "Precious time they could've been searching for my daughter. Outside of relatives and my church family, the only person who would listen to me was you, Jordan," she said, looking me dead in my eyes. "That's the only hope I had until all hope was lost."

That was too much even for me. My fissure cracked, and the tears streamed down my face, but I didn't care enough to try and stop them. Pamela, too. Louise put her arm around her, and the pastors formed a chain, laying hands on her shoulders.

The camera continued to roll. Pam regained her composure. "Yes, the police were wrong," she said. "But I don't have time to be mad at the police. I'm saying to the police right now, in this moment, I need you. I need you to find the man who did this. I cannot rest, I will not rest, until you do."

I'm at the corner of 45th and Calumet Avenue in Bronzeville, where the body of fifteen-year-old Carol Crest High School honor student Masey James was found underneath these "L" train tracks three days ago. Tonight, more than 150 people gathered near the crime scene to remember Masey and to show support for her family, which includes her mother, Pamela, and Masey's father, Anthony James.

When I was starting out, my mentor, a seasoned veteran at the Dallas station, gave me some sage advice: "Walk and talk; no one wants to see you just standing there." Recalling this, I asked George to follow me with the camera and do just that to record the teaser—walk with me as I talked the audience and our anchors in the studio through this sorrowful night. At the conclusion of a nearly twelve-hour day, I would see my hard work distilled down to mere minutes on the air. But that's the irony of this business: long days are chopped up into short pieces and sound bites. No wonder people feel their stories aren't fully expressed. And for what? To set aside enough time to show a funny video at the end of the broadcast to counterbalance the bad news they just heard? Precisely.

But I needed to get as much information as I could to these anchors in the studio.

Will and Iris, I spoke with one woman who told me that people are furious with the way Chicago police dealt with Masey's disappearance, classifying her as a runaway for weeks. This simmer of anger is going to turn into a boil if police don't provide some answers soon. More in my full report later tonight.

It was still light outside. The vigil was set for seven o'clock, but no one really expected it to start on time, given the large numbers of people straggling in on foot. I noted that very few of the people gathering were coming out of nearby homes. This was the time of day when the setting sun exposed the underbelly of a neighborhood in transition, when people were accustomed to retreating indoors for the night. Seniors abandoned their porches and parents called the little kids inside. Then when the streetlights flickered on, the middle schoolers picked up the pace, recognizing they are nowhere near equipped to deal with the kind of stuff that can potentially transpire once night creeps in, so they made their way home.

I thought to myself, *No one wants to be here.* They've come because they've been affected by the fact that a Black child has been murdered and discarded in a field, and because they are worried something like this could happen to their child. They are tired of the constant violence in their communities and the absence of empathy for Black and brown victims—to a certain extent, even among their own people. They weren't eager to stand in a dark street, because even on a night like this and even with a heavy police presence, you could feel a shift in the energy level as the texture and beat of the community, sadly, tilted toward what the media so often portrayed as violence. In a place such as Bronzeville, whose enchantment as a Black mecca had vanished decades earlier and which was now in the midst of regentrification, the daylight concealed the inherent dangers and the nighttime revealed the vulnerabilities that many equated with being on a street corner ruled by people it might not be safe to be around. Tonight, if just this once, they were willing to take the risk, because the unthinkable, the incomprehensible, had happened to one of their own.

I scanned the crowd, assessing people to interview on camera. The aromas of scented candles—apple cinnamon, vanilla, and pumpkin spice—broke the stale tension in the air and spoke volumes about the carriers, from their religious beliefs to their favorite TV and film characters. One teenage girl cradled a religious candle in a long glass cylinder emblazoned with a yellow cross that appeared to glow with the flickering light catching it and softening the exaggerated neon color. Then it hit me: The crowd was predominantly made up of women and children around Masey's age. These kids could be anywhere else, gossiping with their friends about the boy they liked or playing video games. Instead, the horrific nature of this crime broke through their teenage indifference and led them here.

I didn't have a lot of time to conduct what we refer to in the industry as man-on-the-street interviews, which was a funny thought considering I was surrounded mostly by women. But again, that kind of male-dominant terminology was another example of the archaic nature of the business I must fight to thrive in. I had to at least try and squeeze in a few before the program started without allowing the exchange between Pamela and me a few moments ago in Tanya's living room, which I was still processing, to distract me from doing my job.

After the roundtable interview, George waited for me on the sidewalk in front of Tanya's, and the two interns went back to the news truck to label the tape. I was glad when they left, because it gave me a chance to sneak over to Pamela without my colleagues witnessing how emotional, how personal this story had become for me. I hadn't thought about what to say, so I simply took Pamela by the hand and gave it a gentle squeeze. For the first time since that uncomfortable moment when I asked during our one-on-one, "When was the last time you saw your daughter?" we made eye contact. It was brief but intense. No words were exchanged between us, but none were needed. We had an understanding, I now realized, that had been there all along. More of a code of conduct, really, and it was this: I'm too familiar with the way these investigations play out for Black families to abandon her, and she knows that. Expressing her appreciation on-camera was her way of letting me know that she didn't take it for granted. It wasn't necessary for her to say in that moment, and I almost wish she hadn't, but it helped me undo some of the awkwardness between us that, as it turned out, I had invented in my own mind.

The racket around me started to quiet down. Volunteers got busy tidying up the dining and kitchen areas, tossing discarded plates, half-eaten sandwiches, and piles of crumpled napkins into the garbage. The McMillans' foyer grew congested as people made their way out onto the street below. It was time for me to join them, but the smells emanating from the donated food and the Sternos burning the bottom of the aluminum chafing pans connected with my brain, reminding me that it'd been hours since I'd scarfed down that hearty breakfast with Commissioner Clark. I walked over to Tanya and her mother and thanked them again for hosting us.

"Did you get something to eat?" Tanya's mother Patricia asked, pointing toward the dining table. "There's plenty of food."

I reluctantly declined, but her offer legitimized a need in me to be seen as one of them. That I belonged here. Or maybe I just missed my family. Still, I discreetly picked up a cube of pineapple from a fruit plate and popped it in my mouth before stepping out into the chilly air to find George.

The crowd fanned out across 45th Street, spilling over onto the former Ida B. Wells-Barnett playground. The city had made a half-assed attempt to clean it up—performing the bare minimum of a task turned herculean due to years of neglect in order to be able to say it was keeping up its end of the bargain to maintain public land. Overgrown weeds as tall as the Chicago Bulls' latest draft pick still lined the perimeter. Earlier, as I walked to Tanya's from my parked car, I noticed signs tacked to utility poles by the tracks warning of rats, then tried to unsee them as I recalled Dr. Chan's alluding to night creatures as one of several obstacles to collecting useful evidence from the crime scene.

The wind gusted and the temperature instantly dropped about ten degrees. But that's Chicago. I learned soon after moving here to keep an extra jacket and something to cover my legs in the trunk of my car. I felt sorry for the group of girls I spotted wearing shorts, though up top they had on matching warm black-and-gold jackets with *Hyde Park/Kenwood Drill Team* stitched on the back and black berets.

"Hey, George." I pointed. "Let's go talk to them."

None of the girls knew Masey personally, but said they were disturbed and saddened by what had happened to her and concerned about their own safety.

"It's scary, you know. There is a *killer* out there," one of the girls said. "It ain't safe out here in these streets."

I noticed a boy and a girl standing together wearing blue sweatshirts with orange letters and an emblem that looked vaguely familiar. Then it occurred to me I had seen it before; it matched the symbol on a navy blue and orange school spirit flag that I'd noticed on Pamela's front porch for Carol Crest, the STEM school Masey had transferred to on the Near West Side. The one it took her nearly two hours on several buses to reach each day. Masey had attended the school for only under a month, but if these kids came here tonight, there was a good chance they might have known her.

"Hey, George, start rolling. I'm going to talk to these kids over there in the blue-and-orange sweatshirts."

I got their attention as I approached. "Hi, guys! How are you? You go to Carol Crest High School?"

"Yes," they said in unison.

"Carol Crest *Academy*," the girl emphasized with pride.

"Did you know Masey James?" I asked.

"I didn't know her that well," the boy said. "She was in my geometry class. She was really nice, though."

"I knew her!" the girl chimed in. "Oh my God, she was soooo pretty! This is so sad. I cried so hard when I found out it was her."

So did I.

"Can I get a quick interview? What's your name?" I asked her.

"Shawn Jeffries," she said.

"Spell that for me, please," I said, and she obliged.

"And you, young man, what's your name?"

"Maleek Tate. M-A-L-E-E-K T-A-T-E."

"Okay, Shawn, I'm going to ask you if you knew Masey for the camera this time."

She nodded.

"Go ahead," George said. "I'm ready."

RECORDING: "I'm here with Shawn Jeffries, a student at Carol Crest Academy on the Near West Side. She says in the short time she got to know Masey, they became friends. Shawn, what was she like?"

Before she could answer, her face crumpled into tears that streamed down her face. It was unnerving. I swallowed my breath and straightened my back to keep my composure.

"I'm sorry. This is just so sad. We were becoming really good friends," she said, wiping her face. "She was super nice. I just admired her, you know? She was so pretty and so down-to-earth.

Just a real cool person. We ate lunch together, and after school, I walked her to the bus stop on my way home on the days she didn't get a ride."

A ride? A ride from whom?

Pamela never mentioned Masey getting a ride from school. She told me she took the bus back and forth every day. No, wait, or did she? I remembered she described Masey's journey to school, but she didn't mention how she got home. Nonetheless, I followed my gut and I turned around to face George. "Hey, can you turn the camera off for a minute?" I asked and turned back around to face Shawn.

"Did I say something wrong?" Shawn asked.

"Oh no, sweetheart. Absolutely not. I want to ask you something, but not on-camera. Okay?"

"Okay?" she said. "What is it?"

If the person giving Masey a ride factored into her murder somehow, I didn't want to put Shawn, a potential witness, at risk by interviewing her on the air.

"Do you know who gave her a ride?" I asked.

"No, she never mentioned it. I mean, I assumed it was a family member. She usually didn't know if she had a ride or not till the end of the day. But she'd still meet me outside the gym after school and let me know one way or the other," Shawn said.

"Did you ever see what kind of car she got into?" I asked.

"Um, I think I might have once. I really didn't pay that much attention to it, though," she said.

"Did this happen often?" I asked.

"Uhhhh." Shawn thought about this. "No, not that often. Really just here lately."

"Here lately," I repeated. "Like a week or two before she went missing?"

Shawn searched her memory. "Yeah, like, a couple weeks. But not every day. Just every now and then," she said.

My instincts were right to ask George to stop filming. This little girl just might have shared a critical detail that even the police weren't aware of.

"Have you spoken to the police?" I asked her.

"No!" she said, recoiling. "Oh, but wait, I do remember her saying one time her cousin was picking her up."

"That's all she said? Her cousin? She didn't mention a name?" I asked.

"Naw, she just said my cousin."

It was possible these rides were indeed innocent and provided by a family member. The next time I speak to Pam, I'm definitely bringing it up.

"Are you both sophomores?" I asked, changing the subject.

"Yes," the two responded in unison again.

"Okay, thank you, Maleek and Shawn. I appreciate your time."

"Are we going to be on the news?" he asked.

"You might," I said. "These interviews get edited. But make sure you watch just in case."

I pulled out a business card and handed it to Shawn. "And, hey, Shawn, if you can remember anything about the car or the person giving Masey a ride, would you please call me?"

"Sure," she said.

Something told me not to leave without getting her contact information.

"You know, is it okay if I get your email address or cell phone number?" I asked.

The teenager beamed at the idea. "Yeah! That's cool!"

I handed Shawn my cell phone. "Here ya go. Just go in and create a contact."

I'm always amazed at how fast kids can type on a cell phone keypad with their thumbs.

"Done," she said.

Before my feet could move, I felt compelled to ask Shawn for another favor. "Hey, one more thing, Shawn. Promise me that you won't say what you just told me about Masey getting rides from school to another reporter on the air. Can you promise me that?"

"Sure. No problem!" she said.

This wasn't about getting an exclusive; this was for her safety.

"Thanks. You've both been great. I'm so sorry about the loss of your friend. You guys be careful out here."

"Yes, ma'am," said Maleek. "You, too."

The question burned on my brain. Who gave Masey rides home from school? Shawn mentioned a cousin. It could've been a member of Masey's extended family: one of her model-esque, basketball-player-looking relatives; her aunt Cynthia; or this cousin Yvonne, whom I have yet to meet. Maybe even Pamela herself.

I would have to unpack this revelation later. A group of about a half-dozen or so White women grabbed my attention in this predominantly Black and brown assembly.

"Hey, George." I pointed toward them. "Let's go talk to those ladies. Follow me."

The crowd had grown dense, and I had to push my way through the tightly packed bodies like a defensive lineman. "Pardon me . . . excuse me . . . oops, sorry, excuse me . . . can I get past you?" Out of the corner of my eye, I noticed a news camera and a reporter headed in my same direction, and I picked up the pace, determined to get to the women first.

As I drew closer, I noticed the group of women were all

wearing matching pink T-shirts with the words WOMEN UNITED AGAINST VIOLENCE inscribed on the front, but they must not have noticed me while I was rushing up on them. "Hi, ladies!" I said.

One of the women jumped. She gave me a look, rolled her eyes, and rested her right hand on her chest, breathing a sigh of relief. I'd startled the poor woman, who was clearly a fish out of water in this neighborhood after dark. I scanned the area and didn't see the reporter from the competing station. She must have conceded defeat and gone in another direction.

"I'm sorry. I didn't mean to startle you. I'm Jordan Manning with Channel 8. Can I get a quick interview?"

They all gestured toward a short nondescript woman standing a few feet away, wearing a baseball cap over her medium-length brown hair. "You'll want to talk to April," she said.

Of the women standing there, she seemed the least likely to be the leader of the group. She appeared to be surveying the scene herself, craning her neck to see over and around the crowd, which appeared to have grown by at least a third in the last five minutes. At around five-four, she had a hard time seeing over other people's heads.

"April!" one of them yelled to get her attention. "This reporter would like to speak with you."

April turned toward me with a bright, welcoming smile. "Oh, hello there. I'm April Murphy. I didn't catch your name."

"Jordan Manning. Channel 8," I said.

"Oh yes, of course! It's so nice to meet you. I watch you all the time. You're even prettier in person," she said.

"Thank you, I appreciate that," I said.

"April, do you mind if I ask you a few questions on-camera?"

She shrugged her shoulders and nodded in the affirmative. "Sure. That's fine."

"Okay, great," I said.

We stepped away into a less crowded area to give George enough room to frame the shot.

"Boy, it's getting chilly out here, isn't it?" April said. "I hope they start soon. We have a good hour's drive back."

"Yes, it sure is," I said as I secured my earpiece and the battery pack to my belt. "Where are you based? Are you expecting some others to join you? You appeared to be looking for someone when I walked up."

"We're from the Naperville/Aurora area. And no, this is our group for *this* event. I just like to keep my eyes peeled," she said. "You can learn a lot just by observing."

"April, can you say your first and last name and spell your last name, if you don't mind?" I asked.

"April like the month and the common spelling of Murphy. M-U-R-P-H-Y."

"Okay. Thank you. And what's your title with the group?"

"I'm the founder and president," she said.

The jarring light atop the camera illuminated our figures. There was something unreal about the air. The atmosphere metamorphized with the dusk and painted the area around us in black, white, and gray tones.

I'm here with April Murphy, founder and president of Women United Against Violence. She and several members of her group came all the way from Aurora to take part in tonight's vigil. April, what compelled your group to come?

"We're just sick, all of us, about what happened to this child," she said, her cohort nodding in agreement beside her. "We're here to stand with her community and show support for her family. As a survivor, I empathize."

"April, explain what you mean by 'as a survivor,'" I said.

"My mother was murdered during my senior year in high school. It's been twenty years, but it's something you don't get over."

"What does your group do?" I asked.

"We help victims' families in any way we can—financially, if necessary. In regard to this case, though, I am deeply concerned. I've been watching the news coverage . . . or should I say, what little coverage I could find. There have been more stories about the shortage of salt to put down on the roads this winter than about this missing child. This story should have been everywhere," she said.

"I couldn't agree more," I said on the air.

"Honestly, and I can say this, that if I, a White woman, or my White child had been missing, there would have been nonstop coverage."

Did she really just say that? I like this woman.

"How does your group interact with families who've been victims of violence?"

"We provide access to free grief counseling and support from a network of people who understand what they're going through. This is a dark and lonely walk that nobody should have to take by themselves."

"And what kind of help do you hope to provide Masey's family?" I asked.

"Anything we can do, really. Mainly we just want them to know there are people out here who care and who also want justice for their daughter."

"Thank you, April," I said, and turned toward the camera.

Those are powerful words coming from a mother outside of this community who has been touched by this tragedy like so many of the people gathered here tonight to show their love and support.

I gave George a nod to indicate I was finished and turned back toward April. Leaning in close, I whispered, "I can connect you with Masey's mother."

"Really?" she whispered back. "That'd be great. When?"

I *really* liked this woman. Her voice was full of urgency and resolve. She's a doer, not a talker.

"If you can stick around after the vigil, I'll see if I can introduce the two of you tonight. But in the meantime, do you have a card? Here's mine."

"Yes, I do."

If April Murphy meant what she said and could be a valuable, commiserative resource to Pamela, then I would make it my duty to connect these two women. But more than that, to have the support of an organization led by a White suburban mom might just be the lifeline Pamela needed to keep attention on this case. It's a sad reality, but getting the "white seal of approval" could in fact light a fire under the police *and* media.

I examined her business card, which included an AOL email address and a phone number. "Is this your cell number?" I asked.

"Yes, that's it," she said.

"Great!" I said.

I had no idea what shape Pam Alonzo would be in at the conclusion of this event. "If for some reason this doesn't happen tonight, let's touch base tomorrow. Okay?"

"Sounds good," she said.

"Okay, April, talk to you soon."

I made a note to self to be sure to tell the segment producer, "If you have to cut an interview from the footage, make damn sure it's *not* that one."

By now, it was 7:15. The chirp of car doors being locked with remote keys and car alarms silenced with a click of a button could be heard above the raucousness of the crowd, who continued to flow in from all directions. There had to be over two hundred people gathered now. George and I split up as he made his way over to the row of news cameras and I headed for the news van. The cube of pineapple had worn off and I was literally swooning from hunger. There was almost always something to snack on in the news truck.

"Nice work, George," I said. "I'm going to stop by the truck, then move up closer."

"No problem, Jordan. Thanks."

Even though I was wearing flats, the back of my knees felt weak as fatigue set in. I was desperately in need of a sugar rush. As much as I hated to traverse the tightly packed crowd again to get to the van, I hated the thought of passing out on the asphalt even more.

On the way, I caught snippets of conversations from the audience, ranging from the mundane ("Hey, girl, I haven't seen you in forever") to the conspiratorial ("Her mama got a boyfriend? Usually the boyfriend did it") to the somber ("She had her whole life ahead of her" and "I can't even imagine what her parents are going through").

I passed by the kids from Carol Crest, Shawn and Maleek, whom I'd spoken to earlier. Their group had swelled and there appeared to be an adult with them. I wanted to stop, but my stomach told me to stay the course toward the Snickers bar and a bottle of Gatorade I prayed were in the cooler.

Suddenly I felt a tug at my jacket.

"Excuse me," a girl's voice said.

I swung around, but there were so many people standing nearby, I couldn't tell where the voice was coming from.

"Hi! Excuse me!" I heard once more.

There were two teenage girls standing between me and the

person trying to get my attention, but she still managed to reach across them both to ensnare me, then ducked under one girl's arm to plant herself directly in my path.

"Hi," she said in a high-pitched voice.

"Hello. Can I help you?" I asked. I sized her up, unsure if she was a high school student or in college. Her mature face didn't match her very childlike voice.

"You're the lady on TV, right?" she said pointing at me with her index finger, like Marcus had done earlier.

She's a kid.

"Yeah. I'm Jordan Manning. Nice to meet you," I said hurriedly.

"Well, you haven't exactly met me yet," she said.

I'm going to meet this pavement if I don't get some food.

My impatience with the exchange was on 10. "Hey, listen, I was just headed to the news van," but I didn't want to be rude. "Okay, so what's your name?"

"My name is Monique Connors," she said.

"Great. Now we've officially met. Nice to meet you, Monique, but I've seriously gotta go."

"I thought you'd like to know that I was a friend of Masey's," she said. "Well, yeah, I guess you could say that."

Her words halted my movement. The last person who had described themselves as a "friend" of Masey's provided information that could potentially be a lead in this case. But this girl didn't sound so sure that she was even Masey's friend. "There are friends and there are acquaintances," my mom used to say. "A lot of folks don't know which one they are. But you'd better know the difference."

"Oh," I managed as my empty insides twisted, "I'm very sorry for the loss of your friend, Monique. Very, very sorry."

"Thank you," she said.

"But you'll have to excuse me. I really have to get something out of the news van before things get started, okay?"

I reached into my pant pocket. "If there's something you want to share with me, here's my card. Call me tomorrow."

She took the card and stared down at it, looking disappointed. "Okay then, bye," she said in an unnecessarily sassy and dismissive tone.

I nodded and forced a smile and went on my way. I was lightheaded by the time I reached the van and pulled open the side door, startling the interns. "Hi, guys. What're you up to?"

The other intern, named Chad, stammered nervously, "We're labeling the tapes like George told us to do."

"Okay, that's fine. I'm not here to check up on you. Hey, Grace, do you see a cooler in the back?"

"I dunno. I'll check," she said, and hollered back seconds later. "Yes!"

"What's in there to eat or drink? Is there any candy? A Snickers bar?"

"Um, let me see."

Please, hurry.

"There's a bunch of protein bars and a can of pop," she said, using a word for *soda* that is characteristic of Chicagoans.

"No candy?" I asked.

"Nope, I don't see any."

I normally don't drink soda, but today I would make an exception.

"I'll take 'em. I'm dying here," I said, trying not to sound less than gracious to the young woman who had earlier described herself as a huge fan. I managed a smile when she handed me dinner.

"Thanks, Grace. Please forgive me. I'm hangry," I said, and she smiled.

..

By 7:30, darkness advanced and the candles transformed the block into a sea of lights. At 7:32, the family, the Black Pastors Coalition, and the South Side Community Council members emerged from the McMillan home. The women wore T-shirts, like Tanya's, with Masey's image on the front. Tanya had handed me a shirt, too. It would be inappropriate in my role to wear it, but I accepted it from her out of respect.

They lined up, paired off in twos, and locked arms for the brief walk to a makeshift stage flanked by two blown-up images of Masey someone must have just put up: the ninth-grade school picture that was now embedded in my mind and that of anyone who'd seen the posters, and another picture of Masey wearing a backpack and a pink quilted jacket, holding up the peace sign, looking deadly serious, like a model pose. Pamela, who locked arms with her childhood sweetheart, and Masey's gorgeous relatives each carried a single pink rose. Their faces long and somber, they held on tightly to each other so they wouldn't collapse in the street from their overwhelming grief.

A hush fell over the chattering crowd as the family and the community leaders took their places. The stage wasn't large enough to hold everyone, so Masey's relatives walked around and stood in front. Tanya had sent me an email earlier with the order of the speakers, beginning with a prayer by Bishop Toney, who, as he'd done during our interview, set the mood. Louise was supposed to be up next, but instead Pamela and Anthony James stepped up to the front of the stage and someone handed her a microphone. She was visibly shaking and had trouble raising the mic up to her mouth. Anthony had to reach in and hold it steady for her. The atmosphere became eerily quiet except for the resonating sound of traffic swooshing down nearby King Drive, the screech of a passing train, and the occasional squelch of a police officer's two-way radio.

"Hello? Can you all hear me?" she asked. The crowd responded "Yes, sister, we can hear you" before quieting down again. "I want to thank you all for coming to be with us," Pamela said, and turned to her right and placed her hand on Anthony's shoulder. "Me and Masey's father, we are humbled by your presence. I didn't realize how much I needed my community until I saw all of y'all standing here."

Pamela appeared to run out of breath before she got to the end of the sentence. She paused and took a deep breath, and Anthony pulled her in tightly against his shoulder. "I'm so tired," she muttered, struggling to hold up her head.

"When I look out at you," she continued, "all I see is my baby. My beautiful, smart, lovely daughter. Her future had just taken off like a rocket."

Her words reminded me of one of my favorite Stevie Wonder songs.

Pamela lifted her head slightly and caught the gaze of the young woman with blond streaks in her hair I'd noticed hugging Louise. Standing right next to her was Monique Connors. I had accounted for all the other relatives who were present except one, Yvonne, Masey's cousin on Pam's side. Seeing as how this woman looked nothing like the women of the James clan, through deductive reasoning, I concluded she must be Yvonne.

"I don't have a lot to say, because honestly, I'm talked out. But I want y'all to hear me out," she said, managing strength to emphasize: "And that goes for the po-lice, too.

"Our girls aren't safe. I don't mean to scare you just because

I'm going through hell. And this is hell! But a lot of you know it's true. They don't have to go outside their communities for harm to find them; they're getting hurt right here in our community, in front of our eyes, some of them. And we look away. We judge them. We don't protect them. We say, that's somebody else's problem. But that's a lie. Their protection is your problem. And I don't know how I know it, other than to say that God put it on my heart. But somebody knows who did this. This ain't the time to be saying, 'I ain't no snitch.' You hear me? If you know something, tell it! Tell the police! If you're afraid to go to the police, tell somebody who ain't afraid."

Pamela's voice cracked.

"There's a killer among us and he's got to be stopped!" Tears streamed down her face; Masey's dad dropped his head and put his hand over his eyes.

The block was as quiet as a cemetery as Pamela gained the strength to power through. "If you know something, tell us. You don't even have to identify yourself. But tell us. *Tell* us," she pleaded as she regained strength in her voice. "Tell us! Tell us!"

The rest of the family and the community leaders in lockstep also started to shout, "Tell us! Tell us! Tell us!" Some people clapped on each word; some stabbed their fists in the air. I noticed that a couple of police officers standing in the back near the train tracks were also chanting. *Surprising.* That would make great footage, but unfortunately George was facing the opposite direction on camera row, with his lens pointed toward the stage. That little detail, however, had to make its way into my broadcast, even if it meant redoing the teaser I recorded earlier.

Pamela held up her hand, and it took a few seconds to quiet them down again.

"I pray to God that you mean it," she said, her face stern and her lips drawn tight. Louise stepped up to embrace Pamela and Anthony, who handed her the microphone.

"Bless you, Chicago," she said. "I'm Louise Robinson with the South Side Community Council. I want to thank members of the council, Bishop Toney, Reverend Clement Harper, and state representative and pastor Charles Bowman for surrounding this family.

"I'm so glad that I was able to answer the call when the family asked for my help. I said, 'You just tell me what I need to do. You name it. You've got it.' So I called all the people standing shoulder to shoulder with me and the family tonight. That's what we have to do, Chicago. Stand together! Fight back! And for God's sake, speak up!"

I'd almost forgotten about Louise. Since no one had mentioned her and given her credit for her involvement in tonight's vigil, her narcissism rearing up, she did it herself.

It always amazes me when people use other people's pain to promote themselves—even more so when well-meaning people do it, which I believed Louise was. She couldn't help herself.

"We know, though, that sometimes, even when we do speak up, the people who can solve the problem with a simple phone call fail to act. For years, I warned the city that this poor excuse of a playground was going to attract crime."

She wanted people to revere her for trying to prevent something like this from happening, conflating the Park District's neglect with the discovery of a dead body, with no evidence to support her claims. She wanted people to think of her as saving the day, although the playground itself was now a non-issue.

As Louise continued to beat her own drum, I noticed that Pam and Anthony had slipped away across the vacant field next to the McMillan house and disappeared into the darkness.

There would be no introduction tonight between April Murphy and Pamela. Pam had had enough, and who could blame her?

"We've got to do something, Chicago," Louise went on, addressing the crowd as if the entire city was there. "We have to fight. We have to hold the police accountable. We have to hold city hall accountable. And by God, we have to hold ourselves accountable. That's right, I said we have to hold ourselves accountable!"

Some people around me nodded and expressed agreement as Louise leaned into her cadence. A showman, or show woman, as it were. If she hadn't been into community activism, she could have been a great entertainer. Though I must admit that Louise struck the right tone in this moment: an elder stateswoman admonishing her people to hold themselves to a higher standard.

"If you see something, say something. If you know something, tell the police, but don't stop there. Tell the leaders in your communities, too. Because we don't know what the police are going to do with that information. Are they gonna follow up? Or are they going to mischaracterize our children and our families the way they did with this child?

"There's nothing typical about this tragedy. There's a monster among us," said Louise, again evoking the monster reference, which I'm starting to think was her fallback analogy. I didn't mind, though. This time I agreed with her.

9

Ravenous, with the weight of the day still heavy on my shoulders, I started to come down from the workday high and called in takeout from my favorite sushi spot in Streeterville, a touristy neighborhood just east of downtown by the lake. A dragon roll with eel sauce, spicy tuna-avocado maki with roe, and smoked salmon and yellowtail nigiri with extra ginger, paired with a large tokkuri of warm sake at home would feel like a reward for surviving this relentless day. When I was a rookie reporter working the graveyard shift at the Dallas station, driving a used four-cylinder Honda and barely able to afford a one-bedroom apartment, I couldn't have imagined enjoying such decadence—unless someone else was picking up the tab. A fast-food drive-through was more like it for me in those days.

Look at you now, Jordan, driving through Chicago's Gold Coast in a convertible with a turbocharged engine to pick up sushi on the fly.

As it turned out, the day wasn't through with me yet. When I pulled into the garage beneath my apartment complex, someone had parked in the numbered space I pay $150 a month to guarantee is reserved just for me.

"Gotdamnit! Really? Jerk!"

This has happened twice before, and it was just as infuriating then, too. Now I would have to turn around, make a left out of the garage, because you can turn only one way, sit through that long-ass traffic light at Halsted, and make another left to access the uncovered upper parking deck. The odds of finding an empty space this late in the day weren't in my favor. Unlike in Dallas or even Austin, in Chicago a dedicated parking space is a privilege.

I passed by the floor-to-ceiling lobby windows as I drove around to the other side of the building. I could see Bass sitting at the guard's desk. He looked up just before I rounded the corner, stood and waved, then shrugged his shoulders, his palms up and his arms out to the side. His body language told me that he'd probably seen me pull into the garage on the security camera and wondered why I was now headed to the roof.

The driveway to the upper deck is steep and always makes me feel as though I am falling backward. Thankfully, its being a Monday night, there were a few empty spaces for me to park in. I parked in the space closest to the heavy steel door leading to the stairwell. It has been a rule of mine since my early reporting days to favor stairs over elevators. This started as a means to get some exercise, because I hate working out, but it became a safety issue, too, after I read about a woman being attacked and pinned in the elevator of a parking garage. Ever since, I've considered stairs the safest route.

I reached behind the seat to get my heels and debated throwing them off the roof, given how much they'd hurt my feet today. And on top of that, I'm disgusted about the damage to the heel due to the mishap outside Cynthia's house, in need of repair after wearing them only twice.

The upper parking deck was poorly lit. The lamp closest to the exit door has been flickering since the day I moved in. That was two years ago, and I've given up on complaining about it. I'm not up here that often anyway, though, on these rare occasions that I am, I could appreciate that the towering lamps were no competition for the radiant moon, which has a scene-stealing advantage from up here in a cloudless sky. Instinctively, I checked my surroundings before getting out of the car and walking toward the heavy steel door. Just as I yanked it open, the light went off on cue and the cold draft from the stairwell penetrated my bones, a startling reminder it was time-out for parking on the roof. I don't belong here anyway. I pity the person who dared park in my heated garage space again. I might have to go rogue and key their car. No way I wanted to ever wake up to my convertible under twenty feet of snow.

My feet pulsated pain with every step, and although I'd hardly eaten today, my clothes felt like they were tightening around my body. If my parking space hadn't been hijacked, I would be in my apartment by now, completing my transition from work me to home me. I should be de-splintering the chopsticks and stirring wasabi into the soy sauce and savoring the prickly slivers of ginger on the back of my throat. But no. Some foolish person had subjected my feet to a marathon walk to my apartment. Red-hot anger pumped me full of adrenaline, and before I realized it, I had flown past my floor and headed straight to the lobby to tell Bass.

I nearly ran into him when I opened the lobby door. "Oh crap!" I said. "I'm sorry, did I hit you with the door? Are you okay?"

"Hey Jordie!" he said. "No, it's all good. I was just coming up to see about you. Did somebody park in your space again?"

"Yes," I said, pouting.

"Why do you sound like a five-year-old?" He laughed.

"Because I'm mad, and of all *fucking* days!" I said. "Is that grown enough for you?"

Bass is four years my junior, but his congenial ribbing sometimes made me feel like I'm younger than he is.

"What kind of car is it?" he asked.

"I don't know, but it's got a Michigan plate . . . license number . . . BLE . . . 568," I said.

"You wrote it down?" he asked.

"No, but I'm fixin' to so that I don't forget," I said, slipping into my Texas twang.

"You memorized that?" he asked.

"Uh-huh," I said matter-of-factly.

"But you don't remember the car? The color? Nothing?" he asked again.

"I don't know. I don't know cars," I said, giving him my most intense eye roll. "I just need it out!"

"All right, Texas, I'm on it," Bass said, mocking my accent.

"Boy, you better leave me alone," I said, shifting my weight between my aching feet.

"Jordan," Bass admonished me playfully, "nobody calls a Black man *boy* in Chicago."

I rolled my eyes at him once more. "You know what I mean."

Though I pretend to be annoyed, our lighthearted verbal sparring had a calming effect on my mood. These fun-loving exchanges with Bass were reminiscent of one of my besties from Texas—Tyson Holloway. We met in drama class sophomore year and were cast as siblings Tom and Laura during a table read of *The Glass Menagerie*, and the rest is history. Tyson and I became running buddies. I wasn't looking for a brother and he wasn't looking for a sister, but we fell effortlessly into a sister-brother type vibe, nonetheless.

We would lie to our parents that we were studying when we were really at the mall. I got busted one time outside the Limited Express by my aunt Mel, short for Melanie, my dad's baby sister. But Aunt Mel was cool and didn't tell on me. That was the only time we got caught outright, but it didn't slow us down. During our junior year, Tyson's parents, who were older, allowed him to drive to school, and we would sneak off campus for lunch, a privilege reserved for seniors. Sometimes we'd ditch eighth period and slip off to the bowling alley, which had the best nachos, and play Pac-Man and pinball. Tyson had the gift of persuasion. I had my first drink because he convinced a college student to buy me a margarita at Six Flags on our senior trip.

I'm so comfortable around Bass, in part, because he reminds me of Tyson. With Bass, I'm able to strip off the armor I wear out of necessity to the newsroom, where every word I say, every time I challenge the status quo, I could be perceived as angry or too aggressive. Where the shade thrown from colleagues is palpable, where my new dress leads them to wonder how much my contract is worth, not realizing I picked it up at an after-Christmas closeout sale, when newbies like myself finally get time off work to visit family for the holidays. Where I must fight the perception that all I care about are material things, the superficial versus the substantive, because of the car I drive. Where because I'm a woman on television, I am judged differently from men. A man can wear the same suit and tie to work every day, but if I wear a scarf or a jacket too frequently, someone has something to say about it. Where the code-switching I as a Black person must adhere to so that others can feel comfortable around me is so indelible to my professional persona that I hardly give it a second thought. It's automatic.

The side of me that free-falls into Texas vernacular isn't one many people see. It says a lot about the person who brings it out in me. I don't know how to define that quality, but whatever it is, Bass has got it. No pressure. No judgments. No mask. He's more than a security guard who works in my building; he's like my little brother, though he thinks of himself as my big brother, my protector. I'll go on letting him, because I can honestly say I trust him with my life.

"Damn, so you memorized the license plate, though," Bass continued.

"Yeah, it's funny, because I can't even remember my cell phone number half the time. It's a little trick I taught myself," I said.

"Okay, Jordie," he said, looking serious and placing his hands on my shoulders, "if I can't get it out of there tonight, I'll set it on fire."

We both laughed. I needed that.

"And I'm okay with that!" I said, leaning back to look up at him.

"Listen, speaking of fire," he whispered, his forehead wrinkling, "I can roll you one if you want." Bass looked around as if a DEA agent might leap out from behind the marble columns, when he and I both knew that, even in a luxury building like this, at any given moment and on any floor, you could smell that distinct aroma wafting through the air.

"Don't tempt me," I said, and I *was* tempted, but I am accustomed to forgoing such self-indulgences like dessert or one last shot before the bar closes, particularly if I have an early morning. I hear it from friends all the time—"Jordan, you're always putting work above fun. Lighten up"—and I'm sure I'll hear it again when I tell Lisette I won't make it to Saugatuck after all.

"Thanks, Bass Man, but I'll pass. I'm already tired and if I puff-puff, I'll be asleep before the ten o'clock news comes on."

"You always say no," Bass said, looking disappointed.

"That's the trade-off," I said. "I can't do both."

I headed toward the bank of elevators, then stopped and turned around. "If that ass gets out my parking space tonight, hit me up on my cell. You know, I've got that soft top; I don't like my car on the roof."

"Okay, I will. No stairs tonight?" he asked.

"Not the way my feet hurt right now," I said. "I'm about to put my whole face in this sushi and try to stay up long enough to see how my Masey James story turned out."

"Yeah, I heard something on the radio about that on the way to work. That's messed up." He shook his head, his expression somber. I imagine he thought about his own daughter.

I nodded my head and turned to step into the elevator. Just as the doors were about to close, I shouted, "By the way, we still need to talk about you and Sabrina getting married. Your flower girl is right here waiting!"

"Woman!" Bass laughed. "Go to bed!"

..

Finally, inside the apartment, I practically threw the bag of sushi on the kitchen counter, so anxious to begin my ritualistic physical dismantling. I started stripping on the way to the bathroom and dropped my clothes in a pile outside the door. My shape-shifting wouldn't be complete without a hot shower, where I could scrub off the day and the on-air makeup that I had touched up at least a dozen times, and allow it to dissolve along with the stress down the drain.

How nice it would be to step out of the shower and into a big thirsty towel handed me by a lover. It's just not as sexy with a shower cap on my head.

I laughed at the chameleon in the bathroom mirror, unrecognizable from the Jordan Manning of News Channel 8, even from the person I was just a few moments ago. I reached for my home staples—a pair of cotton leggings and a frayed over-size Dallas Cowboy sweatshirt long overdue for replacement—and put the TLC CD into the disc changer and blasted "No Scrubs," my all-time dating anthem.

I turned my dinner splurge into a full-on production, with bamboo place mats and the scalloped appetizer plates that made their way home from Bloomingdale's after a barrage of commercials during hours of TV watching. I set up on the table in front of the camelback sofa and grabbed the bottle of room-temperature sake and the tokkuri on top of the bar cart, filled it to the top, and heated it up in the microwave. Courtney always says, "You should never pour your own sake; someone should poor it for you." Tonight I would pour my own and savor the solace, and thank God for being able to blow fifty bucks on dinner.

I thought about calling my mother but started to doze as the sake worked its magic. I propped my head up on a pillow and lay back on the sofa to rest my eyes, as my dad used to say. I apparently dozed off and was jarred awake by the newscast's theme music and voice-over. I panicked. Did I miss it?

Coming up, Chicagoans descend on the Bronzeville community tonight, remembering Masey James, the fifteen-year-old tragically killed. Channel 8's Jordan Manning was at the scene of the community vigil and spoke with students who went to school with Masey and a group of moms who drove in from as far away as Naperville and Aurora.

Shit! It was 10:06. I missed the first part of the broadcast, possibly the interview with Pamela and the footage of the roundtable. I have the ten o'clock news scheduled to record on TiVo every night. So I grabbed the remote and hit rewind to go back to the beginning.

I moved to the edge of the couch and leaned into the TV as close as I could without blurring my vision. I was glad to hear the anchor, Iris Smith, mention "moms as far away as Naperville and Aurora." That meant the April Murphy interview made the cut. But I was nervous about "students from Masey's school," praying the editor excluded the part where Masey's friend, Shawn Jeffries, mentioned her getting rides from school in the weeks before her murder.

My heartbeat moved to my throat. No matter how many times I've stood in this moment, as a reporter I never stop worrying about the storytelling being sacrificed for time, because they've got to get in other stories or the end-of-show kicker, which sometimes seemed more important than the lives of people who are struggling. Thankfully, that didn't happen. The segment led the news. The first part alone lasted longer than the usual one minute and ten seconds, which is an infinite amount of time in TV. Tracy did an amazing job of editing all the footage. The one-on-one with Pamela, the roundtable with community leaders, and the vigil flowed like a documentary short.

Nice.

I checked my cell phone and was happy to see several congratulatory text messages from friends and colleagues.

Ellen: PHENOMENAL COVERAGE!

I texted back: Thanks, Ellen! It's been a long day. I'll be in an hour late tomorrow, OK? See you around 11.

Zena: Saw your story. Girl, this is unbelievable! You owned it. No one could have reported it the way you did.

Text: Awww thanks, sweetie!

Scott: The piece turned out really nice. Congrats!

"Yeah, whatever," I said out loud. "No thanks to you."

And Courtney: So full of emotion after watching your segment tonight. I know it wasn't easy. Love you, girl.

Love you 2! I texted back.

Ellen, Zena, and Courtney, without even realizing it, had

validated a need in me to feel that the work I do is important, that it matters. That a two-minute clip, for me, is the culmination of ten hours immersed in the inextricable pain of sobbing family members, exasperated community leaders, frightened residents, and insolent cops, all along carrying the knowledge of a terrifying medical examiner's report, then standing at the crime scene where a child was discarded. Who wouldn't welcome an "atta girl" after all that?

My cell phone chimed and Thomas's name popped up.

How was your day?

Before I could text him back, the phone beeped again
WANT SOME COMPANY? the text jumped off the screen like it was in 3D.

Really, Thomas? If you had watched my newscast, you would know how my day was.

I wasn't in the mood to respond. I set the phone down on the kitchen counter and went for the bottle of pinot noir on the bar cart that Amanda had brought over for brunch that we didn't get around to opening. It had one of those screw-off tops that I've come to appreciate. If I'd had to wrestle with a corkscrew, it would've been a nonstarter. But this was too easy to pass up, so I said screw it and poured myself a glass. Feeling somewhat guilty for blowing Thomas off, I walked back into the kitchen and picked up my phone to text him.

I'VE HAD ALL THE SATISFACTION I CAN HANDLE FOR ONE DAY. BUT I'LL SEE YOU SOON. XX.

I plopped back down on the coach, hit rewind, and watched the Masey James segment again. I paused on the shot of the overblown picture of her wearing a puffy pink jacket, holding up a peace sign. As I lingered on her face, the image of the girl next door came into focus. I've always resented that ideal— the girl next door—because mainstream society had always portrayed her as White, blond, and upper middle class, but in reality, she is Masey. And by the way, she's also the White girl with brown hair whose parents have no money. This ideal of the girl next door puts a lot of girls on the back burner, not just girls of color.

How'd this happen to you?

Tears streamed down my face. I leaned forward, and with my face in my hands, I silently asked God, "Send me a sign, Lord. I need to know what happened. And, Masey, if there's another realm that we enter when we die, and I believe there is, beautiful girl, send me a sign." It just might come to this, because I'm not confident that anyone in this world will ever know what happened to you.

Wow! It's come to this. Breaking my own rule not to wake up with alcohol on the nightstand.

I stripped down to nothing but my skin and dissolved into the cool cotton sheets. I closed my eyes, took a deep breath, and forced myself from the depths of despair as I struggled against the inevitability of sleep. I thought sleep wouldn't come easy, but I was wrong. It came so quickly that when the phone rang, just for a second I felt disoriented as I fought against sleep paralysis. I clumsily reached over onto the nightstand for my cell phone. It wasn't there, but the ringing persisted. It took a moment for me to realize the ring was coming from my house phone on the dresser by the window. Only a handful of people have that number. It truly is my "in case of emergency" line.

I got out of bed and felt my way over to where the ring was coming from, my movement stilted and clumsy. Half present, my brain finally registered that it was probably Bass calling to let me know my parking space was open.

"*Mmm* . . . hello?" I cleared my throat.

"Hey, Jordie. It's Bass."

"Hey, is this about the parking space?"

He laughed uncomfortably. "No, not that. You have a visitor."

I turned around to look at the clock by the bed. It was after one A.M. "A visitor? Who?" I said, getting my bearings.

I heard a voice in the background say, "Let me talk to her."

"I'll let him tell you," Bass said.

"Hey, babe, it's Thomas. I'm in the lobby."

I rubbed my eyes and checked the time again. "What's wrong? Why are you here?" I asked.

I heard a throat clearing in the background and muffled voices. *Why was HE covering up the receiver?*

"What are you doing? What's going on down there?"

"Sorry, I'm back, babe. Listen, I know you had a tough, I mean a *really* difficult day. Oh, and I heard about the long walk from the roof."

"Bass told you that," I said. *Why is Bass in my business?*

"My buddy's looking out for me, that's all," Thomas said. "And you, too."

In the background, I heard Bass say, "Uh-uh. I'm Bennett and I ain't in it!"

I laughed.

"What're you laughing about?" Thomas asked.

"I'm laughing at you two co-conspirators," I said.

"Guilty as charged," Thomas said. "But I would love to come up and see you, and maybe even a foot massage?" he said, his voice rising an octave in a rare display of insecurity for fear I'll say no from a man who usually displays confidence.

"Please, baby, baby, please," Bass chimed in, giving his best Spike Lee impersonation while managing to control his laughter.

I'll deal with you later, Bass.

I sighed heavily, letting go of skepticism and giving myself permission to *want* to see him. "Okay, fine. Come on up."

Bass hit the buzzer, and it dawned on me that he was playing coy about Thomas the way I tease him about Sabrina. I could imagine him giving Thomas a thumbs-up with a big smile on his face.

Before I hung up, Bass came back on the line. "Don't disown me. But you would've killed me for sure if I didn't let you know he was here," he said.

I laughed. "Yeah, you might be right. Good night, Bass Man."

What did he expect me to look like at one o'clock in the morning? Vanity kicked in, but there wasn't time to rifle through my lingerie drawer to find something more in line with how I was suddenly feeling. I don't know if it was mixing the sake and red wine, or the urge to be transported to another place, to be someone and something else just for a little while, but I had put my Cowboys sweatshirt back on and pulled on a pair of fitted boy shorts before I heard knocking. By the time I reached the door, I'd made up my mind what was going to happen.

"You look beautiful."

Something seemed different about him. I wanted to say, "This is quite bold of you showing up unannounced," but the creaminess of his flawless skin set off a chemical reaction, a tingling sensation I felt in the top layer of my skin and fingertips. Clearly, we were on the same page about the rest of the night. I wanted to melt into him and him into me. I didn't say a word. I just smiled, took his hand, and led him to my bed.

··

I awoke in a red wine/sake fog the next morning, which was regrettable knowing the day that lay ahead. Thomas was still asleep. For a second I had to remind myself that he was still here. Creeping at one o'clock in the morning was nothing new for us, though I'd always had a heads-up before. Last night was the first time he had spent the night. All night. Though I was glad he took the lead, because he was exactly what I needed last night, his surprise visit would have to be addressed. This isn't the lane we're living in. This is not a monogamous relationship by any stretch. This is a situation-ship. I don't want him to stumble upon something one night that he doesn't want to see and I haven't shared.

My mind turned to the conversations I would need to have in the newsroom today to get what I'm aiming for—a special assignment designation that will anoint me untouchable for general assignment stories.

I turned away from Thomas to check the calendar and then my emails on my cell phone. I'd been scrolling through for a good three minutes when Thomas said, "Good morning." I returned my phone to the nightstand and turned to face him.

"Good morning," I said.

"How long you been up?" he asked.

"Just a few minutes."

"Is this what you do every morning?"

"What?"

"Start your day loving up on that phone?"

"I have to check my emails and text messages, and oh God,

my calendar. That'd be a big mistake not checking my calendar," I said.

"So you just launch in like this?" he asked.

"Yes, and I wouldn't have it any other way."

In a single movement he reached out with his left arm and pulled me to his chest and playfully pecked me on the lips. "This is how you should be starting your day," he said, and took my hand and began to slide it down toward his naked pelvis.

I pulled away. "Cut it out!"

"I wasn't going to do it." He laughed. "I'm just messing with you."

"I should've known this was too good to be true," I said.

Thomas squeezed me tight and our bodies, skin on skin, rocked back and forth.

"I'd love to make you some coffee, but since it's our first sleepover, I don't even know where you keep it," he said. I took it as a slight dig at me for not letting him stay over before.

"It's good to see you smile, though. As a matter of fact, let me look at that," he said. "I don't think I've ever seen that smile before."

"So, what, are you taking credit?" I asked.

"Yeah," he said without hesitation.

"I'm glad you came over last night," I said. I figured I'd play to his ego before making it clear never to sneak up on me like that again. "But don't make it a habit."

His smiled dimmed, which wasn't my intention. Something I know I need to work on is getting better at living in the moment, instead of always searching for the next one.

"I looked a mess last night," I said, deflecting.

"No, you didn't. You looked beautiful."

"You were right about one thing—yesterday was a very difficult day emotionally."

"I kinda figured that after I saw your story," he said.

I leaned away, pulled the sheet up over my breasts, and propped myself up on my elbow, with rapt attention. "You saw my story?" I'd assumed he hadn't.

"Yeah," he said, scooching up in bed and sliding a pillow underneath his head. "That's why I texted you right after it went off," he said.

"Oh." What's the saying? When you assume, you make a what out of who and who? I perked up. "What did you think?" I asked.

"I thought it was kind of fucked up," he said with a sour look. "That mother looked like a zombie. There was no life in her eyes. I don't know how you reporters do that to people. That woman was in no position to be in front of a camera, and you guys were right there in her face."

"That was her choice," I said, abruptly sitting up in bed. "Don't go there."

He had no idea how insulting what he just said was to me.

"I'd better get up and get my day going," I said before the conversation went any further. I turned my back to him and grabbed my phone off the nightstand.

"Wait. What just happened?" he asked.

I turned around and faced him. "You offended me, that's what," I said. "You make reporters sound like thrill seekers forcing people to talk. Like I get paid for tears or something. Pamela Alonzo *wanted* us there. She was using *us* to *her* advantage."

Just then, the sun bore through my bedroom window with a flash of hot blinding light like it was agreeing with me. I ran my hand through my hair and tried to settle down a bit before I went on. "And I'm glad she did, because you know what?"

"What?" he said, pouting like a seven-year-old man-child, his arms folded across his bare, prodigious pectorals.

"This little girl, Thomas, from what I've learned, was the girl next door. *Our* girl next door. Smart, ambitious, beautiful. I'm just baffled how her life came down to *this*."

Thomas sat up and leaned his back against the headboard and drew his knees to his chest in a contemplative pose.

"What?" I asked.

"What I don't get is how come she was riding a bike home that night when it was getting dark?" he said.

"Well, supposedly, she took off before it got too dark out. Her mother told me her cousin was throwing a birthday party for her boyfriend that night and she didn't want her there. The people were too old for Masey to be hanging around, and her mom probably suspected there would be a lot more going on than Masey was ready for. But she let her go to the mall with her cousin that afternoon. So you make a good point. Why didn't she just drop her off at her house?"

"She's probably kicking herself right now," Thomas said, reaching down to pick up his shirt off the floor.

"Or worse, blaming herself," I said. "I drove over to Englewood yesterday before the vigil and tried to figure out the route Masey might have taken. It's not destitute or anything. In fact, it's busy as hell over there. There's a church on every corner. A liquor store on every other block. This section of Englewood is very busy and not always in a good way. The closer you get to Auburn Gresham, the quieter the streets get. It's a mystery. I also feel like Pamela may not have known her daughter as well as she thought. She might've fit in a lot better at that party than her mother realized. Does anyone really know their child? I can think of at least six things I did around that age my mother will never know about."

"Her mother seems like a nice person," Thomas said, pulling his club jersey over his head.

"She is. That's not to say Pamela isn't nice. But I don't just mean her mother. Her cousin, the one she was with that day. That's who I want to talk to," I said. "As soon as possible. Meanwhile, this guy is still out there, and I'm worried he's going to hurt somebody else."

"You really get into this stuff, don't you?" he asked. "Are you a reporter or an investigator?"

"At this point, I'm whatever I need to be to figure this out," I said.

"Okay, police lady," he said. Thomas swung his legs to the other side of the bed and yanked on his workout pants in a single rapid motion, then half laid back down.

"I don't know if I've ever told you this, but along with a journalism degree, I have a degree in forensic science. But not because I want to be a cop. Trust me. I would hope the level of incompetence I've seen by police wouldn't be my MO."

"Well, yeah, I hear ya," he said.

I sensed Thomas was starting to lose interest in the conversation. I recognized the shift. This is where I often struggle in relationships, when my job may seem more important than his, and fifteen minutes after "good morning," we've talked only about my job and the story I'm following and my life, but nothing about his. I've seen it enough times where a guy feels intimidated or says I think everything revolves around me. I've found that the things men love about me are also the things they end up resenting.

Thomas propped himself up on his right elbow to glance at the clock. It was going on eight. "Ah," he said, dropping back down into the pillow.

"What?" I asked.

"Nothing. I've gotta get going."

"Yeah, me too," I said.

As abruptly as it had started, it ended.

..

As much as I wanted to stay in bed for another two hours, when I arrived at the station, the energy inside the newsroom bolstered my spirits, and so did my colleagues.

"Bravo!" Ellen said, clapping as I walked toward her desk.

"You *killed* it yesterday!" she said. "Channel 11 ran an interview with the mom, but they didn't have the community leaders or the great people you interviewed at the vigil. I know Peter wants to talk to you."

"Great! Thanks for the heads-up," I said. I wasn't concerned, though. When Peter Nussbaum, the station's news director, wanted to have a word with me, it was usually good news. And if he really was as impressed with my performance as Ellen just suggested, it shouldn't be hard to convince him to allow me to stick with this story exclusively, even if it meant working overtime and on my regular days off, and pushing the day-to-day police blotter crime stories to general assignment reporters.

"How'd you do working with George last night?" Ellen said with a smirk.

"Good! He was late getting there, but it wasn't his fault," I said.

"You know what I mean," Ellen said, twitching her nose.

"Oh, that. It must have been shower day," I said. "Please don't share that with anyone. He did a great job last night."

"Oh, I wouldn't. Never," Ellen said.

Out of the corner of my eye, I saw Keith Mulvaney, aka Tonya

Harding, coming out of Peter's glassed-in corner office. Ellen and I exchanged dubious looks.

"I wonder what that's all about," I said. Ellen shrugged her shoulders just as Peter leaned halfway out the door and waved me over.

"I've been summoned," I said to Ellen. "Talk to you later?"

"Sure." She smiled, clapped her hands twice, and rested them in a prayer position. I chuckled and headed over to the senior managers' row overlooking Michigan Avenue, with spectacular views of the Chicago River, the neo-Gothic Tribune Tower, and the Spanish Colonial Wrigley Building. I had a huge smile on my face. I felt good, confident. I lived for days like this and decided to enjoy it. You're only as good as your last story, and I was already back at the starting block.

Along the way I received accolades from colleagues. I got a thumbs-up, a nod and a smile, a high five, and a verbal "Kudos!" "Nice job last night, Jordan!" "Thank you." "Great segment last night." "Thank you."

As Keith drew nearer, I scanned his appearance, thinking: *There is nothing extraordinary about him. Not one thing. He's not even handsome. He has no striking features. Not even an air of confidence. No it factor. Even among the most generic men, he fails to rise to the top. What he is, though, is masterful at working the reps. He knows whose offices to stay in and how to skillfully stir gossip and besmirch his colleagues, while concealing his own sins but never his motives. In that way, he is transparent as fuck. In others, he's a human grenade. You don't notice him until he explodes. And yet he doesn't have to contemplate going from network to network to advance his career, even with his marginally successful résumé with no exclusives, no awards, just a penis and a lot of fake bravado.*

I didn't expect Keith to congratulate me on my story, nor did

I want him to. I didn't need his false admiration. I felt empowered and greeted him with a genuine smile. "Hi, Keith. How are you?" I said in my best golf-buddy voice.

"Good," he said, a couple of beats too late, unmasking his inner asshole. My smile broadened into a sly grin. I didn't bother turning around and picked up the pace to Peter's office. I was energized, sensing it was a good time to ask for exactly what I wanted.

I knocked before entering. Nussbaum was sitting on the corner of his desk with his back to the picture window that framed downtown's architectural splendor, his feet barely touching the floor. Peter is about an inch shorter than me when I'm wearing high heels, so I avoid standing too close to him whenever possible to protect his ego, in case it's fragile. I just wish he or his wife would do something about that errant swath of hair that lays across his forehead like half of a bang. It isn't that I'm not fond of Peter. For the most part, he's an okay guy. I'd just like to walk into a news director's office at a major metropolitan news station and see a woman sitting behind the desk, or a person of color. Not since I've worked in television has that ever happened. What has been consistent, though, is there's always a reporter, an assignment editor, or a news director, all of them men, looking for a reason, any reason, to push me off the crime beat. Covering violent crime is often viewed as a masculine pursuit, and a lot of editors assign the top crime stories to male reporters by default. I've seen female assignment editors who are just as guilty of enforcing this unspoken patriarchy. Intentional or not, they need to check themselves. It's one of those hidden assumptions I have to push back against time and again.

"Jordan! Please, have a seat," he said. "I won't take up too much of your time. I just wanted to tell you that I think you did a helluva job last night on a very complicated, very emotional story."

It was unusual for Peter to describe a story as emotional. Masey's murder was so devastating, it pierced the heart of a cynical newsman, and that was saying something.

"Thanks, Peter. I appreciate that. I really do," I said, then immediately launched into my pitch. "You know, last night, I think I might have picked up on a potential clue in this case. I'd like to put my forensic hat on and dig deeper into this story. The nature of the crime, the outcry from the community, *all of it*, demands focused attention. And I'm willing to work overtime, weekends, whatever I need to do to stick with this story, because if we—"

Peter held up his hand and interrupted me. "I'm sorry. I don't mean to cut you off, Jordan," he said.

You'd better have a good reason.

"I see where you're headed, and listen, you don't have to convince me. I'm all in. That's what I wanted to talk to you about. Now, the overtime I'll have to figure out, but look, you've got your finger on the pulse of this story, and what's more, you're in the community, which is a big part of this. So yes, we're in agreement. Stay close. And see what you can get out of Dr. Chan, though I don't have to tell you that, do I?" Peter said.

"Well, exactly," I said confidently. "Dr. Chan is out of the country, and when we last spoke, it sounded like he was going to be gone for a good three weeks to a month."

"Oh, that's unfortunate," Peter said.

"No, it's okay. I'll shoot him an email. He told me that he was sending some evidence for testing to the state crime lab before he left town. Unless he's lying flat on his back somewhere, I'm pretty confident he'll respond," I said.

"Sounds good, Jordan. Thanks for making us look good out there," he said.

"My pleasure, Peter. Thank you."

As I exited Peter's office, something he said struck me as odd. "You're in the community," he'd said. In my mind, that could mean either one of two things. He was acknowledging the way in which I'd skillfully inserted myself into my subject's lives and gotten them to open up—an outsider from Austin, Texas, with no roots on Chicago's South Side. Not even a third cousin. Or he simply meant, "You're Black and they trust you. So you might as well stick with the story."

Either way, he'd given me the green light to take my reporting to a whole other level. And Tonya would have to suck it up. I just pulled off the news equivalent of a triple axel in his face, and there wasn't a damned thing he could do about it.

As I walked back to Ellen's desk to share the good news, I contemplated where I'd test out my newfound freedom first. Should I call April Murphy or Pamela Alonzo? Or should I start with Lieutenant Joseph Samuels—just to see what I can learn from him about the investigation?

"Well?" Ellen said.

I smiled wide and opened my mouth in a silent scream. "I'm on special assignment," I told her. "Well, Peter didn't use that term, exactly, but I'm off the day-to-day crime stuff for now. He's moving that to GA," short for general assignment.

"That's great!" she said, and tilted her head slightly toward Keith, who was looking directly at us. "Did he say anything about Tonya?"

"What about him?" I asked.

"He's a parasite. We know that. He could see this as an opening to push in on your beat," Ellen said.

I paused before responding, because frankly I was slightly

annoyed that she would bring this up. I was still basking in the good fortune that Peter had bestowed on me. Then I spoke slowly and deliberately. "This is the *right* story for me *right* now," I said. "I have neither the time nor the energy to worry about *him*."

Ellen shrugged her shoulders. "Okay, I'm just saying."

"Gotta go. Talk to ya later," I said, and hurried to my desk. By the time I sat down and picked up the phone, I'd decided who to call first. I reached into the side pocket of my purse and pulled out April's business card.

Let's see what you're all about, Ms. April Murphy.

I dialed the mobile number handwritten on the back of the card.

She picked up on the first ring. "Hello?"

"Is this April?" I asked.

"This is April. Jordan?"

News Channel 8 must have popped up on the caller ID.

"Yes, this is Jordan Manning. Sorry about last night. Pamela Alonzo left the area right after she spoke."

"No problem. That poor woman was in no shape to meet anybody last night. Honestly, I don't know how she got her words out. I was awestruck, frankly."

"I know. I was as well," I said.

"The depth of the loss she has suffered, the way it happened, it's enough to stop a mother's heart," she said. "No matter how long I do this type of work, even with my own personal experience as a benchmark, I'm still amazed by the way survivors deal with trauma. I always say, though, the day I get used to it is the day I'm no longer effective as an advocate."

"The women against violence group . . . do you do that full time?" I asked.

"I used to, oh, about the first seven or eight years. But in the last three to four, after my divorce, I had to go back to work. I renewed my life and accident insurance license with the state. The good thing is, I'm able to make my own schedule."

I surmised from her emphasis on *had to* that April's lifestyle changed after her divorce. She might yet be affluent, to a degree, but certainly not like before.

"Oh," I said.

"I have to tell you, full disclosure, I watch a lot of court TV shows. I'm obsessed, really. I'm a little embarrassed to say how much," April said.

She need not be embarrassed around me. Not about that. I understand women's attraction to those types of programs, especially the ones that are based on true crime stories. My theory is that women are drawn to such shows because no matter how strong a front we present, we harbor a fear of something horrible happening to us. The nagging question "What would I do if I were ever put in that position?" is always in the back of our mind. The what-if motivates me to walk up eight flights to my apartment. It's why I took the stairs from the rooftop last night instead of the elevator. The feeling nags me, perhaps more than most, because I confront other people's misfortunes for a living. I've watched people dig through memories turned to ashes in a fire and searched my soul, wondering, *What would I grab if my home were ablaze? What if I lost that one picture of my now-deceased grandparents that I keep in my living room? Or the one of Stephanie and me standing by an ice sculpture wearing those itchy lavender lace bridesmaid's dresses from our cousin Thelma's wedding?*

"I'm still interested in meeting Pamela," April reiterated.

"And I *definitely* want to connect you two, but I can't say right now when that will happen. She still has a funeral to get through, and after last night, I don't know her state of mind," I said.

"Understandable," April said. "I can wait."

I approved of the way our conversation was flowing but was wary of becoming too casual with her, so I switched into my work voice. "Something Pamela said to me the day before the vigil makes me think you won't have to wait long," I said. "She told me that her mission in life is to catch her daughter's killer. My heart sank hearing her say that, because I know how cold cases can, far too often, stay cold. Where does the average citizen get the time, money, and resources and even the media attention required to keep a homicide case on the front burner?"

I said *average citizen*, but I really meant that cases involving Black victims go cold and stay cold, and don't get the same level of media attention, something April alluded to last night. It was a leading question I hoped would help me better assess April's intentions.

"That's where my organization comes in," she said.

Elbows on my desk, I leaned into the phone as if I was talking to April in person.

"Last night, do you remember when you asked me if I was looking for other members of my group to join us?" April asked.

"Yes."

"Well, in fact, I was scanning the crowd for anyone who looked suspicious, hanging around the family, doing a little too much, being a little *too* helpful. A lot of times, a killer will come back to the scene of the crime to see how people are reacting to what he's done. Or they'll hang around the victims' family in an attempt to eliminate themselves as a suspect. Some will sit back and get off on watching the people whose lives they've destroyed pick up the shattered pieces."

I didn't want to interrupt April, but I was familiar with the pattern she was describing. People kill people they know. Serial killers hunt where they live. The boogeyman doesn't drop out of the sky upon his victims. He walks out of his house and kills usually within a three- to five-mile radius, a fact crime shows don't reveal very often. Instead, I listened and waited for an opportunity to ask the question that was burning me up.

"Do you think he'll kill again?"

"I don't know," she said. "But interesting you would ask, because I was about to ask if you thought we are dealing with a serial killer."

Dr. Chan had planted the seed in my mind a few days ago, but that wasn't the first time he'd mentioned a suspected serial killer in Chicago targeting Black women. When he first became special consultant to the chief medical examiner, he told me that he reviewed hundreds of cold cases and discovered a dozen unsolved murders of Black women going back eight or nine years. The victims, he said, were characterized as indigent, homeless, or engaged in intravenous drug activity or prostitution. That shouldn't matter—a victim is a victim. But it could explain why nobody cared enough to find their killers.

"I think it's a possibility, yes," I said.

"Me too," April said.

After a long silence, April spoke. "About a year ago, I teamed up with a group out of D.C., started by a bunch of retired law enforcement officers and prosecutors. They track cold cases. Ever since Ted Bundy, when the FBI first developed personality profiles of serial killers, they've been adding on more crime-fighting techniques, like algorithms to identify patterns of behavior and styles of killing. I'm sorry if that sounds morbid."

"No, not at all. I grew up knowing that I wanted to be a reporter. And one of the people I always envisioned myself interviewing was Henry Lee Lucas. Ever heard of him?" I asked.

"Uh, yeah," April replied. "I got the chills just hearing his name."

Lucas was the notorious Texas serial killer who confessed to more than a hundred murders. Investigators kept him alive because they kept believing his stories about hidden bodies, though not all of them proved to be true. He was by far one of the most despicable human beings on earth, but he wasn't executed. He died of natural causes in prison.

"Listen, when I first moved to Chicago, I drove by John Wayne Gacy's house, just to see it. I was disappointed when I found out it'd already been torn down," I said, relaxing into the conversation. April and I had only met, but eventually, I hoped, she would stop apologizing for being interested in murder and realize whom she's talking to.

"So, all good," I said. "Continue."

"Well, we created a database to store and share information. When we hit upon something interesting, we reach out to local authorities to see if they would consider reopening a case," she said. "Sometimes they do. Sometimes they write us off as crackpots with nothing better to do."

"You said this group is out of D.C., so do they track cases around the nation, or just in the Chicago area?" I asked.

"No, they're national, but in recent years, they have been tracking a growing number of unsolved murders of Black women in the Midwest, including Chicago and the surrounding suburbs, St. Louis and Kansas City."

Oh my God! They've picked up on the same trend as Dr. Chan.

"Did they release their findings?" I asked.

"To the police? Frankly I think they were hesitant because

many of the victims were women who clearly had struggles, some living on the streets trying to survive," she went on. "I know. It's infuriating."

I huffed incredulity. "Did they come up with a profile of the killer or killers? Do they think there's one, two, three? What's the motivation?"

"Unfortunately, they didn't," she said. "I know what you're thinking, but the victims' profiles don't line up with Masey's case. I could be way off base here, but I can't help but wonder how in the hell a girl like Masey James, a good student from a solid, loving family, ended up being murdered in such a terrible way."

She had no idea what I was thinking.

"That's something of an indelicate question, isn't it? How does someone like Masey end up a victim? Aren't victims always victims?"

"Well, yes, of course! It shouldn't matter. All I'm saying is that nothing about the way Masey lived and who she was pointed to her life ending in this way," she said.

I didn't mean to put April on the defensive, but what's the point of collecting the data and then not sharing it? "I agree with you there," I said.

"She's too young for it to have been a crime of passion. No, this is a psycho. Question is, did this guy lose it one day, because he got triggered, or did he plan this?"

I remained silent as I thought about that.

"You think I'm being irrational, or that I watch too many made-for-TV movies, right?" she asked.

"No, not at all. I was just thinking. I'm impressed, really, by the fact you care this much," I said to try and soften what might have felt to her like an attack, not simply my journalistic nature. Still, I hesitated to share Dr. Chan's speculations about Masey's killer or that he, too, had identified a similarly disturbing pattern among Black female victims in Chicago. I told April I had some other leads to follow, and we promised to stay in touch.

Dr. Chan had been gone only two days, but surely they would fast-track this sample under the circumstances. Calling the lab directly wouldn't do me any good. I would need a Freedom of Information Act request and maybe even a court order to get that type of information released directly to a journalist. Even Joey might experience a lag unless he was listed as an investigator on the case.

Dr. Chan was still the fastest way to find out. Rather than email him, I decided to try and reach him by phone. I could tell by the delay and sound of the telephone ring that he wasn't in the country, so I was ecstatic when he picked up.

"Hello?" he said. Dr. Chan usually answered the phone by calling my name, but his caller ID might not be working outside the United States.

"Dr. Chan! Hi, it's Jordan," I said. "I hope I didn't catch you at a bad time."

"Oh, Jordan, hello. Well, actually—" he said before I cut him off.

"Listen, I know it's only been a couple of days, but I'm calling to see if you've gotten those tissue results back yet. You know, the tissue from Masey you sent to the crime lab."

"Well, you said it yourself, Jordan. It's only been a couple days," he said.

"I thought it might be on the fast track. Does anybody else know about it?" I asked him.

"Sure, my assistant. I asked her to get it to the state crime lab," he said. "She knows."

"No, no, I mean, other reporters?"

I regretted the question the moment I'd asked. I didn't want Dr. Chan to think I was accusing him of anything. He'd clearly promised me the exclusive.

"Well, no, Jordan, I didn't speak to anyone else before I left. I told you that," he said.

"I'm sorry."

"Listen, Jordan, I've got to go. You caught me in the middle of something," he said. For the first time, I noticed lethargy in his voice.

"Are you okay, Dr. Chan? You sound exhausted," I said.

"Look, there's no way the results are back already, okay?" he said, sounding slightly annoyed. "Let's talk some other time. I have to go now. Bye."

The call disconnected and I stared at my phone, baffled.

Where did he say he was? Switzerland? You idiot you didn't even think about the time difference. You probably called him in the middle of the night.

My cell phone felt hot and clammy in my hand, but I didn't hesitate to call Joey. It went straight to voice mail. My heart pounded and my mind raced as if I were running out of time. To do what? I didn't know. There were so many aspects of this case to think about. I turned my focus to last night's vigil. I hadn't begun to process what I'd learned there, in particular Shawn Jeffries's revelation about Masey's getting rides from school. I walked back over to Ellen's desk.

"Hey, I'm going to run downstairs and grab a coffee. You want something?"

"Sure," she said. "I'm buying," and reached into her wallet and pulled out a ten.

"Thanks, you don't have to do that," I said.

"Is everything okay? You're scrunching," she said.

When I'm deep in thought or ticked off, my eyebrows curl up like they came with a drawstring.

"No, I'm fine. I'm just trying to process everything from the vigil last night. Monique, Louise hugging Masey's cousin Yvonne. What's their connection? I just feel like everybody knows more than they're saying, and I don't understand why."

"Like what?" Ellen asked.

"Well, first, the young lady from Masey's school named Shawn. She told me that Masey had gotten rides from school in the weeks before she disappeared."

"Really? I don't remember that detail from your reporting," Ellen said, her brows now scrunched up. "Did I miss that?"

"No, you didn't," I said. "I asked Tracy to cut it. I'm not sure even the police know that yet. My instinct told me it might be a clue, and I didn't want to put this girl's life in danger."

"You sure her mother or a relative didn't pick her up from school?" Ellen asked.

"I don't know. Her mother never mentioned it to me. In fact, she made a big deal out of telling me about the long bus route Masey took from her house to the West Side school. And then there was this other girl named Monique, Monique Connors, who said she was a friend of Masey's. Well sort of. That's how she said it, like she didn't sound so sure about that. She was a little off-putting. I didn't interview her on-camera, but I saw her hanging around Masey's relatives later. She was standing next to Masey's cousin Yvonne. That's the older cousin that Pamela said Masey hung around her house all the time. Well, she did. And Louise Robinson knows Yvonne. That's how she got involved in the vigil, I suspect. At first I thought it was because her niece lives across the street from the crime scene, but I think it's deeper than that."

"Wait a minute. You're telling me that Louise Robinson's niece lives across the street from the crime scene? That's one helluva coincidence, isn't it? Did you talk to her?"

"Yes, her name is Tanya McMillan, the young woman I did the live interview with the day the body was found. Next thing I know, Tanya is calling me and telling me about the vigil. I didn't realize they knew Masey's cousin Yvonne until I saw Louise hugging her last night."

"Wow, the world is small, isn't it? In this case, it's almost too good to be true," Ellen said.

It was a coincidence, but I didn't want to make too much out of the dots that connected Tanya to Louise to Yvonne. Chicago is a city comprised of neighborhoods and streets, and people who live in certain neighborhoods, on certain streets, know one another. From what I can tell, besides the trip to school, Masey's life was an amalgam of streets and the houses she'd been in and out of because of where she lived, hung out, and played. As far as the people in her life, only one or two degrees separated them.

"Maybe," I responded. "In either case, I think my next move is to see what's up with Masey's cousin Yvonne."

10

On the way downstairs to grab coffee, I ran into Grace, the intern, in the elevator.

"Oh, hi, Jordan!" she said. She studied me from head to toe. It was almost as though she were visualizing herself in a pair of designer stilettos, fantasizing what her career could be like one day.

"Everything turned out so well!" she said. "I'm really glad I got a chance to work with you last night."

"Well, you didn't actually work with me, but I understand what you mean. Thanks. You did great," I said.

Her enthusiasm rose. "I just had one of my most exciting days since I've been here."

"I assure you every day won't be like that," I said.

"The vigil was amazing!"

A vigil is not amazing. A child is dead!

Inevitably, every year a new string of interns dying to be reporters jump into this business with a skewed view of the job. No one values heart anymore. It's the drama they're after, the thirst for the high five from a colleague congratulating you for "owning someone" in an interview. I know I might sound like an old J-school dinosaur sometimes, but I think schools should require would-be reporters to take psychology classes, or at least some type of counseling curriculum to acquire the empathy they need for the day-to-day, so they're forced to remember these are human beings, not just stories. I realize this is exactly what Thomas was trying to convey earlier, and this ticked me off. It was the equivalent of somebody else calling your baby unattractive. *You* can say that, but another person can't.

I mask my annoyance, because I realize Grace didn't mean any harm and because I could tell she immediately regretted it.

"It's tragic, I know," she said. "Don't get me wrong. I grew up in Evanston, but it's not the city-city."

Therein lies her ignorance. Most of the time, the types of people reporters encounter at work are very different from the ones they grew up around. Like Grace, who has spent most of her life in the suburbs.

I changed the subject. "Who are you working for?" I asked. "Are you making the rounds or are you just supporting the camera crew?"

"Right now George, I guess. Or his boss. Honestly, it's kind of been super low-key. I thought I'd be moving around more, working in different aspects of the newsroom. But so far I've spent the first couple weeks of my internship with the camera guys."

I realized I've never been in Grace's shoes, because she took a different path than I did, and now she was trying to break free of that path. So often people who graduate from prestigious universities take low- or no-paying internships believing they will get a chance to shadow a reporter their parents love on the news or someone they got a chance to meet once. If they're really lucky, they will get help from that reporter or a nice camera guy to make their résumé tape. What they don't know, and nobody tells them, *before* they get here is that between union rules and newsroom management, most of the time that doesn't happen. They're more likely to find themselves on a coffee or script printing errand with that $50,000-a-year journalism degree.

It's a hard pill to swallow because they all want to be in New

York, Los Angeles, or Chicago, and in some cases, they think they can go straight to the network because once upon a time somebody they know or heard of actually did. Reporter legends are a form of urban legend. It happened to this person, so it can happen to me. I always tell recent grads that it's better to work in a small market first instead of a major city. It doesn't matter where; just throw a dart at a map and head toward the first small market it lands on. Newbies are far more likely to get some real experience, actually meet people and get out of the bubble, even if it's just covering the state fair, a high school commencement, or the Fourth of July parade. I smiled to myself, thinking about my mentor back in Dallas, Lucy Hansfield, who successfully fought off a legion of "I'm smarter, prettier, and I graduated from a better college than you" contenders who mistook her for a has-been because she was in her late forties and Black. Lucy is a dyed-in-the-wool city hall reporter, and she kept her coveted spot because she practically lived there, stalking the mayor and council members and hunting for clues in the bowels of the city clerk's office, digging through dusty files because she valued getting the scoop over her manicure.

"Let me look into it for you. Maybe you could shadow me," I said.

Her eyes lit up. "Oh my God, Jordan, I'd love that! Thank you!" she said.

"So, uh, Grace, I'm going to be doing some investigative work on the Masey James case. Some of it will probably be off the clock, so you've got to be ready to roll with me," I said. "Do you have an iPhone?"

"Yes, actually, I just got one," she said.

By now Grace was undoubtedly envisioning herself doing her sign-off from a breaking news report: "This is Grace So-

and-So reporting for blah-blah news." There was nothing more
to explain.

It occurred to me I don't even know her last name.

"I'm going to be knocking on some doors this week, which
can get a little tricky. I'd feel better knowing someone was
recording just in case . . ." I trailed off, because I didn't want
to say, "just in case someone tries to jump me or something
goes wrong," and frighten her. "It's just a good idea to have
back up."

"Oh my God, Jordan, I'd love that! Thank you!" repeating
her exact words from before.

"Okay, I'll let you know," I said as we got off the elevator.
"Oh, and Grace, I'm embarrassed to say but I don't know your
last name."

"Ito!" she blurted out with no ego and no offense taken. "It's
Ito. I-t-o."

Now that I'd identified my apprentice, I had to figure out
how to pull this off and what I hoped to get out of this ar-
rangement. I decided to check out a new trendy coffee bar that
recently opened along the pedestrian walkway by the Chicago
River. Coffee is my water during the day, just as wine is my
drink at night, so it's a wonder it has taken me this long to
try it. Besides, a walk would give me time to think. I crossed
the circular drive by the Booth School of Business to access the
winding metal staircase leading to lower Michigan Avenue.
The sound of CTA buses and drivers laying on their horns to
leverage their way down the congested, luxurious Magnificent
Mile placed my body at the scene, but my mind was someplace
else. Outside a crowded high school gym after the bell for the
final period, waiting on my friend to meet me so that we could
walk to the bus stop together. I tell her, "I've got a ride today."

She scrunches up her face, disappointed. "Again?" she says. She looks forward to our talks after school, no matter how brief. "Okay then, girl, see you tomorrow," my new friend says, and walks away.

If I'm the friend, I'm thinking, *Why can't I walk with her to catch her ride? Why is the bus stop different? Is there something or someone she doesn't want me to see?* Maybe that's it. Masey was hiding something or someone. Was her "ride" at the vigil?

"What kind of car was it?" I had asked Shawn Jeffries, and she responded like a typical teenager. "I didn't pay any attention."

Jordan, you couldn't even tell Bass the color of the car in your parking space last night. Still, I couldn't shake the feeling there was something more to it. Finding out was my new obsession.

I descended the steps to the bowels of lower Michigan, looking behind me as if the way back would suddenly disappear. The upper and lower streets in downtown Chicago are a configuration like no place else. The first time I came down here, I kept waiting for someone to yell, "Get out from down there!" It's dark and oftentimes damp and a little scary at night. It reminds me of the tunnel in Paris where Princess Diana died in a car crash. But it's perfect for inconspicuous parking lots and gargantuan heating and cooling systems for the vast number of high-rise office buildings and hotels on the busy thoroughfare above.

The wind was crisp and strong along the riverfront and fashioned fast-moving ripples across the calm water. Chicago's wind is known as "the Hawk." It nearly blew me backward as I rounded the corner and fought against it to open the static door to the café, instead of using the revolving door. The river wind rushed in behind me and nudged me from behind like a playground bully, drawing a few glares from the patrons.

"Sorry," I said sheepishly and moved toward the counter. As I was about to place my order, I felt my cell phone vibrate in my pocket. I figured it was Joey returning my call. I was wrong. I stepped to one side to take the call.

"You must be kidding me," I said aloud to no one. It was Pamela Alonzo.

"Pamela, hi," I said, at a loss for words.

"Hello, Jordan," she said in a hoarse voice. "I wanted to call and thank you for everything you did yesterday. I saw your story. They can't forget about my baby after that, can they?"

Oh yes they can, and they just might.

"Not if I can help it," I said.

"I just wanted to tell you that I'm grateful. I know I didn't make it easy on you," she said.

"Pam, it's not your job to make it easy for me."

I was anxious to tell her about April. "I'm really glad you called. I thought about calling you, but I didn't want to intrude. Yesterday was overwhelming, and I'm sure you have a lot to do," I said.

"You mean the funeral," she said.

"Well, yes," I said.

"I would if they would release the body, but the medical examiner hasn't done that yet," she said.

What? That's insane. Dr. Chan completed his examination on Saturday; it's Wednesday. What the hell is going on? I had already intruded on Dr. Chan once today, but I felt the urge to call him back and ask him why the morgue had not released the body to the family. I couldn't dwell on that now. Pamela was on the phone, she'd reached out *to me*, and there were some important things I wanted her to know and needed to find out.

"Pam, remember the other day when you told me your mission in life was to find out who did this?" I asked.

"Yes, and I meant it, too," she said.

"I spoke to my editor this morning. The whole newsroom knows how important this investigation is," I said. A week ago, nobody was even trying to cover it.

"That's very different from what I've experienced, Jordan. You and I know that wasn't always the case, but I hope you're right," she said.

Summoning the courage, I blurted out, "Can we meet?"

I expected Pamela to hesitate. I was wrong about that, too.

"At the coffee shop?" she said.

"Are you up for it?"

"I've gotta get out of this house for a while. The walls are closing in on me," she said.

I'd gone this far; I might as well go all the way.

"Pamela, there's somebody I want you to meet. Somebody who wants to help, who *can* help, I think. She's from Aurora. She's a victim advocate."

"Is she White?" she asked, which struck me as odd.

"She is," I said, though it hadn't occurred to me that Pamela might be suspicious of April's motives. "She's been looking into cold cases and working with retired law enforcement officers to reopen cases and put pressure on departments for more than ten years. But I'd rather she tell you her story."

"I can be there in an hour," Pam said.

"Can you make it two hours? I need to see if April can join us. That's her name, April Murphy. She'll need time to get here. In either case, there are a few things I want to talk to you about. See you at two o'clock?"

"You interviewed her last night," Pam said. "Yes, she was interesting. I'd love to meet her. I'll be there."

··

So far today, things couldn't be going any better. After I hung up from Pam, I called April to see if she could meet us. Just so happens, she was already in the car headed to downtown Chicago to drop off paperwork to one of her clients. I asked her if she could meet me at one-thirty. I wanted time alone with her before Pamela arrived to feel her out on this reconnaissance mission.

"Yes, that should work perfectly," April said.

I arrived first and grabbed another coffee, then staked out the booth at the back of the store where Pam and I always sit. With a few moments to spare, I decided to call Lisette to give her the bad news.

"Hey, Jordie," she answered.

"Hey," I said unenthusiastically.

"What's wrong?" she asked. "Wait, I already know."

At times, Lisette can read me better than my mother. Sometimes we finish each other's sentences.

"Yeah, I'm so sorry. You know I would love to go, but it's not a good time for me to get away right now. The good news is I'm on special assignment," I said, brightening.

"Girl, you stay on special assignment. What is it this time?" Lisette asked.

I almost hated to tell her, because by now I must sound like a broken record. "The Masey James case. Nussbaum is cutting me some slack from the day-to-day to focus on it. I don't want to bore you with the details, but trust me, it's good news."

She sighed. "Well, okay. You know I was looking forward to seeing you every bit as much as Mike," she said.

"Some alone time together will be good for the two of you," I said.

"You're right," she said. "I think I'm in love."

"What!" I shouted, drawing attention from the patrons standing at the counter. "Really?"

"It hit me the other night when we were talking on the phone," she said.

"Have you told him?" I asked.

"*No,*" she said. "He hasn't told me yet. I'm not saying it first."

"Okay, well, yeah, I know you," I said, chuckling.

"I dunno. Something about this trip feels different," she said.

"Then I don't feel so bad about not going. You all don't need me there."

Call waiting signaled an incoming from Joey. As badly as I hated to miss it, Lisette's revelation was far too surprising and important to cut her short.

"It's only a three-hour drive, so don't be surprised if you look up and see me waiting for you in the lobby," she said. "Bass'll let me inside."

"Hell, Bass will let you in my apartment!" I said.

Just then, I looked up and saw April Murphy coming through the revolving door. "And I would definitely welcome a visit," I said, omitting *if I can get the time off.* If she comes to town, I'll deal with it then. "We could double-date! But listen, let's talk later. I've gotta go. My meeting just arrived."

"Okay, I love you," she said.

"That's right, you just keep right on practicing those three little words," I said.

"Only after he says it first!"

"Love you, too. Bye!"

April Murphy was almost unrecognizable. She had upgraded her suburban minivan mom look to suburban cool mom in a pair of black faux leather pants, with a matching black half sweater, a half faux leather jacket, a white turtleneck, and red high heel ankle boots. Our eyes met and I waved her over. She was carrying a stuffed brown legal folder.

"Hi, Jordan," she said, extending her right hand while clutching the folder against her chest. "I'm glad we could do this today."

"Thanks for coming on such short notice. Pamela is joining us at two. I wanted us to have some time to talk before she gets here."

"Perfect! Because there's something I'd like to share with you," she said.

"Okay."

"I have a friend who has done some consulting work for the state crime lab. He's my boyfriend, actually," she said with a tinge of embarrassment. "I hate that word."

"Oh," I said, finding her revelation unnecessary. It made me wonder whether she was always this transparent with reporters. No doubt, I wasn't her first.

"Look, the only reason I'm telling you this is because I think he can be of some help to you—and to Pamela Alonzo."

"How's that?" I asked.

"Seth, that's his name. He knows the state crime lab is a shit show of grand proportions," she said, checking around as if someone in the boisterously loud café could overhear us.

"How do you mean?" I asked.

"Noncompliance, ineptitude, downright stupidity," she said. "Just short of malfeasance, and I'm not convinced that's wrong, either."

Pressed for time, I probed. "Okay, what specifically are you talking about?"

She sighed hard. "Jordan, you won't believe how much gets lost, overlooked, improperly assessed. If there's one thing prosecutors and defense attorneys agree on, it's that they are more likely to lose a case in the state crime lab before it ever gets to court."

"Go on," I urged.

April rested her left hand on the brown legal folder. "I've been keeping a record of their mistakes going back ten years," she said and began pulling out data sheets and newspaper clippings. "It's so bad, I've got to believe that some of it is on purpose. I'm talking DNA that could have changed the outcome of hundreds of cases lost or never reviewed, or if it was, the results could be delayed for months. Here, check out this piece in the *Sun-Times*."

April and I leaned in close, our heads nearly touching.

"This is from 2003. Hundreds of rape kits from poor communities in suburban Cook County were never processed!"

"Wow, really?" I said and picked up the clipping. "I hadn't heard about this. This happened before I moved here."

Underneath the clipping was a stack of logs. "What's recorded on these?"

"These are evidence logs from the state's crime lab, from the county's, and from the city of Chicago's," she said, spreading them out side by side on the table. "Look here." She pointed to a line item. "See the entry date of this blood sample? It was from a murder committed during a home invasion. There was a struggle and blood had been collected from the scene that didn't belong to the victim. See the case file number?"

"Yes," I said. "But wait. How did you get these?"

She grinned coyly and batted her eyes.

"Oh," I said. "Never mind."

"Now look at the date recorded by the city's crime lab. June 15, 2001. Right? The results were inconclusive. So the city sent the sample to the state crime lab in Springfield on June 29. Now look at the evidence log for the state. See that case file number?" I nodded. "The evidence wasn't logged by the state until November of that year. You mean to tell me it took five months for that evidence to travel 170 miles down I-55 to Springfield?"

"That's insane!" I said. "Was there ever a result?"

"No," April said, shaking her head slowly. "I looked up the case file. The victim was a seventy-seven-year-old Black man. God bless him, he must've tried to fight 'em off, because he drew blood from his attacker. An arrest was never made in that case."

I looked up at April, bewildered by what she was telling me. "And let me guess, that wasn't an isolated case?"

"You got it! It happens time and time again," she said. "I've tried to get print reporters interested in this story and in connecting the dots. The TV reporters blew me off entirely. The *Sun-Times* and the *Herald* did the rape kit story. But news organizations have short attention spans when it comes to these things. Too scientific; too 'in the weeds,' they tell me. One reporter said his editor asked him, 'How many more stories can we write about government agencies being inept?' The topic grew stale *to them*, and they moved on."

"Meanwhile, the number of cold cases just keep piling up," I said.

"Exactly. That's why in recent years, more private labs have sprung up. Some of the better public labs are run out of the South and Southwest, in cities like Tulsa and Dallas–Fort Worth. We've got to have one of the worst systems in the country. And from what I'm told, law enforcement across the state ain't big on asking the FBI crime lab for help when they're stumped."

April was talking so fast, I could barely keep up to form an opinion. *This is what April wanted to talk to me about? To pitch a story every television outlet in town had already turned down? And why did they? It is interesting.*

"All of this is public record?" I asked.

"Well, most of it, yes," she said.

"Wow, you must be the queen of the FOIA," I said.

"That I am, but I didn't FOIA all of this," she said, the wry smile returning. "Ever heard of pillow talk?"

There's something about lying in bed with someone that makes us vulnerable. When we shed our clothes along with our inhibitions, that can lull even the most esteemed professionals into sharing confidential information that could get them fired if it ever came to light. April, I believed, risked sharing to convince me of her allyship.

"What does Seth do for the state crime lab?" I asked.

"He doesn't work for the lab directly. He accredits public and private labs that have a staff of more than ten people."

Maybe my prayers are working. This guy is the forensic equivalent of a CIA operative. I'm impressed. April's forthrightness melted my skepticism and I felt compelled to share something about myself.

"You know the leading forensic pathologist in Cook County? Dr. Marvin Chan?"

"Of course!" she said, "but I don't know him, personally. Seth has met him. He has a lot of respect for that man."

"Dr. Chan is a *dear, dear* friend of mine," I said. "I spoke with him earlier today."

I felt the need to clarify: "But not pillow talk, let's be clear. We met when I was in grad school."

I was reticent to tell April about the tissue sample that Dr. Chan had sent out for analysis in the James case. Come to think of it, Masey hadn't been the focus of her conversation thus far.

"Interesting," she said. "Does he give you scoops?"

"Well, I wouldn't say that, but yes, he's a good friend." My mother has a saying: "It's one thing to tell your business, it's another to tell someone else's." Dr. Chan and I have several years of friendship on April Murphy. I wasn't about to break his confidence for her on day one. "Dr. Chan is out of the country right now, so I'm not sure how much help he'll be at the moment."

"Hmm. Well, I think we could make quite a pair, Jordan," she said.

You could be a valuable source, April, but a pair sounds exclusive, and that's not what this is. April is amiable, but with sources, especially new ones, I try and do more listening than talking so that I don't inadvertently say something that April could take back to a competitor, unwittingly or not.

"One thing is for sure, after hearing about all this evidence bungling, at such a high level, I'm going to track analysis of evidence in this case very closely," I said.

"Hey, mind if I grab a coffee and a muffin really fast?" April asked.

"No, go right ahead," I said.

"Okay, great. I'll be right back."

"You mind if I look through these?" I asked pointing to the neat brown legal folder.

"No, go ahead. Just keep the pages in order. There's a method to my madness," she said.

I found it interesting that April described the Dallas–Fort Worth crime lab as one of the best in the country. But I suspect further analysis would show that the way crimes are prioritized has a lot to do with it. Chicago crime isn't all gun violence and gangs, but because those crimes occur more frequently, they receive more attention than kidnappings and serial murders.

I'd ignored several pings from my cell phone while listening to April's story. I had three text messages. One from Pamela: I'm parking. One from Joey: What's up? And one from Mrs. Bennett: Hi, Jordan. How are you? Saw your report the other night. Great job! Are you free for dinner Sunday?

Margaret Bennett's husband, Robert, was a college buddy of my uncle Stew's, my dad's much older brother by twelve years. When he learned I was moving to Chicago, he arranged for me to meet the Bennetts. Since then, they've become my great-aunt and -uncle away from home. Mr. Bennett is a financial wiz and has given me excellent advice on my taxes, and Margaret, whom he calls "my Maggie," is a renowned art curator, and she exudes all the elegance, style, and finesse that comes with that title. I relish Sunday dinners with the Bennetts. It makes me feel like I'm back in Texas with my family. After nearly fifty years of marriage, they still seem genuinely crazy about each other and they still look good. A beautiful older Black couple, they're aspirational.

I returned Pam's text: OK, we're both here. I'll see you soon. And Mrs. Bennett's: Thank you, Mrs. Bennett. Yes, I'd be delighted to join you this Sunday. To Joey: In mtg. Call U back.

I looked up just as both Pam and April were walking toward the table. I slid out of the booth and stood up to greet Pam and, no question in my mind, to hug her, too. I held out my arms and she practically fell into them. I stumbled backward a bit.

Out of the corner of my eye, I caught April's sympathetic expression.

"Pamela," I said, releasing my grip. She pulled away. "Have a seat here next to me."

Pamela looked up just as April took her seat on the other side of the booth. "This is April Murphy with Women United Against Violence."

"Ms. Alonzo, thank you for meeting with me today. You have my sincere and heartfelt condolences," she said. "I'll do anything I can to help you. That's a promise."

Pamela dropped her head and looked up, tears welling in her eyes.

"I appreciate that Ms. Murphy, but it's too late to help me. My child is already dead. But maybe we can help the next one."

April took Pamela by both hands. "I know you're right, but that breaks my heart. I haven't lost a child, but I lost my mother to violence when I was in high school. I can't change what happened to her, but I do this work because of her. I guess that's why I can't let it go."

I fought back the tears, because I understood that mandate. I've used it myself to fill the void of having someone you love ripped from existence.

"So you understand, I'm not letting go until the man who did this is either dead or in prison," Pamela said. "They catch your mother's killer?"

"Yes. There was no mystery there. It was her ex-boyfriend. He'd been stalking her for months," April said.

"Glad you got closure. See, I'm afraid I won't live long enough to see that day. I don't have any faith in the police after the way they handled—or I should say, mishandled—my daughter's disappearance. If I heard the word *runaway* one more time . . . I was gonna scream!"

Her voice rose into a near scream. Her mood can change in

an instant, as it did yesterday when I was interviewing her at her "sister-in-love's." But that's to be expected under the circumstances.

"Through all of this, I've begged the police, and I begged them again last night, to do everything in their power to catch who did this. No, I didn't bad-mouth them, because I need them on *my* side. You understand?" Pamela said. "This isn't going to be another unsolved murder on the South Side. And you said the magic words last night on TV, April. You said if it'd been *your* daughter, the police would've handled things differently. I believe you're right."

It was then that April Murphy came into view for me as savvy and deliberate. For surely, it wasn't lost on her that as a White suburban woman, for her to say what she did on the air last night boxes the critics in from describing Pamela as just another angry Black woman complaining about the police. April might not be batting a thousand with media, but she doesn't fit the profile of someone who can be easily dismissed on police investigations.

I drifted away from the conversation for long enough that by the time I sprung back into consciousness, April was boasting about how her group helps victims' families put pressure on police to do their jobs, and the success she's had reviving cold cases across the country, which was different from the series of failures she described to me a few minutes ago.

Pamela and April were getting on well, and I hated to break their groove. But the question that had been burning in my brain since last night wouldn't let me wait a minute longer.

"Guys, I'm sorry to interrupt, but, Pamela, I recall you telling me how Masey got to school every day. We were here, remember?"

"Yes," she said.

"You said she took a couple of buses and walked about a half mile on the final leg of the trip."

"Right," she said.

"Did she take the same route home? Or did she get a ride home from school?" I asked.

Pamela looked puzzled. "No, she came back the same way. I don't get off till six on Wednesday and Thursdays, and I work until seven on Tuesdays, Fridays, and Saturdays," she said. "On Mondays, I pick up Malcolm early from after-school care. His auntie Cyn gets him the rest of the week. I wish I could've picked her up."

It was as I'd feared.

"The reason I asked, Pamela, is because last night I met a girl from Masey's school. She said they were friends. She told me that Masey got rides from school in the days leading up to her disappearance. Not every day, but on occasion," she said.

"What?" Pamela exploded. "From who?"

"She didn't know. She said she and Masey would meet after school by the gym and she'd walk Masey to the bus stop."

"Okay, but she got on the bus, right?"

"Well, yes, on those days, she would get on the bus. But the girl said they'd meet at the gym regardless of whether Masey had a ride or not. She said Masey usually wouldn't know until the end of the day," I said. "But she didn't walk Masey to her ride."

"Masey never got no rides from school!" Pamela said with a look of disbelief mixed with betrayal. "That's a damn lie!"

"Pam, she said she saw Masey get in a car once from a distance, but she couldn't tell the make or model. You know kids. She didn't think anything of it."

"Was she sure?" Pam said, clearly struggling to breathe.

"I have no reason to doubt her. She seemed sincere, and she

was very, very upset about Masey," I said. "I didn't include this in my report, because if there's something to it—well, my instinct told me not to."

"Why haven't the police said anything?" she said.

"I honestly don't think they know. I haven't mentioned it to them yet. I wanted to ask you first," I said.

"Oh my God!" Pamela said. "Oh my God!"

Pamela looked confused and frightened. It was obvious she genuinely knew nothing about this.

"Could a family member have picked her up?" I asked.

"No, not without me knowing about it!" she said.

April shifted uncomfortably in her seat and leaned back away from the table. I felt it, too, the awkwardness of learning at the same time as Pamela this revelation about her daughter. Any parent with a teenager knows their child doesn't tell them everything. But a secret this big, this out of character as a guy picking her up from school? This was a blow, one that might push us closer to the killer but destroy Pamela in a way she couldn't brace herself for, a betrayal of the closeness she believed she shared with Masey.

"What's this little girl's name?" Pam asked.

"Her name is Shawn Jeffries," I said.

"You did interview her. I saw that," April said.

"Yes, but I asked the editor to cut the part about Masey getting rides. Listen, something just told me to protect her. And from your reaction, I think I was right."

"Jordan, your instincts seem on point to me," April said.

"We've got to tell the police," Pamela said.

"I agree," I said.

"I'm calling them right now," she said, and reached into her purse for her cell phone. "I'm calling Detective Fawcett."

As she waited for an answer, a look of disbelief remained

frozen on Pamela's face. "Detective Fawcett, this is Pamela Alonzo. I just found out that someone saw my daughter get in the car with somebody after school. I didn't know nothing about her getting rides from school. Call me."

"It went to voice mail. Oh my God! Jordan," she turned to me, now in tears. "This has gotta mean something. If Masey was getting rides from someone legitimate, someone I trusted, I would've known about it. If we find out who it is . . ."

". . . it might lead us to the killer," I finished.

The three of us sat silent for a moment. I hated to push, but I had one more important ask. "I'd like to talk to Masey's favorite cousin, Yvonne," I said.

"I'm sure Yvonne don't know this. Something like this, she would've told me. She's not crazy," Pam said.

"I understand, but you all are family. Let me see if I can get something out of her that she may not be ready to tell you. She may be too afraid to tell you, honestly," I said.

I instantly regretted the way that must have sounded. I didn't want her to think I was suggesting that Yvonne was lying to her or that this wasn't a close family. But I do know that kids don't tell their parents everything. They get pulled into places and spaces their parents would flip out over if they knew. Pamela's grieving, I know, but she understands what I'm talking about, whether she admits it or not.

Masey might very well have been sexually active, experimented with alcohol and smoking weed or something more. She was, after all, at that critical age.

Pamela quieted down. Just as I was about to clarify myself, she said, "You're probably right. Yvonne does hair out of her house, but I can't imagine she's taking appointments right now. I'll call her. When do you want to go?"

"Later today, if possible," I said.

My cell phone vibrated. It was Joey again. Either he didn't see my text, or it was important. I thought about telling Pamela and April that I have a friend at the police department but decided to keep it to myself.

"I'm sorry, ladies, but I'm going to have to go," I said. "I've got to return an important phone call."

Tears rained down Pam's face. As she struggled to gain composure, I realized she might not be composed enough to figure this out right now. "Okay, I'll get back to you about Yvonne," Pam said.

"What's her address?" I asked.

Pamela hesitated. "I'll text it to you," she said, "but I want to be there when you talk to her, okay? Don't go without me."

"All right. I'll wait to hear from you," I said.

"Cameras!" April said abruptly. "We should be able to get camera footage from around the school."

"Yes, but that's something the police will probably have to ask for," I said.

"Damn right!" Pamela said.

"Pam, if I were you, I'd go straight to the police station from here. And April, please, this has got to stay between the three of us. I just gave up a lot here, so can you promise me you won't share this with any other media?"

"You have my word," April said.

As I got up to leave, Pamela tugged my jacket sleeve. "Jordan, thank you."

I nodded at them and bolted for the exit. Before I got out the door, my finger was already on the callback button.

"Hello," Joey answered.

"Hey, Joe Joe. Sorry, I've been in meetings this morning whenever you've called," I said.

"So what's up?" he asked. "Oh, and before you ask, I don't know anything else about the James case."

"Well, this time I know something you don't," I said as I navigated my way up Lake Street through breaks in the pedestrian traffic.

"Oh," he said, just as the "L" train screeched overhead with the deafening sound of grinding metal and speed. "I can't hear you!"

"Wait, there's a train," I said. "Hold on."

I scanned the block for a sound barrier and eased my way into the archway of a bank building, blocking the entrance, eliciting a dirty look from a patron. "Okay, can you hear me now?"

"Yes. So, what do you know that I don't know about a case I'm not working on." He laughed.

"Very funny. Listen, last night, one of Masey's classmates told me she was getting rides from school every now and then in the weeks leading up to her disappearance. I just shared that with her mother, and her head exploded. She knew nothing about that!"

"You tell Fawcett?" he asked.

"No, not yet, because I wanted to ask the mom first to see if there was anything to it. There's something to it. She called and left him a message."

"Okay, so what can I do for you?" he asked.

"Tell Bartlett! I know it's not your case, but you can just tell him someone who knows you personally reached out. I don't care if you tell them it was me, okay? I just need Chicago PD to get over to that school and see if they can get security video of Masey getting into a car. And they better do it quick, because I'm heading over there now with a camera, and it's gonna be on the news tonight. I promise you."

"Why don't you call him?" Joey asked.

"I plan to! But I thought a detective inside the department could get results faster than a reporter calling in a tip."

"I'm not sure who's the detective, you or me," he said.

I didn't know whether Joey was being facetious or complimentary. But I don't care. I've confirmed a break in the case and planned to run with it, even if it meant police playing catch-up.

"If the school surveillance video exists of Masey getting in this car, it'll look better for the CPD if they've pulled it by the time I break this story tonight."

BREAKING NEWS

Diana Sorano: A day after area residents gathered in Bronzeville to remember Masey James, the fifteen-year-old homicide victim whose body was found on an abandoned playground, News Channel 8 has learned of an important break in the investigation. What police are calling a person of interest. Our Jordan Manning reports.

Jordan: Diana, I'm on the West Side in front of Carol Crest Academy. The person of interest police is looking for was seen picking up Masey James from here before she went missing. It has been almost a week since she was found dead, and this might be the first big break in the case. It's unclear who this individual is, but I am told it's not believed to be a relative or anyone associated with her family. Police are poring over surveillance video from security cameras around the school as they try and get an ID on the car, and the driver.

Diana: Do we know how police learned about this person?

Jordan: It's unclear at this time, Diana, how this came to the attention of police.

If they find out I called in this tip, I'm screwed. I know I did the right thing. I know I did the right thing.

Diana: Thank you Jordan, and we will continue to follow this breaking news.

..

I decided not to wait for Joey to tell Bartlett about Masey's mysterious driver. I called Bartlett the minute we hung up.

"Superintendent Bartlett, hello. Listen, I just learned that Masey James was getting a ride from school on a regular basis. Her mother doesn't know who this person is, and I'm worried he might have something to do with her disappearance."

"I know; Fawcett just told me. He said the victim's mother left him a message. I wonder why she hadn't mentioned this before?"

"Because she didn't know. I told her," I said, "this afternoon."

"You told her? What do you mean, you told her? How would you know this?" Bartlett said, sounding both confused and annoyed.

"One of her classmates," I said.

"You went to her school?"

"No. I spoke to the student last night at the vigil. She told me that Masey was getting rides from school as recently as a few days before she went missing. And today I was talking to Pamela and I asked her if she knew anything about someone picking Masey up from school, and she clearly didn't, because she hit the ceiling," I said.

"Jordan, she was upset, but did she say anything about Masey having a boyfriend? Or any idea who this person could be?" Bartlett asked.

"No. She was completely blindsided."

Surely police would ask Pamela those very questions.

"Do you think it was appropriate to go to a family member—

the child's mother—and ask her something that may or may not be true? You hadn't vetted this. You could have come to me. You know my number," Bartlett said.

I wasn't accustomed to Bartlett admonishing me about the way I do my job.

"Look, you can criticize my tactics, Superintendent, but tell me this, is there one detective in your department who knew this information? I don't think they did. So along with your criticism, how about a thank-you? Because you just got your big break. Look, we're on the same side. I want this person to be caught, I know, as much as you do. But, Superintendent, some of your detectives, they're not impeccable when it comes to following up on cases involving missing Black and brown kids."

I don't know why I expected Bartlett to thank me. Once Fawcett finds out who the tip *really* came from, we might have a fractured relationship for a long time, and it wasn't that great to begin with. Was it worth it? Absolutely.

Now the ball is in their court to find out who this person is. Have they checked the surveillance cameras in and around the school? Or at nearby convenience stores? Have they talked to students at her school? Do your damn jobs! What does it say about their detective work when I was able to accomplish more in an hour with Grace Ito, whom I dragged along to canvass the school and gain some real-world reporter experience, than the CPD had managed in three days. With her youthful, trendy appearance in a bebe cardigan, high-rise jeans, and ballet flats, she blended in with the diverse student body of the STEM school, scoping out opportunities to question students, while I talked to the school's principal, Dr. Evelyn Moss. She refused to go on-camera, because she hadn't gotten permission from the Chicago Public Schools to do the interview. Turns out she wasn't even remotely helpful. I texted Grace to meet me back at my car to give me a quick download before I filmed my lead-in.

"Jordan, you won't believe this! I talked to a student who said he remembers seeing Masey get into a car a couple times after school," Grace said.

"Did she say what kind of car?"

"It's a *he*, and he said it was a sports car, maybe a Dodge Charger, but he wasn't sure. He said he noticed it because one of the rims was missing, and the driver was wearing this 'dope-ass jacket,' he called it."

"Was it a man in the car?"

"I didn't ask him, but I assumed he was talking about a guy from what he said about the jacket and the rims."

"Did he say anything about what the guy looked like?" I asked.

"He said he was a big guy," Grace said.

"As in heavy? Tall?" I asked.

"That's all he said—a big guy. He didn't get a real good look at him. He just saw him in passing," Grace said. "He said he walked his girlfriend to the bus stop and spotted Masey getting into the car as he was crossing the street heading back toward the school for football practice. He said he was running late to practice, so he didn't get a good look at him. Oh, but he said he had a low fade haircut from what he could tell."

"Good work, Grace!" I said. "What's the kid's name?"

Grace looked stricken suddenly, and the color drained from her face. "Oh. Uh, I dunno. I didn't get it."

I closed my eyes and dropped my head, fighting the urge to scream, *You didn't get it? Are you crazy?* Instead, I breathed deeply and mustered a calm "Why not?"

"It was happening so fast. The hallway cleared out after the bell and I had to duck into the girls' bathroom. I don't know!"

said Grace, shaking her head and growing more distraught by the second. "I was afraid of getting caught!"

"Okay," I said, "rule of thumb: always ask the person's name first. Always, always. Got it?"

"Got it," she said.

Masey had a secret boyfriend. But who was he a secret from? Was it just from her mother? Did her friends know about him? Was he involved in her disappearance? My mind went back to my cousin Stephanie's lying to her parents about a band trip so that she could spend an entire weekend with an older man. Is Masey's boyfriend an older guy? The type who hangs out around high schools? Who would Masey have confided in?

Her cousin Yvonne.

My phone vibrated and I looked down and saw a text message from Joey.

I did what you asked, but our cover is blown, he wrote.

I texted back: **WHAT ARE YOU TALKING ABOUT?**

I sighed and shook my head. I wanted to call him, but whatever Joey meant, I would have to deal with it later. Right now I'm focused on Yvonne. All paths were leading to her. Besides, she was one of the last people to see Masey alive.

"What's the matter?" Grace asked.

"Nothing. Everything's fine."

I scrolled through my text messages and checked my email. Still no note from Pamela with Yvonne's address.

"Grace, are you free tonight?" I asked.

"Yeah, I'm available," she said. "What's up?"

"I'm going to ride out to Englewood. I hope by the time I get there, Pamela Alonzo will have texted me her cousin's address, but I think I know where she lives. I want to drive around."

"Okay, I'm in. Just the two of us?"

"Yeah, I sent the camera home. This is investigative journalism, Grace. We're investigating," I explained. "Have your iPhone ready. We can get some pictures, at least."

I texted Pamela: Can we meet at Yvonne's? What's her address? I'm on the West Side. It'll take me about 30 minutes to get there.

I dropped a bombshell on Pam about a mysterious person in her daughter's life. Someone who in fact might have killed her. Pamela has said twice now that she won't be satisfied until he's dead or in prison. Does she have an inkling who it is? Is she at this very moment out looking for him? Or is she having a mental breakdown, curled up in a fetal position and convulsed in tears? Was I expecting too much from a grieving mother? Maybe Bartlett was right.

I took the 71st Street exit off the Dan Ryan Expressway and drove west. I checked my phone—still nothing from Pam. I am now concerned about this radio silence.

Did April say something off-putting after I left the two of them alone? Did Fawcett tell her to stop talking to the press?

I recognized the blond-brick facade of the Fellowship Missionary Baptist Church at Sangamon, Louise's street, but drove past. The next block was Peoria, the street Cynthia Caruthers told me Yvonne lived on, but she didn't know the house number. I kept going.

"What are we looking for?" Grace asked.

I didn't know how to answer her. I was on a wild-goose chase, cruising around a neighborhood I knew nothing about apart from the news stories that all too often tell the worst and not the best that happens, which, again, is part of the struggle I have with what I do for a living. The power we have in the media to paint a perception of a neighborhood as reality by the stories we cover.

Englewood looks different in daylight. Clusters of people are gathered on front porches and steps, and along sidewalks teenagers no different from Masey block the path as if the street belongs to them. And honestly it does. This is the center of the universe for them. Nothing is bigger or more important than where you are from. It's your identity, which is why the death of a young girl from this neighborhood is so painful. It's no secret a blind eye can be cast on the death of someone who "deserved it," but no one thinks this of Masey.

The issue that continues to upset me is if they all know she didn't deserve this ending, then why make it her story? Someone knows something, and now I've dragged this kid Grace into my obsession to figure it out.

I didn't realize I was deep in thought, a full-on daydream, until the driver behind me laid on the horn and passed recklessly on my left, crossing into the opposite lane and swerving over just in time to avoid an oncoming SUV. I had forgotten in the moment that Grace was even in the car until I heard her gasp.

Grace's eyes grew large.

I tried to reassure her. "It's okay. Just somebody in a big hurry."

Grace got her bearings again. "It's kind of sad here. Nothing is open. It's all boarded up," she said.

"Yes, but that'll change in the next block or so," I said. "Watch."

"Hey, there's St. Luke's church! I didn't know it was around here," Grace said, pointing to the iconic sanctuary led by an activist minister who has organized numerous anti-gun and anti-gang rallies in the community. He is always in the news, again proving my point that to someone not from this neighborhood, it could never be so close to what Grace called a "sad" area.

"It's beautiful and bigger than I imagined," she said.

To me, St. Luke's represents the potential of Englewood, a neighborhood of pastors, parishioners, business owners, and residents who also see its potential, and work hard to make a better life for themselves and a better future for their community. If it weren't for divestment in its infrastructure and the interminable drug and gang violence, one could only imagine the possibilities. The brownstones just a few miles down the road on Lake Shore Drive would go for a million dollars or more. Englewood, properly tended, had the potential to raise many ships.

We passed nearly two blocks with nothing but sidewalks and vacant land on either side of the street before coming upon the Miracle Salon, the sole building on its block, its own little island.

"You've gotta love the name, right?" I said.

"Right," said Grace.

I thought about going inside to ask about Masey. Then I remembered Pam saying that Yvonne does hair out of her house, what my best friend in college called a kitchen-tician. Every Sunday a gang of us would pack into someone's dorm room and proceed to relax, braid, and cut one another's hair. If you were lucky, Renée would help you out. If you were unlucky, you got me. I was not that good, but I never had a challenge I didn't meet—that is, until I tried to shave one side of Renée's roommate's hair for an edgy look. It was more of an edgeless look.

I was on Yvonne's stomping grounds. She might know the owner of the salon or the women inside, and the last thing I needed was people telling her that Jordan Manning from Channel 8 was in there asking about Masey. I didn't want the word on the street to be our introduction. I need an ally in her, not an enemy.

A little farther up on the east side of Halsted was a convenience store, the L & H Convenience Mart, that anchored a few stores in a strip mall, including a barbershop that was packed even at this time of day. The L & H sign looked like it had been painted by hand in red letters against a yellow background. I figured there was no better place to start a search with no bread crumbs to lead me. I made an abrupt U-turn, and boom, we were right in front. Now I would have to muster the courage to go inside and do what I needed to do.

Young people milled about in the lot. I could tell, even if they didn't come here to buy anything, they'd come just to socialize.

"Okay, wait here," I said.

"You don't want me to go in with you?" Grace asked. "With my iPhone?"

"No. I'll just be a minute," I said.

Inside L & H, two clerks were barely visible behind the thick plexiglass barrier—a young woman sitting on a stool off to the side, talking on her cell phone, and a young man in his twenties chatting with a middle-aged man buying lottery tickets. I stood back and waited for them to wrap up.

"Good luck. I hope you win," said the clerk, who was brown-skinned with coarse, shiny black hair and an accent that told me he wasn't from this neighborhood.

"Hello," I said to the passing older gentleman. He did a double take as if he recognized me. He looked about to speak, but I could tell he wasn't quite sure, so he didn't say anything. He isn't the first person to be thrown off by my shorter hairdo.

"Powerball ticket?" the male clerk said with a smile.

"Not this time." I smiled. "I'm Jordan Manning with Channel 8 News."

He began to shake his head and held up his hands as if I'd said I was about to hold up the place. "No, no, no, I don't want to be on-camera. I don't want to be quoted. No," he said emphatically.

The irony of the mic being viewed as a weapon is not lost on me. That again speaks to the danger and the power it holds.

"Oh, you won't be." I grinned. "I don't have a camera. I promise. See? Hands free."

"Okay," he said with a glint of suspicion. "What can I do for you, ma'am?"

"Do you get a lot of students in here after school?" I asked.

"Yes, but we only allow three in at once. Otherwise, they'd clean me out," he said.

"What school is closest to here?" I asked.

"There are two. Hilton and Sumner. That's the school for the kids who got kicked out of regular school. What's this about?"

"I'm not trying to get you into anything. I promise. We're just talking. What's your name?"

"Eddie," he said.

"Nice to meet you, Eddie," I said. "Did you know that a student who used to go to Hilton High was found dead last week?"

"You're a detective." It wasn't a question.

"No, I'm a reporter for Channel 8. I'm following the story. I'm just curious and asking people for help. There is no way this should be an unsolved case, don't you agree?"

"I guess. I just don't know what you want from me, what you want me to say," he said.

"I don't want you to say anything, but I would love it if you could share anything you might know or may have heard."

His expression turned remorseful. "It's terrible. I couldn't believe it when I found out. She used to come in here all the time after school with her friends."

"Really? Masey James?"

"Not as much lately, because she changed schools. I was happy for her. But she still came in on the weekends sometimes," he said.

I had to think about how to ask my next question. I didn't want him to think I suspected him of anything. "So you knew about her changing schools. You talked to her sometimes."

"I mean, not really, or at least not for long. I hadn't seen her in a while and asked her, 'Where you been?' and she told me she goes to a different school," he said. "I make conversations with customers, you know. But I didn't even know her name."

If you didn't know her name, how'd you put two and two together that the dead girl was the same girl who came into the store?

"But you're sure it was Masey?"

"Yes, it was definitely her."

"Forgive me, but how can you be so sure?"

"Not to sound creepy or anything, but she was hard to miss. She was a real knockout. Taller than most girls her age. Very polite. I was sorry to hear what happened to her. Somebody brought in posters for us to hang up in the store with her picture. We did it, but after they found her, we took them down right away."

Eddie could no longer hide the way he felt.

"You seem really upset about it," I said.

"It's just so sad, you know. I have a little sister around her age. I couldn't imagine anything happening to her."

"Did you ever see her in the store with a guy?" I asked.

"*Mmm*, let me think. I'm back here most of the time. I don't see everything that goes on out on the floor. Like I said, her and her friends came in a lot. One of them came in yesterday. I'd seen them together a few times. I tell her, 'I'm sorry about your friend.'"

"Do you know her friend's name?"

"I don't know her name," he said, "but she starts saying all this stuff, like, she heard police think some kids did it."

Everything Eddie had said up until this point made sense.

"What'd you say? Some kids did what?"

"Did *it*," he said.

"Killed her?" I asked.

"Look, I don't know. This girl said she heard people talking."

Who is this girl?

"Hey, man, what's taking so long?" said a voice behind me. Eddie looked over at the clerk still sitting on the stool talking on her cell phone.

"Kendall," he said, startling her. "Open the register."

"I'm on my break!" she shot back.

"Break is over now. Get over here!" he said.

"Eddie." I moved closer to the partition. "Can we speak without this between us?"

He pointed toward the opposite end of the counter and I followed his instruction. I met him at the side door. He unlocked it and stepped out onto the main floor. The counter gave him height; he was much shorter up close.

"Okay, so I thought that was very strange, what she told me," he said.

"This girl said *the police* are saying some kids did it? You sure?" I probed.

"I think that's what I heard. I'm sure she said kids, though," he said, sounding unsure as hell. "She said something about a lady telling the police she saw some boys over by where the girl was found."

"Eddie, what did this girl look like who told you this? Can you describe her? Any features stand out? Tall? Short? Fat? Skinny? Long hair? Short hair?" I said in quick succession.

"She's a cute girl. It's hard to tell behind the counter how tall she is. All I see are the tops of people's heads," he said.

"What's her hair look like?" I asked.

"It changes all the time," he said. "It was braided yesterday, I think. Long braids."

"What about her skin tone? Lighter or darker than me?" I asked.

"She's lighter than you. Way lighter," he said. "She's lighter than me." He pointed to himself and chuckled.

"What time was she here yesterday?"

"Very late last night. I don't know the exact time, but it had to be, oh, not too long before closing," he said.

"What time do you close?" I asked.

"Two o'clock," he said.

I thought about Yvonne with her short, blond-streaked hair. That was just yesterday. I doubt the kitchen-tician left the vigil, braided her hair, and hit a convenience store afterward.

"Eddie, I don't doubt she said it, but that makes no sense."

"Believe me, I hear it all day. Kids talking stuff on each other, saying crazy stuff. That's probably all it was," he said.

Patrons began to pile into the store. Some grew annoyed as they waited in line.

"Eddie! I could use some help!" Kendall yelled, getting her revenge for the way he'd spoken to her minutes earlier.

"I've gotta go now, lady," he said abruptly. "I'm so sorry."

"Thank you, Eddie. You've been very nice, and very helpful," I said.

As I made my way to the front door, I heard a car horn honking incessantly. It sounded close. It was mine. When I emerged, I saw Grace holding my phone in her hand waving it. I was so focused on her phone, I'd left my own in the car.

She rolled the window down and shouted, "It's been ringing and ringing, but you told me to stay in the car."

I ran to the car and jumped in and grabbed it from her just as the ringing stopped. The caller was Justin Smierciak.

"You were in there a long time. Your phone rang three times."

"Yeah, well, I wanted to talk to the clerk, but I had to wait in line like everybody else," I said.

"Did you find out anything?" she asked.

My thoughts were so jumbled by the far-out theory Eddie had just shared that I didn't know how to put it into words.

"Masey did hang out here," I said. "I was right about that. The clerk remembers her being in the store often. But that was about it."

I wanted to call Joey but not in front of Grace. I only hope that when Joey said "our cover is blown," he didn't mean I could no longer count on him for the inside scoop, because I needed it now more than ever. My instincts were telling me that the rumor mill was working overtime to pump out such a ridiculous story about kids being involved in Masey's murder. Sometimes the streets talk faster and louder than any news network. As for Justin, he calls me after five o'clock only when he's looking for somebody to go grab a beer with. Before heading back toward downtown, I decided to circle a couple of blocks along Peoria and Sangamon.

"What are we looking for now?" Grace asked.

I suspected that by now Grace was growing impatient and wondering what the hell she had signed up for by agreeing to this ride-along.

"Sometimes you don't know what you're looking for. But you know it when you see it, like the convenience store," I said, putting on my mentor hat. "Investigative journalism requires patience. You have to trust the process. Some clues jump out at you. Others you have to dig for and get your hands dirty."

"You have to be brave, too," she said.

I laughed. "Grace, were you scared back there?"

"A little," she said.

I guess I can respect the fact that such a scene felt different for her. But long before I became a reporter, I decided that I couldn't go through life being afraid of people, especially not my own. How do you treat someone with dignity and respect in your reporting when you fear them or their circumstances? It's one of my frustrations, and it's not just White reporters. I see profiling in media cross racial and economic lines more than folks in my business would ever admit.

I turned left onto Peoria Avenue. "I just want to drive up and down a couple blocks, and then we'll head back."

The 7100 block was quiet. Just about every other house had boarded-up windows, and there were very few cars parked along the curb. The 7000 block was the same. Half of it was taken up by a school building. I headed toward Sangamon. It, too, was uneventful. I passed Louise Robinson's house. Cynthia said Yvonne lived about a block away, but she never specified parallel blocks.

Maybe Yvonne lives across 71st.

At dusk, I pulled out onto 71st and this time turned south down Peoria. There were more boarded-up homes and a few people sitting outside those that weren't. The end of the block was busier. There were cars parked on both sides and a large group of people was congregating in the middle of the street.

Grace looked frightened. She placed one hand on the dash and the other on the door handle. I wasn't crazy about driving through the crowd, either. I flicked my headlights on and off to warn them of the approaching vehicle. Nobody moved until I was right up on them. Driving about 5 miles an hour, I surveyed the scene. Men and women, mostly men, standing around listening to loud music. Then I noticed someone I was sure I had seen before: a young girl with long braids wearing an oversize white leather jacket with silver spikes and studs on the back and along the sleeves. She turned toward me just as I was driving past. It was Monique Connors. I caught her eye just as I sped away through a clearing. I don't know if she recognized me or not.

"Oh my God," I said.

"What?" Grace asked.

"That girl standing there with the white jacket on," I said more to myself than to Grace. "I met her last night at the vigil."

I started putting the pieces of the puzzle together. Pamela had compared Yvonne's house to Grand Central Station, and from what I could tell, this residence fit the description. Grace's witness at Carol Crest had described the driver as wearing a dope-ass jacket. And Eddie had described Masey's friend as way lighter than me with braids.

It was hard to tell as it grew dark, but the girl in the white studded jacket did appear to be a lighter complexion.

That's Monique. I'm sure of it, and I'd bet dollars to donuts that's Yvonne's house she's standing in front of.

"Oh shit, Jordan!" Grace said. "Look!"

The street came to a dead end. No sign. No warning. I couldn't turn left or right. I was completely blocked in and would have to practically drive up into somebody's yard so that I could turn around and head back down the way I came.

"Calm down! I'm sure this happens all the time," I said.

"I didn't see a sign saying this was a dead end," Grace said.

"Me either. Take out your phone and turn off the flash. Try

to angle it up to get a picture of the girl there in the white jacket."

"Are you sure?" she asked.

"Yes, do it! Hold on!"

I turned to the left and rolled my window down halfway, waving my arm out the window to signal *Sorry, excuse me*. At least I hoped they would take it that way.

"Get ready. There she is," I said.

Grace did as I told her, but Monique made it easy because she was standing in the middle of the street, pointing right at me. "What are *you* doing over here?" she shouted. "It's that reporter!"

Then I heard someone say, "Get out the street!"

I stuck my hand back out once more as a thank-you, switched on my headlights, and tore down Peoria doing about 40 miles an hour. My only regret was that I was too busy trying to get out of there to look for a car with a missing rim. There was no way I was circling back.

I pulled back onto 71st Street. Not convinced that someone from the group hadn't decided to follow me, questioning my intentions, I sped up to 45 miles per hour until I made it to the entrance ramp to the Dan Ryan and headed west toward downtown.

"Whew!" I sighed. "Was that exciting enough for you?"

Grace laughed nervously. "Yeah, pretty exciting."

"Did you get the picture?" I asked.

Grace checked her phone. "I put it on speed snap, so I got several shots. That jacket really shows up in the dark. Look."

I glanced over carefully as I drove. Grace had captured the girl's face. It was blurry, but I was convinced it was Monique. Frankly, her reaction gave her away.

"Who is she?" Grace asked.

"Somebody I met at the vigil last night," I said. "We've gotta go back to Masey's school and find that kid you talked to today."

··

It had been a long day of discovery with emotional minefields exploding all over the place. After all I'd put Grace through, I figured I at least owed it to her to drop her off in front of her apartment on the Far North Side.

"Check your phone; I sent the pictures to your phone," she said with one foot out of the car. "Thanks, Jordan. This was interesting."

"That's one word that comes to mind," I said half joking, half still in shock.

"Oh, and Grace, remember what I said about the football player at Masey's school. You know what he looks like; I don't. The good thing is, at least we know he's on the football team. It should be easy enough to stake out practice to find him," I said.

"Okay, but I made up an excuse today so that I could get out of work early to go to the school with you, remember? I'm not sure if I can pull that off two days in a row," she said.

"Let me worry about that. I'll figure something out," I said. "Good night, and thanks, Grace."

"Good night," she said.

On the way home, I took one of the most incredibly scenic routes that any city has to offer down Lake Shore Drive. The view of Lake Michigan, even on those infamous brutally cold days, is awe inspiring. How could a place so beautiful hide such ugly secrets? Would the silence surrounding Masey's death melt away like the sheets of ice soon to arrive over the lake? I thought about calling Pamela, but my persistence might make things worse. Surely she saw my text messages. I can't imagine her phone not being fused to her hand, the grip of a mother waiting for answers she needs, but at the same time, wants to ignore. Learning who killed her daughter won't bring Masey back. The absence of an answer might even allow for her to pretend it was all a dream—or more aptly put, a nightmare. I regret not driving past her house when I was in her neighborhood to see if she was there. But that would have required an explanation of why I was hanging around the area. My heart rate picks up unexpectedly and a wave of anxiety ripples through my body. The what-ifs start pounding so loudly in my head, I debate pulling over.

What if Pam is shutting down?

What if April Murphy is a fraud or an opportunist who just wants to be on television?

What if Masey wasn't the girl her mother thinks she was? What if there was a dark side to her life I'd have to reveal to her family and the viewers at home?

What if Ellen is right and Keith Mulvaney uses my absence from the day-to-day crime beat to carve out a place for himself or take it over?

Why has this case gripped me so?

Is this really what I want to be doing?

As I tally the sum of my career, my review extends to my personal life. What am I doing with Thomas? Am I wasting his time or is he wasting mine? If one more person asks me about motherhood and settling down, I'm going to scream.

The flood of fear is broken only when it occurs to me that I can't remember the last time I ate something, but instead of stopping for takeout, half recovered from the nervous system overload, I decide that the bag of potato chips and the bottle of cabernet sauvignon I can visualize sitting on the kitchen counter will do for the night.

Then the unmistakable ring assigned to the one and only who grounds me brought me back to earth.

"Hi, Mom."

"Hey, my lovebug. What's going on? I haven't heard from you in a couple days."

"I've been busy working on that case. I have good news!"

"What?"

"Nussbaum pulled me off everything else so I could just focus on it," I said, stopping before saying too much about how I intended to exercise that privilege with the Worrier.

"Are you working the same hours?" she asked.

"Basically, that means I'm working whenever I need to—which is practically all day. But it's okay," I said. "This was my first day. It was interesting."

Again, not the most accurate description that comes to mind, but it will do.

"I'm sure you haven't eaten," she said.

I laughed. "You're right, I haven't. I'm actually going to cook when I get home, and I'm almost there now, Mom."

Lie number two. I'm not cooking, and the "interesting" part of my day would have her on the first flight here to hug me if I shared the details.

I pulled up to the automatic garage gate and waved my key fob over the reader. The mechanical arm bounced slightly in the high wind, despite the structure protecting the entrance on all sides except for the driveway.

"Can I call you when I get inside? I'm pulling into the garage. And nobody better be in my parking space like last night."

"That's still happening? I know you were not pleased. I hate that roof," she said.

"Tell me about it," I said.

You're really in that big of a rush?

As I pulled forward, a car was right on my bumper and practically hit me, the driver too lazy to pull out their own key fob, I guess.

"These people in my building! Either they're forgetting their key fob and slipping in behind you or the guests of folks in this building are in too big of a hurry to wait and get buzzed in. It's so annoying!"

"You're annoyed every time I speak with you." Mom laughed. "When are you going to get a vacation?"

"Remember I'm coming home for a week for Christmas, Mom. And I haven't completely ruled out a girls' weekend getaway before that. Lisette might be here in the next couple of weeks," I said.

"If Lisette comes to town, you're just going to end up entertaining her. That's not giving you a break," Mom went on. "I know you, how you are . . ."

If every other conversation with my mother wasn't about my taking time off or taking better care of myself, I might have been too distracted to notice the car that slipped in behind me was now following me up the spiraling drive to level 8. I know most, though not all, of the people who park on my floor. But I don't recognize this driver, though I can see even through the tinted glass that he is Black.

I felt a little uneasy and thought about passing by my space to see if the driver would continue to follow me. But why risk the guy pulling into my spot? Then I would have to confront him, and I don't want to deal with that. So I turned into my $150-a-month parking space, number 048, and the driver kept going.

See, silly? That man wasn't thinking about you. Jordan, did you really just have one of "those moments"? The brainwashing that we chide White people for all the time? You see a person of color and suddenly they are suspicious. Did I just play the role of the purse-clutching White woman on the elevator? The poor man did nothing.

Mom continued her tirade, regaining my attention. "All you do is work, work, work," she said. "I thought you belonged to a union."

I laughed. "I do, but, Mom, listen, I'm about to get to the hallway and lose my connection. I'll call you when I get inside, okay?"

The cell service interrupted her far better than I could. "You'd better," she said. "Okay, I *will* call you back if it's not too late."

I'll miss seeing the Bass Man tonight but was relieved to be able to walk from my car directly onto my floor and down the hallway to my apartment, unencumbered by my habit of allowing other people's grief to enshroud me, then trying to drown it in a bottle, or by tired feet or a lover's need for attention and approval. Tonight maybe I will cook after all. I'll get some sleep and rise early to plot and put into play a strategy that will best utilize my instincts and allow me to swerve around the lies that threaten to throw me off the trail of a killer. This time the scent is too strong not to follow it, and so is my determination to arrive at the naked truth.

..

I decided to give Pamela another chance to respond before showing up at Yvonne's house without her, and to my surprise, finally she picked up the phone.

"Hi, Pamela, I'm just checking on you. I didn't hear back from you yesterday. How did things go with April after I left?" I asked.

"April is a beautiful person. She has a good heart," Pamela said.

Pamela's words were kind, but I sensed tension.

"That's nice. I'm happy I connected you two. Are you sure everything's okay?"

"I saw your last report," she said, her voice dissolving to a thud I recognized as disappointment. "I thought you would've told me before you said it on the air."

"Before I said what?" I asked.

"What we talked about . . . Masey getting picked up. I was hurt," she said.

Huh?

"But you already knew I had this information."

"You're not a mother, Jordan. You wouldn't understand. It makes me look like a bad mother that I didn't know who was picking her up," said Pam. "You know as well as I do, people are already looking for a reason to blame me, turning me into one of those moms you people in the media seem to enjoy taking advantage of."

"Pam, I'm sorry that you feel that way, but I would never portray you as an irresponsible mom. I'm at a loss for words right now."

It never crossed my mind that Pamela, under any circumstances, would have perceived what I consider simply doing my job as a betrayal. Though this is a reminder to me of the inherent risks of getting too close to the people I'm reporting on. I'll do any and everything I can to help her, but at the end of the day, it's my job.

"That wasn't my intention, Pam," I said. "I'm sorry you see it differently, but I'll have to leave it there."

"Uh-huh," she said.

I think we both recognized that we need each other. Our

alliance, however fragile, may be the only way this case gets solved.

"Pam, I really need to talk to Yvonne, and I need you to go with me. I have some time this morning. Can you meet me at her house at ten-thirty?"

"I can't; I have something to do. I'm taking Malcolm to counseling."

"My heart breaks for Malcolm. I can't imagine what he's going through emotionally. But, Pam, we have got to follow up on this lead."

"All right, let me see what I can do. Give me about an hour," she said. "Will it just be you, or is a cameraman coming with you?"

"No, just me."

"Okay, I'll text you her address."

..

No surprise—Yvonne's house was located right where I'd been the night before. I made a U-turn and parked directly in front of the house. I looked for Pamela's car. Even though I'd gotten a head start on her, in the back of my mind I kind of hoped she'd arrived early so we could have a chance to smooth things over. But her early arrival would probably have set off a whole new set of problems. The sight of her in the neighborhood would have led to a swarm of neighbors surrounding her, offering their sympathies and demanding to know what the police were saying. The attention could set off alarm bells. A reporter at Yvonne's house . . . does that mean there's new information? Is there a break in the case? What do they know about Masey's killer?

As I walked around the car to the sidewalk, my gaze was

initially fixed on the front door, but the sight of a man talking on the phone loudly as he emerged from the basement stairs caught my eye. We stared at each other. Pulling his cell phone away from his face, he asked in a suspicious and protective tone, "Can I help you?"

His pristine White Sox hat, slightly tilted to the right, concealed a portion of his face. He was definitely not a pretty boy. His features were strong, his face narrow. From what I could see, a perfectly groomed beard complemented his chiseled face. The long-sleeved thermal shirt he was wearing revealed a body not nearly as well groomed as his beard. He reminded me of a guy who played ball years ago who now leads a more sedentary lifestyle.

"Hi. I'm actually here to meet Pamela Alonzo," I said.

"Pamela Alonzo don't live here," he said.

"I know. I'm meeting her here. I'm Jordan Manning from Channel 8."

"Oh, you're that reporter. Yeah, she's upstairs. Go on up and knock on the door."

That reporter.

"All right, thanks."

I walked toward the house past two tricycles resting on their side in the grass. Along the walkway was a faded hopscotch chalk drawing that led to the porch steps. Yvonne's house was by far the best kept on the block, a welcome sign of life in a blighted area neglected by an uncaring government and people's desires to move out and move on, resulting in uninhabitable homes and buildings that should have been torn down a long time ago.

I see movement in the curtains covering the window near the front door. Whoever's inside knows I'm here. Before I could knock, Pamela opened the door. She understandably has looked weary since the day I first met her, but today she looked especially worn down. The dark circles under her eyes had deepened and her hair was brushed back in a ponytail, frizzy edges framing her face, a shadow of the defiant woman who addressed the crowd at the vigil. There was no point in asking how she was. I already knew.

"Come on in," she said.

I tried to make eye contact with Pam to get a read on how she was feeling after our earlier conversation, but all I saw was a mother at a breaking point. My search was abruptly interrupted by a jolt from a piercing scream.

"Imani," said Pam, exasperated, with her head in her hands. "Oh my God!"

Yvonne walked through the open doorway connecting the kitchen to the dining room. Biting her upper lip, she looked pensive and strained, but from her quick steps I sensed a resolve in her. "Have a seat, Jordan," she said.

She wasn't trying to avoid the conversation. She was ready for it.

"It's nice to finally meet you, Yvonne," I said, and gently waved to Imani, her face covered in tears. She clutched her mom, clearly upset, and now there was a stranger waving at her.

"So you're a hairdresser," I said.

"Well . . . yes," she said, glancing at Pam. "My boyfriend, Manny, Imani's father, has a barbershop in the basement and I do hair upstairs. But please, don't mention that. We're not licensed."

That's the least of my interests.

Yvonne leaned down to put Imani in her bouncer seat, then sat back on the couch with her head down and her hands in her lap. Her blond-streaked bangs nearly covered her eyes.

"Yvonne, you were one of the last people to see Masey," I said. "What was she like that day before she left on her bicycle?"

Before she could answer, Pamela interjected. "I miss my baby so much. Just looking at Imani with Yvonne, I think about how Masey was always over here, making videos for her MySpace page with her friends. Yvonne would do her hair for her. She had a different style every time she came home. How did we get here so fast?"

"What were her videos about?" I asked.

"She'd do dance routines and model clothes. Half the time they were my outfits," she said.

"The rest of the time they were mine," Yvonne chimed in. "And her hair had to be on point."

"Yep," Pam said, brightening up a bit. "She wanted to be a star. She wanted to be famous. I wanted her to focus on the gifts God gave her, her beautiful mind, her intelligence. Masey was so smart. I told her: 'You want to be as pretty on the inside as you are on the outside. Don't rely on your looks, or how fine somebody tells you that you are.' But all she talked about was being famous, being a model/actress and moving to L.A." Pam went on: "I guess that's part of growing up. But I admit she looked a little too grown up for me at times, especially in those videos. And I told her: 'Ease up on the mascara. You don't need all that makeup.'"

Yvonne was listening, but she seemed to be somewhere else. She moved around nervously. Imani held her arms out to her mother and Yvonne picked her up, looking agitated and breathing heavily. Her body language was unsettling.

What's going on here?

Yvonne was clearly having a moment, and not the same

moment that Pam was experiencing. Tears streamed down Yvonne's face. "I'm sorry . . . Pam," Yvonne said. "I loved her so much. You know I did."

Something felt off. I got the feeling that Yvonne's *sorry* had nothing to do with what Pam was talking about.

"I know this is devastating for both of you. I can't pretend to imagine what this is like," I said. "Yvonne, I'm trying to get some answers here. I'm worried that the more time that goes by, the less likely we are to find out what happened to Masey."

I rephrased the question. "Yvonne, what do you remember about that day? Anything stand out before Masey left on her bike to go home?"

"I really don't," she said. "There was nothing different about that day. Nothing. I've gone over it a thousand times in my head. Nothing. There was nobody in the area I didn't recognize. No cars I hadn't seen before. Nothing."

"Do you have any idea who might have done this to Masey?" I asked.

"No," she said flat out.

"Did you see my report yesterday about someone picking Masey up from school?"

"I didn't see it, but I heard about it. They're saying someone was picking her up from school all the time?" she asked.

"Nobody said all the time, but people at the school said at least a couple of times, yes," I said.

Yvonne paused and rubbed her temples with her fingers. "Pam," she said, choking up, "I'm sorry. There's something I've got to get off my chest."

"What?" Pam asked, leaning back and tilting her head inquisitively.

"Masey really wanted to be famous," Yvonne reiterated. "She was constantly talking about modeling and acting, and making a demo of professional quality, you know. Something she could send to a studio."

Pam interrupted. "Like the stuff on her MySpace page."

"No, you don't understand," Yvonne said. "I think her wanting to be famous might have gotten her in trouble."

"What do you mean, it might have gotten her in trouble?" I asked.

Yvonne's sobbing grew louder, and she had to pull herself together before she could continue. "Mase . . . she met this guy named Terrence," she said, catching her breath. "He, uh, he told her he could produce her video, and he had contacts in the recording and modeling industries that he could show it to. Masey told me how dedicated he was to helping her and how he promised to focus on her and make it happen."

"Masey asked me if she could do a recording session with her friends, and I said, 'No. I want you to focus on this new school I prayed for you to get into,'" Pamela said. "You saw her. How much more adult she'd started to dress. You weren't suspicious?"

"Sure, I was concerned, this grown man wanting to help her. What did he want in return? But Masey assured me he hadn't tried anything, and he just wanted to help her. So I talked to him myself to see what he was about. He may hustle a fifteen-year-old, but he wasn't going to fool me."

"You weren't her mother, Yvonne. That was not your decision to make."

"Where did she meet him?" I asked.

"Here, at my house," she said. "Manny cuts his and his roommate's hair. He's not from here."

"And you're sure he wasn't trying to mess around with her?" I asked.

"No, no, no! It wasn't like that at all. He was acting like he was her manager. Manny says he's corny as hell, a wannabe. He did make a lot of promises. Not just to Mase but to her friends, too, about his studio and his connections. He even offered to pay me to do Mase's hair and I said, 'Why would I take your money? I do her hair for free.' But I'm pretty sure he gave her money to buy that pink bomber jacket she had pictures taken in."

I recall seeing that photo at the vigil and thinking Masey looked like a model in it.

"How old is this man?" asked Pamela, now incredulous.

"I'm guessing almost thirty."

"Thirty! You let my daughter hang out with a thirty-year-old man!"

"Pam, I swear there was nothing going on like that. Masey would've told me."

"Did you ask her?" I asked.

"Of course!" Yvonne insisted.

Pam grabbed her head, then slammed her arms back down on the arms of the chair.

"But then I started hearing from my customers that he was a fake. He'd taken this one girl's money to pay for studio time and she never heard from him again. He don't have any money. He's been living with his boy for a couple years, and sometimes he stays with this older woman, his girlfriend. Turns out that was her car he's been driving. He's broke. He's a phony."

"Do you think he had something to do with Masey's murder?" I asked.

"Honestly, no, I don't think so. He's a con, but nobody on the street says he's violent. He did show us pictures of him with this big Grammy-winning producer once. He said he had the guy's number and that they hung out. He made it seem like he was the man and that with his connections Masey could make it in L.A."

"How much time was she spending with him, Yvonne?" Pam asked.

"Not a lot. One time he took her and a few of her friends over to the South Shore to do a photo shoot. I went with her. The pictures came out beautiful. That part was legit, I know. It was just that one time. I wouldn't have let her go alone, and that was only after I'd checked him out," Yvonne said.

"If you don't think this Terrence hurt Masey, then why do you think her wanting to be famous got her in trouble?" I asked.

"I said *maybe*," she said. "He might've owed people some money. I'm just speculating. But maybe he took money from the wrong people and they came looking for him, and Masey got caught up."

"Do you know his last name?" I asked.

"Bankhead."

"You say he's not from here. Where's he from?"

"He mentioned something about living in New Mexico for a few years before coming to Chicago."

"So you think it's possible that Masey was collateral damage for something he was mixed up in?" I asked.

"I dunno. I just had to say something," she said.

"*Now* you say something!" Pamela screamed. "Now you say something! God damn you, Yvonne!"

"Pam, I'm sorry. You're right, I should've. Please don't hate me," Yvonne pleaded.

The situation between Pam and Yvonne was escalating, but the conversation raised more questions.

"Where does he live?" I asked.

Before Yvonne could answer, Pamela interrupted. "If they were after him, why would they want to hurt Masey? How would they have connected them?"

I know from the many stories that I've covered that the wicked watch, and they strike when they think nobody's looking. In Masey's case, that would've been the day she left Yvonne's at dusk on her bicycle.

"When was the last time you saw him?" I asked.

"At Manny's birthday party. He was here late that night. He couldn't have done something to Mase and been here at the same time," she said.

"But you think it's possible somebody who was after him recognized Masey and caught up with her?" I asked.

"It's possible, I guess. Manny said he was always flashing cash. One minute he'd say he won it gambling, the next he'd just gotten a record deal. At one point he even claimed he had all this real estate."

"Wait—but you said he was strapped for cash," I said.

"Well, that's the thing. We were hearing on the streets that he owed people money. But whenever he was around here, he wanted people to think he was ballin'."

But if this guy Terrence isn't who he says he is, what else is he hiding?

"Yvonne, I'll ask you again, where does he live?"

"I don't know."

"Who else does he hang out with?" Pam said.

"I don't really see him with anybody other than his roommate. Like I said, he's not from here," Yvonne said.

"What's his roommate's name?" I asked.

"Brent," she said.

"What's his last name? What does he do?"

"Carter. I don't know," she said, becoming more aggravated by the second.

I leaned in and looked Yvonne square in her eyes. "Yvonne, stay with me, okay? Stay in the moment."

She nodded her head.

"I'm curious, what kind of car does he drive?" I asked.

"A gray Camry. I've seen Terrence drive it sometimes when he didn't have the other car."

"What kind of car?"

Yvonne sighed. "It's hard to describe, like it was customized or something. Kinda sporty. A grayish purple color."

"Did you notice if it was missing a rim?"

"No."

"Has he been around here since Masey disappeared?" I asked.

"Yeah, Manny cut his hair about a week after she went missing. Manny told me he kept saying how messed up it was, but it seemed like he was trying to downplay how close they'd gotten recently. That bothered Manny, him acting like he didn't know her all that well."

"So Manny let him off the hook? He just let him act like he didn't know her? Did he confront him?" I asked.

"No, he didn't."

"But why?" I asked.

"I don't know." She shrugged.

"Did Manny spend much time around Masey?" I asked.

"What are you trying to say?"

"I'm not trying to say anything. I just wonder why he wouldn't have confronted Terrence."

"This is some bullshit!" Pamela shouted, and leapt out of her chair and headed toward the basement in search of Manny.

"Pamela! Pam! Wait!" Yvonne pleaded.

The last thing I wanted to do was to get caught in the middle of the family argument that I sensed was about to happen. But there's so much more I needed to know, so I followed Pamela and Yvonne as they rushed to the basement. It felt damp down here and smelled of the type of astringent used to sanitize clippers and combs. Manny's shop consisted of a single barber chair, a television bracketed against the wall, and an adjacent room with another television and folding chairs lining the wall. Magazines were stacked on a side table. But no Manny.

"If you'd given me a chance, I would've told you he's not cutting today," Yvonne said.

"I saw a guy outside as I was coming up. He had a White Sox hat on. Was that Manny?" I asked.

"Yes, that was him," Yvonne said.

Pamela was now sweating from the sprint and the fear and adrenaline that had to be rushing through her body after all she'd just learned.

"Pam, come on, have a seat," I said, gently draping my arm around her shoulders. "Try to settle down. Let's get through this."

"No, we need to go back upstairs," Yvonne said abruptly. "He'll be back soon."

"Okay, that's fine. Let's go," I said.

Once upstairs, I jumped right back in. "Yvonne, did Terrence ever pick up Masey from school?"

"If he did, she never said anything to me about it."

"But it's possible?" I asked.

"Yeah, I guess," she said. "But like I said, Masey didn't keep secrets from me."

Yvonne thinks she's the cool cousin that the young girls come to for advice and gossip and even to share their secrets. I thought back to my cousin Stephanie, what it was like when we learned that she'd lied to everyone to meet up with an older guy on what was supposed to be a school band trip. She didn't even tell me. Even now it stings when I think about it. I thought she trusted me most.

I go back to the question I had asked before. "Masey was over here quite a bit. Were she and Manny pretty close, too?"

The question struck a deeper nerve the second time. Yvonne's teary eyes of regret were transformed into a ferocious stare now directed at me. "What are you trying to say? Why do you keep asking me that?"

"Look, Yvonne, I'm trying to put together how many people were in Masey's circle to figure out how she ended up dead in a field, naked and left to rot!"

Pamela's expression imploded like a building taken down by dynamite, and I realized I'd crossed the line.

Jordan, get a grip!

In that moment, I was embarrassed by my reckless choice of words. But I had to try to shift into reverse, leave this terrible moment behind, and back out of my confrontation with Yvonne. I needed to keep the focus on Terrence.

"Yvonne, we're all here for Masey. Nobody carries a greater weight than Pam, and I know you're hurt, too."

Masey's real life—as opposed to the life everyone thought she was living—is now the story and the path to learning the truth. Piecing it all together, I'm starting to believe that Masey was in fact dating this guy. Or at the very least, he lured her with promises of making her famous. I feel certain he was the person who'd been picking her up from school. But what set him off? Did they get into a fight? Did he try to have sex with her and she said no? Did he force her? Did he silence her to keep her quiet about the rape? Of course this is all speculation; there is no evidence. It could be him, but it also could be Manny. It could be anyone.

Yvonne handed Pamela tissues from the Kleenex box on a nearby table. Grief was so thick in the air, it was hard to breathe. My visit here began with Imani crying her eyes out, seeking comfort from her mother, and would end with two mothers comforting each other. I was relieved to have an excuse to escape.

"Pam, I've got to get back to the newsroom. I'll be in touch. Yvonne, thank you so much for everything. I'll let myself out."

When I reached the door, I felt a tug on my arm. Pamela was right on my heels.

"Yes, Pam?"

"Are you going to report this on the news, too?"

"Report what?"

"All this stuff about this guy," she said, then more discreetly so Yvonne wouldn't hear, "and Manny."

"No," I said, shaking my head.

She let go of my arm.

As I walked to my car, I glanced back at the basement steps where Manny had emerged an hour before. Enough time had passed that maybe he'd return soon. Perhaps I should wait. I looked around for Manny one more time and paused to take a beat to process, as best I could, everything that had just happened before I got in the car. I'm drained, I realized, but there was still more to do. I called Joey and got his voice mail.

"Joey, it's me. Listen, we don't have time to be mad. I need your help. I have some more information in the Masey James case. Masey's cousin just told me about a guy named Terrence Bankhead. He had some type of relationship with Masey. Her cousin said he's about thirty years old and moved to Chicago from New Mexico, but she doesn't know where he lives. And while you're at it, can you check out Masey's cousin's boyfriend Manny Walker? Talk to you later. Bye."

It hit me that the answer to what happened to Masey James could be terribly obvious: a beautiful girl being taken advantage of during an impressionable time in her life by the wrong guy. To my knowledge, only one person could confirm the driver of the car Masey got in that day, and that was the football player Grace talked to at Carol Crest.

··

The next day, Joey still hadn't returned my call. So I left him a neutral message—"Hey, give me a call when you get a chance"—before heading to my doctor's appointment. I was sitting in the waiting room when my phone vibrated. I was supposed to turn my cell phone off in the waiting area, but I never did. Switching to vibrate was the best I could do. I looked down and saw that it was Baby Smierciak.

"Jordan, where have you been? I called you last night."

"Yeah, I'm sorry I missed your call," I said. "What's going on?"

"You're never gonna believe what just happened this morning!" Justin said excitedly.

"Hold on. I need to move somewhere more private," I said.

I rose to step out into the hallway, eliciting daggers from the waiting room receptionist for my noncompliance.

Your boss never turns off his cell phone. Give me a break.

"Justin, what's up?" I asked, safely away from waiting room ears in the chilly hallway.

"Something big's about to happen in the Masey James case," he said.

"What do you mean?" I asked, my heart racing.

Did police find and arrest the mystery driver?

"I heard on the scanner that police had reopened the streets surrounding the playground. So I headed right on over this morning to see if I could get some pictures. Well, sure enough, the street was open, though the yellow tape kept me pretty far back. I went across the street to set up my shot, right? And this woman comes up and starts asking me a bunch of questions. We started talking, or I should say, *she* started talking. Telling me she told police she'd seen some kids over on the playground where the body was found. They'd scrounged up some sticks, she said, and were squatting over something. She identified two of them—the Harvey brothers, she called them. She said they go to her church. She told me that police picked them up for questioning, then came back to her house yesterday and asked her if she could identify them from a lineup of photos. Jordan, she told me that police said a positive ID was all they needed to charge them."

Eddie from the convenience store was right!

"Charge them with what?" I asked incredulously. "You said *boys*. How old are they?"

"Not sure about the charge, but the lady said the Harvey brothers go to Ida B. Wells Prep, which isn't far from the crime scene. Jordan, it's a middle school!" Justin said.

"Get out! You mean they think the killer could be as young as a sixth grader? This is unbelievable! Where are you now?" I asked.

"I'm headed to police headquarters," he said. "I'm gonna stake out there for a bit to see if charges are announced."

"All right. I'm at the doctor's office, but I'll probably see you there . . . soon."

I went back inside the waiting room and tapped on the receptionist's window. "Excuse me, I'm going to have to reschedule," I said. "I'm really sorry, I have an emergency."

The receptionist rolled her eyes. "Wait here," she ordered.

My cell phone vibrated in my hand. I didn't recognize the number, but after what I'd just learned, there was no way I wasn't answering it. The receptionist returned.

"Excuse me," I said.

"We have a no-cell-phone policy," she said loud enough for everyone to hear.

"I'm sorry . . ." I said, checking out her name tag, "Christina, but I don't have a no-cell-phone-policy kind of job. Excuse me, I'll be right back."

I stepped back out into the chilly hallway. "Hello? This is Jordan Manning."

"Ms. Manning, I hope you're sitting down, because you're not going to believe what I'm about to tell you," said a woman whose voice I didn't recognize. "In about an hour, the Chicago PD will announce charges against three boys, one thirteen-year-old and two eleven-year-olds, in the death of Masey James. The thirteen-year-old and one of the younger boys are brothers. I've seen your coverage. That's why I'm calling you."

The Harvey boys.

"And you are?" I asked.

"My name is Adele Constanzo," she said. "I'm their attorney."

12

BREAKING NEWS

Diana Sorano: We begin tonight with breaking news. There has been a stunning development in the investigation of the murder of fifteen-year-old Chicago honor student Masey James. Our Jordan Manning reports.

Jordan: Diana, it is indeed stunning. Cook County state's attorney Chandler O'Brien just announced felony murder charges against three middle school students, a thirteen-year-old and two eleven-year-old boys. The gravity of the charges in a crime Superintendent Donald Bartlett described as "unspeakable" against suspects so young is sure to send shock waves across the city and the rest of the country.

Video of O'Brien: The suspects have been identified as three African American males—two age eleven and a thirteen-year-old. All reside in the South Side community of Bronzeville less than a mile from where the victim's remains were found. The thirteen-year-old is charged as an adult with aggravated murder, kidnapping, and desecration of a body [audible gasps] . . . and the two eleven-year-olds are charged with accessory to murder after the fact. The older suspect has been remanded to Cook County Jail and the younger suspects are being held in juvenile detention, all pending arraignment.

Reporters hurled questions at O'Brien, a gangly man about six-five with thinning salt-and-pepper hair. Typically devoid of emotion, today he seemed troubled.

"Please, please, let me finish and then I will take your questions and answer what I can. The suspects will be arraigned tomorrow," he shouted over the disorienting noise. "However, due to their ages, the proceedings will be closed."

"Why are they closed if the thirteen-year-old is being charged as an adult?" a reporter called out, freeing others to chime in.

"Excuse me, the proceedings for the younger suspects will be closed at my request," O'Brien said.

The murmurs from reporters in the room grew louder, and Bartlett, standing next to O'Brien, held up his hands and appealed for quiet.

"I understand the seriousness of these charges begs a lot of questions. But make no mistake, this was an unspeakable act. The charges reflect that. And however unconscionable it might be due to the suspects' young ages, we owe it to Masey and her family to see justice done. Thank you, but that's all we have at this time."

O'Brien had promised to take reporters' questions but seemed content to follow Bartlett's lead and end the news conference then and there. Reporters protested as the men, joined by Detective Fawcett, turned to walk away.

It was my voice that grabbed their attention. "Detective Fawcett!" I yelled. "What about the mysterious driver you were looking for two days ago?"

Fawcett seemed to lean toward me, and even with the distance between us, I felt the piercing stab of his gaze dead in my face. Without a word, he turned and nodded to the department's public information officer, Linda Folson, who took the podium as the prosecutor and the lawmen walked away.

"This concludes today's news briefing. We will keep you informed of updates following the arraignments."

Hell no! You don't get to just walk away after dropping a bombshell like this!

"Wait a minute, Linda. So this is it? The investigation is over? Police aren't looking into any other leads? What is the evidence? The motive?"

A chorus of questions rained down, all of them ignored, failing to break her stride as she seemed hell-bent on leaving. Then suddenly, as though it occurred to her that her abrupt departure would play out on every newscast, she turned around and repeated, "That concludes today's news conf—"

"Linda, are police looking into other suspects?" I pressed. "Three children—because that's what they are, *children*—have been charged with taking part in the savage murder of one of their contemporaries. By themselves?"

Folson turned, stone-faced. "Does the media have any other questions?" she said.

"Can you answer my question, please? Are the police looking at other suspects?"

"Jordan, you're not the only reporter in the room," Folson shot back.

Clearly you have no intention of answering any of our questions.

"Is it true that two of the suspects are brothers?" I asked.

The room suddenly fell silent, but within a beat, every reporter in the room wanted to know the answer to that question.

"Brothers?" "Is that true?" "Are the eleven-year-olds twins?" my colleagues asked.

I almost felt sorry for Linda. Something had compelled her to stick it out and take the beating on behalf of the men she worked for. But clearly she wasn't authorized to tell the media what we begged to know, or she did not know herself.

"We will be issuing a statement tomorrow following the outcome of the hearings. I'm sorry but that is all I can share at this time," Folson said, and finally exited.

Jordan's sign-off: Diana, as you just heard, it's unknown whether police have abandoned other potential leads in the case, like the one I reported just the other day about a mysterious driver who'd picked Masey up from school. However, my sources have confirmed that two of the suspects are indeed brothers. The thirteen-year-old and his younger brother. This is Jordan Manning reporting.

An unspeakable act committed by children. Is this what the Chicago PD wants us to believe? Want Pamela Alonzo to believe? Then Satan might as well open his mouth and swallow this city whole. I could picture it now, one high-rise after another tumbling down his red throat.

..

I don't know why Adele Constanzo chose to tell me, and not other reporters, that two of the suspects are brothers. It wouldn't have been difficult for an astute reporter to find that out, but it did give me a leg up to be the first to report it, though I wouldn't have done so based solely on Justin's second-hand account from the neighbor.

The siblings thickened the gruesome plot and spawned an unfathomable perception that two adolescents brought up in the same household could become killers before even earning a driver's permit. That Black boys barely old enough to stay at home alone on their parents' date night, Black boys who are endangered in ways that even Black girls aren't, Black boys who are presumed guilty until proven innocent, are capable of being murderous kidnappers who desecrate bodies in their spare time between the school dismissal bell and church on Sunday.

"Jordan, you could fill a notebook with the mistakes and presumptions that the CPD and the prosecutor's office have made in this case," Adele Constanzo told me. "Can you meet me at my office today after the news conference?"

"I'll come straight to you," I said, "with a camera, if you're in agreement."

"Absolutely."

..

After a few days away from the beat, I was happy to see that the "camera" the desk assigned to the news conference was Scott. After Folson left the room, I was just as anxious to clear out of there. A reporter from one of the local newspapers had the nerve to ask me, "Where'd you hear two of the suspects are brothers?" I smiled at him, shrugged my shoulders, and walked over to Scott.

"Let's bounce," I said.

In the news truck, I was reluctant to ask Scott *What happened the other day?* or *Are we okay?* I was too caught up in the moment. And after the way I'd gone after Fawcett and Folson, so was he.

"You were an attack dog!" Scott said. "Did you see the way Fawcett looked at you? And Folson. What was that about?"

"Fawcett, no surprise there. But they were all cowards to leave Folson twisting in the wind. For a minute there, I thought she might've grown a conscience. She's so rigid, though, more likely she counted to ten and bolted."

"What do you think about these kids being charged?" he said.

"It's bullshit! But I cannot believe that police or the prosecutor's office are satisfied they've found Masey's killer. If these boys were involved in her death, they got help from someone older. Or they're taking the rap for that person. They at least would've needed to have a vehicle to dispose of the body. Dr. Chan said Masey was killed somewhere else and dumped in the field. How would little boys pull something like that off?"

"I agree, it's pretty damned desperate," Scott said. "Where are we headed, anyway?"

"To get some answers, I hope, from the boys' defense attorney."

Scott looked at me curiously.

"Adele Constanzo. She called me about an hour before the news conference . . . on my cell phone," I said.

"Wha-a-at? Someone you know?" Scott asked.

"No. I asked her how she'd got my number. You know what she said to me?"

"What?"

"'What kind of a shitty investigator would I be if I couldn't get the number of a reporter who wanted nothing more than to take my call?'"

"Oh, so she's a little full of herself?" Scott said.

"I didn't take it that way. I googled her. She's a second-generation Cuban American. Graduated from Berkeley. She was recognized two years ago by the NAACP for her justice reform work."

"I'm surprised I haven't heard of her," Scott said.

"Yeah, me, too, but she's been pretty low-key the last two years. Her bio says she has a three-year-old son. Maybe she took some time off," I said. "At any rate, Adele Constanzo wants to use me to advance her agenda, and I think I'm going to let her."

We parked across from Constanzo's Loop office building and proceeded up to her spacious yet unpretentious office on the thirty-third floor. If I didn't know better, I would've thought we had walked into the headquarters of a children's charity. Many images of young people decorated the walls.

A receptionist announced our arrival, and Adele strolled out mere seconds later to greet us, suited and booted and camera ready.

"Ms. Manning," she said. "Thank you for coming."

"Ms. Constanzo, it's nice to meet you. This is Scott Newell."

"Please follow me," she said.

Her office was around the corner, sparsely decorated save for a life-size painting depicting sad brown faces with piercing eyes that seemed to be staring right at me, crying for help.

"Ah, the painting," she said. "Haunting, isn't it? It reminds me who I'm fighting for."

She took a seat behind her desk. Adele Constanzo is a picture of contrast. The sternness of her voice belies her disarmingly youthful appearance, but her strident attire—no color, no texture, no thought put into it—is professional and to the point, much like her personality.

"When I first started following your coverage of Masey's disappearance, I could not have imagined that I would become involved in this case."

She looked at Scott. "I'm sorry, Mr. . . . . ?" she asked.

"Newell. But you can call me Scott," he said.

"All right, Scott, do you plan on turning that camera on?" she said, and then to me: "You want a taped interview, yes?"

"Absolutely!" I said.

Her style was a bit harsh but quickly forgotten once she started to tell me about the accused and how they got trapped in a tunnel of misperception, errors, and lies. It was such a familiar parable, I could almost finish her sentences.

The day the body was discovered, a neighbor, an older African American woman, called 911 to report that she'd seen three African American boys hanging out beneath the "L" tracks. Not just once but three separate times the week before the sheriff's inmates discovered the body.

"She told police they were behaving suspiciously," Adele said.

I suspect the neighbor, like so many have done, may have fallen into the trap of believing Black boys congregating in a field must be up to no good, even though she is Black herself. It's part of what we have been conditioned to view as the criminal profile. And sadly, that profile is often a Black boy.

Adele continued. "The third time she spotted the boys, she recognized two of them. The family attends her church, and she knew all of them by name. Police apprehended the brothers when the family arrived at church last Sunday, put them in the back of a squad car, and told their parents to meet them at the police station. There police questioned them with their parents present, but we don't know what the officers said to the boys while they were in the squad car."

The boys admitted they used the playground sometimes as a shortcut but denied hanging out there.

"Tell me about the boys. Have either of them ever been in any trouble?" I asked.

"Interesting that you should ask. When the older boy was in the sixth grade, he got expelled for bringing a kitchen knife to school in his backpack," she said. "At that age, kids go through a lot of changes, you know. He said he was being bullied, and out of fear, one day he walked past the kitchen and grabbed a knife from the drawer on the way to school."

I shifted in the seat. The attorney picked up on my discomfort.

A knife is not sounding good.

"I'm not talking about a switchblade, okay? I'm talking about an ordinary kitchen knife and a kid who was afraid of being jumped after school. Was it the right decision? No. But it doesn't make him a criminal, either. He made a mistake."

I would have to mask my feelings better around this woman. She was a mind reader.

"His father emphasized that he was certain his son never would have used it. Carrying it made him feel safe. But he was expelled and sent to an alternative school to finish out the semester. He was allowed to return to his regular school in the fall. There hasn't been one incident since then."

"Do police know about this incident?" I asked.

"The stepdad figured he'd come clean so they could all go home. And that night they did. But then, the next day, a police cruiser was waiting for the kids outside their school. This time, the younger boy's friend was with them—the other eleven-year-old. He lives with his grandmother. His mother got mixed up with the wrong guy and she's serving seven years in a federal penitentiary in Missouri. Mi—". She almost slipped and said his name but caught herself. "This boy is part of a program that takes children of incarcerated adults to visit their parents in prison.

"The boys said police convinced them to take a ride to the playground to demonstrate how they cut across the field. They said the police were nice to them but kept asking the same questions over and over. Obviously, as an attorney, I would never have allowed any of this to happen. They even asked the oldest boy if he liked girls, and 'Have you ever seen your dad hit your mom?' I think the police were trying to assess their tolerance for violence against women, but it was inappropriate. The boys said the police never mentioned a body, and neither did they."

Constanzo said the boys told their parents what had happened. The brothers' stepfather was livid that police talked to the boys without him or his wife present, and especially because they'd asked if they'd ever seen him hit his wife. He called the department to complain, and a detective and two officers followed up and came to the family's home that night. A more affluent couple with their lawyer on speed dial, or simply more educated about how to handle these matters, wouldn't have answered the door.

"The stepfather let them in, and that's when things got worse," she said. "Their questions started to sound more like accusations when the detective asked the boy if he still had the knife he took to school.

"The stepfather had had 'the talk' with his son about how to deal with the police. But the boy is terrified of them. For whatever reason, that night he tried to run to his room, but one of the officers grabbed him. The stepfather intervened and things escalated. There was a tussle and the stepdad, Bernard, was tased in front of his wife and his kids in his own living room."

"Oh my God, that's horrible," I interjected. "What evidence do they say they have? Did they search the home?"

"They did."

"And did they find anything?"

Constanzo clasped her hand together under her chin in a prayer posture. "Police checked the boys' room and found a sharp kitchen knife under the oldest's bed. They confiscated the knife, shoes, jackets, backpacks, and other articles of clothing from both houses, and the crime lab matched DNA from the crime scene."

My poker face was becoming harder to maintain by the minute.

"First, let's look at the situation, the timing of their visit. The stepdad complained to the brass. Next thing he knows, police are at his house. As I see it, they were there to intimidate them," Constanzo said. "They didn't have a warrant and no probable cause to go after these kids other than they are Black."

"Wasn't the neighbor who reported them to police also Black?" I asked.

"Your point?" she asked.

I was just thinking out loud. I didn't feel like explaining. "Are you saying they illegally searched the house?"

"I'm saying it was a trap," she said. "They took advantage of the situation, arresting the father and the older boy as a way to get around the fact they didn't have a warrant. They found a kitchen knife under the boy's bed, took it and ran with it."

"Why did he keep a knife under the bed?"

"Weren't you ever afraid of the dark as a kid? Or slept with a butcher knife next to your bed as a single woman? I sure have," Constanzo said. "It's little consolation, but when you're frightened, it can help you sleep at night."

The next day police questioned the eleven-year-old at home and got him to admit that they had come across the remains one day while taking a shortcut through the park.

"Again, he thought if he told the truth, he'd be okay. They instantly treated the boys like murder suspects," Constanzo said. "They didn't get the benefit of the doubt. That happens a lot in families where somebody is already behind bars and the adults don't know who to call if they feel their rights are being violated."

"Why didn't they tell anybody about the body?" I asked.

"I can't explain why these kids discovered a body, didn't report it, then went back to the scene more than once. But that is precisely what happened."

My eyes grew wide. Being placed near the scene was one thing, but discovering the body and going back for another look was creepy.

"You'll connect the dots of what I'm telling you when you read the petitions and the indictment against the older boy. Their ages should be a factor, but not to investigators or the state's attorney. I admit the circumstances are strange, but you can't charge kids with murder for behaving strangely."

"Do police think the boys knew Masey?" I asked.

"I don't know what police think, but I can tell you unequivocally no, they didn't know her. They're kids; they didn't even know a girl was missing."

I put two and two together. The person who turned the boys in must have been at the vigil, and someone overheard her talking about police focusing on the kids.

"Have police made a link between the kitchen knife and Masey's murder?"

"Again, the kitchen knife incident happened almost a year ago. This is a kid who was afraid of a bully," she said.

And now one bad decision could become the sum of his life, assigning him a label that allowed the police officers who came to his home to judge him and his stepfather, a journeyman carpenter and a deacon at his church.

"Anything else you'd like to share?" I asked.

Constanzo shook her head. Scott turned off the camera and began to pack up.

"Thank you, Adele. Can I call you that?" I asked.

"Sure."

"Just curious. Who was the detective who went to the family's house?"

"I'm sure you know him. His name is Fawcett."

"Mitch Fawcett," I confirmed. "Yes, I know him."

"He's a real asshole," Constanzo said. "That's off the record."

"I still don't get it. What evidence are they saying connects these boys to the crime?"

I understood her perhaps not wanting to divulge that on the air, but I needed details, because nothing she'd told me thus far had changed my mind about what or who the police should be focused on.

Adele Constanzo stood up and made her way to the front edge of her desk, both hands at her sides to prop herself up in a power pose I am certain she has used in court many times, adding a level of seriousness to what she was about to say.

"This is off the record, too," she said. "There are reasons other than what goes bump in the night to explain why kids keep knives in their rooms."

"What do you mean?"

"The older boy. He's going to be named, so I might as well tell you. Derek. Derek Harvey," she took a breath. "He was assaulted at camp. I don't know all the details, but his parents think it was one of the young adult counselors. He developed a form of PTSD."

"When did this happen?" I asked.

"A couple years ago. His parents don't believe he's ever told them everything that happened."

Then the expulsion and now this? It's too much for any child to bear.

..

This Is a News Channel 8 Special Report

So shocking were the charges against the three boys that a national media firestorm descended on Chicago. The Windy

City has been castigated for its culture of violence and has been accused of being an urban war zone. By any standard, this case was extraordinary. Blaming a crime so vicious on children was about as tone-deaf as singing a legendary Chicago blues song about heartbreak and a no-good man at a wedding. But it fed the media monster obsessed with violence in major cities that have large African American populations. Chicago, Baltimore, Detroit—the bull's-eye shifted from one to another of them, and these tragic stories fed into media markets where people devoured them. When I first got into the business, "If it bleeds, it leads" was the watchword of newsrooms. A way to boost ratings off someone else's pain. It sounds heartless, I know. It's not deliberately callous but a conditioning of the mind to forget that the "blood" once ran through a person. Because you can't have blood without a victim.

A portion of my exclusive interview with Adele Constanzo was carried by the national network. It lasted just twenty-five seconds (yes, I timed it—a habit), but it was still a dream come true. Mom was thrilled to see my coverage in Austin but disappointed that I wasn't featured in the clip.

"That's not how it works, Mom," I told her. "Locally, the story is mine, but the network has its own national correspondent here, Grayson Michele. Remember? I told you I met him at a journalism conference a few years back. I've admired him since I was in undergrad. He reached out to *me* to get a handle on the story."

For someone like Grayson to seek my advice was a confidence boost, matched only by the call I received from the network's executive producer congratulating me on getting the scoop.

"Mom, I just pulled off one of the biggest exclusives of my career, thanks to this attorney."

"That's wonderful, sweetheart," Mom said. "What did your boss say about it?"

"Ellen, of course, gave me kudos, but Nussbaum blew me away. Here's this White news executive from the more conservative northern part of Illinois. You know what he said?"

"What?"

"He told me he doesn't think the boys did it. He doesn't believe for a second that police got it right. That's unusual coming from someone who has nothing in common with these kids. No reason to give them the benefit of the doubt."

In fact, Nussbaum had spent his career turning a blind eye to the constant dehumanization of Black men and boys by the media. And yet there he was, no proof, only his gut, telling me they were innocent. It reminded me of the power of the job. It's not about making or breaking someone's day; it's the ability to make or break a system that can destroy someone's life if they are innocent. It's also about humanizing people and not being used as a weapon against the lesser-thans and the have-nots.

I felt a strange vibe, though, in the newsroom. Some of my colleagues moved robotically around me, diverting their eyes. Keith's negative energy was noticeable. It wasn't just the way he looked at me. His dismissive posturing was practically a snarl. If he thought I was passively waiting for the "atta girl" from him, he clearly didn't know me at all.

Around the city, a different type of storm was brewing. Radio shows, from the morning talk hosts to the evening drive-time jocks, between playing the hits, invited Chicago's angry and outraged citizens to call in. The outrage was bolstered by an editorial in the *Sun-Times* that called out police for glaring early signs of a very problematic case. Not to mention the lack of transparency at that sham of a press conference, which only fueled this combustible moment taking place yet again in this city. It was different this time, not isolated to the black community or the neighborhood and the few streets where the boys grew up or the church they attended. The air was thick with tension everywhere. A Black child was dead. Now three Black children were charged with her murder. Chicago braced itself for social unrest, and protesters shutting down Lake Shore Drive or tony Michigan Avenue like it did when a quarter million or more marched against an anti-immigration law pending in Congress a year ago.

With tensions running high, the station signed off on my making an appearance on the highest rated urban radio show in the city. While enormously successful, the show was typical in many ways, with two hyper-opinionated guys occasionally chastised into playing nice by a bold, unapologetic alpha female who spent much of her time shooting down their borderline misogynistic comments and standing up for the women listening in. But when it was time to pivot, like now, *The Get Up with Gil Show* abandoned its shtick for substance, recognizing its powerful contrast with mainstream media when it came to directly impacting Black lives.

The timing of these interviews could be a blessing or a curse. It would give me breaking news to talk about but would come with an expectation of more answers than I had to give as the first reporter to break the story.

"By now, most of us have heard about the three boys who've been charged in the murder of Masey James. One of the kids got in trouble for bringing a kitchen knife to school earlier this year. So now that makes him a murderer?" Gil Thompson opened with what sounded more like a statement than a question. "We're so lucky to be joined this morning by Jordan Manning of Channel 8 News. Welcome, Jordan."

"Thanks, Gil. I'm happy to be here," I said.

Gil sighed. "Whew, there's a lot to unpack. Let's start with the evidence. What proof do police say they have that points to these kids as the killers?"

"Gil, we don't know. Police have been very tight-lipped about what evidence they have connecting the boys to Masey's murder and even how they obtained it. We've heard about the knife incident, but what does it mean? They found a kitchen knife in the home. So what? People have kitchen knives. The lack of transparency has left people to imagine all types of scenarios, even the possibility of police planting the evidence," I said.

"The father told police his son took the knife to school because he was afraid for his own safety. He didn't hurt anyone. Our kids can't make mistakes," Gil said. "Jordan, I just read an article about the number of Black children in elementary school who are expelled for things that a kid in a White suburb would get detention for. But our kids get kicked out completely for the year, left to run the streets."

"Many things will be uncovered here, Gil. Your listeners, our viewers, are waiting to hear, at least right now, what comes out of the indictment against the thirteen-year-old and the juvenile petitions against the younger boys. And if it's not as clear as police are saying, heads are going to roll."

Heads are going to roll. Did I just say that? Check yourself, Jordan.

I mustn't be too emotional in my responses. I don't need police shutting down on me, or someone making it appear as though I'm more interested in proving the police wrong as opposed to accepting the sad possibility that they've arrested the right people, no matter their ages or their race.

Gil asked, "What's it like to cover a story like this as a Black reporter?"

Oh boy, here we go.

One of my pet peeves is something my colleagues and I have talked about many times. This is the perception by the police and others, including our newsroom colleagues, that Black reporters are incapable of reporting on what's happening in our community without bias. We instantly become part of the story if the suspects or victims are Black.

I took a deep breath, not knowing how to answer. Would it sting as much if the victim were a White girl Masey's age? Was it supposed to hurt more because Masey looked like me? There was no answer I could give that would make everyone happy.

"A victim is a victim. I care about everyone, Gil, I do. But I'll admit that this feels more personal, because when I look in the mirror, I know that Masey could be my sister, my cousin, or my child one day. So yes, it does hurt in a different way."

"Jordan Manning, thank you for coming on the show today. We'd love to check back in with you, because it doesn't look like this case is going away anytime soon."

"Thanks, Gil. It's been a pleasure."

"Oh, and before you go," he said, "you're still not married, are you?"

Just like that, he shifted from discussing a serious topic to taking a parting shot, demonstrating the true artistry of the radio morning show hosts, who were masterful at this. Bass, if he was listening, would have a field day with this. But I didn't mind because it was a break in the weight and the pain of it all.

"You're all up in my business, huh, Gil?" I retorted playfully.

"Hey, you know how it is when you get around family," he said. "This ain't the Channel 8 newsroom, okay? You're around family now, and family will get in your business."

Family.

"No, Gil, I'm still single," I said. "Happily single."

••

AM News Radio: The scene is building outside the Cook County Juvenile Justice Division, where dozens of residents, led by local activist Louise Robinson, have gathered in protest over the shocking murder charges brought against two eleven-year-old boys in the murder of Masey James.

After I left Gil, I made it back to the newsroom in time to grab coffee and hop in the news van with Scott and another cameraman to cover the growing unrest outside juvenile court during the hearing of Cecile Harvey and his best friend, Michael Blasingame. Derek Harvey, thirteen, was to be arraigned tomorrow at 26th and Cal. Father and son were both arrested the night of the scuffle with police, but Bernard Willis was released on a recognizance bond. Derek spent the night in adult lockup, where he remained in isolation for his own safety.

"Are you ready for this day?" Scott asked.

"How could anybody be ready for something like this?" I replied.

Police directed traffic as bodies and vehicles converged, moving at a crawl along the boulevard leading up to the courthouse. Parking was a scarce commodity, but luckily spots were reserved for news crews and we pulled up right in front amid the protest. As important as this case was to them, other cases were being heard here today, cases equally or more important to the individuals and families dealing with the heartbreak of losing a loved one to violence, or losing one so young to the system, struggling to come up with the bond money to bring them home and to get on with their lives.

For me, it would be a day of waiting around to do a live hit by the courthouse steps for the noon newscast, which I didn't appear on all that often. But for big stories like this one, I'm locked on them all day. The station sent Keith to sit in on the hearing. The state's attorney objected to media attending, and cameras are never allowed in juvenile court. But the chief judge granted permission for reporters to sit in and take handwritten notes once they agreed to temporarily surrender their cell phones.

While the boys' hearing was going on, I covered the protest and made a beeline to Louise Robinson, who was at the center of it all, bullhorn in hand, leading a chant: "Save our boys! Save our boys!" And "What do we want? Justice! When do we want it? Now!"

The boys' hearing concluded with them being remanded to custody in juvenile detention. Keith shared his notes with me, though it clearly pained him to do so.

The boys were named in the petitions, though protocol dictated the media not publicize them. All bets were off, though, for Derek, because he was being charged as an adult.

··

News anchor Iris Smith: Two eleven-year-old boys were officially charged this morning in the murder of Masey James. Our Jordan Manning reports from Cook County Juvenile Court.

Jordan: The hearing for the two eleven-year-old boys wrapped up here just over an hour ago. As you can see behind me, protesters are still here but not nearly the number that staked out the courthouse before the hearing. We now know that the two boys, as you just said, will be charged with accessory to murder after the fact, a felony. They will be held in Cook County juvenile detention. As for the thirteen-year-old, the older brother of one of the suspects, he will be arraigned tomorrow in adult court. At today's hearing, we learned that DNA evidence collected from the spot where the body was found matched evidence taken from the boys' shoes and clothing.

Iris: Jordan, any word on a motive?

Jordan: That remains a mystery, and police are saying very little. But activist Louise Robinson had plenty to say during a protest march that she and members of the South Side Community Council led here earlier today. She told me, simply put, that the dots don't connect.

Video clip of Louise Robinson: I'm here to save these boys. They are much younger than Masey. They've never attended the same schools as Masey. There is no link between these boys and Masey. Not one. When would they have encountered her? Where would the crime have taken place? These charges are an insult to our intelligence, and we demand that police go back to the drawing board, or wherever they need to go, to find out who did this. There's nothing anybody could tell me to make me believe that these children are the perpetrators.

Jordan: Iris, Louise Robinson and other protesters I spoke with earlier want to know what happened to the police following up on the mysterious driver that witnesses saw Masey getting into the car with after school.

Iris: Have police offered an update on the driver? Has that person been cleared?

Jordan: That's part of the problem. The protesters here feel police are laser focused on the boys. It's a horrific case they want to close. And now the people here are accusing them of rushing to tidy it all up.

..

After a nerve-racking two days of brutal radio silence, Joey, clearly not acknowledging the urgency behind my voice mail, finally called me back, and we agreed to meet, immediately, at a gas station south of downtown. I pulled up behind him, leaving some space in between our cars. I was on 10 when I got out of the car.

"Did you get my message?" I asked.

"Yeah, that's why I called you back," he said bluntly, telegraphing that I had work to do to mend this fence. "I'm still on duty, so I don't have a lot of time," he said, which explained his badge dangling from a chain around his neck and his casual plainclothes attire—loose-fitting jeans, a flannel shirt, and Timberlands.

The distance between our cars, I began to feel, was symbolic of the distance I sensed between us.

I haven't seen Joey in months. He really is a handsome man. That's what you're thinking about, Jordan, in the midst of all that's happening?

"Did you find out anything about those guys?"

"Yes, but we need to talk about Bartlett and what you did first," he said.

He is still irritated with me.

"What happened that day? What did Bartlett say?" I asked.

"Bartlett didn't say anything; it was Fawcett. I passed the message on to him. I said I'd do it. Why couldn't you wait for me?"

"Joe, I'm sorry, but you have to understand—"

"No, Jordan, you're the one who needs to understand! Stay in your lane. You're doing too much. You could end up doing more harm than good. You are a reporter, okay? You are not an investigator. I get it. You went to school and you studied forensics, and now you think you get to play both roles. That's not how it works. Get your pen and your pad and write a story instead of trying to make the story about you."

"Who uses a pen and pad? I have a laptop." My sarcasm was disarming. Knocked him right off the soapbox he was prepared to stand on until I raised the white flag, which I did to keep things moving. He gave me the side-eye and shook his head, and we both laughed.

"Joey, okay, I'm sorry. Are we okay?" I reached over and caressed his forearm. "Because I need you. I really need you."

After a brief silence he said, "Don't say that. I might take it the wrong way."

All right, that came out of nowhere.

I withdrew my hand, and after I didn't respond to whatever point he was trying to make, he continued.

"Okay! So I got your message about Terrence Bankhead. I didn't find anything on him. You've got to get me a birth date or an address or something."

"What about Manny?" I asked.

"Jackpot! His real name is Emmanuel Walker. He's done time. He was convicted of aggravated battery back in 2003. He spent a few months in Cook County Jail before being transferred to Joliet."

"How long did he serve?"

"Almost two years. He just got off parole in May. That's how I was able to connect him to the address you gave me."

"Who did he beat up?"

"The details in the report were kind of sketchy, but it had something to do with an altercation with a girlfriend."

"Yvonne?" I asked.

"No, I can't remember the name on the police report, but it wasn't Yvonne. He pled guilty to the charge. There haven't been any incidents since then. According to his parole officer, he went to barber school and he cuts hair somewhere," Joey said. "But I'll find more on Bankhead. Everybody's got a footprint. I just need more time."

"You're exactly right. I didn't get a chance to tell you, but Yvonne said he lives with someone named Brent Carter. Both go to Manny to get their hair cut. He cuts hair in his basement, by the way."

I thought back to Yvonne's vibe when she said we should go back upstairs before Manny returned. She seemed more eager to get out of there than she was to confront him about Terrence.

"They all know one another. So now what? Have the police questioned Manny? I'm hearing nothing on the ground."

"I have to be careful. If the department finds out I'm leaking information to you, it doesn't end well for me."

"You don't believe those kids killed Masey, do you?"

"Hell no!"

"Police are no longer looking for the driver who was seen picking her up from school?"

"Not sure. I've been trying to find out. Nobody wants to tell me anything anymore. Fawcett put the word out, I think, that I'm leaking to the press. They're focused on the kids. I went to

Bartlett and told him I'd gotten a tip about the mystery person picking up Masey from school."

I wonder if that was before or after I spoke with Bartlett.

"I'll follow up today," Joey said.

"One more thing," I said. "There's a kid at Masey's school who may be a good eyewitness. He's on the football team at Crest."

"Oh yeah? They've got a really good squad this year," Joey said. "What's his name?"

"I don't know. I didn't talk to him; an intern did. She was so unprepared, she forgot to ask him his name, and she wasn't able to fully describe him. So, it's probably a dead end at this point."

Joey dropped and shook his head, appearing as broken and frustrated as I was becoming by the endless roadblocks. I started to walk back to my car, then turned and asked, "Are we good?"

Joey closed the space between us and rested his hands on my shoulders. "We are as long as you promise to stay away from Manny Walker's house. Because if detectives do show up to question him, he'll know who tipped them off."

13

The case against the boys has an emotional grip on people across this city. No matter their occupation or zip code, Chicagoans throw it into the conversation, from beauty shops and barbershops on the South and West Sides to the posh residences along the Gold Coast that at times feel far removed from the realities of life for most city residents. So when I got the email with the subject line "MANDATORY TOWN HALL TONIGHT AT 6 P.M.," I had an inkling of what the meeting was about. Chicago's newsrooms aren't nearly as diverse as the city is. Ellen, in fact, is the only high-ranking female news executive at Chicago's four major networks, and there's not one general manager who is Black, Latino, or Asian. So whenever a high-profile case touches the live wire of race or gender, the trepidation reporters feel over saying the wrong thing and being called out for it can lead to animus that spills over into the work environment. With unprecedented murder charges lodged against three Black minor children, it's quite clear we are sitting on a powder keg. Before that toxicity spills over into the newsroom, Ellen and Nussbaum called this meeting to hear from their staff.

Ellen knows that in the eyes of the people in the community, our coverage has put us on the same side as the police, fueling a perception that we're somehow all in it together. That we're not scrutinizing the police nearly enough. We're just taking their word for it. They have no idea that behind the scenes, TV reporters and journalists at the local papers have been scrutinizing the hell out of the police. But that doesn't always come through in the coverage.

I was just about to step away from my desk to head to the meeting when my cell phone rang. *Who is this?*

With everything that's going on, I can't afford not to answer a call.

"Hello?"

"Jordan, it's Yvonne Alonzo. Do you have a minute?"

I didn't give Yvonne my number. She must have gotten it from Pam.

"Sure, I was just headed to a meeting, but . . . what's wrong?"

Yvonne sounded breathless. I could practically hear her heart beating through the phone. "Terrence came over, and he and Manny got into a fight."

"They got into a fight? What happened?"

"After you left, I couldn't get it out of my head, ya know, why Manny didn't question him more about what he was doing with Masey. When he got home, I confronted him. He got real defensive at first. 'Why are you asking me this all of a sudden?' I told him after me and Pam talked to you, a lot of things didn't add up."

"But how did he end up in a fight with Terrence?"

"Manny blew up. He kept saying, 'I don't need this shit!' and 'Why are you talking about me to reporters?' But I was like, 'You mean, it never crossed your mind he could have something to do with Masey?' And he said, 'We're going to straighten this out right now.' Then he called Terrence and Terrence came over. I overheard Manny talking to Terrence on the phone. The way he sounded when he asked him to stop by. The fact he came over so fast, Terrence had to know what Manny wanted to talk to him about," Yvonne said. "I was surprised how calm he seemed when he got here."

"So then what happened?"

"Terrence met me and Manny downstairs in the barbershop. He seemed caught off guard that I was with Manny. Before we could say anything, he said, 'Man, I'm gonna get that money I owe you.' Apparently, Jordan, Manny lent him a thousand dollars. Manny told him it wasn't about the money; it was about Masey. Terrence blew up. 'Look, man, I'm so sorry about what happened with her, but what's that got to do with me?' That's when Manny said, 'You act like you hardly knew her, but that's a lie.' Before Terrence could respond, Manny asked him: 'Were you messing around with her?' Terrence just stood there. He wasn't saying nothing at first, but then he tried to leave. He told Manny he wasn't gonna have this conversation with him, and that he was out of here. Manny stood in front of the door and flat out asked him, 'Did you do something to her?' Terrence was like, 'Get out of my face with that bullshit, man. Are you crazy?' And Manny *lost* it. The next thing I knew, Manny had him on the floor, beating his ass. I was screaming at Manny to stop. I don't know how Terrence got out from under him, but he took off running. Manny tried to run after him, but I grabbed him and begged him not to follow him. He could've had a gun in the car. I just begged him to let him go! Let him go!"

"And did he?"

"He had no choice. By the time he got to the top of the stairs, Terrence was in his car. He yelled out the window that he was going to call the police and 'Your ass is going back to prison!'"

This is the worst thing that could've happened. If Terrence does make good on his threat and calls the police and they come for Manny, my name might come up, and I don't need detectives knowing I was over there talking to Yvonne and Pam.

"Yvonne, I'm so sorry that happened. Are you okay?"

"Yeah, I'm fine."

"Where's Manny now?"

"He's in the kitchen with some ice on his hand," she said.

"Call me if the police show up at your house, okay? Sorry, but I've got to get to this mandatory staff meeting. I'll call you later."

I have less than four minutes to get to the newsroom town hall. I grabbed my cell phone and called Joey on the way upstairs to tell him what happened, but he didn't answer.

What is with this guy, never answering his phone?

"Joey, I just heard that Manny and Terrence got into a fight. I'm heading into a meeting. Call me!"

I made it to the town hall just under the wire. The editorial staff was packed tightly into the large conference room overlooking the theater district, Broadway in Chicago. The email from Ellen and Nussbaum described the event as a time for people to vent but also be reminded that we have an obligation "to follow the facts wherever they lead," a journalistic cliché if ever there was one.

I grabbed a seat next to Simone Michele, the daughter of veteran reporter Grayson Michele. Although Simone was the beneficiary of nepotism, she was a strong reporter in her own right. I liked Simone a lot and wished we had more time to spend together, but with her working the overnight shift, it just wasn't possible.

She greeted me warmly. "Hey, Jordan, how've you been, girl? It's so good to see you!" she said.

"You too!" I replied. "Remind me that we have to find a way to make these drinks happen one day."

Nussbaum, as important as it was to have this conversation, recognized it was Friday evening, and people would be somewhat distracted, thinking about how long it would take them to get home on the Kennedy Expressway in the notorious evening traffic. So he opened the meeting at six on the dot.

"Good evening, everyone. Thank you all for coming," he said.

Simone whispered in my ear, "Like we had a choice."

"I know you all want to get home. But clearly, if I didn't think this was important, we wouldn't be here," Nussbaum said, then launched into his spiel about how Chicago is the lead story nationally, and there are concerns that violence will spill out onto the streets if police have wrongfully accused these boys of murder. "Now, with all these national reporters coming in, I want to make sure our newsroom is a united front and everyone feels liberated to speak up and talk about the impact this case is having on all our lives, professionally and personally."

Then I heard my name.

"Jordan, I'm calling you out. You've been on this story since the beginning. I know you think we failed off the top for having a blind spot when it came to covering the story and giving it the attention it should've received from the start, and you were right," Nussbaum said. "And those are the things we have to come to grips with. What kind of baggage are we carrying into the newsroom? And are we as guilty as anybody else of valuing one type of person over another?"

Some of my colleagues nodded in agreement while others grimaced, disagreeing with Nussbaum's blanket statement. Not everybody recognizes their bias, and rubbing their noses in it doesn't make it any better.

"But now we're faced with this awful set of circumstances of children accused of murder. Not gang violence, but a savage murder of an innocent girl. And I imagine, some of us are experiencing disbelief much like what we're hearing about in the black community."

"Disbelief over what? That they were charged?" Keith interjected.

A voice in the crowd said, "Do you know how many people were sentenced to death row in Illinois alone who were innocent?"

Keith didn't answer the question. Instead, he responded, "You really need to give the police a break. They're doing the best job they can. This idea that all cops are bad cops or ready to set up some kids has been overplayed. There are some bad apples, I'll give you that. But there are also plenty of bad apples in the hood."

Both his tone and his choice of *the hood* didn't play well among his peers, eliciting groans and exasperated sighs.

Ellen jumped in and went for the jugular. "Keith, be careful. I know you think every situation is an audition for your cable news show. But we're trying to have a productive conversation here based on facts, not what-about-isms."

"Wow!" I said, louder than I meant to. Simone discreetly hit my thigh with a swift *pop!* reminiscent of the way my aunt used to correct me in church when I was playing too much and distracting the entire pew from the sermon.

"Look, the police have done very little to help themselves," I said. "None of the evidence that they have provided explains why these boys are in custody right now. And to be honest with you, I don't believe they did it."

"Why? Because they're Black?" Keith asked.

"No, Keith, because I've been talking *to* people, not talking *about* people. I've actually been doing my job. Not to mention that I have the ability to see them as innocent before proven guilty, whereas someone like you struggles with that, and I'm sure you're not the only one in here."

"You act like the only way a person can understand someone

is if they're from their neighborhood. That's ridiculous!" Keith said.

"Am I from their neighborhood, Keith? Am I from their neighborhood? No! I'm not even from Illinois."

"So, let me ask you, what proof do you have that they didn't do it?" Keith asked.

"The same proof I had that Masey James wasn't a runaway— they don't fit the profile."

I'd allowed Keith to bait me into a sanctimonious posture. We were dominating the conversation, and I sensed our colleagues were growing irritated with us both. So did Ellen.

"Guys, guys," Ellen intervened. "This is not about the two of you or your egos. This isn't the type of honesty we were hoping for."

Keith, not interested in defusing the situation, went into attack mode. "Hey, Jordan, since we're opening up, why don't you tell us how you took an intern out on assignment and put her life in danger."

His words hit me like a sucker punch. My eyes narrowed to an infuriated squint. He wasn't finished.

"You're questioning my integrity? Your professionalism is in the toilet and your career should be, too, given what Grace said happened when you took her out."

No good deed . . .

"Screw you, Keith!" I said. "And speaking of toilet, excuse me, I'm going to the ladies' room."

But I had no intention of going to the bathroom. I was headed to my car in the garage before I said something that could get me fired. Before I reached the elevators, I heard Ellen behind me.

"Jordan! Jordan! Wait! Stop!"

I didn't want to talk to Ellen. I felt her ego comment was

unnecessary. How dare she put me in the same category as Keith, someone we both despise.

"What?" I turned around. "Are you sure you can stand my 'ego' long enough to have this conversation?"

"All reporters have egos, Jordan," she said. "I just said what everybody was thinking. What *did* happen with Grace?" she went on. "What did he mean by 'You put her life in danger'?"

"Her life wasn't in danger, Ellen. Any neighborhood that has more than four Black people is dangerous to him."

"What was she doing with you in the first place?"

"I was mentoring her, okay? She jumped at the chance to go with me to the area where Masey lived to see if I could get some leads."

"So you're telling me you took her after work with no one knowing. Just the two of you? To investigate? Are you crazy?"

"I know you don't expect me to answer that, do you?"

"Have you lost your mind? She's an intern! We barely let them leave the building to protect the station from litigation. If something were to happen to one of them . . ."

"I ran into her, okay? I wasn't thinking. You're right. She shouldn't have been out there," I said.

"And you probably shouldn't have been out there, either. You're a reporter, Jordan, not a cop," she said. "It was reckless and irresponsible."

Her words stung. "That's not what happened. I need to go back in there and clear this up."

"I think it's better if you don't," she said as I started to walk back toward the conference room. "Go home and get some rest. I'll clear things up. Trust me, nobody is dying to be on Keith's side. You've been hitting it pretty hard lately. Take a load off for the night."

I nodded but still felt bruised. My newsroom BFF just reminded me that she's still my boss. I guess it was a fine line at times. This was one of them.

"Yeah," I said. "That's exactly what I need to do."

··

Before leaving the station, I texted Thomas. **U still at the gym? Heading over for a workout.**

I hadn't been to the gym in two weeks and was surprised Thomas hadn't been hounding me by now. Certainly the ridiculous membership fee to belong to an exclusive club with the occasional celebrity sighting, on a reporter's salary, should be enough motivation. Even with an advanced degree, I wasn't earning anywhere near what Chicago's legendary Black news anchors were getting paid, some with multimillion-dollar contracts.

The membership is a waste of money if I don't use it. And if I'm being honest with myself, I joined more for prestige than health reasons. The workout clothes I keep in my trunk are a charade. I don't even know if they fit anymore.

I pulled into the garage of the gym—I mean *the club*—and took the stairs up to the rear access door to the women's locker room. Weekdays between nine A.M. and two P.M. it's packed with women in designer workout gear skipping lunch for a midday sweat and affluent professional housewives attending one-on-one Pilates sessions. Then they stay for a heavy dose of juicy gossip as plentiful as the chilled, logoed water bottles they hand you at the check-in counter, which resembles the concierge desk of a five-star hotel.

At nearly seven o'clock on a Friday, the after-work crowd had cleared out and I practically had the place to myself. I went directly to the treadmill room, where TVs lined the wall, and I cringed at the thought of one of my taped reports airing while I was getting my heart rate up. There were a few dedicated stragglers working out late, as evidenced by the grunting and the sneakers screeching across the multiple basketball courts where city council members stripped off their suits to go up against former ballplayers and a mix of characters. It's anyone's guess what they do for a living, but they can afford the membership.

Just as I was elevating the incline on the treadmill, I heard a voice behind me. "You can do better than that. Push it! Come on!"

It was Thomas in all his delicious grandeur in a tank top, showing off his nearly perfect body. *Who am I kidding? It is perfect!*

"You're never here this late," he said. "What's going on?"

I said through panting breaths. "It was . . . either . . . the treadmill . . . or murder. I chose the treadmill."

"Rough day, huh? Bet I know how I can make it better."

I gave him the side-eye. "Is that all you ever think about?"

"Baby, that's all you allow me to think about."

Thomas was being particularly flirtatious. He kept staring and smiling at me. I almost wanted to ask him if he had a secret, but instead, I said, "You're in a good mood tonight."

"Maybe I'm just happy to see you," he said.

There's not a chance in hell I'm finishing this workout.

For someone who badgered me about getting to the gym more, he seemed more interested in distracting me, and didn't seem to mind when I finally gave up and pushed the decline button over and over in a series of beeps, lowering the belt back to zero and slowing to a stop.

"I need a salad. Walk with me up to the café."

I stepped off the belt and Thomas's eyes scanned me from

head to toe. I shook my head. "Don't be so obvious. You're not supposed to be fraternizing with the guests."

I headed toward the elevators. "Uh-uh," he said. "Let's take the stairs."

"Fine," I huffed.

"So who are you trying not to kill?" he asked.

"I'd rather not talk about it," I said. "I just want to get a salad to go and veg on my couch."

We made it up the mezzanine-level café/smoothie bar just as it was about to close.

"What do you want, babe?"

"I'll take a number five with balsamic," I said, and reached into my zip compartment for my credit card.

"I've got it, babe," he said, instructing the cashier. "Charge it to my account."

It was a nice feeling, being taken care of. I just never want to feel like I owe anybody anything.

"I'll be off in an hour," he said. "You want me to come by?"

"Let me see how I feel in an hour. It's been a rough day. Call me before you leave, okay?"

He stared at the ground. When he looked back up, his smile had evaporated. "Why can't you ever just say yes the first time? Huh? Why do you do that?"

"If I have to answer right now, it'll be a hard no. Is that what you want?"

"A *hard* no," he said, raising his right brow with a devilish grin. "The last time, I seem to remember you saying a good . . . hard . . . *yes!*"

I shook my head. "Wow, you went there? Okay. We'll see. Call me."

"Well, at least let me walk you to your car," he said.

It was almost eight o'clock when I pulled out of the garage.

The endorphins from the workout, even though I hadn't put in my usual thirty minutes, kicked in, and I started to feel better, more clearheaded. I'd told Yvonne that I would call her back, but I assumed that wasn't what she expected. After the brawl, Yvonne was searching her mind for what to do next, afraid her man could be on his way back to jail. Maybe she reached out to me hoping for some advice, but I didn't have any answers for her. If Terrence filed a complaint and the police had arrested Manny, she would have called back. Or Joey would have called to let me know by now. That much I was certain of. So I decided to hedge my bets and wait to hear from Joey.

I turned on the radio in the middle of Lauryn Hill's "Killing Me Softly," and my shoulders, tightened by stress, relaxed. It wasn't looking good for Thomas. All I could think about was taking a shower and settling into bed just as the city was coming alive. Groups of friends walked vibrantly down Restaurant Row, while others congregated on the sidewalk waiting for a table at a new high-end diner. No longer in my twenties, I couldn't be further from that energy. Jockeying for a reservation or mapping out which bars to hit on the weekend didn't appeal to me as much as it used to. Dinner at home or at one of my girls' places with a couple bottles of wine, laughing and talking as loudly as we wanted to without worrying about someone overhearing us and calling a gossip columnist to spill the beans on the lady from the news, made for a much more pleasurable evening. But tonight, it would be just me and my salad watching the evening news, then lights out.

I pulled into the driveway, reached into my console, and grabbed the key fob, my golden ticket home, easing into the garage. Lauryn sang me up the spiral drive, and I turned up the volume as the song climaxed and cruised to the eighth-floor landing. Then my moment of Zen was shattered—someone had parked in my space again.

"Fuck! This cannot be happening! What the hell is wrong with people?"

I pounded on the steering wheel as I drove past the gray sedan, eyeballing the Illinois license plate JLV 5491. My head throbbed and my face grew hot with anger. This time, I decided, I was going to file a complaint with the board, and, in fact, would compose a letter and email it tonight.

"This is ridiculous! I cannot believe this shit!"

I fumed all the way down the driveway back to street level to access the roof.

Thank God it's not raining or snowing.

As I exited the garage, I caught a glimpse of Bass having an animated conversation with someone at the guard's desk. Bass talked to everybody. It was his favorite way to pass the time on the night shift.

On the deck, as I feared, nearly all the spaces closest to the door accessing the stairwell had been taken, and I had to park in the farthest corner away. I turned down the radio just in time to hear my phone ringing. It was Joey.

"Hello?" I answered, sounding angrier than I meant to.

"Hi, what's wrong with you?" he said.

"I'm sorry," I said, turning off the engine. "Someone parked in my space again tonight. This is the second time in a week! Pisses me off! Excuse the rant. Did you get my message?"

"Yeah, I did. So these two guys came to blows? How bad was it?"

"Yvonne told me Manny was on top of Terrence beating him in the face and head, so pretty bad."

"What set him off?" Joey asked.

"Yvonne confronted Manny about letting Terrence off the hook when he acted like he barely knew Masey after she disappeared. That obviously was a lie, because he'd bought her an expensive jacket and took her and some of her friends on a photo shoot."

"What? A photo shoot?"

"Yeah, I didn't tell you. This guy passes himself off as connected in the entertainment world. Music, fashion, you name it. Manny called him and asked him to stop by. Terrence thought it was about some money he owed him, but Manny asked him if he did something to Masey. When Terrence acted nonchalant, Manny flipped out on him. Yvonne said Terrence threatened to call the police."

"He ain't gonna call the police, Jordan. If he did, they would ask what happened and his dealings with Masey would come out. What's a thirty-year-old man doing hanging with a bunch of teenage girls and buying them clothes and shit? Manny should've beat his ass for that alone. A man who just got off parole wouldn't risk going back to prison if he didn't think this guy hadn't done something."

"Or maybe he just has a short fuse," I said. "He did go to jail for battery."

"Well, now you know why I told you to stay from over there. It's dangerous, Jordan," he said. "Guys like Bankhead disgust me. I'll find him."

I started to gather up my things to get out of the car. "Okay, Joe, thanks for calling. Let me get inside my apartment. I need a reset."

"All right," he said. "Good night."

My hands full, I got out of the car, struggling to carry the food, my gym bag, and my extra-large tote at once. I could use another hand or could just make another trip, which wasn't going to happen. My thighs couldn't handle the burn.

The release from my workout, however brief, and my thirty seconds of Zen on the drive home were long gone. Right now all I want to do is eat my salad under the covers and be done with it. And as crazy as this day has been, some things never change. The light near the access door was still broke, only now instead of flickering, it was completely out.

Damnit, how hard is it to fix a lightbulb?

I pulled a pen with a flashlight at the tip that I picked up at the dentist's office out of the tote and used it to help illuminate my path. *Who knew it would come in handy?* Steps from the heavy steel door, I heard a man's voice.

"So you're still not married, Jordan?"

I looked around. "Excuse me?"

Gil from the radio morning show had razzed me about my marital status during my appearance. "Gil?" I turned around. "Is that . . ."

I felt an explosion of pain in the middle of my forehead, then another to the back of my skull. I spun around and fell backward. My head hit the pavement so hard it bounced off the concrete.

"You fucked up, bitch! You fucked up!"

The fall knocked the wind out of me. I couldn't even scream. I was disoriented, and what little I could make out in the darkness was blurred. Before I could recover, the force of his fist struck me hard across my right cheek.

Dear God! What is happening? Help!

There was another blow to my forehead. He was saying something, but I couldn't make it out. The next thing I felt was his body on top of me. He was yelling, crushing me, cutting off the little bit of air that remained in my lungs. I felt something warm running down my nose and mouth. Everything was moving in slow motion but rapidly at the same time. I could feel his warm breath on my face as he continued to shout words I couldn't make out. But I could feel his rage. He closed his hands around my neck and pressed down. I would've fought him if I could, but I was overpowered, gasping for air. For the first time in my life, I thought *This is it. This is how I die.* And the world went dark.

14

I woke up in an ambulance, awash in a blinding antiseptic light, a siren screaming and bouncing around my skull like a banshee straight out of hell. A blurry, muffled figure hovered above. "You're going to be okay."

But I was unable to respond. All I could see, feel, and smell were the moments following the initial blow. Hot breath on my skin. Hands as rough as sandpaper around my throat. A crushing weight on top of me, stunting my breathing, and that smell. Industrial, oily, like an accelerant. I gasped for air. If my arms hadn't been strapped to my sides, I would have reached up and touched my face, felt my own breath against my skin to remind myself that I was still alive. My reliving it was broken only by the calming words "Ms. Manning, you're safe now."

A man with dark hair and glasses came into focus. He was wearing a navy blue collared shirt, and there was a patch on his sleeve with the American flag and the four-star Chicago flag crisscrossing a flame or a snake. I couldn't tell which. I tried to lift my head, but a bolt of pain shot through the base of my skull and out through my forehead.

All I could hear was my attacker's assertion: *You fucked up. You fucked up.* My thoughts were dizzying.

Who called the ambulance? It must have been Bass. I bet he's freaking out right now.

My brain fog lifted, and the day's events replayed like a sizzle reel. Yvonne confronted Manny. Manny beat up Terrence.

Manny's been violent before. The only two people who would have thought I'd fucked up were Manny and Terrence. But I'd never even met Terrence. What did Manny tell him?

My next recollection was the jarring motion as the gurney was pulled out of the ambulance and rolled through sliding glass doors, then parked in the hallway up against a wall.

Where's my phone?

I felt around the gurney to see if someone had left it by my side. I was in too much pain to sit up and look.

Did the assailant take my phone? Was I robbed? But why would a mugger say that I fucked up?

It was cold and much, much too bright in the hallway. My adrenaline was on a sliding scale, fluctuating between extreme highs and lows. I closed my eyes, and all I could see was red behind my eyelids. I tried to turn my head, but it felt like an hourglass, heavier with sand on one side than the other. After a few minutes, someone wheeled me into an emergency room cubicle and sealed me in with a closed curtain.

Moments later, the curtain was whisked away and a woman with short blond hair and a voice so buttery smooth, I wondered whether she'd ever done voice-over work, walked in and got right in my face. "Jor-dan. Jordan Manning," she said, speaking loudly. "Is that your name?"

I nodded and pulled down the oxygen mask as she asked me what seemed like a never-ending series of questions. What year is it? Where do you work? What city are you in?

I was sore, but my cognition returned rapidly and so did my need-to-knows. "Can I speak to one of the officers who was at the scene?"

"Just try to relax. You're okay now," she tried to reassure me.

"Where are my things? My purse, my phone. I need my phone."

"Just try to relax, Jordan. It's going to be all right."

"No! You don't understand, I need my phone!"

I sat up a little too quickly and my neck snapped back like I'd been lassoed. Aware of my surroundings, I didn't want to bring attention to myself, so I gritted my teeth to suppress all parts of my body telling me to scream. My face was numb, reminding me of that strange sensation after waking up from dental surgery before the novocaine had worn off.

Is my chin still on my face? I think so.

I brought my hand up to my right cheek and was suddenly terrified of what I must look like. The last time I got punched in the face was in the fourth grade, by a boy. I went crazy and tried to scratch his eyes out. Before it was over, the teacher had to pull me off him.

There's no way they're going to let me on the air tomorrow. Are you actually more worried about how you look right now after what just happened?

"Ms. Manning, you need to lie down," the nurse pleaded. "You likely have a concussion. Please! Lie back down."

I tried, but that just made the pain worse. "I can't. It hurts too much. Just let me stay like this. Is my phone here?"

The nurse told me my belongings would arrive soon.

"How did they find me?" I asked.

"Someone who lives in your building discovered you and a guy who works there. You were both unconscious," she said.

"What's his name?"

"I have no idea. I'll see what I can find out, okay?" the nurse said, speaking to me in a soothing tone of voice like she would a child about to get her first shot. "But you need to lie down for me first, okay?"

"And please, see if you can locate my phone. I need my phone," I said.

"Will do, just sit tight. My name is Maggie, by the way," she said.

"Thanks, Maggie."

After she hadn't returned ten minutes later, my patience was worn thin.

What's taking her so long to get the answer?

A rush of adrenaline took me from the sitting position to thrusting my legs over the side of the gurney. Before I knew anything, I was up on my feet, wobbling across the floor and clutching the privacy curtain to steady myself. I pulled it open slightly, and then I realized I was only a few feet away from the nurses' station located in the center of the room.

"Excuse me," I blurted as I got closer to the desk nurse tapping away on a computer. "I'm trying to find out the name of the person who was found with me."

The desk nurse was far less congenial than Maggie. "Ma'am, what are you doing up?" she scolded me. "You need to go back and lie down."

"Please, you don't understand. I need to find out. Who is it?" I pleaded.

A rush of fear took hold of me that it was Bass. He probably saw me drive up to the roof on the security cameras. He had ventured upstairs to escort me down before, like the time the access door got locked accidentally. Tonight maybe he went up to check on me and ran right into the assailant. It was the only logical explanation.

Oh my God! What happened?

Tears poured down my face. I could no longer feel the pain from my injuries. A panic attack surged through my body and I felt unsteady on my feet.

"You're not okay," she said. "You need to be checked out. Now get back to your room, or I'll have to call security."

"My God! Can't somebody tell me who it is?" I screamed.

"Ms. Manning, I've got a name for her," said the nurturing voice of Nurse Maggie, appreciated far more now than before. "Harold Brantley. He works security in the building."

Bass.

"How is he? Where is he? Can I see him?"

"He's being prepped for emergency surgery," Nurse Maggie said. "Apparently, he was stabbed during the attack."

Just like that, the wind was knocked out of me for the second time tonight. I clutched my chest and my body lunged forward as I burst into an avalanche of tears.

"You know him," Maggie said. "I'm so sorry, but you really need to lie down and let a doctor examine you."

She took me by the shoulders, but my feet wouldn't budge. "Do you have my phone?" I asked.

"Your belongings should be here very soon," she said. "Okay, back to bed now."

"I've gotta make a call. Can I use that phone?" I asked, pointing to the phone on the supervisor's desk. "Please, it's urgent!"

"Ma'am . . ." started the desk nurse.

"Ple-e-a-se!" I cried. But my sobbing and begging only made the desk nurse more strident.

"Come on," she said. "Let's go!"

She got up to walk around the desk. While her back was turned, I reached over and grabbed the phone and dialed Joey.

Please answer. Please answer.

"Samuels?"

"Joey! It's Jordan," I managed to say through my sobs.

"What's wrong?"

"I'm at Northwestern. Someone attacked me at my apartment—"

"In your apartment?" he asked.

"No, not in my apartment. In the parking lot," I said.

"Ma'am! You cannot use that phone!" said my now nemesis of the ER.

"Wait!" I said, holding my hand up to her. "I'm talking to the police!"

She stood defiantly in front of me with her arms folded. Her mouth was moving, but I wasn't focused on what she was saying. The other nurse held on to my left elbow, trying to nudge me toward my ER pod.

"Jordan! Can you hear me?" Joey said. "What happened?"

"And Bass was stabbed!"

"How badly are you hurt?"

"I'm in the ER," I cried. "Please, get here fast!"

"Okay, that's it," I heard Nurse Ratched say from behind. "I need some help over here getting a patient back to her room!"

Just then, I looked up and saw Ellen rushing toward me.

"Jordan, my God, are you okay?" Ellen gently wrapped her arms around me as if I would break. "What are you doing up?" she asked.

I was determined to stay up on my own two feet, but I felt flush, faint.

"What are you doing out here?" Ellen asked again. "Oh, Jordan, look at you!" she said, placing a hand over her mouth.

"Excuse me," the other nurse said, "if this is a friend of yours, can you convince her to get back in bed? She hasn't even been seen by a doctor yet."

"Sure," Ellen said. "Come on, Jordan." She wrapped her arm around my shoulders and guided me back to the gurney. I climbed under the sheet. Nurse Maggie cradled my head, taking the pressure off my neck, and slowly lowered me back onto the pillow.

"What were you trying to do out there?" Ellen asked. "Jesus!"

Ellen had no idea who Bass was. He'd become like a little brother to me. Learning that Bass had been seriously hurt felt more injurious than the beating itself.

"Ellen, you don't understand. I just found out my friend who's a guard in the building was stabbed during the attack," I explained. "He's one of the closest people to me in this town, and I need to know where he is right now. Where is he having surgery? What floor? This is all my fault."

"No-o-o," Ellen said. "You can't blame yourself for this. He tried to save you."

"How do you know that?"

"You know some of the best sources are paramedics and people who work at the hospital, right?" she said. "The *Sun-Times* got wind of what happened and called the desk to confirm that you were the victim. They probably picked it up on the police scanner. They knew even before we did. I called your mother, by the way. Don't give me that look."

The next-of-kin rule. When you're unmarried, your emergency contact is none other than your mom.

I grimaced. *She's freaking out right now.*

"Ellen, this wasn't a random attack. He kept saying, 'You fucked up.' He was there for me. He was waiting for me."

"But why?" she asked.

"It has to be connected to the Masey James case," I said. "A lot has happened." I took a deep breath and told Ellen how I believed Masey had gotten entangled with an older guy, about the fight between Terrence and Manny, and about my suspicion that either one or both of them could have been involved in Masey's murder and tonight's attack.

"Otherwise, this is one helluva coincidence. And I don't believe in coincidences," I said.

A swell of confusion floated across Ellen's face. Frozen, half confused, half in disbelief, she lit into me. "What in the hell were you thinking?" she said, pacing the room with her hand pressed against her forehead. "If you wanted to be a cop, why did you become a journalist?"

Okay, is there a sign on me that reads "Jordan, you're not a cop"*? Because if I hear this one more time . . .*

"You could've been killed!"

Ellen morphed into the personification of tough love. She was furious with me but at the same time deeply concerned, as was I, that someone was out to shut me up. "I know you're dedicated, but you've gotta ease up. It's no longer you *might* get hurt. You *did* get hurt!"

"Ellen, there are three little Black boys locked up right now on murder charges," I said. "They didn't do it. You know—"

Ellen interrupted. "Jordan, we can deal with that. But Keith was right. You put Grace in unnecessary danger, and I was willing to give you the benefit of the doubt. The case is important, but you've been reckless and impulsive. This is the second time I've had to call you reckless today. What don't you get? I don't know how much longer I can defend you."

The curtain rustled and a woman in a white coat walked toward me. "Hello, Jordan, I'm Dr. Tina Patel," she said, extending a hand. "How are you feeling? Looks like you've been through a terrible ordeal. Let's have a look at you."

Dr. Patel was the escape I needed from the wrath of Ellen, whose anger had gone from a simmer to a boil. She was about to explode.

"Can you excuse us for a moment?" the doctor asked.

"Can you see if you can track down my phone?" I asked Ellen. "Please?"

Ellen nodded yes as she glowered at me, trying to conceal her anger from the doctor.

It only now occurred to me that I hadn't looked at my face. Based on Dr. Patel's reaction, I wasn't sure I wanted to.

"Dr. Patel, if it's all right, can I go to the bathroom first?" I asked.

"Sure. There's one just around the corner to the right."

I scooched across the floor in my hospital-issued nonslip socks and gown to the tiny bathroom. I felt like I was crashing, so I closed the door and leaned against it to steady myself, then reached out and grabbed the sink and lifted my eyes. I didn't recognize the person in the mirror. My top lip was so swollen that it almost completely covered my bottom lip. A cut above my right brow dripped dried blood and my right eyelid was half closed. I turned my head and there was the literal imprint of his fist fused into my cheek, as if my skin was some type of mold. Right then, any doubt that remained that this attack wasn't random was removed. I'd been the victim of pure rage, not simply in the wrong place at the wrong time. Whoever did this came for me, and he found me.

My eyes bloodshot red, all cried out, I made my way back to the examination room. I read in Dr. Patel's face that she had sensed I was visibly more shaken when I returned than when I'd left. I'd worked hard to prove that I was more than a pretty face. But the reality was that in television, the way I look was tantamount to my ability to work in this business and advance to the next level.

"Are you okay?" she asked.

All I could do was shake my head no.

"Let me get a look at you," she said.

Dr. Patel examined me, paying attention to every contour of my face like a sculptor. "The good news is you don't need stitches," she said.

I breathed a sigh of relief. *Thank God!*

"But I would like to run a CT scan to rule out any bleeding or clotting on the brain. So I want to keep you overnight."

Great.

"Beyond that, I think you're going to be fine, at least on the outside."

As she turned to leave, I snapped out of my own lassitude to ask her what she knew about Bass.

"Dr. Patel, there was someone brought in with me named Harold Brantley. A nurse told me he was in surgery, that he'd been stabbed. Can you get some information on how he's doing? Where he is?" I asked.

"Yes, the nurse told me you'd been asking about him. I checked right before I came in. He's in pretty bad shape. Worse off than you. He's still in surgery, so I probably won't know anything for another hour or two. Just pray for him."

I'd never heard a doctor say pray for someone. Prior to today, I'd never been in the hospital for anything in my entire life. Every interaction I'd ever had with a doctor, other than a routine checkup, had been on my beat or during an exchange at a news conference, where information was guarded and answers were given in stark, often emotionless detail. And here she was telling me to pray for Bass. Pray for what? Was he dying? What did she know?

"So it doesn't look good? Is that what you're saying?"

"I'm not saying that at all. I'm not in surgery with him. I'm not his doctor and you're not a family member. I'm just saying pray for him. I'll be back to see you soon, Ms. Manning. Try to get some rest. Excuse me."

Dr. Patel left and Ellen walked back in.

"I've got your phone," she said, handing it to me, the Holy Grail that it was. The battery was almost dead, but I could read the long list of calls and text messages I'd missed.

"I need to call my mom," I said. "Ellen, thank you. Thank you so much for finding my phone." I hoped my gratitude would soften the edge that Ellen could care less about trying to conceal.

Mom answered on the first ring. "Jordan, where are you? Are you okay?"

She wouldn't let me get a word in, stopping only to tell me that she was filling Daddy in on the other line.

"I'm fine, Mom," I said. "There have been some robberies in the neighborhood and I was in the wrong place at the wrong time. But I'm okay. The guy was looking to steal cars and I stumbled into him."

"I'm flying there as soon as I can get a flight out," she said.

"The doctor said I can go home in a few minutes. Click over and let Dad know everything is okay," I said.

"Hold on," she said.

Ellen mouthed, "You're lying to your mom."

"Shush!" I said.

Mom clicked back over. "Between you and your father trying to keep me from coming there, I'm over both of you."

"I'll admit it was scary. But I live in a big city. Things happen. But I promise, they're letting me go home soon. And the Bennetts are going to come by."

The Bennetts didn't even know what happened, but I knew that mentioning them would back Mom off me a bit. And it turned out, I would have to cut our call short anyway, because two uniformed officers stepped into the room.

"Hey, Mom, I've got to go, but I'll call you later. I love you."

I relayed to them everything I remembered about what happened. Because I'd come in close contact with my assailant, the officers asked if I would submit to having my fingernails scraped for possible DNA evidence. In a surprise attack, it was quite possible that I might have scratched my assailant or ripped off pieces of his hair.

After they left, I wanted to call my friends, but Ellen and our unfinished business loomed over me like a helicopter parent. It would have to wait, though, because we were interrupted again on this, my unlucky lucky day.

"Jordan." Joey moved from the curtain to my bedside at warp speed. I could tell he was visibly taken aback by what he saw. My vanity kicked in. Realizing that I wouldn't be able to go on air any time soon was one thing, but I didn't want a man to see me looking like this, especially one who'd earlier today gazed into my eyes, flirting with me.

Before he could comment, I launched into my theory of what happened. "Joey, this was not a random attack. This was not a robbery. This had something to do with Masey, and I think they've been following me. A couple days ago, a guy followed me as I pulled into the garage."

"Why didn't you tell me?"

Honestly, it had just occurred to me that the car that slipped in behind me and trailed me to my floor saw precisely where I parked.

"I think I was set up. These guys all know each other, and they're all connected to Masey's disappearance."

Joey said, "Jordan, you may be right. I finally got some information on Terrence. Before he lived in Chicago, he lived in Albuquerque."

"Yeah, Yvonne told me he moved here from New Mexico."

"Right, well, things probably got a little too hot for him out there. He was arrested a few years ago for breaking and entering. I spoke with the prosecutor, and she told me that a sixteen-year-old girl lived in the house. They believe he'd been stalking her, but his attorney struck a plea deal and he was sentenced to a year's probation. Then he moved to Chicago after that. But while they were investigating him, they uncovered a lot of creepy behavior toward young women. They also found out that he and the girl knew each other. Now, the girl would never admit it, but her friends told the prosecutor there'd been something going on between them."

"Was he molesting her?" I asked.

"The prosecutor believes it was more like grooming, but the girl was under his influence and never revealed much more than that," he said. "But that's not all I found out. That story didn't rest well with me. So I talked to one of the detectives out there. Some years before that, he was questioned about a fifteen-year-old girl who was found dead under a bridge overpass. She'd been sexually assaulted. She was killed in a wooded area not far from her home, and her naked body was found in a fishing riverbed along a lightly trafficked trail on the outskirts of Albuquerque. No evidence was ever recovered. It's been a cold case ever since."

"Jesus! How'd you find this out so fast?"

"I've been working with a few informants. This one guy, he owes me—a lot. He told me he'd heard rumors about Bankhead and underage girls. A lot of the stuff he was mixed up in out in New Mexico followed him here. His name has come up in one of those chat rooms where folks with an ax to grind put shady characters on blast. A former cop outed him on a website. He tried to get ahead of it after he moved here, telling his side of things, but I hear a lot of guys here don't like him. He doesn't have a lot of friends. His circle is pretty tight. Just him and this guy Brent."

"Did you get an address for him?"

"Not yet, but he has a little storefront office space Uptown. I don't know what he uses it for."

"Well, he's supposed to have 'connections' in entertainment," I said. "What about his roommate?"

"This guy's a ghost, a real loner. I'm not even sure Brent Carter is his real name," Joey said.

I don't know why, but my mind went back to that bizarre conversation the day of the vigil with Louise Robinson when she talked about a Red Moley character. She said, *If there's one, there's probably two.* Louise knew Yvonne. I wonder if she knew anything about these two guys.

"This is going to sound crazy, but I was at Louise Robinson's and she started talking about, and I'd never heard of this before, the legend of Red Moley."

"The legend of Red Moley? You never heard of that?" Joey asked.

"No, I haven't. Must be a Midwest thing."

But now I was beginning to wonder why Louise mentioned it in the first place. Was it possible that Masey's involvement with these men was an open secret? Did these people know all along what was going on in Masey's life?

..

National news anchor: We have a strange update in the case of three boys charged with the gruesome murder of a fifteen-year-old Chicago girl. The reporter who broke the story has been the victim of a brutal attack. We go now to correspondent Grayson Michele in Chicago.

Grayson: Last night, News Channel 8's Jordan Manning was discovered unconscious on the upper parking deck of her apartment building. I'm told the thirty-year-old suffered severe bruising to her head, face, and neck. She is in stable condition at Northwestern Memorial Hospital. A security guard in the building who interrupted the attack on Manning was stabbed by the assailant and remains in critical condition. Both were discovered by a tenant a little after 9:30 P.M. last night. Police declined to say whether security cameras captured the attack. There are no suspects in custody, but I've heard speculation of ties to Manning's coverage of the troubling murder case. The three suspects, two eleven-year-olds and a thirteen-year-old boy, remain in custody.

I awoke to more than sixty text messages and some forty missed calls, including from Justin, who'd gotten wind of the attack on the police scanner; Thomas, who grew concerned after he drove by my place and saw police cars and ambulances outside but couldn't reach me; and my local family circle—Courtney, Zena, Amanda, María Elena, and the Bennetts. I discouraged them from coming to the hospital, telling them "I'm in a secure room, and I'll be home later today anyway." I won that battle with everyone else, but Courtney wasn't deterred. I'd never known her to take no for an answer or been anyplace her physician's credentials couldn't get her into. Courtney had the forethought to bring me a change of clothes and slippers to wear home. The gym gear I had on during the attack was taken into evidence to test for hair and skin follicles. She also worked her contacts at the hospital to get me in to see Bass, flashing her badge to access the secure ICU wing.

Before I went in, Courtney did her best to prepare me for a new reality. Bass's injuries were far more severe than what had been shared. He was stabbed in the gut twice by a sharp object that nicked his abdominal aorta, causing life-threatening internal bleeding.

"Closing that wound was critical. That's why they took him

into the OR immediately," Courtney explained. "If it'd been more than 40 percent severed, he would have bled out in a matter of seconds."

Bass is lucky to be alive.

"He hasn't regained consciousness. It could be because they put him in a medically induced coma to give his brain a rest and a chance for the swelling to go down," Courtney explained.

"His brain?" I asked.

"He sustained a blow to the head," she said.

The air left my lungs, and I thought back to what Ellen had said. "He tried to save you." No, he did save me, and now he was fighting for his life because of it.

Seeing Bass lying there with tubes coming out of his arms and body and a machine doing the breathing for him was surreal.

"Can he hear me?" I asked Courtney.

"Possibly. Just say what's in your heart," she said.

I took him by the hand and intertwined his long, bass-playing fingers with mine, the closest we'd ever been, our most intimate moment. I held the rail with my other hand, anchoring myself to his bedside, and leaned in close to his ashen face.

"Bass, it's Jordan." The tears and sobs turned on instantly. "I'm so sorry."

A respirator covered half his face and his chest expanded, then sank at once, again and again. "It kills me to see you like this. I'm okay because of you, but you're lying here because of me. I feel horrible."

I'd played a dozen scenarios in my mind of how it happened. Bass opened the door, saw a man on top of me, choking me. He pulled him off, they scuffled, and then . . .

"You're like my family, like a little brother to me, and I know I should've told you that before now. How important you are to me. I love you, Bass, I do. And I'm going to find out who did this, and you're *going* to be okay."

The only response was the beeping of monitors and medical machines surrounding his bed.

"You saved my life. I can never repay you. But I'm going to be there for Sabrina and the baby until you get out of here. I promise. You fight, little brother. You're my hero."

I wanted to stay longer, but Courtney convinced me that the best thing I could do for Bass right now was to go home. I left behind my card with a note on the back for his folks and Sabrina. "Don't hesitate to call me if you need anything." But I left the hospital still clinging to guilt, with more questions than answers.

Who did this to Bass and me? To Masey? And are they one in the same.

15

Diana Sorano: Good afternoon. Our lead story this hour: outrage in the black community builds as police provide few new details on the latest bomb to drop in the case of Masey James, the young girl found dead nearly two weeks ago. There are disturbing new details to report about one of the boys charged in the case. You may recall three boys have been in custody since last week, two eleven-year-olds and a thirteen-year-old. We now know the thirteen-year-old boy has been attacked while being held at the Cook County Jail.

Keith Mulvaney: Diana, Derek Harvey is being treated here at the jail's infirmary. There is confusion over why a boy his age, even though charged as an adult, wasn't in protective custody. I spoke with his parents, who are outraged and sickened by the inhumane way they say their son, whom they've not been allowed to see, has been treated. As you recall, Derek's father had his own run-in with police when the boys were being questioned. This case has been fraught with problems from the beginning. And now we have a thirteen-year-old attacked by inmates. We're headed from this location to talk with Derek Harvey's parents. We'll have more on the evening newscast. Meanwhile police have not given us any more details on how or why the boy was attacked.

Diana: Thank you, Keith.

You have got to be fucking kidding me!

After watching that insincere piece of garbage—"Fraught with problems": Yeah, right, Keith! You sure didn't seem to care about the problems associated with the investigation when we were in the town hall—I could hardly stomach this fourth cup of coffee. My overwhelming sense of helplessness was dwarfed only by my rage and by my need to do something and do it now. And the subject of my red rage was Louise Robinson and her insane Red Moley story. Was Louise playing me? That story came out of nowhere. Was it her delusional way of dropping a bread crumb? She said, *If there's one, there's two.* And now I was wondering if there could be two men involved in Masey's death.

What was she getting at?

The caffeine did wonders to help pull me out of my painkiller haze. And after Keith's disingenuous report and the suffocation of being in this apartment, I was off the couch in seconds, tearing off the pajamas I'd been wearing for the last two days. There was one person I needed to talk to, and I was on my way to confront her.

I was just about to reach for the pair of jeans and a sweatshirt on the chair, but I wanted Louise to understand this was not a casual call, so instead, I turned to the closet and the work clothes I hadn't seen in three days.

Am I ready to be Jordan Manning the reporter again?

I grabbed a skirt, my blazer, and some heels, then darted into the bathroom to apply just enough concealer and foundation so that I didn't look like I was at death's door. The urgency of my mission quickened my steps toward my car on the upper deck. This was the first time I'd gone near the scene of the attack. I opened the access door to the roof and a wave of fear and anxiety rushed over me. I walked past the last thing I remembered seeing before blacking out—the light fixture with the flicker that had provided my assailant the cover he needed to carry out his surprise attack. It looked different in the daytime, as if nothing had happened. There was no sign of the blood that poured out of Bass's body. It'd all been power-washed away. And for the first time in my life, I felt like a victim. I had always been able to empathize with victims but had escaped such a fate. The weight of what someone who'd been attacked or raped must feel in court, or at any point having to relive what happened to them, was real for me now, too. After Stephanie and Jaden, I always thought I understood, but it was one thing to say that you could imagine what it felt like and another when it happened to you. The gravity of the moment left me with but two choices: Go back to my apartment or face this new reality.

I refuse to live in fear.

Nonetheless, I couldn't get out of there fast enough. I clutched my keys with the largest one protruding between my first and second fingers, poised and ready. If someone was to attack me again, they'd lose an eye at the very least.

Pulling out, I felt like a getaway driver, hell-bent on making it across state lines to freedom. The lack of traffic meant I didn't get the beat I needed to collect my thoughts. What were the odds? I'd lived here nearly three years, and I couldn't recall making it anywhere in Chicago this fast. But in record time, I was outside Louise's.

Now what? I'm at someone's house, unannounced, ready to confront them on something I'm not even sure about.

To soften the blow of my abrupt arrival, I called her.

"Hello," she answered.

"Hi, Louise, it's Jordan Manning. I know this sounds strange, but I'm outside your home. Are you inside?"

"You're outside my home?"

"Yes. I really need to talk to you."

"They sent both of you?"

"Both of us?"

"Your coworker Keith is coming over here to interview me about the Harvey boy being attacked in jail," she said.

"What time is he coming?"

"In about forty-five minutes," she said.

"That's fine. I won't be long."

Louise went silent. I didn't know if that was a yes or a no, but either way, I didn't care. I made haste to the door, which this time wasn't answered by Marcus but by Louise herself.

No way is she prepared for what I am about to say to her.

"What can I help you with?" she asked.

"It's not what you can help me with, Louise. It's what you can help me understand. Can we sit down?"

"Sure. Come in," she said, and directed me to the sofa. From a distant room, I could hear the distinct sound of a video game. *Marcus.*

"I'm sure you've heard about the Harvey boy," Louise said.

"Yes. Horrible. Heartbreaking. But that's not why I'm here."

"My phone's been blowing up all morning," Louise said, seemingly ignoring what I'd just said, rocking back and forth in her chair and looking around. "I've called an emergency meeting of the South Side Community Council tonight, and I've got a million things to do."

Louise's awkward, almost nervous demeanor was a far cry from that of the confident person I'd encountered here before. I got the feeling she didn't want to talk about whatever she thought I was here about. But with Keith on the way, I didn't have time for small talk, so I launched in.

"Louise, what do you know about Terrence Bankhead?"

Half stunned and half the Louise I remembered, she looked askance at me and leaned forward. "What do you mean?" she said in an unnecessarily defiant tone, which I gave right back to her.

"Louise, I'm not here to sugarcoat this. So let me spell it out for you."

I leaned in closer to make it clear that any bullying tactic she was debating would not work on me.

"Terrence Bankhead was hanging around Masey James. I've learned that Terrence has a roommate. When I was here last, you brought up to me this story out of nowhere about Red Moley. And I remember you saying very specifically 'If there's one, there's two.' I think these two guys had something to do with Masey's murder, and maybe the attack on me and my friend, too. Now you look me in the face and tell me you don't know anything about them."

Louise sat straight up in her chair. "Jordan, that's a big question. Do I know anything about them?" She faked a laugh. "I know something about everybody. You do know who I am."

Her transition from near fragility to hubris was remarkable.

"And that's exactly why I'm here. What do you know about Terrence?"

"Terry? I've heard of him, but I don't really know him. He's friends with my nephew."

Nephew? Could it be?

"Is your nephew Brent Carter?"

Hearing the name, Louise shifted from defiance to confusion. "How do you know Brent?" she asked.

"I don't know him. I just know that he and Terrence are roommates. I've been able to uncover some very disturbing things about Terrence. We've tracked him from New Mexico

to Chicago. I believe he was having an inappropriate relationship with Masey. I need answers about him, and I suspect police will, too, very soon.

"So," I said, ready to lower the boom, "what has Brent told
you about him?"

Louise sneered, looking agitated. "I don't know what you
want."

"Do you really want to look like you are hiding or protecting
these guys?" I asked. "Louise, you told me about the legend of
Red Moley. They come in twos. You had no reason to tell me
that story, and now I think I know why you did."

Louise rested her mouth against her hand like Rodin's *The
Thinker*, shaking her head vigorously. "Uh-uh, Jordan, I don't
know what kind of cop routine you're pulling here," Louise said.
"But I'm not new to this. If you're asking me if I know anything
about Masey's relationship with Terrence or Brent, I don't."

"I don't believe you, and I'm not leaving until you tell me
what I need to know," I said, leaning back on the sofa and folding my arms.

Louise was silenced by my directness, which was surprising.
This was a woman who didn't understand what it meant to be
quiet.

"Okay, fine. You don't know Terrence." I shrugged. "But you
do know Brent, your nephew."

"He's always been a good kid. I've known him his whole
life."

"Well, of course you have—he's your nephew," I said.

"I said he's *like* my nephew. He's not actually related to me.
But he's family. I was very close with his mother. She was like
a sister to me. She died when he was just a baby. He was only
eight. I don't know what else you want to know about him."

"I want to know everything you can tell me about him as an adult, not a kid. How often do you see him?"

"He comes by occasionally to check in on me to see what's going on," she said, her speech growing more measured.

"What's his relationship like with Terrence?"

Louise shot me a look, then tried to pivot. "Like I said, I don't know Terrence, but what I do know about him, I don't like."

Is she throwing Terrence under the bus?

"I've heard about New Mexico, and I've heard stories here, too, but I don't know anything about him and Masey. And just so you know, yes, I brought it up to Brent, and he said there are a bunch of haters and gossips out here who are jealous of him because he's making moves."

"What kind of moves?" I asked.

"They're building this entertainment company," Louise said.

"They?" I asked.

"They're in business together," Louise said. "Signing people to music deals, modeling contracts. Managing acts. Helping people get from Chicago to L.A. They're doing well. They even have an office in Uptown."

They're doing well? If Louise knows enough about their business to know they're doing well, then she knows something else, too.

Louise was now a fish on a hook, and I didn't need her to wiggle off. I needed her to stay right where I had her and to keep talking. So I worded my next question carefully.

"Louise, like you said, you hear and know everything. So does that mean you knew young girls have been going into that Uptown office?"

Her eyes glowed red. "What are you trying to say?"

"Where there's smoke, there's fire. You're not stupid, Louise. You know exactly why they have those girls going in and out of there. Name me one star they've made. Name me one person they've taken to Hollywood. No. They are luring girls like Masey there. And you know it."

Her mouth tightened and she stood up and pointed toward the door. "Get out of my house."

"Why are you protecting them?" I asked pointedly. "Because you're not doing a good job of it right now."

"I said get out of my house!" she yelled.

Louise's screeching rebuke must have been louder than the video game, because Marcus flew out of a room down the hall. "Grandma, are you okay?"

"You told me that Red Moley story, Louise, because there's got to be some part of you that feels guilty," I said.

If there's an ounce of decency in you.

"Jordan, you need to leave," Louise said through gritted teeth.

Marcus looked confused. "Grandma, what's going on?"

"Nothing!" Louise said, glancing over at Marcus. "Jordan, get out! Right now!"

I got up to go, but when I reached the door, I turned around and looked at her and fired off a rebuke of my own. "You'd better search your conscience, lady, if you have one."

I bolted out the door, seething over the very real possibility that this self-appointed, self-righteous, fiery community activist and so-called women's advocate may very well have known about two men preying on underage girls. She might not have known the extent, but at the very least, she knew it was perverse. That Red Moley story was so random, it was as if her guilt unmuzzled her against her will. Now that she'd been called out for it, instead of seeking redemption, she'd taken a hardline stance. Could it be that she loved Brent and his deceased mother to the point that she'd betray her own conscience? I thought back to Commissioner Clark's revelations about Louise Robinson. Little did he know, he'd barely scratched the surface.

..

My work in Englewood far from finished, I turned down 71st Street and made a quick right onto Peoria to Yvonne and Manny's. There were two cars parked out front, possibly belonging to customers of theirs. I admired their hustle and hoped they wouldn't regard my dropping by as a bold intrusion.

"Who is it?" said a muffled voice behind the door.

"Yvonne? It's Jordan Manning."

The door flung open, and the concerned look on Yvonne's face reminded me of what I must look like. It was one thing for Yvonne to have heard the report, but another to be one of the few people who had actually seen me face-to-face.

"Are you okay?" she stood back and sized me up. "What are you doing out and about?"

"No . . . I mean, yes. Physically, I'm fine. But, Yvonne, I need answers."

"Sure." She nodded. "Come on in. Follow me."

She led me through the kitchen, where a woman was sitting under a hair dryer and a young girl was mixing color over the sink. Baby Imani was content in her high chair, mesmerized by what I caught at a glance was *Sesame Street*.

"Don't worry about that right now," she told the girl. "Watch Imani for me. I'll be downstairs."

"How much longer for the dryer?" the girl asked.

"Give it twenty minutes."

Halfway down the steps, Yvonne called out, "Manny! I'm coming down!"

"Okay, come on! I'm by myself!"

"I'm not!" Yvonne said. "Jordan's here."

Manny, sweeping up hair from his last customer, stopped what he was doing. He turned around, broom in hand, and dropped his head. "Sister, I'm sorry," he said, appearing genuinely remorseful. "You and that brother who got stabbed . . . that shoulda never happened."

"Thank you for saying that," I said.

"I don't think it was random," he said.

"Neither do I. What do you know?"

"Let's go in here and sit down," he said.

Manny arranged three of the waiting room chairs in a semicircle. "I hope you don't think I had anything to do with that." His eyes were full of regret, a far cry from the hard stare he had given me the first time we met.

"What do you want to tell me?" I asked.

"Actually, we want to show you something," said Yvonne. She pulled a photo album off the shelf behind her, unmoored an image from one of its pages, and handed it to me. The photo was of a man and a girl I recognized as Masey. She was sitting on the man's lap with her legs crossed, her arm slung around his shoulders. The man's arm was wound behind her body, his hand resting on half her bottom.

"That's Terrence," Yvonne said.

The photo eliminated any shred of doubt in my mind that Terrence was having an inappropriate relationship with Masey.

"You've had this all along?" I asked.

"No, I found it in the plastic pumpkin Masey used to keep her nail polish in. I was looking through it two nights ago and found it in an envelope at the bottom," Yvonne said. "I stuck it in the album for safekeeping."

Masey was keeping it hidden.

"This picture . . . it didn't come as a shock to you, though, did it?" I asked.

Yvonne dropped her head in her hands and started to weep. "I got caught up."

"Caught up how?"

"Being her best friend instead of her big cousin. Instead of looking out for her," she said.

It occurred to me then that Yvonne and Masey's relationship reminded me of mine and Stephanie's, except that Stephanie fulfilled her role as big cousin. Yvonne really wanted Masey to see her as the cool cousin, the big sister you could tell anything to, the vault.

"I wanted to be supportive of her dreams, you know?" Yvonne continued. "I wanted to believe . . . that he was legit."

"You never heard any of the rumors floating around about Terrence? You, Manny?"

Both were silent.

"Yvonne, you told me yourself he was from New Mexico. He was in trouble there all the time."

"Hell, I've been in trouble," Manny interjected.

"I'm well aware," I said. "But the kind of trouble he got into in New Mexico is not usually something you do once and never again."

"I get it," Manny said.

"Folks are always talking about how Black girls are the most unprotected people on this earth," Yvonne said, "but when the time comes, they look away. You can't talk about other people if you're doing the same thing."

And that's precisely what you did.

"But didn't something feel wrong? I mean, why didn't you take it seriously?" I asked.

"I don't know. But I am now," she said. "I'll have to carry that regret with me for the rest of my life."

Yvonne and Manny were repentant of their mindlessness. I saw in them what I didn't in Louise, a sense of obligation to try and figure this out, to be redeemed.

"What are you going to do with this picture? Has Pamela seen it?" I asked.

Yvonne glanced over at Manny, who dropped his head.

"Look, if you didn't trust me, you wouldn't have shown me this. And if I didn't trust you, I wouldn't be here," I said.

"Pam is in denial," Yvonne said. "After the boys were charged, she didn't want to hear no more about Terrence."

The mother who had pleaded with the crowd at the vigil "Tell us what you know. This isn't about being a snitch. Tell us!" had turned a blind eye herself.

"What about his roommate? I hear they're in business together. You think he's part of this?"

Manny looked surprised. "Really? I thought Brent worked for Terrence. I ain't never heard either one of them say they were business partners."

Interesting.

"What's Brent like?" I asked.

"He's quiet," Manny said casually, but Yvonne, I noticed, was having a visceral reaction.

"What's wrong?" I asked her.

"Oh God!" she said and started shaking.

"What is it, babe?" Manny asked.

"You know Monique?" she said to Manny.

"Yeah."

"Monique Connors?" I asked.

Yvonne said, "Yes. How do you know her?"

"It was a chance encounter at the vigil. As I was walking through the crowd, I ran into this young girl who described herself as Masey's friend, 'sort of.'"

"They were more than 'sort of' friends. They actually got closer when Brent, her brother, started getting his hair cut here," Yvonne said.

"Oh, they're brother and sister?"

"Yes."

Yvonne raised an eyebrow and said, "I'm thankful to God I didn't have a brother like that."

Manny turned to look at Yvonne like he was unsure about what she was talking about. I stared at her, bracing myself for the point she was trying to make.

"I don't know how you're going to feel, Jordan, about me not mentioning this before. Manny doesn't even know. As a woman who has had something like this happen to me before, I just didn't want to tell anyone what she shared with me. It's her secret."

"What secret? What are you talking about?" I asked her.

"The young girls like to tell me everything. I don't know why. They just trust me and they tell me everything. Maybe it's being in the chair, me taking care of them, doing their hair, and making them feel comfortable. You know what they say about beauty shop and barbershop talk. You become a therapist, and I'm a therapist big sister."

"Yvonne, I need you to get to the point," I said. "What did she tell you?"

"Monique hates her brother and she's also afraid of him. She can't stand him."

She paused.

"Monique told me a couple of months ago that when she was younger, Brent used to come in her room and touch her." She swallowed and lowered her gaze, recognizing again the impact of what she was saying and triggering memories of her own.

Manny squeezed his forehead and rubbed at his temples. I grabbed Yvonne's hand, left to console her, as women often do in these moments, and sympathized with what she was feeling, having just admitted that she, too, had gone through some type of trauma.

"How long did she say it went on?" I asked.

"She didn't say how long exactly. She just said for years."

Our girls were not safe. I'd heard that thousands of times. But to appreciate the full extent of what that really meant was almost too much to bear.

"Do you have a picture of Brent?" I asked.

Yvonne was in no shape to answer. Her whole world had turned upside down. She was emotionally destroyed.

"Hold up," said Manny. "Let me look in this box at the pictures from the cookout last summer. I know he was there, and we have a bunch of pictures."

Manny shuffled through the box of loose images and finally handed me a picture of six men posing around a picnic bench at a park, looking like they were having the time of their lives.

"There." Manny pointed to a man in the middle of the group who was in full floss mode, smiling away. "That's him."

The man in the picture was a sharp contrast to the monster Yvonne had just revealed in his awful form. Tall with a medium build, he smiled broadly, confidently, leaning against a picnic table with his arms folded and a beer in one hand. There was something about his eyes.

"Can I have this?" I asked.

Manny said, "No, I need to keep it in case the cops come around."

I pulled my cell phone from my purse and snapped the photo with Brent and the one with Terrence and Masey.

"What are you going to do with that?" he asked.

"I just need it for something," I said. "The question is, what are you going to do with these photos?"

Yvonne looked at Manny again, as if she were waiting for his permission.

"Yvonne, look at me!" I said. "There are three little boys whose lives are at stake. What are you going to do?"

She looked up and finally said, "Give them to the police."

"Right! Don't wait for them to come around. Do it. Today," I admonished her. "Okay?"

She nodded.

"Have you told me everything you know?"

They both nodded.

"Yvonne, are you going to be okay?" I asked.

"Yeah," she said.

"I want to thank you both so much. I know it must've been hard for you to share this."

As I got up to leave, Manny said, "Wait, before you go." He grabbed a miniature filing cabinet on a nearby table and pulled out a business card. "In case you're interested," he said, and handed it to me. "This is Terrence's card."

"Mad Cash Talent Management," I said. "What a stupid name."

The card listed an address.

I don't know whether Manny read the determination in my face or misread the wince of pain that followed from my still tender, swollen cheek, but in his search for redemption, he said, "If you wanna check it out, let me know. I'll go with you."

..

I already knew before I left Yvonne's that there was no way in hell I was going to rely on her to turn over the photo of Terrence and Masey to the police. That errand was all mine. And although I knew it was dangerous to be texting while driving, I wasted no time forwarding the incriminating picture of Terrence and Masey and his office address to Bartlett and Fawcett on the way home.

TERRENCE BANKHEAD. CHECK HIM OUT. THIS PIC SAYS IT ALL.

Then to Joey.

THIS IS TERRENCE. CALL ME. LOTS TO SHARE. WE NEED TO TALK ASAP!

The traffic I'd missed on the way to Louise's showed up with a vengeance, providing the stop-and-go I needed to fire off one more text, to Sabrina, to get an update on Bass.

ANY CHANGE? I tapped out with my right hand while holding the steering wheel steady with my left.

Thomas had called, but I wasn't in the frame of mind to deal with him. I hadn't seen him since before the attack, though he'd called several times, full of regret that he hadn't been with me that night. There wasn't anything he could have done anyway, even if I'd agreed to let him come over. He still would've been too late.

After what I'd learned this afternoon, there was no doubt in my mind that I was 100 percent ready to be Jordan Manning, the reporter, again. The repugnance I felt at Brent Carter's years of sexual assaults on his little sister and Terrence Bankhead's grown-man hand cradling Masey's teenage bottom in that photo fueled my rage. In my mind, I wandered off to a dark fantasy where I ran into him and brutally beat him into confessing.

My empathy for the girls and Yvonne, too, held my thoughts in place long enough that I didn't have time to focus on my own trauma as I pulled into the garage, instinctively now looking for any car that seemed remotely out of place.

Safe inside my apartment, I locked and unlocked the door for what seemed like a dozen times, testing the security and the sanctity of my own home as I'd never done before. I peeled off my work clothes and slid into the stunning silk kimono that Mom gave me after years of begging. Dad had bought the *kakeshita*, or wedding kimono, at one of the temple markets in Kyoto, Japan, while serving in the Army. Why I chose today of all the days to wear it I wasn't sure. But in the moment it made me feel as if my parents or something higher was wrapping me in a literal security blanket. Pacing around the apartment was doing little to tamp down my racing thoughts, which randomly bounced from "Is my door locked tight?" to "Should I move?"

As if someone had concealed a camera in my walls, watching and waiting for the right time to call, the phone vibrated, shimmying across the table. It was one of maybe five people I felt up to engaging.

"Hey!"

"Hey yourself! You sound good. How are you feeling?"

"Great, Ellen. So great, in fact, I'll be back at work tomorrow."

"Jordan, who are you kidding? This 'fake it till you make it' act is not impressing me."

"Ellen, put what you think you heard to the side. It's not a request; it's a demand. I need to return to work."

"O-kay," she said, relenting in a way that was unlike her, but perhaps knowing that if I was anxious to get back in the hot zone, there was a compelling reason for it, which I expected her to ask me about next.

Instead, Ellen posed the most authentic question I'd heard in a long time. "I hate to ask, but how do you look? Peter's not going to let you back on the air if you're still bruised up."

And there you have it. It's TV, not radio. Male or female, you knew what shade of eyebrow pencil to use and how to lay the foundation on thick when you needed to, and you were always ready with a makeup bag stuffed to capacity. This wasn't hard.

"Nothing makeup won't fix. It'll be fine," I tried to assure her.

"O-kay," she repeated, still unconvinced. "I guess I'll see you tomorrow then. Good night. Oh, by the way, there are still no leads on who . . ."—she paused—"Who . . ."

"Attacked me?"

"Yes. I called our comms contact at police headquarters, but nothing new. I'm sorry, Jordan."

I really had nothing more to say, so we both hung up, not wanting to linger.

I'd expected a return text or call from Joey by now. He had been MIA the last couple days, pulled into investigating a string of home invasions that turned deadly the other night when a fifty-seven-year-old homeowner took on the burglars and was shot to death. I was anxious to talk to him, so I took a chance and called.

"Hey, Jordan. How're you feeling?" he said.

"Joey! Thank God! You won't believe what I found out about Louise Robinson and Terrence and his roommate Brent today," I said, nearly running out of breath before getting to the end.

"Found out? Haven't you been resting all week?" he asked.

"Never mind that," I said. "Listen, did you get my text I sent a little while ago?"

"No, I hadn't looked at my phone yet. Hold on," he said.

That was nearly an hour ago. I should be used to it by now. Apparently, police detectives weren't as attached to their cell phones as reporters. I didn't have to wait long for his reaction.

"I do be damned," he said.

"I admit, I wasn't surprised, but having seen this . . . there are no words."

"Have you shown this to Bartlett? How'd you get it?"

"I sent it to Bartlett and Fawcett, but no word yet from either of them," I said, avoiding his other question, but Joey wasn't having it.

"Where'd you get this, Jordan? Masey's mother?"

"No. From Yvonne." I hesitated because I knew what would come next. "Okay, so I went over there."

"Jor-dan! What is wrong with you? You can't be this smart and so rash at the same time!"

"Listen, there's more," I interrupted. "I stopped by Louise Robinson's house, too. Remember I told you about that crazy Red Moley story? I got a weird feeling about that. Well, it turns out Louise knows Terrence *and* Brent. She said Brent is like a nephew to her. She was close to his deceased mother."

"Wait, what?"

"She practically threw me out of her house, Joey. But hold on, I'm not finished. She said Terrence—she calls him Terry—and Brent have a talent business together. She's heard stories about Terrence's troubles in New Mexico and asked Brent about it. But he brushed it off as haters are gonna hate."

My home phone rang. It was the security desk. "Hold on a minute, Joe. Yes?"

"There's a Thomas Fountain here to see you," the guard said. *Really?*

"Okay, let him up, I guess."

Great.

"I'm back."

Joey struggled with what to say next. "Um, I'm knocked off my feet. So Louise Robinson is mixed up in this from all sides."

"I'm not saying she knew about Terrence and Masey. But I think her feelings for Brent have clouded her judgment. When I pressed her about it, that's when she threw me out."

"She didn't put her hands on you, did she?"

"No. She just yelled for me to leave. I think she's scared."

"Speaking of the Harvey kid," he said, "don't be surprised if you don't hear from Bartlett and Fawcett. There's so much heat coming down on them right now over those boys, you're the last person, I'm sure, they want to talk to. Especially about anything to do with other potential suspects."

I could feel my temperature rising with my frustration. "Why are they so hell-bent on keeping those kids locked up? I don't understand, Joey. We can't let those boys take the fall."

"I've gotta get an address on these guys," he said. "The most recent one I could find on Bankhead was in Pill Hill. He was living with some woman there."

Pill Hill was once an affluent Black neighborhood that earned its name from the proliferation of Black doctors who made their homes there in the 1970s.

Knock-knock-knock.

Damn it, I don't have time for this.

"Just a minute!" I yelled.

"You got company?" Joey asked.

"Yeah, a friend stopped by unannounced," I said. Then it dawned on me that I'd been doing that to people all day, so this was karma coming back to bite me.

"I'm going back to work tomorrow," I said. "Joey, I can't let this go. I know too much. There's one more thing."

"Do I need a drink first?" he asked.

"That's not a bad idea, actually," I said. "Brent was molesting his sister."

"Where are you getting that from?"

"Yvonne. It's a long story, but it's true. She had no reason to make it up. Too much detail for it not to be credible."

Joey let out a long, sorrowful moan.

Knock-knock.

"I'm coming!"

"Okay, and now I know too much, too, to let this go," Joey said. "But please, don't do anything else without me, you hear? Promise me?"

"All right, I promise."

"Mean it this time!" he scolded.

"I'll call you in the morning," I said.

"Let me call you," he said. "I'm working late tonight."

"Fair enough. Good night."

When I opened the door, I expected Thomas to be in gym clothes. He was in a suit, holding flowers.

What is happening?! He's not a suit kind of guy. What was he trying to prove?

"Hey there," I said. "Where are *you* headed?"

"Straight to you, beautiful," he said, and gently lifted me off my feet with one hand and spun me in a half circle before setting me back down for a lingering hug.

If bad timing had a photo, this was it.

"I've missed you," he said. "How are you feeling?"

I smiled. It was the first true smile in more than a week, and honestly, it kind of hurt.

"Thomas, thank you for the flowers, but I have to get to work."

"Work?" he asked. "Jordan, you were just attacked. Why are you working? Are you back on air? Look at your face!"

Realizing his words had landed like a kickboxer's reverse roundhouse, he course-corrected. "You still look beautiful. Sorry, Jordan, but you can't put work over health. I know I play second fiddle, but you can't put yourself behind the job."

God, I know he cares, and in another life this would all be so perfect. But in this life, this moment is a distraction.

His face shifted from hopeful to defeated. "You don't care, do you?" he asked.

"Care about what?"

"You don't care if this kills you. You don't care about your relationships, your joy . . ."

"You're overreacting. There's a dead kid, and I know who did it. What am I supposed to do? Sit here cuddled up with you waiting for this guy to kill again? And it may be connected to this," I said, pointing to the bluish black bruise staining the side of my face.

Thomas stood just past the doorway, flowers still in hand. It was a sad picture. "Let's go sit in the living room," I said, an invitation meant to restore some of his dignity.

I might as well settle down. There was nothing I could do at this very moment with all this information. I'd launched Joey, I'd called Bartlett and Fawcett. Even Ellen knew. Making Thomas leave this second wouldn't move the case forward one inch.

"Can I get you a glass of wine?"

"Jordan, have you ever seen me drink?" he asked.

I paused, realizing I'd spent nights with this man for nearly a year and we'd done things that made me blush just thinking about them.

"See, Jordan, that's my point. You know nothing about me. You don't notice anything about anyone but yourself and your stories. You claim to be the most observant person around, yet you see nothing, including the love right in front of you."

Love?

I almost looked around to see who else was in the apartment, because surely he couldn't be talking to me. The silence of the moment left us both awkwardly searching for the next move.

"I could use a glass of wine," I said.

From the safe distance of the kitchen, I circled back to the L word. "Thomas, I know you were worried about me, and I know it had to be scary not knowing all the details and hearing it from what felt like a million miles away. But don't let the heat of the moment twist you up in knots."

"Jordan, are you human? What android raised you?"

I shot him the "Are you talking about my mama?" look that I'd mastered in the third grade.

As I walked back over to Thomas, my wineglass half full, I was swept away by his vulnerability. It took a lot for him to dress up and come over with daisies, no less, which were my least favorite flowers. Not having the heart to keep the intensity going, I sat down, inching closer for the kiss we both wanted despite the heated words and hurt feelings.

His warm skin, his loving hand, his total being—all of this was more important than he would ever know and perhaps more important than I'd anticipated. And just like that I led him to the place where we felt ourselves to be equals, the place where our relationship thrived the most.

I laid on my bed still wearing the kimono. Thomas discarded his suit in a pile on the floor and crawled into bed with me before I could debate whether or not it was right, and our bodies merged into one.

One glimpse in the mirrored closet doors reminded me this was real, a moment that I deserved, never mind what he needed. I rocked him over onto his back and climbed on top, admiring his incredible features, his kind eyes.

My own eyes filled with tears. It was a sweet release, but it wasn't love.

..

"Can I get you some water?"

Thomas's words awakened me from the instant, dreamless sleep that overcame me following our lovemaking.

"I'm good? How are you?" I asked in my groggy voice.

"I'm great," he replied, seemingly forgetting the barrage of judgment that proceeded this moment.

I reached over onto the nightstand and grabbed the TV remote. "Don't be mad," I said. "Mind if I turn on the news?"

As he shook his head, it wasn't clear if he was giving me permission or simply signaling that he understood that I would never change.

Evening anchor Steve Schwartz: Tonight the parents of Derek Harvey, the thirteen-year-old boy charged along with two other minors, including his younger brother, in the death of fifteen-year-old Masey James, break their silence following the brutal assault on their son by adult inmates in Cook County Jail. Our Keith Mulvaney spoke with them at their home earlier today.

Marcia Harvey-Willis's face was the picture of fear and anxiety. That was all she was capable of feeling while both her sons were locked up and branded as monsters.

While the real monsters roamed the streets.

Keith: The assault on Derek has inflamed already tense rela-
tions between the African American community and police.
Activist Louise Robinson, who has been at the center of the protests over the charges against the boys, called an emergency
meeting of the South Side Community Council tonight, but
then canceled it along with a scheduled interview with Channel 8 earlier today.

I got to her. She's scared.

"Jordan, what's going on with this case?" Thomas asked to
my surprise.

"That's why I have to get back to work tomorrow. I know or
I think I know what's happening."

He rolled over and sat up in the bed and started to get
dressed. "Let me get out of your way," he said.

His reaction was abrupt but true. He was in my way. Our
dalliance had caused me to temporarily shift my focus away
from things that truly mattered. But I didn't feel the need to
double down by putting it into words. I wrapped myself back
up and walked him to the door in his now-crumpled suit, his
shirt no longer perfectly tucked in.

Before he left, he had one parting shot. "Can you at least put
the flowers in water?" He nodded toward the kitchen counter,
where they'd sat since he arrived.

"I will. They are lovely. I'll put them on the side of my bed,"
I said. "Good night. Drive safe."

The good night kiss felt different from the hello kiss a short
while ago. This one was cold and distant. I stood in the doorway and watched him enter the elevator without a look back, a
smile, or a wave.

..

Damnit! I forgot to remove my makeup last night!

I threw back the covers and leapt out of bed almost involuntarily. If Thomas could see my face right now, he would consider himself a lucky bastard. I stomped into the bathroom, giving the door a healthy nudge with my foot. Air rushed into my lungs, and my chest started to heave. The *me* that I wake up to before I become the version of Jordan who wears the mask that grins but doesn't lie and speaks the least intimidating version of the King's English *needs* this time to herself.

Just as I sat down to pee, my cell phone rang and nearly jolted me into standing up way too quickly. "Hurry up! Hurry up!" I said, ordering the urine stream to end. I rushed from the bathroom to grab the call, thinking it might be Joey, but it was Justin.

"Hey, Justin. Is something up?"

"Jordan, I hope I'm not bothering you."

"No, of course not. What is it?"

"A body. Just heard it over the scanner," he said, then laid out the details like he was reading directly from a police report. "Black female . . . found behind a dumpster at a small barbecue spot . . . 79th and State . . . partially burned . . . wrapped in heavy plastic."

16

"Describe the perp."

Thinking back on a grad school lecture by Dr. Chan on the tenets of profiling a serial killer, I walked through the steps in my mind to establish a profile of Masey's killer.

Was he an (a) loner or (b) socially competent?

I would say *b*. The killer was streetwise and comfortable in society. He made friends easily and he probably knew his victims. They might even have liked him, trusted him.

And motive? Was it (a) a lust kill, (b) a calculated attack, or (c) a crime of opportunity?

It was hard to say. Maybe all of the above. He was ritualistic, that was for sure, cutting up his victims, burning their bodies postmortem, and wrapping them in heavy-duty plastic that he probably kept at home or picked up at a work site.

Was he an organized or a disorganized killer? I would say organized. He killed his victims in a set location, then transported and disposed of their bodies elsewhere. Although this time, instead of trying to conceal his crime, he left the body out in the open on purpose.

So does that make him psychotic or psychopathic? There was no doubt in my mind he was a psychopath, the same man who'd killed Masey James, only with his latest victim, Tania Mosley, he changed his modus operandi. He wanted her to be found quickly, so he left her body just visible enough to be spotted the next time a restaurant employee took out the garbage.

"When an organized killer changes his pattern, there's usually a reason," Dr. Chan taught me. "Either he wants to get caught, he's playing a game of cat and mouse, or he's angry."

"Why would he be angry?" I'd asked him.

"Something didn't go right for him. He wanted it badly, but he couldn't get it. Or it could be that his heinous acts haven't drawn the attention that he'd hoped they would. Maybe somebody or something took the focus off his actions, so he lashed out."

It all made sense. Masey's killer didn't want to get caught, but he watched and thrived off the thunder, and the boys being charged with Masey's murder had stolen it from him. But was he angry about that or something else? I believed he was angry because of something he wanted and didn't get, and he satiated himself not just by taking a life, but by mutilating his latest victim even more savagely than before. He was sending a message. He was pissed.

I ran the killer's profile through my mind over and over again. It felt like I was in one of those infuriating dreams where I would attempt to dial a phone number but for the life of me could neither complete the action nor give up trying. I believed Masey's and Tania's killer and the man who attacked me were one in the same. When he was unsuccessful in his attempt to take my life and Bass's that night on the parking deck, he found another life to take.

After I hung up with Justin, I texted Scott the address of the crime scene and asked him to meet me there. Then I called Ellen.

"Sorry to call so early, but it's important. I just got a tip that another body was found overnight by a dumpster outside a restaurant . . . It's Masey's killer, I know it. He wants to steal his thunder back! I'm headed to the scene now."

"Jordan, do you think it's wise that this should be your first story just coming back to work?" she asked.

"Ellen, the kid gloves you and Peter are handling me with have got to come off at some point, so it might as well be now," I said. "I'm back on the story."

I showered in record time. To get out the door faster, I threw my makeup must-haves into my already tightly packed in-case-of-emergency cosmetic tote to apply on the way to the scene. The barbecue place floated in the middle of its ample parking lot like an island. A retaining fence in back separated the restaurant from a string of retail stores to the west, but the north and south entrances were accessible from the street, a four-lane boulevard with a wide concrete median. It wasn't someplace where people hung out.

No witnesses.

It was a sobering thought that I could have ended up like poor Tania Mosley. The nineteen-year-old former high school track star had been one of millions of teenagers who faced home-lessness on their own the past five or six months, trafficked by predators and working the streets. For that, her mother kicked her out of the house. Now she was angry and full of regret, insisting that she never stopped loving her daughter, pleading with the community to help find the killer. It was a repeat epi-sode, only this time I scored an exclusive with her mother later that day, solidifying my place in the Chicago media lexicon as the reporter who landed the ratings-boosting tearful interview with the grieving mother.

The similarities between the condition of Masey's body and Tania's were too striking to ignore. I made the deduction even without the inside scoop from Dr. Chan. I missed him and wondered when he would return. After the last ill-timed call, I emailed him instead.

"Dr. Chan, how are you? So much has happened here. Another body was found, the MO similar to Masey James. When are you coming back? I was attacked last week. I think I was being watched. I'm fine now. But I think I got too close. Call me."

I was prepared to deal with the damsel-in-distress treatment in the newsroom, where I had gained a kind of celebrity status that forced me to field the same types of questions over and over from my colleagues, oozing sincerity with their puppy dog expressions and pats on my shoulder. Their concern, I believed, was genuine. I just didn't like being cast as a victim.

Two days later, Bartlett and Fawcett were still ignoring my calls, emails, and text messages, and I'd reached my limit. I drove over to police headquarters early that morning and stood outside by the employee entrance and waited for Bartlett to arrive at work. He got out of his car, red-faced and perspiring. Any attempt he'd made to appear like he was in control was long gone, the awful magnitude of what was unfolding breaking him into a thousand pieces.

"Jordan, you don't have an appointment and I don't have time to talk to you this morning," he said, walking past me with his head down.

"Bartlett! Bartlett!" I said, walking alongside him. He wouldn't even look at me. "So let me get this straight. You're okay with three little boys sitting in jail after seeing that picture of Terrence Bankhead with Masey James?"

Without so much as a word, he swiped his badge to access the secure door. "Can I quote you on that?" I yelled after him facetiously. "What happened to you, Bartlett?"

When I got back to the newsroom, there was a note on my desk from Nussbaum: "Come see me."

"Yeah, Peter, what's up?"

"Jordan, you can't go around harassing the chief of police," Nussbaum said.

I'd never figured Bartlett to be the type to run and tell my boss on me.

"He called you?" I said, finding it almost comical. "And since when did stalking an authority figure to get a quote become harassment? I'm a reporter. It's what I do."

"Ellen should have handled this, so now I'm handling it. You came back to work too soon. Take another week off the air," he said. "And stay away from Bartlett."

"I don't want to take a week off," I said.

"It's not a suggestion," he said.

Off the air? Okay, fine. Off the story? I don't think so.

··

My relationship with Joey was growing and changing. He started to see me as an equal and also as an asset, something of a role reversal for us. And thankfully he'd stopped lecturing me about backing off the case, but not about being careful.

"Morning, Jordan."

About a week after my interview with Tricia Mosley, Tania's mom, our two prime suspects appeared to have fallen off the face of the earth.

"Joe, have you got a location yet on Terrence and Brent?" I asked.

"Naw, I think they ghosted that office," he said.

"Is there another tenant in there now?" I asked.

"I didn't say that. They just haven't been around. It was under surveillance, but the North Division just pulled off the patrol yesterday."

The police are pulling back. Meanwhile, three innocent boys are still locked up.

"Why?"

"Resources. They put a squad on the building during the day and one at night. But nothing's going on, so they pulled them off," he said.

With Dr. Chan's absence, it took almost a week to get a copy of the autopsy report on Tania Mosley.

Cause of death: strangulation/asphyxiation.

Was the victim sexually assaulted? Yes.

Condition of the body: partially clothed, second- and third-degree burns. There was no evidence of smoke in the windpipe or lungs, indicating the fire took place postmortem.

A diagram on the report showed the placement of each wound. The brutality was unimaginable. During her final moments on this earth, she was subjected to the cruel and inhumane madness of her killer. The deep slash across her throat detailed in the report nearly decapitated her. The sketch of her wounds did not come close to the words explaining her injuries. The tiny X marks seemed insignificant until I read that they were all stab wounds.

I didn't take being off the air as being banned from the newsroom. So I dropped by to pick up a few items from my desk and noticed Keith sulking around more than usual. The invigorating feeling he'd experienced on the crime beat during my absence was about to come to an unceremonious "you are not relevant" kind of ending. So Keith did something about it.

Ellen was just emerging from a closed-door meeting with newsroom brass. "It finally happened," she said.

"What did?" I asked, sitting on the edge of her desk.

"Keith threatened to quit if Nussbaum doesn't split the beat," Ellen reported.

"Let him. What did Nussbaum say?"

"He's thinking about it, Jordan."

Keith had sucker-punched me once again. I leaned close to Ellen's face so only she could hear what I was about to say. I got on my soapbox yet again, explaining the obvious misogyny in the industry. It reeked like a rotted skunk. "Let's all imagine, Ellen, a woman—any woman in this building—pulling that stunt."

I was shaking, close to tears, I was so mad. But even Ellen, a successful woman who had made it in this business, would hold tears against me.

"I said he was thinking about it. And you'd still be on the beat, you'd just be sharing it. Look, what happened to you, that scared the shit out of Peter."

I narrowed my gaze at her.

"Don't look at me like that. I hate myself for letting the words even come out of my mouth. But, Jordan, you have been reckless."

That was the third time Ellen had used that word to describe me, but this time, something inside me snapped. It was as if the tether that connected us two women, floating in a space dominated by males unconcerned with our job satisfaction or advancement, had suddenly been severed.

She must have felt it, too, because she swung her chair back around and faced her computer, proffering me no chance at a rebuttal. Nussbaum had given her the task of delivering the news. I'd seen this movie before. "Thinking about it" was Nussbaum's lily-livered precursor to a done deal. He'd exploited my relationship with Ellen, a relationship that, it turned out, was a clumsy two-step, and she'd just stepped on my foot in the middle of a competition.

Nussbaum, the coward, left the office early, his assistant said. It had all been settled with zero input from me.

Reckless, you call it, Ellen. Feckless, I say to both of you.

April Murphy left a voice mail for me a few minutes ago. I owed her a callback and needed an honest-to-goodness distraction to keep me from writing my resignation letter.

"Hello?"

"Hi, April, how are you? It's Jordan," I said, noticing right away that I needed to correct my tone.

"Hey, Jordan. What's wrong?"

Too late.

"Nothing," I said. "I was in a meeting when you called. What's going on?"

"I was just calling to see if there was anything I could do to help," she said.

Funny you'd ask.

Her timing was impeccable. When I'd met with April at the coffee shop, I didn't tell her about the tissue sample Dr. Chan had taken from beneath Masey's fingernails to be analyzed. But when I finally received the autopsy report for Tania Mosley, I inquired about the result. The sample had been logged into evidence, but no results could be found.

"Maybe there is something you can do, April. Dr. Chan had taken a tissue sample, I think it was skin or blood or something, from beneath Masey James's fingernails. Nobody at the medical examiner's office can track down the results, and Dr. Chan is still out of town. I had a fingernail scrape at the hospital after the attack, but the results didn't match anything in the crime database. If my results are in, then surely they should have the

results on Masey James. Can you see what you can find out?"
I asked her.

"I'm on it," she said.

"Thank you so much. Have you talked to Pamela Alonzo?"

"Pam and I talk about twice a week," she said.

After the attack, Pamela sent me a text message to wish me
well and had said she hoped I'd feel better soon. But I hadn't
spoken to Pamela since that day at Yvonne's when Terrence
Bankhead's name first came up.

"Did she mention the name Terrence Bankhead?" I asked.

"No, who's that?"

"He's a suspect. You and I need to catch up. Let me know
what you can find out about this sample, and let's try and get
together sometime this week," I said.

"Okay, sounds good."

I should be relieved that Pamela hadn't called. That she'd
hitched her wagon to April and cut me loose. But I was still
bothered by what Yvonne had told me about Pamela's not wanting to hear anything else about Terrence, her turning away
from the truth.

I felt a headache coming on, and I massaged my temples and
forehead and closed my eyes. I was furious over what Nussbaum was planning to do and at Keith for talking him into it.
But the exchange with Ellen had cut me deep.

"Jordan?"

I looked up, and Grace Ito was standing at my cubicle. I tried
to mask my exasperation with her, but the eye roll couldn't be
contained.

"I deserve that, I guess," she said.

"No, that wasn't directed at you. It's just been a long day.
What's going on?"

"First, I'm so sorry about what happened to you," she said,

a single tear rolling down her face. "I never said you put my life in danger. Those were Keith's words, not mine. I told a few people at the Billy Goat one night that you'd taken me out on a story. But I told them it was exciting. I never said I was scared."

"Were you scared?"

"Yeah, but I never would've admitted it to them. I respect you so much. You are my hero."

Well, this was just great. For a second time today, I was fighting back tears in the workplace. Grace's words were not what I'd expected. I'd attended my fair share of mentor programs and "women must stick together" summits. But there was nothing like hearing someone looked up to you because of the work you put in.

"I have something else to tell you," she said.

"What?"

"That kid I talked to at Carol Crest . . ."

"The one whose name you didn't get?" I said, unable to resist the dig with the gentle nudge of a big sister.

"I know who he is now," she said.

My ears perked up. "How?"

"He's on the football team, right? Sports started covering those games, because they're now a favorite to go to state. I went out on that shoot. He's the star running back."

"What's his name?"

"Demetrius Turner."

"Did you talk to him?"

"No, I couldn't get close. But it's him, I'm sure of it. He has his hair twisted in the front with blond highlights on the tips. He's number 28."

I checked the clock above the city desk. It was 2:25. School didn't let out until 3:30.

"Grace," I said. "Thank you, and I believe you, and I believe in you."

..

I hailed a cab over to Carol Crest Academy and instructed the driver to drop me off by the football field. I arrived moments before the dismissal bell and took a seat in the bleachers. A coach or team staffer wearing a Crest Academy sports jersey with a whistle around his neck and carrying a clipboard exited the tunnel leading to the locker rooms. Once he was on the field, he spotted me and headed my way. I could tell by his determined stride he was coming to confront me.

"Hello, ma'am. Can I help you?" he said.

"No."

"Well, are you waiting for someone?"

"Yes, I'm waiting on my ride."

"Are you a sub?" he asked.

While I thought about how to respond, I pretended not to hear him.

"I'm sorry, what did you say?"

"Are you sub?" he said.

I nodded. But he wasn't satisfied.

"Practices are closed to the public," he said.

It occurred to me that with the state championship within its grasp, the coaches were on the lookout for spies from other teams stealing plays and assessing the biggest threats on the Crest squad.

"I know you don't think I'm here to steal secrets, do you?" I feigned a laugh. "See these?" I said, proffering a foot. "I'm wearing four-inch heels, not Adidas."

He folded his arms and smirked.

"I'll be out of here before practice starts. I promise."

He would make a terrible reporter; he gave up way too easily. He strutted back to the field, satisfied with his "investigation."

Ten minutes passed before the first ballplayers jogged out onto the field. I moved off the bleachers and stood against the wall in the tunnel leading to the locker rooms. Once Demetrius made it out onto the field, it'd be too late.

A group of players finally emerged from the pit, trash-talking, cursing, and smacking one another in the back of the head the way immature boys do. Because they were clustered together, it was hard to make out the numbers on the front of their jerseys. Then I remembered Grace said Demetrius had blond highlights at the end of his twisted hair, and suddenly there he was.

"Demetrius!" I called out, and the kid stopped as if he heard a fan calling out for an autograph.

"Over here." I waved to him and he turned in my direction.

"Isn't she a reporter?" I heard one of the boys say.

"Hey, Turner! What're doing, man? That's a reporter!"

"Aw! Okay, damn," Demetrius said, and turned in the other direction.

"Demetrius, wait!" I said, chasing behind him. "I'm not here about football. Demetrius, remember the Asian girl you spoke with a couple weeks back about Masey James?"

He stopped and let his teammates file past him, then stepped toward me. "Yeah. I remember her," he said, proudly stroking his fully grown-in goatee. "What about it?"

"She told me that you saw Masey James get in the car with a guy after school. Can you describe him?"

"You talking about Terrence?"

My eyes widened. I couldn't believe how matter-of-factly he just identified the driver who'd been giving Masey rides from school: the man I'd suspected all along.

"You know him?"

"Yeah. I see him at the barbershop sometimes," he said. "That was her dude."

"Whose?"

"Masey's," he said like there wasn't a thing in the world wrong with a thirty-year-old man being a fifteen-year-old girl's "dude."

"You do know that Terrence Bankhead is a grown man?" I asked.

He shrugged. "Hey, got nothing to do with me."

"Why didn't you tell my colleague his name?"

"I don't know her," he said, shrugging his shoulders.

You don't know me, either. Oh, but I'm a Black woman. I get it.

He started to walk away, then turned and asked, "Are you coming to the game?"

"No, I don't cover sports. But good luck, Demetrius."

What happened to right and wrong? Had values been canceled? What the hell was wrong with people?

Terrence Bankhead had groomed Masey James in broad daylight. She hid their picture in the bottom of that silly pumpkin, but she might as well have taped it to her bedroom mirror. They were an open secret. Not even a secret, really, just open. And to think that nobody told her mother, nobody told an adult who could have intervened, nobody tried to save her. Vampires walked the streets in the daytime, surrounded by people who could've grabbed a stake or a cross to dispatch them but didn't do a damn thing.

I pulled the Mad Cash Talent Management card from my wallet and walked toward the United Center. It would be easier to hail a cab from there, but I lucked out about a block away. I wasn't headed back to the newsroom but to Uptown.

"The 4700 block of North Racine," I told the driver.

I sank down into the too-low back seat of the taxicab, my knees practically in my chest, and texted Joey. JUST GOT CONFIRMATION, TERRENCE IS THE MYSTERY DRIVER.

What I failed to mention was that I was headed to Terrence's office. Terrence, I now realized, was smart. Smart enough to notice the police surveillance. Smart enough to notice when it stopped.

Uptown wasn't a neighborhood I'd frequented since moving to Chicago. It was known for its iconic bars and music venues—such as the Green Mill, the Uptown Theatre, and the Aragon Ballroom—that helped to cement Chicago's reputation as a hotbed of emerging musical talent.

Terrence's office was located in a run-down building next door to the Riviera, an aged but popular concert venue that primarily booked alternative and acid rock bands. The Uptown area came alive at night, so there weren't many places open during the day for me to duck into and keep watch from a safe distance. I walked up and down the block until I noticed a woman wiping down the counter of a bar called the Python. The door was open, so I walked in.

What if Terrence and Brent are in here?

I shuddered. I hadn't really thought this through, had I? My reasoning was sound. They were liable to recognize my car if I was driving around the area. I could be more clandestine moving around on my stilettoed feet.

"Good afternoon. What can I get for you?" asked the tattooed bartender. She had multiple piercings and a nose ring in the shape of a bat with a fake diamond stud on the side. I sat at the bar, which gave me a direct line of sight to Terrence's office building.

"What kind of wine ya got?" I asked, though my expectations weren't high in a place with a wall of dart boards.

"Here, take a look at the menu," she said.

"Thanks."

I swiveled the barstool around to face the street and held the menu up close to my face, just below my eyes. There was no sign of life in the building.

What a dump.

"Did you find something you like?" the bartender returned.

"You know, um, I'll have a draft beer," I said.

"We've got Leine's Red on special," she said. Leine's was short for Leinenkugel's, a local brewery.

"Okay, that sounds good."

I could have used something stronger, but the ice-cold beer soothed the burning sensation in my belly. *Fear.*

"Pardon me, but that building next to the Riviera . . . do you know what's in there?" I asked the bartender.

"Yeah, it's some sort of artists' loft," she said. "Musicians, painters, dancers, jewelry makers . . ."

"Wow, really? All that's going on over there?" I asked her.

"It looks better on the inside," she said. "Well, not by much. A friend of mine lives over there."

"Oh, so people live there? It's not a commercial building?" I asked.

"It's kinda both," she said. "That's what it's for. Most artists just starting out can't afford to pay rent for a studio *and* an apartment."

"Oh."

"Can you excuse me for a minute? I've got to get something from the back," she said.

"Sure."

Now it made sense why Joey couldn't find an apartment or house address for Terrence and Brent. They probably lived there, at least part time, and stayed with family or "girlfriends" the rest.

Joey would be furious with me if he knew I was this close.

Just as I began to reconsider the wisdom in coming here, a bluish-purplish car pulled up in front of the building. I hopped down off the barstool and stood by the window to get a better view. Two teenage girls and an older woman got out of the car. The driver, a man, repositioned the vehicle closer to the curb and was just getting out of the car when a CTA bus pulled up and stopped right in front of the Python.

"Damn it!" I said out loud.

"Everything okay?" the bartender asked.

"Yeah," I said, "I just remembered I'm supposed to be somewhere. Let me take care of this," reaching for my wallet to hand over my credit card.

Laughing at my credit card over cash, she said, "Don't worry about it. It's on the house. The fee for the credit card charge is more than the beer."

"Thank you. I appreciate that."

By the time I'd turned back around, the bus had pulled away, but the occupants of the car were gone. I left the Python and walked down to the traffic light to cross Racine Avenue. My phone vibrated in my coat pocket.

"Joey."

"Hey, I got your text. Who confirmed it?"

I had to think for a moment, I was so preoccupied with the reconnaissance.

"The driver. Yes. This kid at Masey's school, a football player named Demetrius Turner," I said.

"D-Turn?" he asked.

"You've heard of him?"

"Yeah, he's a big deal in high school football right now," Joey said.

Chicago is a big city, but the degree of separation between its residents made it socially the size of Mayberry.

"How did you—" he started to ask.

"It's a long story, but check this out. I think Terrence is back."

"Back where?"

"His office, or should I say his studio. I think they live there part time. A bartender across the street told me it was an artists' loft."

"Where are you right now? You sound out of breath."

"I'm walking up Racine. Can you meet me over here? I think that was him that I just saw pull up in front of the building accompanied by three women. Hold on."

I pulled the hood of my jacket over my head to conceal my face. "There's a purplish car sitting out front." I walked past the car discreetly and gazed down at the tires. "The car's missing a rim! It's him! I think it's him, Joey!"

"All right. Stay put. I'm all the way out in Avondale. It'll take me a half hour to get there even with my emergency lights on," Joey said. "Wait for me. I'll hit up the North Precinct to send a squad car."

"Okay," I said.

I was never good at waiting. What was Terrence going to do to me in front of three witnesses? I had to get in that studio. I couldn't rely on the North Precinct or Joey to make it in time before Terrence left again.

I pulled out my cell phone and drafted a text to Joey, I'M GOING IN, but didn't send it. I sized up the building. A scaffold snaked up the facade and a two-by-four hung conspicuously over the front entryway. I opened the door and walked into a small lobby with black-and-white-tiled flooring. To my left was a directory with long-ago varnished brass buttons and the names of studios and individuals handwritten on slips of paper crammed to fit into the narrow slats. Not one of them read Mad Cash Talent Management.

Like a lot of old buildings, this one had that putrid sewer stench, a combination of sour drains and rotten eggs. The building was eerily quiet, making my heels sound like firecrackers as I walked across the tiled floor.

Ding!

A narrow elevator opened up at the end of the hall. I put my head down and drew my neck back into the hoodie like a turtle retracting into its shell. Through my periphery I saw that a White man with a scraggly beard and matted dreadlocks that were holding on to his stringy hair for dear life had stepped out of the elevator. He paid me no mind and disappeared down a staircase at the other end of the hall. I turned around and followed him but went up instead. The steps creaked so loudly, they sounded like they were in pain, threatening to prematurely announce my arrival. By the time I got to the second floor and reached into my purse to find my keys to form a weapon, I could hear music and the immature musings of teenage girls, then footsteps that shook the ancient wooden floor like an earthquake. A woman who looked to be around my age emerged from around the corner. I apprehensively kept walking, and when we were about to pass each other, she said, "Hi."

"Hi," I said back.

"You look lost," she said.

And you look like the woman who just got out of the car out front.

"Can I help you find something?" she said. "This place is a maze."

I could say no or I could make up a name. I decided to improvise.

"I'm looking fo-o-o-or Mad Cash Talent Management?" I said, sounding intentionally unsure of myself.

"Good news! You made it," she said. "Is Terrence expecting you?"

Before I answered, I paused to see if she recognized me. "Yes, I think so," I said. "I'm not sure if he got my message."

"Okay, well, come on in and have a seat in his office. He'll be with you in a minute," she said.

"Thanks."

"What's your name?"

Damn it, I knew she was going to ask me that.

"J," I said. "Everybody calls me J."

"Okay, J."

"Is there a bathroom?" I asked.

"Yeah, yeah. Just to the left of Terry's office," she said.

I walked through the sparsely furnished room Terrence Bankhead called his office and wondered how anyone in their right mind would believe this guy was legit. I'd seen chicken houses in East Texas with more swag. The plaques on the wall looked like they'd been printed off the internet, and crooked photos of celebrities that Terrence in no way had anything to do with decorated the area: Michael Jackson, Mary J. Blige, Johnny Gill, and Toni Braxton.

People believe what they want to believe.

The bathroom was fairly clean but cluttered. The wastebasket needed emptying, and a constant drip-drip-drip of the faucet explained the tea-colored brown stain that encircled the drain. I went in and locked the door behind me, then pressed send on the text to Joey. I wasn't sure what I was looking for, but I would know it when I found it. The overflowing wastebasket seemed like a good place to start. I reached inside my purse and pulled out a state-certified evidence collection kit complete with swabs, fingerprint lifts, zip-top bags, and most important, gloves. The bin was full of crusty paper towels and balls of toilet paper. Near the bottom, I came upon a used condom, which I gathered up with tongs and placed in a zip-top bag, and a large Band-Aid with a substantial amount of dried blood, which I collected, too.

I heard voices outside the door.

"Who'd she say she was? J? I don't know no J. Where is she at now?" said a man's voice.

"She said she was going to the bathroom," she said.

"All right. Put the girls in the studio so they can work on that verse," he said.

"Okay," the woman said. "Hey, Tashena and Robin, come on! Let's go!"

The next thing I heard was a knock at the bathroom door.

"J?" a man said. "Come on out."

"Just a minute." I knew the minute I stepped out of the bathroom, it was on, and I didn't have the friendly receptionist in the room with me anymore as a witness.

"I don't do drop-ins, lady. Appointments only," he said from the other side of the door. "Come on out."

I took a deep breath and pulled the hoodie off my head. Fear was not a luxury I could afford at this moment. Strength was all I had, and I wasn't sure about that. I unlocked the bathroom door and stepped out to meet Terrence Bankhead at last. His back was to me, but he turned around when he heard my heels clacking on the floor.

He looked and dressed young, in black jeans and a white T-shirt, with a black, red, and white jacket that resembled a race-car driver's.

A dope-ass jacket.

It took him a moment to recognize me. "What the fuck are you doing here?"

I didn't know if it was what I already knew about him or those thick eyebrows of his practically growing into a unibrow, but he looked sinister, like a snake about to strike.

"You know who I am?" I asked him.

"Yeah, I know you," he said. "You're that bitch on TV who got her ass beat."

Right then, I started praying that the squad car would show up.

"Wow, that was hostile," I said, struggling to hold my poker face. "How do you know that I'm not here to make you famous?"

"What are you doing dropping my name to the police?" he asked me.

How did he know about that?

"Terrence, I'm here for one reason. To find out what you know about what happened to Masey James," I said.

"What makes you think I know anything?" he said.

"Are we gonna play this game?"

"Who the fuck are you? A cop?" Terrence rose out of his chair and took three steps in my direction.

"Don't come any closer," I said.

"Bitch, this is my house!"

His quickness to anger told me everything I needed to know about how my being there made him feel.

"I'll tell you why I'm here," I said, stalling. "I know that you were picking Masey up from school. Somebody saw you and identified you. Oh, and I told the police that, too."

He stood there silent.

"And another thing," I said, taunting him, "there's the matter of a picture of you with the victim with your hand on her ass. How old was she? Fifteen? That's statutory rape."

I don't know where my courage was coming from. Maybe it felt good to be the one launching the surprise attack this time.

"You're lying," he said. "But I know one thing," he said, taking a step closer, "you better keep my name out your mouth."

"So you have a mole inside the police department?" I asked him.

Terrence was about to take another step toward me when my cell phone rang. I answered it immediately and held out my other palm in a "stop right there" pose.

"Hello?"

"Jordan, where are you? Are you okay?" It was Joey.

"No! I'm not okay," I said, enunciating my words carefully. "I'm at Mad Cash Talent Management, next door to the Riviera on the second floor. Terrence Bankhead is in the room with me, and I feel threatened. You're here? Good."

"You need to go," Terrence said. "Get out!"

I slipped past him and turned to face him while I was still on the phone with Joey. The creaky steps I had climbed moments earlier announced a new arrival. I held my breath and my heart pounced in my chest.

"Police!"

"In here!" I called out.

Terrence looked panicked. He scanned the room, but there was only one way out and I was standing in the way. He ran toward me, and I screamed and flung myself up against the wall to get out of his way.

"Police! Stop! Put your hands up!"

I heard a body drop to the floor. Terrence's screams followed. The woman who'd greeted me came flying out of the studio in the back, flanked by the two girls. "Oh my God. Terry!"

She ran into the hallway. "Freeze!"

The next thing I heard was her body drop to the floor and more screams. Police used tasers to subdue them both.

"Angela!"

The girls tried to follow her.

"No! Don't go out there!" I said, blocking the door so they wouldn't suffer the same fate. "You're gonna get hurt. Stay here and put your hands up."

"We haven't done anything!" one of the girls pleaded.

"It doesn't matter! The police are here! Put your hands up and stay still!" I ordered them.

"Police!" said one of the officers who entered the office. "Up against the wall!"

I knew enough about police raids to know that whoever was in their line of sight was guilty until proven innocent. I thought about the cell phone I still held in my hand and dropped it to the floor. A Black woman had already been shot to death by police in this city in a similar situation.

"That's my phone! I'm Jordan Manning with Channel 8! I called you! I called you!"

"Yeah, that's her," said one of the officers.

I reached down to pick up my phone.

"Jordan! Jordan! Talk to me!"

"Joey, I'm okay," I said. "We got him!"

Without any evidence, in two days, Terrence Bankhead will be back on the street.

"Terrence has an alibi," said Joey the morning after his arrest. "He couldn't have killed Tania. He was out of town."

"Yeah, but that doesn't let him off the hook for Masey's murder, and Brent could've killed Tania," I said.

I would love to tell my attacker, "You thought you were taking me off the field, but not being on the air—no scripts, no deadlines, no live shots, no meetings with reporters—freed me up to block, tackle, and beat you before you could strike again." Joey promised to pay Louise Robinson a surprise visit today to try and establish cause to win court approval to run a wiretap on her phones. I bookended his efforts by getting all the dirt I had on Terrence into the hands of Adele Constanzo, anonymously. All I needed was a burner phone and a Starbucks to hit send from, drop it in the trash bin, then out. She couldn't know it was from me, but I made it detailed enough so that she would know the source was credible. Adele didn't suffer fools gladly. Even if she knew it was me, she would never tell. Her heart was with the boys and whatever it took to free them.

If my instincts were correct, Adele would light the fire and spread allegations of police negligence to cast doubt on her clients' guilt. But in the evidentiary world, her accusations would amount to conjecture. I needed something that would stick.

I forwarded April the lab results from my nail scrape the night of the attack with a note: "I have a favor to ask of Seth."

April called seconds later.

"Can we meet today? I have something for you, but I have to give it to you in person," I said.

"Is twelve o'clock good at our spot?" she asked.

"That'll work, and invite Pamela, but ask her to meet us at twelve-thirty," I said.

The coffee shop was packed, the worst time to be passing a bloodstained Band-Aid and a used condom in evidence bags across the table. April and I leaned in, nearly bumping heads as we tried to conceal the zip-top bags with our bodies.

"How soon do you need the results?"

"Yesterday," I said.

"You want to see if there's a match with your labs, I take it," she said.

"Bingo! That's why it's so crucial that we track down the missing tissue sample from Dr. Chan."

Just as April asked me, "Where and how did you get these?" I looked up and saw Pamela bouncing toward us with her hands shoved in her pockets and her shoulders up around her ears.

"Whew! The Hawk is out today," she said.

Pamela unraveled a huge scarf from around her neck and sat down in the booth next to April. I could not miss a new accessory laying along her collarbone, revealing a delicate but poignant gold necklace with letters that spelled out *Masey*. The message was clear: Masey would not be a forgotten girl.

"How are you doing, Jordan?" she asked with genuine sincerity.

"Much better, Pam. Thank you for asking," I said.

We ordered coffee and I waited until Pamela sank into its warmth before getting to the point of her being here.

"Terrence Bankhead is in custody," I said.

Pam froze mid-sip and set her mug down.

"For what?" she asked.

"He's a person of interest. Pam, I confirmed it—he was the man picking Masey up from school."

Pam went somewhere else in her mind for a moment, then finally spoke like her words had been on back order. "But those boys have been charged," she said, which reminded me that they hadn't been yet the last time I saw her.

"Pamela, you don't really believe they're guilty, do you?" April asked.

"Is this what you asked me to come down here for?" Pamela asked.

I didn't know how I knew it, but this was exactly the way I thought Pamela would react. She was still in the first stages of grief—denial. I couldn't judge her for it. I understood she was trying to do in death what she had been unable to do for Masey in life—protect her virtue and safeguard her reputation. She wanted Masey to be remembered as the flourishing honor student, not the girl who got killed because she was out here "being fast."

With a lawyer's precision, I made the case against Terrence, unsure of whether my words were landing or bouncing right off her until I said, "If you file a complaint against him, they could hold him a little longer. Pam, the picture of Terrence with Masey is—"

"You know what, Jordan," Pam interrupted, "all due respect, but that's not for me."

"Pam, three innocent boys are in jail," I said.

"Who said they were innocent?"

"Don't you want the person who did this—"

"Listen to me," she interrupted again. "Those kids discovered my baby's body and came back to poke at it with sticks like they'd found a dead animal. I couldn't give a damn about them!"

I hated what this was doing to her, and I hated being the one doing it. There were no guarantees any of my efforts surrounding Pamela would matter. Joey warned me that even if she filed a complaint against Terrence for inappropriate contact with a minor, he could potentially bond out the same day. But surely murder raised the stakes, so I kept pushing.

"Have you seen the photo? I have it on my phone."

"I don't want to see it!" she yelled. Then she stood up abruptly and wrapped the giant scarf around her neck.

"Pam, please," I said.

"Come on, hon, sit back down," April pleaded. "We're not against you, we're here for you."

Before I could drop the hammer about Brent's molesting Monique, the girls around Masey's age I saw at the studio, Terrence's threatening demeanor toward me, and the CPD's unwillingness to pursue other leads, she walked out without saying another word, and I knew then we'd lost her.

··

Despite Nussbaum's predilection to split the crime beat, I didn't presume that my special assignment status had ended. So I avoided him and the newsroom. Back at my apartment, my cell phone blared a ringtone so distorted the call sounded like it was coming from the other side of the world.

"Hello?"

"Jordan!" said a familiar voice.

"Dr. Chan!"

It'd been a couple of days since I'd emailed him, and I wondered why I hadn't heard back. "Where are you?"

"I'm still in Switzerland. I think my emails got delayed. I just got yours with a bunch that showed up this morning."

"When are you coming back?"

"Today. In fact, I'm in the airport. You know I would have called you by now," he said, apologetic. "What happened? You said you were attacked. By whom?"

The background noise at the airport threatened to drown me out.

"Dr. Chan, I think I know who killed Masey James, and I was attacked for getting too close to the truth," I said.

"Are you all right?"

"I'm fine, but that tissue sample you took from beneath Masey's nails is missing and no one can find the results."

"That should've come . . . ago . . . it . . . and I . . . matter . . . self," Dr. Chan's line was breaking up.

"I can't understand what you are saying. Dr. Chan?"

The call dropped.

"Damn it!" I tried to call him back and I got his voice mail! Seconds later I got a text from Dr. Chan.

Boarding. Home tomorrow. Will track results. Don't get your hopes up. Might be nothing.

..

Just like that, Louise Robinson reemerged, piggybacking off Adele's stinging rebuke of the police and the prosecutor's office to incite the community's anger, using her bully pulpit to stay in the news and keep the focus on Terrence. Whether she knew it or not, I wasn't sure, but Terrence's alibi in the Mosley murder had turned the spotlight on Brent as a suspect.

"I asked her about Brent, of course. Jordan, that dude is the love of her life," Joey said. He filled me in on his drop-in visit on Louise. By the time he left, he said he was convinced. "There's something really sick about that relationship."

"Do you think you can get the wiretap though?"

"Fingers crossed," he said. "Oh, and I pulled his juvenile file. His full name is Alexander Brent Carter. He spent some time in juvenile detention for stealing a car when he was fourteen. He was found guilty of petty theft a half-dozen times. But his record gets darker. When he was twelve, he was accused of sexually assaulting his eight-year-old foster sister. If he'd been a year older, he probably would have faced charges. Guess who his foster mother was then? Louise Robinson."

..

In less than twelve hours, police would have no choice but to release Terrence Bankhead, and there was still no sign of Brent Carter.

Adele's allegations of gross incompetence, malfeasance, violation of civil rights laws, you name it, against the CPD and the state's attorney's office burned like a brush fire through the city. Some people were ready to wage all-out war, if necessary, as the boys languished in custody. Peaceful protests turned contentious. How long could the pot boil before steam needed to be let off? If there was anything worth fighting for, it was a child, the righteous justification for whatever would come. Bartlett and O'Brien were in a pot and the heat was on. A news briefing was called to respond.

"There are people who want to try this case in public, but that's not how this works," said O'Brien, flanked by Bartlett. "It was irresponsible and unethical for attorney Adele Constanzo to put such severe allegations out in the public square without any evidence to back them up. In my opinion, she should face disciplinary action up to and including disbarment."

He called Adele by name. The heat wasn't just on, these guys were on fire.

Joey called me shortly after the news briefing. Although the clock was winding down on the police's seventy-two-hour hold on Terrence, his many, many years of luck, going back to New Mexico, had finally run out.

"Robin Okoye, sixteen. She was at the studio, office, whatever, that day. Her parents learned she was there and all hell broke loose. Under pressure from them, she fell apart and told them the secret she wasn't supposed to tell."

"What?"

"She was dating Terrence, and they were having sex," he said.

"A kid can't have sex with an adult! That's called rape!" I shouted, feeling the acid rise from my stomach. "So now what?"

"He's being charged with aggravated criminal sexual abuse and criminal sexual assault. He goes before a judge tomorrow."

"What time's the hearing?"

"One o'clock."

"Okay, I'll be there. Thanks, Joey."

I texted April: What's the ETA on the labs? Then Dr. Chan. Are you back?

I'd preemptively sent Dr. Chan my lab results from the hospital with a note: "For comparison." About an hour later, he called back.

"Jordan, I got your lab results. I'm at the medical examiner's office. Can you come by?" he asked. His voice captured the seriousness of it all. I knew the answer. I just needed confirmation.

"Give me twenty."

The building was closed for the day. Dr. Chan waited by the employees' entrance. I was astounded by his appearance. He was almost unrecognizable. His cheeks were sunken and his skin was grayish.

"Hello, Jordan. It's good to see you."

I knew he could tell that I was thinking that he looked awful. He hugged me and patted me twice on the back, something he'd always done. Other than that, he wasn't himself. Underneath that fleece jacket, I could feel that he was nothing but skin and bone.

"You have questions, I know," he said. "Let's go to my office."

Now I was more worried about Dr. Chan than the lab results. We walked through the quiet corridor to his office, which was startlingly bright and dingy at the same time.

"What's wrong?" I asked.

Hiding nothing and not attempting to shield the truth, Dr. Chan revealed he was battling pancreatic cancer.

His words struck me like an avalanche.

How many bad things can happen so close together?

"I was in Switzerland participating in a clinical trial. As you can see, the treatment was harsh, but it's working. I'm back home for a short period of time and I made you a priority."

I would have asked *Why didn't you tell me?* but I probably would have kept a terrifying diagnosis like that to myself, too.

"You're going to be okay, though, right?"

"My prognosis is good. Don't worry about me."

The air that had been sucked out of the room slowly returned.

"So what's going on?"

"Good news. I found the sample."

"Ah, that's great!"

"It wasn't lost; it never left. It was misfiled. Stupid bureaucratic error."

"It was misfiled? So it hasn't been analyzed?"

I hadn't felt this type of rage in a long time. Misfiled? How does that even happen? Would that have happened if Masey was a rich White kid? Misfiled?

Dr. Chan brought me out of a dark tunnel of disgust. "There

was enough blood to extract DNA and establish a blood type. Jordan, it—"

My cell phone rang. It was April.

"I'm sorry, just a minute, Dr. Chan, this could tie into what we're talking about."

I answered. "April, you got something for me?"

"Are you sitting down?" she said.

"Yeah. What is it?"

"You're a very lucky young lady," she said, "because the blood type on that bandage and the blood from your labs are both AB negative and a perfect DNA match."

Let's get these animals!

I put my phone on speaker so Dr. Chan could listen in.

"Wait, that's not all. There were two blood types indicated on the bandage. The other was B positive."

"How could that be?"

"I don't know," she said.

"What about the condom?"

"The blood DNA and the semen don't match," she said.

"Did Seth certify the results?"

"He's doing the paperwork now," she said.

"Has he checked the FBI database?"

"That's next on the list," she said.

"Wow! Okay, this is incredible! There's a new development: Terrence Bankhead is being charged with sexually assaulting a sixteen-year-old girl. He has a hearing tomorrow at one o'clock. I need those certified results ASAP to get them to the police so the state's attorney can introduce them into evidence."

"Okay, I'm on it."

"Thank you, April, I've gotta go. I'll talk to you later."

Dr. Chan, hearing it all, looked gobsmacked. "Have you discovered new evidence in the James case?"

"Yes! It's a long story."

"What I was about to tell you was that the blood under Masey's nail was from her attacker, not her. She's B positive, but the blood under her nail tested—"

"AB negative?"

"That's right! The same as the tissue from your labs. The rarest of all blood types."

I was speechless. I needed a minute to take it all in. But Dr. Chan said the words I couldn't get out of my mind.

"The same person who attacked you killed Masey James."

..

I asked Joey to meet me at the same gas station where we had met before off the Congress Expressway.

"Joey, has Terrence had a cheek swab?"

"No," he said. "There's no physical evidence connecting him to the assault, only the victim's statement."

"There could be. Let's go sit in your car."

"You know something I don't?" he asked.

"Actually, I do," as I adjusted the heat without even asking.

"Really? You're cold?" He laughed.

"I am freezing! Look, I didn't trust the system, so I kind of took matters into my own hands."

I brought him up to speed. By the time I was finished, he sat there quietly, pensive. When he finally spoke, he said, "Who are you really?"

"This is who I am."

"Then you're in the wrong business."

I wonder about that, too, sometimes.

"So how am I supposed to get all this into evidence? Say, 'A reporter gave it to me'? The defense will take it apart."

"They'd have a hard time explaining how the victim's DNA ended up on that Band-Aid. But if it comes to that, you're in luck. I earned my crime scene investigator certification a year ago," I said. "Just haven't been able to put it to use until now."

Joey flashed me a look I'd never seen before. "Get outta here!"

"Yeah." I shrugged. "I'm certified in Texas, too."

"But you're a reporter," he said.

Can you stop saying it like it's a disease?

"Well, technically, I'm on leave right now."

There was something else I thought about.

"If Brent was in the foster care system, the state should have his medical records with his blood type listed. Can you see what you can get from DCFS? They won't give it to me."

..

Pamela might be lost, but I wasn't ready to give up on her yet. How could anyone be in their right mind after what she'd gone through? I texted her details about Terrence's hearing, the time, the courtroom, and the case number. I REALLY WISH YOU'D COME.

The table was set for Terrence Bankhead to go down at last. I wouldn't have asked her to attend if I thought he had a card in the deck that could beat the rap.

walking 2 u.

By the time I read Pamela's text message, she and Cynthia Caruthers were walking up the courthouse steps at five till one.

"Glad you could make it," I said. I was so happy to see her, I wanted to smile, but this was neither the time nor the place. Pam nodded, but apprehension was written all over her face.

We went through the revolving door. The security check-point line was disappointingly long. Before we got in line, a sheriff's deputy opened a lane and flagged us over and people trailed us like a swarm of bees. Everything had to go into the scanner—our coats, purses, cell phones, even my reporter's notebook. I cleared the metal detector first and waited for Pamela and Cynthia on the other side. Pamela took the longest to get through. Her studded belt set off the alarm and she had to strip it off and go through again.

I hadn't even noticed the people behind us. But when I saw Pamela reach into one of the bins at the end of the table, then heard her scream, I recognized Robin Okoye.

"Excuse me! Excuse me! That's mine!" Robin said.

I looked over Pamela's shoulder to see she was holding a red lacquered pendant in her hand. It was in the shape of a heart with a gold rose in the center, like the one Masey wore in her high school picture.

··

"You've heard of serial killers collecting trophies, haven't you?" Dr. Chan posed the question to the graduate student lecture hall. "Jewelry in particular."

The pendant was a family heirloom. It had belonged to Pamela's grandmother. Her grandfather bought it in the Virgin Islands and had *My love, Sarah*, inscribed on the back. There wasn't room for much more than that.

"Now, some serial killers, usually psychopaths, gift people who are close to them with their trophies. Why?"

"It's a source of pride," I blurted out. "And they get to relive it all over again."

Robin Okoye testified she found the pendant in a drawer at

Terrence's office and she took it. "But he knew I had it," she testified. "I wore it around him."

Terrence's DNA swab matched the semen in the condom but not in Tania's rape kit. She wasn't one of his so-called protégés. But that didn't mean he wasn't involved in her murder. I'd come to the conclusion that as useful as Louise's monster story had been at connecting the dots, it didn't put Terrence and Brent in the proper context. I'd come up with a better story. They were more like the man-eating Lions of Tsavo, two males that did something male lions never do: they hunted together and killed for sport, terrorizing African railway workers until they were themselves hunted and slain. The lions, maneless, were actually on display here in the Field Museum. With Terrence so irrevocably ensnared, Brent was beleaguered and alone for the first time in a long time. It wouldn't be long before he went back to a place that was familiar to him, where he could do no wrong.

"Got the wiretap!" Joey texted me for the twenty-fifth time today. Later he told me he was subpoenaing Louise's cell phone records. If anyone subpoenaed my and Joey's phone records, we would be guilty as charged, with the barrage of text and phone calls between us these past few days.

Law enforcement hadn't been listening in on Louise's phone calls even twenty-four hours before Brent called.

"Hey, Mama Lou," he said.

"Alec, you all right?"

"Anybody been around asking about me?"

"No," she lied.

"Yeah they did. The police been over there, haven't they? And reporters?"

"Boy, those people came here to talk about me, not you."

Joey played the surveillance tape he recorded on his cell

phone while we sat in an unmarked car outside police head-quarters.

"It sounded like she called him Alec," I said.

"Remember his first name is Alexander. Alex, maybe Alec, sounds better to her. She said it again. Listen."

"Alec, just stay low for now, baby, okay? Nobody's got nothing on you."

"This is gon' come back on me!" he said, growing upset.

"Not if you do what I tell you."

"Okay, Mama Lou."

"Call me tomorrow."

Joey was right about the ick factor.

"What now?" I asked him.

"We're holding steady," he said. "We need her to slip up. But when he calls, he's always on the move and we haven't been able to lock in a location."

We both looked at each other, trying to get our nerves up to do something that could potentially blow up both our careers. To get the Band-Aid entered into evidence, I was going to have to come clean with Bartlett, who was about to have some serious troubles of his own. A potential career-ending reckoning and degree of scrutiny he had never experienced before. He knew it, too, and I used it as leverage against him.

It was just the three of us in Bartlett's office when I told him about the physical evidence and Brent's alleged assault of Monique, whom Joey found out was his half sister, the daughter of his estranged father who abandoned him to the foster system after his mother passed away.

"This blood evidence will exonerate the boys. If I wasn't sure of that, I wouldn't be here," I told Bartlett. "You've got one more chance to get it right. A little less than three days."

"What's happening in three days?" he asked.

"I'll be back on the air."

It was a veiled threat meant to scare the crap out of him. Bartlett was someone I used to hold in high esteem, for a man in his position. Now I realized he was a tool of the system, ineffective and weak, which was ironic for a man with so much power. Even under the threat of media exposure, he didn't use his position to expedite the bureaucratic process to get the charges dropped against the boys, and neither did O'Brien. They were minuses, canceling each other out, a latent distrust now between them over what the other might say or do, and the boys were paying the price with their freedom.

Self-preservation was the infinite barbed-wire fence between the truth and lies. That was why I trusted and followed the science. DNA I could count on, but when it came down to people doing the right thing, it was a toss-up. Here, once again, the science prevailed. Brent's medical records identified his blood type to be the infrequent AB negative, and his fate was set in motion.

News anchor Iris Smith: We begin with breaking news, as the Chicago police launch a massive manhunt for the man suspected of killing fifteen-year-old honor student Masey James and attacking Channel 8 reporter Jordan Manning and another man. Our Simone Michele has the story.

Simone Michele: Iris, police say they have evidence connecting a Chicago man, Brent Carter, also known as Alexander or Alec, to homicide victim Masey James. He is also a suspect in the murder of Tania Mosley, nineteen, of Chatham. Both victims were sexually assaulted, suffered similar types of wounds, and were killed at different locations and their bodies discovered elsewhere. Carter, twenty-two, is also wanted for the assault on

News Channel 8 investigative journalist Jordan Manning and Harold Brantley, a security guard, who remains hospitalized. Police warn residents that Brent Carter is extremely dangerous. Now the damning evidence against Carter has also deepened the case against his close friend and business associate, Terrence Bankhead. A judge revoked his bond late yesterday.

One more day before I was back on the air, but I was already working on my Day One story, reunited with my other partner in crime, Scott Newell, and hunkered down with Joey and other members of the team tracking Brent Carter and capturing footage of their operations.

I'd convinced Bartlett and Fawcett that after the department's mishandling of this case, transparency was their only hope of repairing the CPD's maligned reputation, for which they had no one but themselves to blame. Fawcett didn't like it, but he was in no position to object.

A manhunt of this scale for a serial killer was unprecedented in the black community. Brent Carter and Terrence Bankhead were this community's Hillside Stranglers, and another bombshell was about to drop—the culpability of their fearless leader Louise Robinson. The wiretapped conversations between Brent and Louise were just as damning to her, but they weren't moving police any closer to finding him.

"Jordan, look, you can't stay up all night," Joey said. "If something happens, I'll let you know. Go home."

I could use a break from sitting around a stuffy conference room with eight police officers, some of whom hadn't bathed in twenty-four hours. But I wasn't exactly comfortable going home, either, with the man who had attacked me on the loose.

"Are you up for an all-nighter?" I asked Scott.

"Is there food involved?" he asked.

"I'll take that as a yes."

We pulled up stakes around 2:30 A.M., and drove over to the White Palace Grill, a throwback to a 1950s diner, open twenty-four hours a day. We parked ourselves in a booth beneath a painting of iconic Chicagoans like Mayor Richard M. Daley, Harry Caray, and Michael Jordan playing cards.

"Do you think this guy is dumb enough to show up at Louise's house?" Scott asked before shoving a forkful of waffles and pork sausage into his mouth.

"I don't know, maybe," I said. "He's starting to mentally break down. There's no telling what he might do. I'm worried that, backed into a corner, he might kill again."

If Brent had figured out that police had made the connection between him and Louise, then he probably wouldn't be calling her. Then again, he was desperate.

"Mama Lou, I fucked up! I fucked up!" he said during the last wiretap call capture. You could hear him pacing back and forth on what sounded like a wood floor.

"This ain't your fault, baby," Louise said. "Terry took advantage of you."

Ain't his fault? Lady, are you crazy?

Louise was Brent's devoted ally and protector. If he couldn't go to her, where else could he go? Surely not back to the Uptown office and studio where his partner was caught. Was there a woman? Nobody seemed to know much about his private life. I checked in with Manny and Yvonne to see what they might know.

"I never saw that dude with a woman," Manny said. "I never saw him around anybody, really, except for Terrence and Monique."

Just before first light, after driving around for what felt like an hour or more to kill time, Scott and I were headed back to police headquarters when a text came in from Joey. HE'S MAKING HIS MOVE. WE'RE GOING IN.

GOING IN WHERE? I texted back but he didn't respond.

"Scott, I think police are headed to Louise's. Let's go!"

By the time we pulled up, police had the alleys on both sides blocked off with squad cars, unmarked vehicles, and barricades. Scott and I abandoned the van and walked just across the street from Louise's house as they were bringing her out in handcuffs swearing and vowing revenge. But as soon as she saw Scott and me standing there with the camera aimed right at her, she cut her words off like a spigot, glowering at me with hatred and disgust in her eyes.

I didn't turn away from her glare. Once she was placed in the back of the squad car, I lifted the mic and turned to the camera to record what I hoped would be the first take in this growing saga.

"Police have taken community and political activist Louise Robinson into custody in connection with the manhunt for murder suspect Alexander Brent Carter. Robinson, it's been learned, was Carter's foster mother through most of his youth, and has been in contact with him since a warrant was issued for his arrest."

The squad car took Louise away. I looked to my left and there was Fawcett, walking in my direction, not trying to avoid me as usual.

"Detective, what just happened here?"

"Think you can turn that camera back on," he said, pointing to Scott. "You're going to want to get this on tape," he said.

..

Brent showed up at Louise's house on foot and took off in her car, after she no doubt gave him her car keys. He collided with a truck accessing the on-ramp to the Dan Ryan. Then he jumped out of the vehicle and fled on foot.

"Damn it, we almost had him!" Joey said. "He won't get far."

"Any idea where he's been hiding?"

"We're trying to get Louise to talk. But she's totally shut down. She's ruined."

And so was Brent Carter. Abandoned by his father and mother, traumatized, he took his anger out on anyone around him he felt dominion over, only to become lackey to an older man who surely would have abandoned him, too, eventually. Who *had* abandoned him, in essence, locked away, probably for good. And the mother figure who tried to make up for what he'd lost, defending him to a fault but doing him no favors.

Where would he go? The place in time where life had been good to him.

My mind went back to Denton County, Texas, and Jerry Branahan. He'd kept his soon-to-be victims hidden away at an abandoned house he used to live in with one of his foster families.

"Joey, check Brent's DCFS file. Where was he living when Louise was his foster mother?"

··

The Simeon Towers high-rise apartments were a relic of the Hyde Park community, but prime real estate, nonetheless, just a short walk to the lakefront and the famous Promontory Point. The north tower was still occupied, but the south tower had been severely damaged in a fire three years ago that left dozens of families homeless. Now it harbored a fugitive. In many ways, the south tower was like the Ida B. Wells-Barnett playground, which had been left to fester until it became a good place to dump a body. That the same eyesore was used by the fugitive's mother figure to make a name for herself was a stunning turn of events.

Oh, the ties that bind.

HE'S IN THERE. LOUISE IS ON PHONE WITH HIM RIGHT NOW, Joey texted.

Police surrounded the building, certain they had zeroed in on Brent's location with a now-cooperative Louise Robinson. I texted Justin, **GET OVER TO THE SIMEON APTS, SOUTH TOWER RIGHT NOW! FUGITIVE CORNERED,** returning the favor for all of the dozens of times he'd given me the heads-up.

Scott and I were the only news crew present, recording what we hoped would be the final scene of the manhunt like a feature film, for once without being shooed away by the police. They needed the public to see it all at some point if there was any chance of regaining a sliver of trust back. They had already charged the wrong suspects. People might be open to believing they'd done it again if the proof was not there for all to see.

"Tracy, I've got confirmation Carter is in the building. We need to go live! Now!"

"Okay. Hold on!"

Come on!

"Scott, get ready."

"I'm on it!"

A team of a dozen or more black-clad officers arrived and poured out the back of two SWAT vehicles.

"Okay, here we go," said Tracy. "Cue."

Diana Sorano: We interrupt to take you to the scene unfolding in Hyde Park where police believe they have murder suspect Alexander Brent Carter surrounded. Our Jordan Manning is live on the scene.

Jordan: Diana, a SWAT team just arrived here outside the Simeon Apartments, and as you can see, they are now hacking their way through boarded-up doors and windows to enter the abandoned building where police have confirmed murder suspect Alexander Brent Carter is holding up.

Diana Sorano: Jordan, I can't imagine what you're going through right now as you're watching this all unfold. This is the man who allegedly attacked you now so close to being captured.

Jordan: What's more shocking is the bizarre turn this case took overnight. Police ended up at the home of community activist Louise Robinson, who was foster mom to Carter from around age nine to sixteen. Part of that time, they resided here, in the south tower of the Simeon Apartments. Now Robinson is accused of trying to help him elude the police. Carter came to Robinson's home early this morning and tried to escape in her car, which police believe she willingly gave him, before crashing at the Ryan and 71st Street and fleeing on foot.

Diana: This is just unbelievable!

Co-anchor Cal McKinney: To think, Diana, it was Robinson who led the public outcry in recent weeks over the arrest of the three boys from Bronzeville who were charged in the James murder.

Jordan: Cal, remember she also organized the vigil for Masey James weeks ago and stood alongside Masey's family. Now, it is not known whether Robinson was aware of Carter's crimes, but her affection toward him has certainly impacted her judgment.

Pop-pop-pop.

Jordan: I do believe those were gunshots we just heard coming from the south tower.

A police officer ran over toward me and Scott. "Go! Get back! Get back!"

Scott walked backward, but not for a second did he take the lens off the south tower.

"Jordan, look up!" he said.

I saw what looked like a man walking back and forth near the edge of the roof, talking on a cell phone. Then he stopped, raised his arm, pointing a gun.

Jordan: Can you see this? The suspect is on the roof of the building, and he's pointing a gun . . .

Pop-pop.

One of the bullets sounded as if it ricocheted off something made of metal. Then Brent Carter stepped up on the ledge, held his arms in the air, and surrendered, his body in free fall until it hit the ground.

18

Jordan: Today, we close a very sad chapter, remembering the lives of Masey James and Tania Mosley, both victims of Alexander Brent Carter. In the end, Carter took his own life, after confessing his crimes and saying his goodbyes to disgraced community activist Louise Robinson, the woman who'd raised him, who tried to help him escape, and who now faces criminal charges for aiding and abetting a fugitive. Today there's also reason to celebrate, as the Bronzeville community welcomes home the eleven- and thirteen-year-old boys who were wrongfully accused of Masey's murder.

Although Derek Harvey had been charged as an adult and his name had been announced in connection with Masey's murder more than a dozen times, the innocent boy, who would turn fourteen in a few days, deserved to resume his place in obscurity. At least I hoped that one day he could.

Diana Sorano: How do the families plan to celebrate, Jordan?

Jordan: I asked their attorney today what this day was going to be like for these two families. This is what she had to say:

Adele Constanzo: People were willing to destroy these boys. Justice is more than just being set free. The city will pay, but for now, Jordan, this is a day to be thankful.

Her voice cracked, and the no-nonsense attorney's tears of joy could no longer be contained. Neither could mine. When I arrived in the newsroom, my colleagues erupted into applause.

Nussbaum approached me and offered me his hand. "You made us look like rock stars out there, kiddo," he said.

"Thanks, Peter."

And as far as splitting the beat was concerned, that problem took care of itself.

"Keith resigned this morning, by the way. He got offered a position at a cable network based in Atlanta."

Where he would be even lower on the totem pole than he was at Channel 8.

"Well, I'm happy for him."

As I was about to walk away, I turned back around and said, "What's that you say? A raise? Yeah, we can talk about that. Oh, and one more thing," I went on. "I'm taking a few days off for a little R&R."

Things between Ellen and me still felt strained. But some wounds needed time to heal, and today that was something I was short on. I had a celebration of my own to get to.

I picked up two giant helium balloons on the way up to the rehab center. But Bass's room was already filled with them. He was sitting up in a chair with a chest harness strapped around his body.

"Jordie!"

"Bass Man!"

"Ah, don't hug me too hard," he said. "You see this?" He pointed to the vest. "It'll be part of my wardrobe for a little while. It's holding me together."

"Don't pay any attention to him," said Sabrina, who held their daughter, Holly, in one arm and hugged me with the other.

"Can I get a hug?" I asked Holly, who nodded and wrapped her little arms around my neck.

"Mommy, I've got to go to the bathroom," she said.

"You two need a minute anyway," Sabrina said.

I sat down next to my adopted baby brother and took him by his hand, and I thanked God over and over again.

"You know that night . . ."

"You don't have to talk about it," I said. "I already know what happened. You saw me come in, and when I didn't come downstairs, you came looking for me."

"Nope!" he said playfully, and we both laughed.

"I did see you come in, that's true. I had a package for you at the desk. I left a note on your door, but when you didn't come down or call, I went to your apartment. When you didn't answer, then I went upstairs."

None of that mattered now.

"I love you, Bass."

"Love you back, girl."

I looked around the room like I had lost something.

"What're you looking for?"

"The preacher man. Ain't y'all getting married today?"

There was a wedding in the offing, just not Bass's. When I told Lisette I was taking a couple of days off, she said, "I'm on a plane." We met Courtney, Zena, Amanda, and María Elena at the Four Seasons for brunch.

"Are you sure you don't want to go to my favorite spot?" Lisette asked.

"The District? Yes, I'm sure," I said.

She ordered two bottles of champagne. "One won't be enough," she said. "I have an announcement to make. So grab your glasses, ladies."

She turned around the plain gold band on her finger to reveal a 2.5 carat diamond. "You're going to be a sister-in-law," she said.

Our shrieks and laughter filled the room. It felt good to smile again, to move away from the dark end of the street and the terrible secrets and consequences when people came face-to-face with the evil that was always watching.

"I raise my glass to you, Jordan," said Courtney. "Here's to saving lives."

According to Joey, I had earned the respect and trust of many of his colleagues at the CPD.

"I owe you," he said. "I don't know how I can ever repay you."

"Just keep answering my calls," I said.

It might take some time for home to feel like home again. And who knows? I might be ready to move by then. I carried home in my heart, a place I could go to and feel the warmth and satisfaction in the knowledge that I was serving a calling and a purpose larger than myself.

In the Windy City, the curtain fell on fall's finale, and winter's opening act was ready to make its debut. This Texas transplant would be ready, too, on those unrelentingly frigid, snowy days to trade in my purple trench and cute bolero leather jacket, even my stilettos, for a pair of warm boots, earmuffs, and a shearling fur-lined coat. It was not what you were accustomed to that mattered, it was how well you could adapt to survive.

I was curled up on the sofa under the velvety soft yellow throw Mom gave me when Darth Vader's theme song, "The Imperial March," rang out of my cell phone. Baby Smierciak deserved to have his own special ringtone.

"What's happening, Justin?"

"Don't make any plans today, sis," he said. "It's going to be a long one."

Breaking news . . .

ACKNOWLEDGMENTS

While this book was written in the midst of an unimaginable time for all of us, the story lived within me for decades as I covered stories that shook my core and rattled my faith. There are so many people and organizations who lifted me up when the last pages of this book weighed heavily on my heart. On some days, I underestimated how the very nature of this novel would result in sleepless nights. I could not have made it without a dedicated team led by my loyal and inspiring WME book agents, Eve Attermann and Suzanne Gluck, who worked alongside the ever-present superagent Bradley Singer, who partnered with me on my Emmy-winning and Emmy-nominated daytime talk show and now this novel. To my assistant and now dear friend Lizzy Levine, I am honored my son will have someone like you to offer him advice when it's time for him to find his lane and career. You make me so proud. Thank you for every email "moved to the top" so I would not miss a thing. You know I hate being late, and you made sure I kept my obligations on all fronts.

When I said out loud to the team at William Morrow that I wanted to write a crime series, they greeted the unexpected dream with open minds and unwavering support. Carrie Feron, Executive Editor, SVP, and Asanté Simons, Associate Editor; my publishers Liate Stehlik and Jennifer Hart; my marketing team of Kaitlin Harri and Sam Glatt; my publicity team of Danielle Bartlett and Kelly Rudolph; my production team of Pamela Barricklow, Elizabeth Blaise, and Shelby Peak; and my sales team of Andy LeCount, Christine Edwards, Ronnie Kutys, Mary Beth Thomas, Michael Morris, and Carla Parker:

your patience as I taped my show from home after our studio was closed and your ability to sandwich our meetings between teaching my toddler to go from crawling to walking and transitioning from formula to finger food qualifies you for sainthood in my mind.

Thank you to my "other brain," Shawn Taylor. On days when my own brain would not focus, you kept me steady and the mission clear. Writing this novel on Zoom was not part of the plan, but seeing your pixelated face in that little square daily as I downed my sixth coffee before 10 A.M. are memories I cherish. And we even found time to exchange recipes and tips on raising boys.

Last but never the least, to my dedicated family and friends: thank you for giving me the space and encouragement to think outside the box. You helped me defy the expectations of what is possible. From the first words written to the very last, you were there when I bugged y'all and called and texted all hours of the night to collect your opinions.

To all the reporters who see the human and not the headline, especially those who "cover crime": I salute you. No one can see or experience what you have and not be impacted. Without tireless souls like you, so many other souls would not be able to rest in peace.